The Ethereal Circle

Nicholas Cooper

Also by Nicholas Cooper

A Hand in God's Till
Kamala

Nicholas Cooper

The Ethereal Circle

The sweep of love, loss and redemption across two continents

The conclusion to the trilogy, beginning with:
"A Hand in God's Till" and "Kamala"

Typeset by Nicholas Cooper
Body Type: Adobe Minion Pro 10.5/12.5pt.

Cover design
by Nicholas Cooper, .
Copyright © Nicholas Cooper 2022

www.nicholascooper-author.co.uk

*This book contains scenes of a sexual nature with some violence and strong
language.*

Dedicated to Anna, my daughter,
who cared and supported me
following my heart surgery.

Kyle, Maggie, Sarah and William
for all their love.

Angie,
my co-traveller in life.

All those awakened souls,
who have entered my life through
the recent times of oppression and discord.

Acknowledgements

Thank you to the many people who travelled with me and whose real identities have been masked by the veil of fiction and are now growing old with me.

Thank you for the Tibetan blessing, inspired by the words of the Venerable Thubten Chodron.

Pierre Kosmidis, The Nazi occupation of Greece 1941-44: An endless list of crimes, atrocities and bloodbaths.

Synopsis

THE ETHEREAL CIRCLE is the final novel in the trilogy, which began with "A Hand In God's Till", followed by "Kamala".

It is late 1970, and time for Adam to leave the mountain retreat where he had settled following his overland journey from England to India.

He must now contemplate the return via the same precarious route, made more so by the coming of winter.

He is hoping to be re-united with Belinda, from whom he set off months earlier with her blessing.

But, circumstances intervene and he finds himself in the heart of Bombay, where he brushes with the criminal underworld and a new-found lover.

By way of corrupt officials and the funeral pyres of Benares, he eventually starts the long journey back to Europe and the realisation of his greatest fears.

Ultimately, many years later, India beckons again, raising the spectre of Adam's past and a final decision that has to be made.

*I*n times of darkness, when doubt and fear are unwelcome companions, look to your infinite self, which prevails beyond and through all matter.

You are more than flesh and blood with no boundaries, always and forever.

Nicholas Cooper

One

O VER FIFTY YEARS have now passed since I lay with Kamala on that rainswept night in India's Himalayan foothills.

Like most distant events, it took on a dreamlike quality that, nevertheless, underpinned and nudged those things that subsequently occurred.

At seventy-something, I would supposedly be deemed an old man by many, but physical strength remains and a mental agility that sweeps me through the years to those reality landmarks.

In many respects, none of it is real. I only have this moment as my pen glides over the paper, drafting the words that bring those moments alive.

Yet, the more I try to think about the present, the more I am drawn to the past and the inevitable tricks of the mind, meandering from one event, year or encounter to another in no particular order, recognising that each is a piece in a huge, three-dimensional jigsaw, without which completion would not be possible.

In the midst of an hysterical world, driven to the brink of insanity by a supposed pandemic, where no-one has seen bodies in the street, whistle-blowers tell of empty hospitals, idle staff and empty ambulances driving round the block with their sirens blaring, is it any wonder people are confused.

The majority have been sucked in by a huge lie, emanating from corrupt puppet governments and mainstream media, perpetrating an evil agenda that few believe exists because it's not on the six o' clock news.

The human interaction we have always engaged in, without flinching, is now buried beneath newspaper columns of fear as people hide behind flimsy Chinese masks that have no purpose other than to suppress the will and challenge the immune system, while dividing communities at measured distances.

How can one avoid being drawn back to times when people were kinder and more trusting, unaware that a wicked elite was hellbent on eventually driving the world into darker levels of economic slavery and using vaccines for population control?

I had travelled overland to India in those hippy driven days of 1970, compelled eastward in search of a spiritual teacher who would reveal the secrets of life.

In an old British hill station, a three and a half mile bus ride up the winding road from Dharamsala, I had found something of those secrets.

Within the tranquility of the former judge's bungalow, high above the village, amongst the pines and cedars, I had practised disciplined meditation techniques, taught by an elderly geshe, whose ascetic life played out in a stone hut in the shadow of the mountains.

At the same time, I was learning the mysterious practise of tanka painting.

My painting master lived elsewhere in the village with his wife and daughter, Kamala. She was a teacher in the village school, who had introduced me to her father on my arrival in McLeod Ganj.

I had become mesmerised by her beauty and openly pursued a relationship until that night in a remote colonial bungalow.

In the early hours, as moonlight cast its spell across the pillows, I had watched the gentle rise and fall of her body, her slightly parted lips, her unblemished skin highlighting blushed cheeks and those long, black plaits, threaded with turquoise beads.

I was grateful for my good fortune.

She was the picture of youth and innocence, compared to those girls I had known in London over the previous three years.

Belinda was one such girl. I'd met her dancing on stage with Arthur Brown, the "*God of Hellfire*" at UFO, the hippy club, in

London's Chalk Farm.

A wild weekend led not only to the loss of my innocence, but also the discovery that Belinda was in the early stages of heroin addiction.

Not long after, having taken some bad *stuff*, she was rushed to hospital, only to eventually discharge herself and disappear.

It was two years later and just a few months prior to setting off for India that I eventually found her, living in a village near Cambridge, cured of her addiction and a completely transformed woman.

She had almost died whilst in hospital and that experience had prompted her spiritual awakening, metamorphosing her into the calm and aware woman I had since come to know and, slowly, love.

My departure for India had been hard for both of us. I didn't have to go, but the lure of the East had been tugging at my soul ever since I had first dropped LSD, which had revealed to me the all embracing and eternal Light and Oneness that *is*.

Belinda had her young son, Harry, by a previous relationship, and was beginning to practise herbal medicine as a means of making a living.

I had vowed to return to her but, when Harry heard of my imminent departure, he asked, 'You will be coming back?'

To which I replied, 'Of course I will. God willing.'

'What does God willing mean?' he asked his mother.

'It is if God wants Adam to return to us.' Belinda said.

'Why wouldn't he?' Harry asked.

'Perhaps God has something else he wants Adam to do, darling.'

Harking back at those words and seeing Kamala beside me, I wondered just what was God's plan for me. My thoughts were now with Belinda, separated by 5,000 long miles back overland to England.

Kamala and I had previously recognised the differences between our cultures and the impact these might have on our relationship; the unshared memories of growing up, the humour and, of course, for me a language that I could not make head nor tale of, save for a few choice words. Yet, even with that realisation, my love was divided between these two so very different women; each of whom had enriched my life in their unique ways.

I wondered what they might make of each other; particularly as now Belinda had awakened to her true self.

'Good morning, Kamala,' I said, as she slowly opened her eyes and stretched her arm across to touch my face with the tips of her fingers. She smiled in her contentment as I gently kissed her hand, but the bright light of day had already filled the room, casting the night away. Unlike my first night with Belinda, it had passed with an ethereal intimacy such as I had never known before.

Wrapped in each other's arms, we fell asleep fused into a sublime oneness. I had thought of her as being too precious to taint with the complications of sex, yet our love was strong and the warmth of our bodies brought us ever closer together. At that moment, the rest of the world mattered little.

The bungalow belonged to an English painter, who'd stayed on after the fall of the Raj. Kamala had hidden herself away there for some weeks as she grappled with the dilemma of our relationship. I'd then stumbled upon her quite by chance on my return from a hike into the mountains.

When I had previously kissed her a few weeks earlier, she had seen that as a signal to suggest marriage; a suggestion that had immediately cast doubts on our future. I had visions of being stranded within an alien culture with a painting style, beautiful as it was, void of any freedom of expression. Such a contrast to the psychedelic posters I had been creating and selling in London.

Furthermore, I did not feel ready to immerse myself in years of meditation practise, ritual and dogma that, even then, I realised was not leading me any further in my quest to understand who or what I was.

Kamala had suggested living in London, where I felt sure something of her inner beauty would be swallowed by the pace and expectations of a life she would be totally unprepared for.

'Kamala, you know I have to leave,' I said, shivering as I left the bed and started to dress.

She sat up, the blanket falling away to partially expose her small, but full rounded breasts. Tears were filling her eyes.

'I had hoped it would not be so, but I too have been thinking and understand that we must part. I am sad Adam and wonder how things might have been, but know we have been brought together for this short time to fulfil a destiny, to experience the love of each other and then to pass on to other things. This is the nature of life.

Its purpose is not always clear and often we only see the purpose of something many years later. One thing is sure. Our souls are tightly bound and we will be forever in each others hearts. I love you, Adam.'

'I, you too,' I replied, as I rolled back into the bed and held her to my heart.

We lay entwined until late morning, our tears mingling with our kisses.

'I'll pack and leave in the morning,' I eventually said. 'There's an early bus to Pathancot. Are you going to stay here or go back to your parents?' I asked, when we finally left the bed.

'My parents. I have to see about getting my job back. Perhaps I'll meet a nice Tibetan boy.' she said, with a resigned chuckle.

We walked in silence back to her parents' house, where her mother was outside washing clothes in a wooden tub. She had always been cordial towards me and, I thought at one time, might even have welcomed me into the family. But, the silence that Kamala and I were projecting spoke volumes, telling her things were no longer all right.

Tears were still in Kamala's eyes, triggering once again my own tearful response. Holding her hands before me, I looked into those dark wells of love, 'You have taught me so much over these months, Kamala. Your laughter, your gentleness, kindness and unconditional love. Why should I ever want to leave you? Yet, I know I must.' I brought her closer to me and held her tightly, as if for the last time.

'Wipe those tears,' I said, sniffling as I spoke.

She pulled a handkerchief from her sleeve and dabbed her eyes.

'See you tomorrow morning, perhaps?' I asked, hopefully, still not fully resigned to our parting,

I turned to her mother, putting my hands together and bowing slightly, before starting up the path back to my room in the bungalow.

This was to be a sudden departure but, with the cold winds of winter now blowing in earnest down from the mountains, I was ill equipped to stay much longer and my money was already running low. The brown macaque monkeys I had fed and watched all summer with anthropomorphic zeal were now being replaced by their larger more aggressive grey cousins descending from the higher reaches.

The rest of the day was spent saying my farewells. To the monks to whom I had taught English. To my spiritual teacher and his protegé. Mrs Kunga in whose restaurant, I had my last bowl of toupa soup and noodles. Finally, it was to Mr Nazeri in his store, where he grudgingly accepted the eleven rupees for the eleven days of November I had been in my room.

There were many others who had enriched my life over the previous four months, not to mention the remaining travellers and seekers, who occupied other rooms in the bungalow.

The cook in the nursery, who had shaven my head a month or so before, bought my little kerosene stove, adding a little more to my funds, which would have to see me back to England.

I had met an Indian in Tehran, who had given me an introduction for work in the Bombay film industry. What guarantee there was, I knew not, but felt it worth the journey there to find out.

CHAPTER
Two

I WAS WOKEN AT HALF PAST SIX by Hugo, my French neighbour in one of the adjoining rooms. At seven, Yeshe Denpo, one of my Tibetan English students, came to tell me he wanted me to join him and my other student, Yeshe Thubten, for breakfast in the village.

He helped me finish packing, rolling up my sleeping bag and taking a last look at what had been my home for the previous four months, before shutting the door and setting off down the winding path to the village, passing for the last time familiar pines, oaks and cedars.

In Yeshe Thubten's room, butter tea was poured and a clean white napkin removed from a plate to reveal Tibetan bread, butter and marmalade.

We talked of my journey ahead, letters to be written and the times we had spent together. When the hour came to go, they readied themselves for a traditional farewell, standing with backs to the door facing me. In turn, they placed a white Tibetan khata scarf around my neck, followed by marigold garlands, 'Because we are in India,' they said. Each clasping my head, they brought it down to touch their foreheads.

I was already quite emotional at the prospect of leaving and, all the while, wondering with a little apprehension whether Kamala would be there to see me off.

Weighed down with khatas, perfumed garlands and my luggage, we made our way up the street to the bus stand, where villagers were already assembled to see me off. I didn't realise I had made such an impact in the short time I had been there, replicating something of the farewell ritual I had just gone through, as I clasped hands and smiled tearfully. All the while, I was scanning the crowd for Kamala, hoping the bus would be delayed just to give me a little more time.

Then I saw her serenely passing through the crowd, her blue chupa dress hugging her curvaceous body. A blue and purple paisley scarf was wrapped around her shoulders, while large silver earrings embedded with coral and turquoise matched large beads of coral around her slender neck.

Kamala had surpassed herself. She stood before me in all her beauty, this angel of love and light, who was moments away from leaving my life; perhaps for ever. She too had brought a khata, not just any old one, but one made from the finest white silk, which she stretched up to place around my neck. Then, holding my head between her hands, she gently pulled me towards her, first touching our foreheads together, before pressing her lips firmly to mine.

A cheer rose up from those around us. Our love had been acknowledged as, without fear of censure, we wrapped our arms around each other and continued to kiss unashamedly to the delight of the now clapping people.

The horn sounded as the bus came up the road, turned in the little village square and stopped alongside us.

As we pulled away from each other, the space widening between separating fingertips, tears continued to trickle down our cheeks.

'I love you, Kamala. This cannot be the end,' I whispered, to which I collected my things and climbed on board the bus. Finding a seat and looking down on her softly smiling but distraught face, I was reminded of my farewell to Belinda as I sat on the bus leaving the little village near Cambridge at the start of my journey to India.

The last few people took their seats, the driver put the engine into gear and we pulled away, gliding past Kamala and down the hill. As with Belinda, I rushed to the back, waving through the rear window as I watched my angel disappear amongst the prayer wheels and stupa beyond.

Strangely, I felt an acceptance that a decision had been made and I was really leaving. Nothing more could be achieved if I was to stay, at least for the present. These had been some of the happiest, most perfect and important days of my life and yet, perhaps presciently, I was now passing the old English church, decaying amongst the trees, the grass growing higher and wilder over the gravestones. What would I find if I was to ever return?

Through Forsyth Ganj and probably my last glimpse of Tibetans gathered together in a large group, down through the cantonment and into Dharamsala.

The bus stopped to collect more passengers, giving me a chance to stand outside for a while, to take a long last look at those mystical mountains that rose so high above the flat plains towards which I was now on my way.

As we pulled out of Dharamsala, I still felt the love and purity emanating from that place where I had left Kamala , but there was a new excitement as I realised that I was now back in India and all that suggested.

Newly ploughed fields stretched out on either side as white oxen, yoked to crude wooden ploughs, pulled the blades through the rich soil. Irrigation ditches fed in water, turning the brown soil ever darker.

In the villages, traders had laid out colourful stalls of fruit and vegetable subji on the wide impacted verges, while tired, fly plagued horses drew decorative tongas laden with passengers and merchandise.

A stretcher was being prepared to take a body to a funeral pyre as old men slept beneath shady trees and young children carried their even younger siblings in their arms, one hand held out for paise.

Through deep river ravaged ravines, the road twisted on as the hills became gentler and the landscape less verdant. In yet more villages with crudely thatched straw roofs, women washed clothes at the communal pond, where green stagnant water contributed little to cleanliness. Cows wandered freely about the road, saddhus collected alms and white shiva temples stood in the midst of eucalyptus glades.

In just under three hours, we were driving into Pathankot and the railway that would take me to Delhi. Through streets lined with time worn shops and stalls, where the rich, poor, young, old,

Sikhs, Hindus, Moslems interwove in an endless cacophony of daily business.

Bicycles, cars, rickshaws moved at a snail's pace in an endless cycle of noise; shouting, blaring horns and indeterminate banging and clattering filling the humid air in stark contrast to the silence of the early hours in the mountains. *What had I left behind?*

The station offered no relief from the chaos as I tried to get a reservation for the night sleeper, being sent from one window to another, until I completed a final form and eventually held a ticket for the train leaving at eleven o' clock that evening. With almost eleven hours to wait before its departure, I had the day ahead of me.

As was so often the case in such situations, food was on my mind and I soon found myself sitting inside a restaurant, open to the street, the food bubbling away in large aluminium vats over open fires. Compared to the high standards of Mrs Kunga, the place was filthy. The candy stripe walls were smeared in dirt and grease. The proprietor, in dark glasses, a grubby white vest and matching candy striped shorts, was running about giving loud orders and equal abuse to some of his customers. Beneath the stone staircase leading upstairs, a barefoot boy of ten or eleven was squatting in front of a bowl of greasy water, washing the endless flow of dishes.

Despite the unhygienic conditions, the lunch of dal, rice, vegetable curry and chapatis caused me no unwanted reaction.

The heat and noise of the afternoon offered no enticement to wander the streets, instead I took the short walk back to the station.

Unrolling my sleeping bag in a relatively quiet part of the platform, I sat for some time watching the world go by.

The red turbans of the ubiquitous porters, balanced trunks, baskets and bedrolls, bobbing up and down the platform's length amongst the waves of humanity. Their clients tended to be well heeled Sikhs or Hindus in immaculate western suits or traditional kameez tunics and baggy shalwar trousers tapering to the ankles, the whole look finished off with black lace-up shoes and no socks. Their wives followed, full of self importance, in exquisite saris and often luridly made up faces.

Elsewhere, an itinerant population of poorer Indians sat on small bundles waiting for a train to arrive. Wizened old men with long white beards, women in well worn saris, squatting on their haunches and children, many of whom were carrying younger brothers or sisters. Amongst these were the beggars, sitting dispirited and broken or wandering up and down the platform with hands outstretched.

As each train arrived, a surge of people moved as one towards it, giving little opportunity for arriving passengers to disembark before piling in to find a seat. Inevitably, there were casualties as some fell to the ground to be trampled or even slip between the train and the platform.

The porters, more skilled in the process, threw luggage in through open windows before diving into a gap to secure a seat for their customers.

It had been nearly eight months since I'd left Belinda behind in England and, although I'd written several times, I needed to let her know that I was on my way home, explaining what had happened since telling her about Kamala.

11th November 1970

My Darling Belinda,
I hope this finds you well and happy.
I'm sitting on the station platform in Pathankot writing this, having left McLeod Ganj early this morning.
A lot has happened since I last wrote.
After much to-ing and fro-ing, I finally got an audience with the Dalai Lama.
Apart from his secretary and an interpreter, I was alone with him and asking questions for nearly forty minutes. He then signed a book he had written and stood for a photo. I won't know whether it has come out until I get back to England.
You remember I mentioned Kamala, the Tibetan girl I had got to know.
Over the weeks, she has been a great inspiration to me in a very different way to yourself.
Her story was heartbreaking as she and her parents had escaped over the Himalayas from Tibet, eventually arriving in Nepal a month later. Because of the arduous journey ahead of them, they

had no choice but to leave her frail grandparents behind at the mercy of the brutal Chinese, not knowing what was to become of them, so she has a lot of sadness in her life.

Despite our closeness, we both realised that we were divided by too many cultural differences to make it work and I finally said goodbye to her this morning.

I'm now making my way to Bombay to see if there is any work in the film industry as I've been given an introduction and told that they're always looking for extras.

After that, I'll be starting the arduous journey back overland to you and should be there sometime in January.

In a couple of days, I'm hoping to be in Agra and the Taj Mahal.

Send Harry my love and hoping to see you both before too long.

With all my love,

Adam xxx

As I finished, I looked up. Before me stood an elderly Tibetan monk, his mala beads being passed one by one through his fingers. A smile flashed across his face and I was immediately transported back to the hills and Kamala.

The day wore on into evening, trains came and went as the sun sank, highlighting the criss-cross of railway lines that led out of the station. Fluorescent lights flickered on and a few radios could be heard above the usual din, pouring out the unmistakeable singing and brash instrumentation of Indian film music. Elsewhere, some were bedding down to catch a little sleep before the train arrived.

As the clock ticked round towards eleven, the train drew into the platform and, with my carriage and berth numbers in hand, I was able to board the train with relative ease to find my bunk and haul myself up. It had been a long and emotional day as the engine pushed out into the now darkened wilderness that I had so often gazed at from my porch in Nazeri Cottage. As sleep pulled its veil across me, I lay remembering how, only forty-eight hours earlier, I had been entwined in Kamala's love with no thoughts beyond that transcendent union.

Three

IT WAS ABOUT SEVEN NEXT MORNING as I awoke to the long passage past the suburban towns and villages of Delhi. A couple of hours later, I was rolling up my sleeping bag and out on to the streets, making my way down to Connaught Place, where I wanted to leave my heavy rucksack in storage.

Cox and Kings, founded in 1758, was one of India's oldest companies; holding travel, banking and insurance amongst its activities, during and since the days of the Raj. Now, I was leaving my rucksack with all my non-essentials at ten rupees for a month, knowing that I must soon be starting my journey back to Europe before winter set in.

By early afternoon I was on my way to Agra, first taking a tuk-tuk out to the ring road, where I started to hitch. How odd it seemed, after my months of relative solitude and peace, to be standing once again by the side of a hot, busy road in anticipation of a lift onwards to a new destination.

Within moments, a lorry stopped and took me a few miles before dropping me in a small village, where one of India's ubiquitous Ambassador cars took me forty miles south to Faridabad. The car's owner was laid out on the back seat, one leg in plaster, following treatment in Delhi, while the driver, a paid employee, was dressed in grubby kameez and waistcoat, smoking strong cigarettes all the way as I sat alongside him in the front.

The part of town where I was dropped, consisted of a few chai shops on either side of the road and a collection of transport companies.

'Why don't you go and ask in one of those workshops?' an obliging Sikh suggested when he saw me standing by the side of the road. 'I think you'll find there is a ninety-nine percent chance of a lift all the way to Agra.'

'Your English is excellent,' I told him.

'Well, thank you very much. I lived in England for two years between nineteen fifty-seven and eight.'

'Where were you?'

'Notting Hill in London. Do you know it?'

'Do I know it? I only lived there for the last three years before coming to India. You must have lived through the Rachman days with the overcrowding, high rents and the riots.'

'Yes, I lived in Tavistock Crescent backing onto the railway line. It was pretty grim, sharing a toilet and kitchen with so many other people. It was possibly worse than India at times.'

'I know it. Did you know a landlord called Blaum?'

'You knew him too?'

'I didn't know him, but I knew he was working with corrupt police.'

'Yes, like Rachman, he was a very wicked man.'

'I've recently heard that he's in prison now,' I concluded.

Crossing the dusty road and asking in the only two workshops where I could find anyone, I was told by a mechanic, whose head was deep inside the bonnet of a battered lorry, to return at four or five o' clock.

An hour or so passed, drinking chai and eating biscuits, until I realised that there was no lorry coming and that the mechanic had probably misunderstood me. By chance, another lorry took me a few miles further through the flat, parched and largely uninteresting landscape; its vastness and scanty crops interspersed with the occasional tree. How quickly the earth had dried after the monsoon.

In another village, I found myself the centre of attention as I waited for a lift in the vortex of dust swept up by successive blasts of hot air blowing in from across the plain. Some teenage schoolboys gathered around, staring at my oddness, whilst a couple of others asked about my travels.

'Bus go Agra six clock,' one of them told me, bravely trying out his limited English.

The sun was already low in the sky as I waited for its arrival, drinking yet more chai and waving off the flies. The bus's arrival threw up yet more dust, almost concealing it in the swirl of ochre particles that permanently covered everything else nearby. As I ran after it, my things in hand, the door was flung open, allowing me to bundle in to the cheers of the awaiting passengers, who moved aside to let me sit. I was overwhelmed by my reception with even the conductor waiving my fare.

An air of conviviality pervaded the bus and even those that weren't shouting and joking sat with mellow smiles on their faces. As the excitement died down, I got talking to a young Sikh.

'I am assistant manager of nearby dairy farm. We are having most very modern production facilities,' he told me with great alacrity. 'I am Jaikaar Singh. Are you wishing to visit Agra?'

By now the sun was a red ball on the horizon, draining the colour from the countryside and casting everything into stark silhouette.

'I am hoping the bus will be there tonight.'

'This bus is not going as far as Agra. You need to change to one other.'

Jaikaar could see me visibly wilt with that revelation.

'If you go tonight, you will be arriving in Agra very late. Better you wait until the morning. You stay in my home tonight. Yes?'

Always keen to see how other people live, I happily accepted his invitation.

On arrival at his village, a few miles before Mathura, Jaikaar hailed a bicycle rickshaw and we travelled the short distance to his home, past small street stalls and chai shops, their kerosene lamps and fluorescent strips lighting the street and causing long shadows to flit across our path.

He lived in one room of a house with an adjoining kitchen for forty rupees a month, light included. For an extra fifteen rupees, a woman cooked his meals.

'It is very economical for me and very adequate.'

It was indeed "*adequate*". A single bed ran down one wall, a table with two chairs was tucked into a corner, doubling as a dining table and desk with a small angle-poise and some papers, neatly piled.

A bookcase contained a limited collection of Indian paperbacks, together with copies of Oliver Twist, Great Expectations and the Complete Works of William Shakespeare.

Finally, there was a wardrobe and open shelf unit on which were displayed four different coloured turbans.

I had always thought the Sikhs wrapped a long cloth around their heads, as I had seen being done in Afghanistan and Iran. But, these were substantial *hats*, suitable to co-ordinate with differing suits of clothes.

'Who is that?' I asked, pointing to a framed reproduction of what looked like an eminent sikh.

'That is Guru Gobind Singh, the tenth Guru and one of our most very famous spiritual masters and warriors. It was he who founded our Sikh warrior class called Khalsa.

Every initiated Sikh must be having the five K's, as we call them. Firstly, we must all be observing the Kesh, so we cannot cut our hair or beard. Then there is the Kangha or wooden comb,' he said, pulling his from a pocket to show me. He then shook his wrist to show me his steel bracelet. 'This is the Kara, which can be made from steel or iron. Under my trousers, I am wearing some shorts called the Kacchera. Finally,' he said, holding back his jacket and revealing the brass hilt of a curved dagger in its sheath, 'this is the Kirpan.'

As we talked, the door from the street opened and a boy of about seven or eight, barefoot and in grubby shorts, brought in two glasses of chai from the nearby chai shop.

'Guru Gobind Singh fought for the rest of his life to protect Sikhs and Hindus from the oppression of the Mughal Empire, under the brutal Aurangzeb. In battle, he was losing two sons and his other two, aged five and eight, were being tortured before being bricked up alive inside a wall.

Years later, after Aurangzeb's death, our Guru was tricked by a Moslem commander and murdered by an Afghan assassin, leading to years more needless war…

A knock on the door interrupted the conversation.

'It is my friend, ' Jaikaar said. 'We are going to his house now to eat.'

Jaikaar introduced me to his friend, Vanjeet, who smiled and placed his hands together in a namaste, leading us out through the streets, the air now diffused with the smell of a divine blossom.

'What is that smell?' I asked.

'We call it, "raat kee raanee" in Hindi. It means "Queen of the Night".' Jaikaar said, pointing to a nearby tree, its branches entwined with an abundance of delicate, intensely white flowers and long peripheral petals. 'It only comes out at night and is giving this intoxicating smell.'

In Vanjeet's house, we were greeted by his mother and two sisters, who sat us down in soft armchairs that circled a thick pile rose patterned rug.

The sisters stood mesmerised by my presence before joining their mother to prepare some dahl and chapatis in the kitchen.

With three large rooms, a hallway, bathroom and kitchen, the house was large by many standards. Books filled the shelves around the walls, together with pictures of Sikh holy men and a decorative wall hanging depicting the Golden Temple in Amritsar.

'So, you are hoping to go to Agra tomorrow?' Vanjeet asked.

'I would like to think so,' I replied. 'I'm trying to see as much of the rest of India as I can before I start the journey back to England. I've been living in the mountains in Dharamsala for the last four months, but it was time to leave.'

'Where are you flying from?'

'I'm afraid I'm not flying,' I laughed. 'It will be the way I came - overland.'

'Winter is nearly upon us. Do you have warm clothes?' he asked, glancing at the flip-flops on my feet.

'Those I must arrange before too long,' I answered, only too aware of how ill equipped I was for the journey and the possibility that my hosts might just think me a little mad.

The food was brought in and put on a low table for us to help ourselves.

As the men tucked in, I was conscious that the women were not eating.

'Are you not having some?' I asked.

Vanjeet's mother waved her hand to indicate that she and her daughters would not be partaking.

'It is the custom,' interjected Jaikaar.

As we ate in silence, I could not help but look at the two daughters, their heads covered in pink and green chunni headscarves, edged with simple gold embroidery.

They cast their heads down and giggled, eventually telling their mother of their embarrassment.

'My sisters are pretty?' Vanjeet asked.

'I'm sorry, if I have embarrassed them, but they are both very beautiful.'

The girls blushed and giggled once again as I put my hands together in an apologetic, Namaste gesture.

The moon was almost full as we returned to Jaikaar's room and I helped him bring in a charpoy bed from the street before we finally turned in for the rest of the night.

Jaikaar woke me at six thirty with chai and two boiled eggs, before putting me in a rickshaw and asking the driver to ensure I got on the eight o' clock bus for Agra.

The dark leathery skin of my driver, bulged above his straining calves as he pushed down on the pedals propelling us slowly out across open fields, their monotony only broken by a solitary whitewashed temple.

Our arrival at the main road coincided perfectly with that of the bus.

The vast landscape stretched far to the horizon on all sides although, nearby, the land appeared much more fertile, supporting a patchwork of green crops and healthy looking trees.

The cultivation was still down to the peasants, driving their teams of white oxen, slowly and resignedly pulling crude wooden ploughs through the hard soil, where patches had been irrigated with monsoon water collected in reservoir ditches.

Now and then, shimmering in the heat, could be seen a small village, a clump of trees or an ancient shrine or beacon tower; survivors from the Mughal dynasties that once ruled these plains.

On the fifty mile journey, we sometimes passed through a village where buffalo wallowed in a pond, women in colourful saris beat clothes clean on a rock and the children swam and splashed, exuding yelps and joyous grins.

Whitewashed houses, set into the ochre soil, principally built from mud and straw, supported tufted thatched roofs made from reeds gathered at the pond. Outside, columns of blue-grey smoke rose unwaveringly into a cloudless sky, while pots of water boiled in readiness for chai.

Temples stood garlanded in red and orange flowers, as red flags hardly fluttered in the still air from long bamboo poles fixed to the roofs.

A short stop in Mathura, amid what was now becoming the all too familiar bustle and noise of the Plains, before passing out once more into open country for the final leg to Agra.

The approach road revealed many more ruined castles and temples with domed roofs and golden spires, sparkling in the sunlight.

It wasn't until I'd left the bus that I realised I'd been dropped in one of the least salubrious parts of the city, somewhere on its outskirts, where metal beaters and basket weavers plied their trade and I was once again the object of stares and giggles.

The sun was by now high in the sky and the heat tangible as I set off toward what I hoped would be a more central part of the city. Down a myriad of narrow streets, turning off here and there into little alleyways, I was followed by a chorus of children, mostly barefoot and raggedly clothed, asking the ubiquitous questions regarding my country of origin, whilst holding out hands for a few paise.

Crossing the railway line, treading carefully to avoid the many small piles of shit, both animal and human, I was once again within narrow streets where vendors called out to attract my attention to their pots, metalware, coloured cloth, cigarettes and food.

Onwards into streets lined with more run down and makeshift buildings, here playing host to car mechanics and electrical repairers and where the gutters and side alleys were home to the poorest of the poor.

A sudden flash of bright daylight drew me down a narrow track between some buildings and out into the open. The River Yamuna lay before me, a mere trickle despite the late monsoon, flowing between expanses of mud on both shores, where lorries were being loaded with rocks retrieved from the sediment.

Nearby, the British-built iron railway bridge spanned the river and, through its arches, beyond on the far bend, my eyes settled upon the fabled Taj Mahal. Its white marble dazzled in its intensity as I soaked in the sight of this fairy tale building, not quite believing what I was seeing.

As I walked further along the bank, its presence seemed to take on a hypnotic power, drawing me ever closer.

This shrine to lost love, built for Mumtaz Mahal, the favourite wife of The Emperor, Shah Jahan, was even now rousing memories of what I had left behind in the mountains. Did I not have a lost love? Not one brought about by death, but by indecision and guilt. It was now only three days since I had last seen her face, the tears, for which I was responsible, streaking her rosy cheeks.

What would be my monument to her? The memories of our time together? The projections for the rest of my life of what might have been had I stayed to cherish and protect her?

For Shah Jahan, his last days were a tragedy. He had been recovering from an illness, only to be usurped by his third son, Aurangzeb, the same Mughal king who had later caused trouble for the Sikhs. Jahan passed the last eight years of his life a prisoner inside the nearby Red Fort, where he was forbidden worldly pleasures, but found consolation in being able to look out towards the Taj where his love had been buried.

As if to mock the solemnity of the story, before me stood two Indians in the most surreal image I had yet seen on all my travels. One of them, with a white stubbled chin and in a long brown overcoat, was blowing up coloured balloons to create an enormous cluster, tied together and waving in the breeze. The other had a battered and tarnished brass sousaphone over his neck, his pursed lips blowing out an unknown tune across the mud flats in the direction of the Taj. It was indeed an image that would have befitted any Federico Fellini film.

Curious to identify with something of Jahan's ultimate plight, I left the river and took some steps up to the Fort.

Decorative tiles and carved filigree patterns embellished the enormous blocks of red sandstone that, in the main, formed this mighty construction of high walls, gateways and ornate Mughal towers. The inner core was mostly laid to lawn, broken by neat gravel paths, shrubs and trees. Concentrated along the eastern edge, facing the river, lay the various palaces, amongst them the white marble, Muthammam Burj, built by Jahan for Mumtaz during her lifetime.

Here, ornate carved panels lined the walls, some in plain marble, others ornate floral designs inlaid with coloured stones. An open terrace ran along one side and in one corner, I stood where Jahan had laid on his death bed looking across the river to the Taj, where his greatest love lay waiting for him to join her.

My tears returned momentarily, as empathy stirred the sadness of their tragic love.

A ten minute rickshaw ride along a tree lined road brought me to the main entrance of the Taj, where the mayhem of tourist coaches, food stalls, money changers, post card sellers and travelling musicians shattered the tranquility that should have prevailed. Ignoring all this, I bought my fifty paise ticket quite unprepared for what I was about to see.

Through the silhouetted framework of the towering Mughal arch that marked the entrance, there it was, this symbol of love from one man to his wife. The intensely white marble octagon and dome floated breathtakingly above the symmetrical gardens of Paradise that fronted it. Carefully trimmed lawns, shrubs and softly swaying trees in blossom gave strong contrast to the building, while two lines of cypress trees straddled the narrow rectangular pool stretching all the way to the lower terrace, as fountains shot thin jets of water joyfully into the air.

Removing my flip-flops, I climbed the steps to the upper terrace, the doorways, minarets and immense onion dome now soaring monumentally over me as I crossed the warm tiles underfoot to the balcony overlooking the river. From here I could take in the high doorways and marble panelling, decorated with floral imagery and exquisitely calligraphed extracts from the Koran.

Whereas the exterior had been built to stun the senses, the interior was designed to calm the spirit. The gentle whispers and footsteps of others circled the inner sanctum, rising to the high domed ceiling, vibrating constantly until they disappeared in the depths of space. Side by side sat the replica marble tombs of Mumtaz and Jahan; hers being the smaller and placed in the exact geometric centre of the chamber, each decorated with finely cut inlaid stones.

Below this chamber lay another, where the real tombs were sited. Amid walls of plain white marble, the sarcophagi for both lovers sat silently for all eternity to mourn, each more exquisitely adorned with floral lapidary than those immediately above them.

It was to be the night of the full moon and I knew that I had to return.

Drifting reluctantly out of the gardens with the Taj at my back, I entered the forecourt outside the main entrance where visitors of yore would have dismounted from horses and elephants before visiting the tombs. Through the south gate and I was into the bazaar where I ventured to find food and while away the hours until darkness had fallen.

In a small restaurant, open to the street, I encountered the first western girls since leaving Dharamsala, one English, the other French.

Talking of home and our time in India, I had no appetite for pursuing anything beyond the temporal moment. I had put so much energy into my days with Kamala, only to see them slip through my fingers as my insecurity and fear of the unknown had got the better of me.

The loss was eating away at me just as I had lamented my leaving when I had abandoned Belinda in England all those months before.

I could still go back to her, but then?

As we talked about nothing in particular, I felt ever more distant from my two companions. Everything seemed so unimportant. Months earlier, on my journey out, in just such a situation in Italy or Greece, I would have engaged intensely, telling stories, joking, even flirting, but I just didn't have the energy nor inclination. I was emotionally drained and desperately needing a compass to my life.

Something truly magical had entered my life in the mountains; a sense of well being, belonging, optimism and positivity. Now, I was just wandering through this vast expanse that is India, an impoverished tourist taking in sights, before embarking on the inevitable journey home.

Where indeed was home now? Having lived all my life in England, I had supposed that was where I should be. But, this journey and all it had encompassed had created a restless spirit, searching for a nebulous transition to something that transcended earthly being.

Yet, I remembered how empty both the Tibetan painting and the meditation had left me. Whilst I felt that emptiness was something of a goal to achieve, the negation of ego and the desires of the flesh, I still felt a restlessness and inadequacy. The sense that this awakening should be something more, perhaps accompanied by a celestial chorus.

Before too long, an orange glow encompassed the sky, turning more intense by the moment, until the sun sank and the stars began to emerge against a deep ultramarine background.

It was time to return to the gardens.

The forecourt was surprisingly empty, leaving just the three of us to pass once more through the main gate to the gardens beyond.

The moon had not yet risen and the Taj was barely visible; its outlines merging with the darkness of the sky and the sequinned stars.

Two old men sat guarding people's shoes on the lower terrace, a hurricane lamp illuminating their sun dried unshaven faces. We joined them for a beedi, sitting on the tiled floor, still warm from the day's sun, as a few people came and went, too impatient to wait for the moon to rise.

Word eventually came that it was rising on the western horizon. Climbing the last few steps to the upper terrace, the moon was looming, huge and bright over the mosque; one of two identical buildings flanking the Taj.

Being some time before the orb would reach its optimum height, we chose to wait inside the upper tomb chamber, listening to the palpable silence and echoes of the occasional sound reverberating around the dome.

Meditation seemed the obvious thing to do. Drawing on my experience with the Tibetans, I sat cross legged on the hard tiled floor, enveloped by the peace and the projections of ornate filigree patterns being cast around the walls from the enormous brass lamp hovering only a few feet above the two lovers' tombs. In that half light, I thought of Jahan and Mumtaz in the lower chamber, reaching out in the darkness, touching each other's ethereal fingertips.

Here, indeed, was the greatest symbol of that intense love felt when one is consumed by the presence of another. Giving of yourself entirely for the happiness and well being of that person.

The moon had risen a little higher by the time we returned to the terrace, illuminating the dome a little brighter. The girls felt they had seen enough and returned to their hotel. With no such comfort to go to, I slipped beneath the darkened arches of the former guest house on the eastern side of the terrace and rolled out my sleeping bag.

Sleep was hard to succumb to. With so much going on in my head, I was seduced once more by the silvery blue light that now cast its spell across the tiled terrace. Standing alone, only in the company of Mumtaz and Jahan, I took in the magnificence of this structure, now crisply delineated in a monotone of blue against the night sky and the myriad of stars beyond. Out across the gardens, I could clearly see the cypress trees and the darkened water of the pool, all colour sucked out of them by the moonlight.

Kamala was once more on my mind as I returned to my sleeping bag. How I would have loved to hold her in my arms in this very place at this very time, silent save for our breath and beating hearts. In this light, the Taj had taken on the character of a mothership, beckoning to take us away to a distant planet - a place of eternal love and peace.

Four

T HE SUN WAS RISING OVER THE TAJ as I awoke, bathing it in a pinkish-orange light and then to a gleaming white as it rose higher in the sky. The gates had opened at sunrise and a few visitors were already wandering about the grounds, so it was no trouble mingling and making my way to the exit, turning for one last look.

As with those last seconds with Kamala, I felt I was leaving something precious and beautiful, tinged with deep regret.

A rickshaw took me into the city, waiting whilst I had some tea and toast in a small chai shop, before taking me on to the station.

The fake student card I'd picked up in Istanbul was still standing me in good stead, earning me a fifty percent reduction on a thirty-five rupee ticket to Bombay.

There was time for a shower before the train arrived at eleven and I boarded directly into the dining car to avoid the scrum in third class.

With a comfortable window seat, I was able to take in the passing countryside while stretching out lunch until the train slowed at the approach to sidings and goods trucks where, sprawling across a high sandstone plateau, the vast ramparts and domed towers of Gwalior fort overlooked the city.

Time had come to resume the rest of the journey courtesy of third class. I was off the train before it had stopped, chasing up the platform and pushing through the clamouring crowd until I had squeezed into a small space by an outside door in one of the corridors. My sleeping bag provided some semblance of comfort as I settled in amongst the press of feet, knees, cooking pots and bedrolls for a twelve hour journey ahead.

The countryside passed, ever-changing, as we rolled on. The still vast plains stretched at first to the horizon, occasionally broken by a range of craggy hills, sometimes topped with a small Shiva temple, a long abandoned castle or an ashram; blood red flags fluttering from long poles atop the buildings. One temple stood out in particular, being totally white and reached by a long, absolutely straight staircase rising from the level of the plain, like something from a child's drawing book.

This monotony continued for much of the rest of the day. There were few fields, but what there were had been well cultivated. Most of the people to be seen were cow and goatherds, driving their animals across the dusty plain from one pasture to another.

A road was being built alongside the rail track. Women dug out the earth nearby with steel hoes and carried it on their heads in shallow baskets to the road where the men were engaged in levelling it out for mile after mile.

As darkness slowly stole the day, the setting sun painted a purple to orange splash across the turquoise sky. All the while, we were passing alongside dense woods where, in small village clearings, people had lit fires outside their huts in readiness for cooking the evening meal.

Glowing in the failing light, the flames highlighted the darkened faces of the villagers tending them as, occasionally, splinters of burning embers were spat upwards with the curling smoke until they too were absorbed into the darkness.

And so the hours passed, occasionally catching the eye of a companion squatting against the carriage wall, dressed in leather sandals, grubby cotton dhoti and a woollen blanket around his shoulders, dispassionately staring into space. Offering him a beedi, he would smile, exposing gaps in his teeth, while moving his head from side to side in that inimitable Indian fashion as a gesture of thanks.

A squatting village woman, dressed in a busy patterned sari and choli top, embellished with brass nose ring, earrings and numerous coloured bangles around her wrists and ankles, would be feeding her family with chapatis, rice and curried vegetables brought on the journey in small aluminium containers.

It was an opportunity to look at the map and try to comprehend where I was and where I was going - almost an analogy for my life at that time, for I felt a certain air of depression hovering over me. Whereas, I had travelled optimistically through numerous hardships to arrive in the peace and tranquillity of McLeod Ganj, to have found Kamala and to have stayed rooted for four months, I was now heading aimlessly to see a *"bit more of India"* but with no tangible objective. All the while, I knew I was eating into precious funds that would be needed for the *"journey into darkness"* as I eventually set off for Europe at probably the worst time I could possibly be travelling.

At the next station, the door was flung open and I was invaded by a host of clamouring bodies in a surge that forced me to stand up. Small bundles, arms, and legs came bursting in with such rapidity that I eventually had to apply some reciprocal force, pushing them back whilst trying to close the door. 'Bas! Bas!' I shouted, but to little avail. It was only as the train started to pull out of the station that I pulled in the few who were still standing on the footplate and shut the door, pushing them into the toilet so that I could resume my seat on the floor.

But, that was the decider. I'd noticed that some Buddhist stupas in a place called Sanchi were not far off the main rail line so, when the train pulled in at Vidisha, I collected my things and left, glad that I would not have to endure the rest of the night to Bombay. Sanchi was only ten miles away on another line and I could get an early train the next morning.

Food was waiting in a restaurant behind the station as was plenty of water, off the station waiting room, where I could wash off the grime and soot that had blown back from the engine.

A charpoy lay empty in the waiting room, inviting me to unroll my sleeping bag and catch some much needed sleep.

At five next morning, I was waiting for the train to Sanchi, huddled round an open coal burner in the station master's office in the company of five railway workers, dressed in overcoats, scarves and ear muffs.

The ten minute journey brought me to the tiny station adjacent to the village; a mere single street with a government tourist bungalow and a rest house run by the Maha Bodhi Society of Ceylon.

Leaving my things in the station, my first stop was breakfast in the single chai shop. My early arrival meant the water had only just been put on the fire and a man, dressed in vest and cotton shorts with a white bushy moustache, was still busy milking the buffalos standing passively outside.

From the village, a short walk took me up the incline and the long flight of steps that led to the crest of the hill, where the stupas stood amongst swathes of cut grass, flowers and trees. On all sides, the plains stretched out to the distance, broken occasionally by gently rolling tree covered hills. A steam train chugged along the track I had recently left, the sound of the surging steam mingling with the birdsong and prevailing silence.

One stupa dominated all others, built in the form of a dome, a giant stone blancmange rising some fifty feet and one hundred and twenty in diameter, built by the Emperor Ashoka to contain some of the Buddha's ashes in the third century before Christ. At each point of the compass, rose an ornamental arch, carved with episodes from the Buddha's life.

A walkway with a stone balustrade circled the dome, accessed by an anti-clockwise stairway. On top, a stone spike held three diminishing concentric stone circles, surrounded by a square balustrade. As with all the construction and carving I had so far seen, it was exquisitely executed by highly accomplished craftsmen, whose skill with crude tools outshone much of what could be achieved in the present day.

Elsewhere, smaller stupas and temples dotted the site, far more than I had time for as I knew I had to press on to Bombay and the possibility of work.

Green parrots fluttered amongst the trees and women with baskets of soil were repairing pot holes in the paths as I returned to the village. Although much of the site had fallen into disrepair, there remained a peace and tranquility that had survived the trauma of the ages.

It was to be eight hours to Jalgaon, passing ever more high plateaux, thicker vegetation and numerous towns and villages. Rattling over girder bridges, spanning vast rivers, now just trickling their way to the Arabian Sea, goats and cattle drank from the narrow channels winding down through the drying mud.

At Bhusawal, night had fallen and one of the passengers explained the profusion of bananas being passed through the open windows as we waited in the station.

'It is the largest banana producing centre in the whole of India, if not the world,' he told me with great pride.

The endless supply certainly kept prices low as I bought twelve for twenty five paise, around threepence farthing in English money.

'They will doubtless be much cheaper in the markets,' he concluded.

It was still only nine o' clock when we pulled into Jalgaon, my departure point for the fabled caves of Ajanta.

Another night in a first class waiting room, complete with adjacent shower and I was ready for the next day.

A young boy of twelve hard spent years woke me at five thirty and gladly went to buy two chai and biscuits for us both with the money I had given him.

He was so typical of thousands of such young boys I had seen and spoken to over the months of travel. Dressed in the ubiquitous shorts and vest, a shock of straight black hair swept across his forehead, he returned holding the two glasses with a look of intense concentration, ensuring not a drop was spilt. The biscuits had been placed in his grubby pockets, but this was of no concern to me as he sat beside me sipping the tea, crunching his biscuits and talking in French. Unlike most young people who only wanted to visit their cousin in Rochdale or Hounslow, his burning ambition was to go to Paris.

The sun rose in a blistering red ball over the acres of banana plantations as the bus set out for Ajanta, passing villages where it seemed people universally earned their living by way of bananas.

The Ajanta cave complex is set into the cliff face of a horseshoe of volcanic basalt, below which lies a picnic garden and a tumbling river, strewn with rocks and boulders. The exterior appearance of roughly hewn rock and colonnades marking the entrance to each cave, belies the magic within.

A pathway extends round the horseshoe, where some thirty caves had been constructed over a period of nearly seven hundred

years since the second century before Christ. Some had fallen
into disrepair, whilst others stunned the senses with the shear
majesty and audacity of concept as I entered one after the other,
where cathedral like interiors had been dedicated to the Lord
Buddha. Hefty columns supported intricately carved lintels with
depictions from the Buddha's life, extending deep into the rock,
not unlike the basilica of a European church, where now a huge
carving of the Buddha would oversee the space. Nothing had been
constructed in the traditional sense; all having been *revealed* by
the painstaking removal of the rock that held these sublime places
within its ancient core.

It was hard to believe that such fantastic and immense creations
had been lost to the world until stumbled upon by a British officer
during the course of a tiger hunt in 1819.

Throughout these temples and monastic spaces, fine paintings,
rich in colour and detail, represented the past lives of the Buddha
and successive Buddhist deities. However, in places, damage had
been caused by time and vandalism and now restorers were at work,
whilst other Indian artists, commissioned by the Government,
were stood at easels painting faithful copies.

It was to be another long bus journey to reach Aurangabad, from
where I planned to pick up the train again to complete my journey
to Bombay. Amongst the assortment of Indians at the stop, a
westerner with a rucksack was waiting.

'Hi, man,' I said, 'are you heading for Aurangabad?'

'Sure, then on to Bombay,' he replied with what I suspected to be
a southern American accent.

'Been on the road long?'

'Ah flew into Calcutta about a month ago. Ah've been around
Benares, Delhi, Amritsar, and down through Rajasthan. Now, it's
on to Bombay before ah probably fly on to Ken-ya.'

The bus rolled in to a stop and people clambered on, but it was
standing room only for the two of us.

'That's quite a trip you're on.' I said, as the bus pulled out with a
jolt. 'Are you going on to Europe before you fly home?'

'Ah should think so. Ah want to visit London.'

Holding tightly to one of the leather grips hanging from the
ceiling, I could crouch down occasionally to see the passing

countryside; a rough terrain of undulations, wild grass and shrubs with the very occasional field carved out of the wilderness.

Small forts and look-out posts, some with towers and a moat, told of past eras when great armies had fought across these vast spaces. From the time of the epic Mahabharata over a thousand years before Christ, to Alexander the Great, the Guptas, the coming of the Moslems and the great Mughal Empire and finally the British, all had left their mark on the land and the people who inhabited it.

A stop for an orange and a pee at the bus station in Sillod saw several passengers disembark, freeing up seats for the remainder of the journey.

'I've not said, hello.' I eventually said. 'My name's Adam.'

'Liam. Pleased to meet you,' he replied.

'Where're you from?'

'Myrtle Beach, South Carolina.'

I looked puzzled.

'Nah, not many folks have heard of it either. Right on the Atlantic seaboard. It's beaches, amusements, golf courses, souvenir shops. It's holiday paradise for America. It's a dump really.'

'It must have something going for it,' I said, intending to redeem it a little.

'Ah've lived there all ma life, so Ah suppose Ah've got used to it and bored with it. They've done lots of things over the years; Pirateland Adventure Park, Fort Caroline, a Wild West theme park. We've got the Camelot movie house and WKZQ-FM radio, which plays the coolest contemporary rock, the Doors, Airplane, Beefheart. Other than that, it's just one long flat beach, the Ocean and then flat, flat, flat as far as you can see.'

'You've got family there, I suppose.'

'Ah grew up an orphan. Ma pa and mom were killed in a pile-up, when Ah was eight.'

'My God, Liam, that's awful. I'm so sorry.'

'That's okay. Ah've had time to get used to it. Ah had no other folks to go to, so Ah was brought up in an orphanage.'

'What about adoption?'

'I guess Ah was too old for that. No one wanted an eight year old. Still, Ah've been lucky. It was a Christian foundation with good people, who were kind to me. They always had a cake and presents for ma birthday and Christmas was always great with the other kids. We had trips and Ah learned a lot in school. But it was never a real home.'

'Girlfriends?' I asked. He was, in my estimation, a good looking man. A little older than myself, just under six foot with searing brown eyes, weathered skin and brown to black curly hair that extended well over his ears and neck. His beard was bushy, but his full lips still evident behind it. He had adopted a sage green Indian kameez and sandals and seemed quite comfortable in his attire, although I had perceived a certain strain in his gait.

'Ah've had a few, but they all want babies and a chalet in Myrtle Beach. Ah'm just not ready for that just yet. That's why Ah'm here. Ah think Ah'd die living there all ma life.'

'What about Vietnam?'

'Flat feet. Simple as that. You may have noticed that Ah walk with some pain.'

Aurangabad was displaying its ancient heritage from the moment we entered the outskirts. Mosques, temples, old forts and castles, all in varying states of disrepair; some crumbling and overgrown with any plant life that could survive in a vacant crevice. Other structures still felt the daily tread of man.

Passing through one of the old gateways in the weathered city wall, we were confronted by the crush of shabby looking street stalls and even more wretched people, who simply existed from one day to another by way of the odd job or begging.

Even within the bus, I was conscious of the incessant noise and the gamut of human experience written on the faces; suffering, greed, hostility interspersed by the occasional smile.

In dark, litter strewn alleys, comatose bodies lay sleeping their days as an escape from the hunger and misery and, yet, some veiled their suffering with games and laughter.

Small groups of men sat in circles on the edge of the road playing endless games of cards. The luckier of them scrounged a living of sorts selling roasted peanuts, battered fruit and the juice of crushed sugar cane.

Further up the economic scale in more substantial shops, open to the street, traders plied their diverse wares; silks, cooking equipment, medical supplies and the plethora of miscellany.

Then there were the restaurants from the cook to the waiter to the boy off the street, who sweeps the floor and washes up for a few paise a day. All of them surviving in proportion to what they have.

Up against a wall, its aged and filthy render crumbling, an old man sat in his rags, his eyes rolled back into his head, a withered hand stretched out seeking the pity of some passer by.

Young children did the same, both girls and boys carrying their near naked siblings, often only a few months old, empty, pitiful looks hanging in their eyes. For them, there appeared no way out.

From the moment they drop from their mothers' wombs onto a cold, filthy pavement and progress to the funeral pyre, they would probably know no other life.

All this poverty, coalescing with the sticky heat, the fetid smell of rotting refuse, excrement, dead rats and dogs, so potent it stifled the brain.

This was real India. That which has cursed so many lives over the centuries, eternally exacerbated by famine, disease, floods, caste and corruption. Technological advances don't change these people's lives to much extent, for the opportunities are few. They are what they were born as. The destiny of the rich and privileged is variable and even perhaps undesirable, whereas for the poor, destinies are certainties with little chance to rise up the ladder. Poverty is a way of life with barely enough money to buy the air they breathe, let alone the opportunities to escape their lot. All are susceptible to the disease of corruption which invariably arises from jealousy and greed, whilst inevitably leading to fear, despair, violence and often death.

Each man has his price, each feeding off the next. From the manager in a Government office to the beggar in the street, appropriating assets in order to enhance their own.

In only the previous year, a group of militant Marxist-Leninists, calling themselves the Naxalites, had been causing havoc in West Bengal. Emanating from poor land workers, where slow starvation had led to rebellion and violence. Their targets had been tribal leaders, police and local government workers, who they blamed for their inherent poverty and suppression of land rights.

Many innocents had been murdered and homes and offices set on fire, causing much consternation and fear in the areas where the rebels were prevalent.

Arriving at the railway station, Liam wanted to visit the tourist office as he craved somewhere comfortable for the night.

'I'm okay in the station waiting room,' I said, 'I sleep just as well there as anywhere. Besides, it's free and I'm not doing anything while I sleep, so what does it matter where I am as long as it's reasonably warm.' The nights had been getting noticeably colder, but they were probably balmy compared to what possibly lay ahead on the journey home.

'Ah'm gettin' on you know. Ah'm twenty-eight next birthday.' Liam told me. 'Let me see what they have.'

As I waited outside, my eyes were suddenly filled with a radiance and overriding joy as I caught sight of a half dozen smiling Tibetan men and women, selling artefacts from stalls on the far side of the road. Despite their sorry state, their heart warming smiles and spirit of perseverance brought me as much excitement as my first encounter in Kangra over five months before.

To me, to see just one Tibetan face gave me more hope than a thousand Indians. Like a ray of brilliant light in a sea of claustrophobic darkness. And amongst those faces, in the dimming light, I swore I had seen Kamala once more.

Liam rejoined me soon after.

'They've suggested a place not far from here,' Liam said as he rejoined me. 'Do you want to give it a try?'

I followed him through a myriad of streets, jostling with the crowds, rickshaws and sacred cows, only to arrive at what seemed to be a holiday camp without the funfair. The place comprised an ugly, utilitarian block on four floors, with over four hundred rooms. A young man showed us to a room with a high window, two beds and a shower down the corridor. Resembling a prison cell without the bars, the room was heavy with the smell of DDT and mosquito nets still hung over each bed. Peeling yellow paint clung to the walls and a single bulb hung from the ceiling. Six rupees for a night of prison air.

'I'm sorry Liam, but I can't sleep here, breathing this crap all night,' I asserted. 'I'm going back to the station.'

'It'll do me,' he replied.

Liam's need for comfort of sorts was clearly greater than mine, but I still joined him for dinner in the canteen, where we were able to get dal, rice and subji.

'Mind if I join you?' a disembodied, but refined English voice interrupted us.

A woman in her twenties in white blouse and khaki shorts stood beside us with a tray in her hands.

'Sure,' I said.

'I don't often get much conversation,' she said as she pulled up a chair and laid her meal out on the table. 'I'm Jen. Where are you guys heading?'

'We're catching the train to Bombay tomorrow,' Liam replied.

'Well, I'm driving to the Ellora caves tomorrow, then on to Bombay. You're welcome to join me.'

'Thank you, we'd like that,' I spoke on behalf of both of us.

I could see that Liam was already infatuated.

Jen was no more than six feet, slim, athletic and tanned with strong, well shaped legs. She'd tied her chestnut hair above her head in a bun, exposing her long neck and defined jawline. Black kohl enhanced her hazel eyes, her nose turned up a little at the end, while her mouth, when she smiled, revealed a perfect set of teeth. It was clear from the beginning that Liam was trying to avoid staring at her breasts, defined by the open blouse and cleavage.

I left them to it, agreeing to meet the next morning at eight and made my way back to the station, settling down on a padded seat in the waiting room, where the station master was considerate enough to turn out the lights.

Morning arrived soon enough and the three of us set off into open countryside in Jen's Land Rover, glimpsing the hills towards which we were heading, from between the growing number of assorted trees.

Jen confidently handled the single track road, anticipating dangers from ox carts, and oncoming cars and buses, making use of the impacted sandy verge to enable others to pass. I admired this woman who, on the one hand, came across as quite conventional and unaware of the alternative culture I had been immersed in over the previous three years, whilst having a strong mind of her own and bags of determination; a quality not often found amongst many of the stoned hippy chicks who had flitted around Notting Hill Gate.

'Where've you been travelling?' I asked, once we were underway.

'Like I was telling Liam last night, I'd been working as a nanny for a couple of years in Melbourne, then picked up this crate in Singapore. I've now driven just over five thousand miles up through Burma, East Pakistan, Calcutta, Benares, Delhi, Agra to here.'

'By yourself?'

'I had a boyfriend at the start, but I dumped him in Mandalay. I caught the bastard sleeping with a local girl. I've had a few hitchhikers but, by myself, yes. When I get to Bombay, I've arranged with a shipping firm to take me and the crate on to Mombassa.'

'That's where you're heading, Liam.'

'Yes. we've already discussed it. Ah can get a berth on the same boat.'

That's a stroke of luck, then.'

Liam nodded and smiled a little smugly as if he knew he'd landed on his feet.

'Are you then going back to England, Jen?'

'No, I see Kenya as my home. My parents are still there with the coffee plantation. I was only sent to England for boarding school. Millfield. Do you know it?'

'Of course. We used to play them at rugby and athletics. I was at school in Somerset.'

An hour later, we were drawing into the open space before the Ellora cave complex, carved into a one and a half mile cliff face, rising from ground level and sloping back to its highest point of well over a hundred feet, where yet more extraordinary carvings represented the three principal religions; Buddhism, Hinduism and Jainism.

Immediately before us rose the most prominent of all the carvings.

The Kailasa, was not a cave at all but a huge Hindu temple, dedicated to the Lord Shiva, carved down and back into the basalt cliff and said to be the largest rock carving in the world. The guide told us it was two hundred and eighty feet in depth back into the rock face, one hundred and sixty feet in width and an incredible one hundred and six feet in height.

From the pinnacle of the temple, every god, dancer, elephant, lion and pillar had been carved out of the solid rock. A broad courtyard surrounded the temple, extending on three sides into a continuous arcade or cloister, its outer perimeter supported by hefty square columns.

The three of us were aghast at the achievement and there were another thirty-three to see, most much smaller in size, but each no less an outstanding physical and audacious achievement. Estimates suggest they were constructed some six hundred to a thousand years before Christ, harnessing an army of craftsmen and labourers to complete the work.

As we walked around the site, through vast halls with vaulted ceilings, in and out of monastic cells and circumnavigating huge carved lingams, a flirtatious exchange was taking place all the while between Liam and Jen. Their fingers twisted and twirled playfully as coy looks and giggles were exchanged. Occasionally, one or the other would disappear behind a pillar, before jumping out like a young child to touch the other, the hands sometimes lingering on an arm, torso or bottom.

Something was blossoming and I only hoped they wouldn't be seeking total isolation before we had reached Bombay.

I had nothing to worry about as, following a bite to eat, we set off on the remaining one hundred and fifty miles of the journey.

The terrain was still flat to the horizon, save for high plateaux rising up on either side to provide a modicum of relief from the miles of monotony.

Occasionally, we would pass through a village where thousands of red onions had been piled high, waiting to be packed and transported to market.

Not much was said as the miles slipped by, each of us in our own thoughts; Jen and Liam possibly thinking about Jen and Liam, while I considered my options in Bombay, the preparations for the journey home and, of course, Kamala. I needed to write to her, to tell of my adventures so far and to reiterate my love, explaining the paradox of loving her, yet leaving her for a five thousand mile mid-winter overland journey to Europe.

As afternoon passed into early evening and the plateaux were being cast into silhouette behind a canvas of diffuse purples, reds and oranges, we considered stopping in a small town for the night and going on to Bombay in the morning. But, the miles led one to the other and, before too long, we were entering the outer suburbs.

The smell hit us first, none of us able to discern exactly what it was other than decaying matter in the streets and alleyways.

Tall blocks of flats rose toward the stars while cars streamed in a steady flow on all lanes of the dual carriageway. We were coming to the city once more, the big city, which already felt overwhelming.

Further into the bowels, I could glimpse something of people's living conditions. Much older and smaller apartment buildings lined the road, as countless bare electric bulbs illuminated dingy rooms. Yards of washing hung out to dry on iron balconies. Men, women and children milled inside the rooms or leant over the balcony with a cigarette, mesmerised by the traffic and lost in their thoughts.

On ground level, children played games, tagging each other and running down dark alleyways that separated the blocks. Gaudy pictures decorated bland walls, families ate their evening meals or settled for some rest from a weary day.

Deeper we drove into this netherworld, the lights becoming brighter and more abundant, street lights, cafés, shops, cinemas, everywhere light in the darkness and as much noise to accompany it. There was no going back until we eventually arrived at the sea front, where the vast colonial, Taj Mahal Hotel overlooked the sea and the Gateway of India, the triumphal arch built to commemorate the arrival of George the Fifth and Queen Mary for the Delhi Durbar in 1911.

Finding a room for the night was not quite so easy as the drive in. One hotel in the streets immediately behind the Taj was nine rupees a night without breakfast, the Salvation Army offered a bed, three meals a day and afternoon tea for twelve rupees, but was already full. In another, just up the road, one double room remained. Jen and Liam's body language said no more.

'You have it,' I said. 'I could sleep in the Land Rover and look after it for you.'

'Is that such a good idea?' Jen replied, a little hesitantly.

'I'm not going to drive off with it, if that's what you're thinking, besides I can't drive anyway,'

'Okay, if you're sure you'll be all right.'

'If I could just have a shower in your room, I'll be fine.'

And so I settled for my first night in Bombay stretched out across the front seats of a Land Rover, while those outside, unfurled blankets onto the pavements with the rubbish and the rats.

Five

I WAS AWOKEN by rocking and multiple tapping on the windows, accompanied by much excited yelling and laughing. A sizeable crowd of boys and young men had gathered around the car and, like a goldfish in a bowl, I was the centre of attention, prompting me to rapidly slide out of my sleeping bag and into my jeans, retaining as much modesty as possible. Gathering a few small coins together, I eased the door open and stepped out into the street, dispensing paise as I did so. Of course, this meant those at the back followed all the way to the door of the hotel in the hope of more.

Joining Jen and Liam for breakfast, I told of my early morning encounter.

'You did lock up, didn't you?' Jen asked anxiously.

'Of course,' I replied, dropping the keys into her hand.

'Liam and I are moving into the Salvation Army after breakfast,' Jen informed me, 'then we've got to take the Rover to a garage for a service, so we'll probably be gone most of the day. You can leave your things in our new room, if you wish.'

Thanks. I've got things to do myself, so enjoy your day,' I replied.

I thought it a little strange that, having covered so many miles already and with a boat journey ahead before the last leg home in Kenya, that they should be having a service here. But that was their business. As we got up from the table, I noticed they gave each other a glance that told me all was perhaps not well. They seemed a little nervous and lacking their usual energy, as if they didn't really want to move into the rest of the day.

The Sunrise Café, just back from the seafront, was a little like the Pudding Shop in Istanbul, a cool meeting place for western travellers, where ideas and addresses could be exchanged.

Amongst the Indian customers, an assortment of westerners sat sipping juices, incongruous in their faux sadhu attire and an unsettling air of aloofness. The Sunrise was also one place where "scouts" came from one or other of the many film studios in Bombay to look for "extras".

I had put my hopes on being selected ever since I'd been given a letter of introduction by an Indian in Tehran and the Sunrise presented a further opportunity.

Some chai and another breakfast later, two clean-shaven, thirty something men in dark suits, white shirts and ties came in looking around as if searching for something specific.

'Are you from the studios?' I asked.

'We are RK Films,' said the taller of the two in a snooty English accent, his dark hair immaculately brushed across his head. 'I have to tell you that there is no work at the present, but if you come back in a couple more days, there might be something.'

With this disappointment and the rest of the day ahead of me, I felt it was time to follow up the Tehran letter and the address of an uncle given me by an Indian woman I'd met in Notting Hill. These were the seeds I imagined would bear fruit.

A bus took me to a run down area in the north of the city where I eventually found what turned out be a shop selling televisions and radios. The place was gloomy and empty save for a young Indian woman who recognised the name and gave me a residential phone number to ring.

Finding a phone in a kiosk by the side of the busy road, I was defeated by the clatter and had to resort to ringing again from the nearby post office.

'Hello, Mr Kapadia?'

'Yes.'

'My name is Busk,' I said, slightly raising my voice as if to give greater clarity to my call. 'I was given your name by your niece in London. She tells me you might be able to help me get some work in the film industry. I am an artist and very good with my **hands**.'

'I have no niece in London.'

'But, I have the correct phone number, yes?'

'I am telling you, I have no niece in London.'

'Can you help me find work?'

'I have no niece in London and have nothing to do with films.'

'I'm very sorry, but I don't understand how I was given your business address with your name attached to it.'

'I have lived here with my family for over thirty years and tell you I have no niece in London,' he repeated, then hung up.

I was confused by the conversation and the disembodiment of Mr Kapadia from the address and the number the young woman in the shop had given me. Perhaps, there had been a falling out for some reason and the family had disowned the woman in London. I was puzzled and once more disappointed.

Returning to the street, I found myself wandering past shops selling brightly coloured and variously patterned material where ladies, young and not so young, were being discretely measured for their new saris. Down another alley, passing shops selling books, maps and art materials, I was suddenly emerging into the midst of what appeared be a vast slum.

As far as I could see, and probably beyond, makeshift homes had been constructed from whatever found materials could be acquired; corrugated iron, old bricks, wood, cardboard and plastic. Some clearly had the mark of a skilled builder, sometimes rising to two stories with windows and ladders. Others appeared to be ramshackle and unlikely to withstand much harsh weather, especially during the monsoon.

In places, pride shone through by way of tubs of soil in which grew a few flowers, vegetables or herbs. Strategically placed communal water pumps provided essential supplies for drinking and basic hygiene whereas, elsewhere, women were still washing clothes in adulterated pools. A rainbow of coloured fabrics and assorted garments hung from makeshift lines or had been draped across roofs and doorways.

Children ran naked through what appeared to be shit and slime while, in partially concealed places, people were openly defecating. Pregnant dogs lay basking in the sunshine, flies buzzing around their mud encrusted coats. An all pervading stench of excrement and the plethora of human activity hung over the area, in places combining to make a retch inducing cocktail.

Yet, I was curious and, as a line of excited children assembled behind me, I ventured further along the narrow mud lanes that wove in a grid of sorts between the closely clustered houses, almost precluding the light in places by their proximity to each other.

There was industry, that I could not have imagined. Small potteries produced hundreds of disposable terracotta cups for the chai sellers. Some were embroidering clothes, diligently and painstakingly with a needle and cotton, whilst others pieced together cuts of fabric with the benefit of a hand driven sewing machine. Leatherworkers turned out intricately decorated belts and bags as young boys stripped insulation from coils of copper wire ready for recycling.

The slum was a veritable hive of activity, but remained to my eyes a crucible of entrapment and found it hard to believe that anyone could actually escape this purgatory.

It was only a short train journey to Bandra, skirting the western perimeter of the slum which, from the train, I was now able to see more clearly and truly grasp its immensity. An irregular patchwork of coloured roofs stretched to a faint distant point, encompassing so much of India's greatest social predicament.

The hotel address I had been given was a short walk from the station, but still necessitated passing slum like accommodation and open ditches where both human and industrial effluent mingled in an unholy fusion

The hotel, which turned out be more of a men's boarding house with bars at the windows, was decorated outside in well worn and peeling blue paint, its cracked walls, plant growth and dismembered drainpipes all added to the perceived state of disrepair.

A sweaty man in a yellow nylon shirt with dark khol around his eyes showed me up the dimly lit stairs, myself following in his malodorous wake. Arriving at the landing with its cracked tiled floor and hand rubbed walls, a padlock had been attached to my contact's door. The receptionist rattled it against the catch a couple of times, to no effect.

As I was leaving, the next door on the landing opened and a short spivvy man with a pencil moustache peered out.

'Can I be of service to the sahib,' he asked.

'I was looking for the man who lives here,' I replied. 'I was told he could help me find work in the films.'

He looked at me as if he had had this conversation a hundred times before. 'You will be finding he is not in the position to be offering the work and he is not here for another four days. But, come, drink chai with us.'

I thanked the receptionist and joined the man in his room.

Two single beds ran along opposite walls with a coffee table in the middle; one of its spindly legs repaired with rounds of tape. A high window cast a diffused light through the begrimed glass.

'This is my good friend, Rahul, he is very good journalist with the Indian Express, he said, pointing to a chubby, clean shaven young man in shirt and cheque patterned lunghi, sprawled along the length of one of the beds. I took his clammy hand and smiled.

'I am Ishaan. I am musician with the films. I am drummer. Here, you have my card.'

His name was neatly printed, together with his profession - "Bungo Player", over which he had used a blue biro to change the typo from a "u" to an "o".

'I go for chai,' Rahul said, lifting himself from his bed and leaving the room for the time it took to reach the street and return with three steaming glassses.

'So you are wanting to be in films,' Ishaan asked.

'I'm retuning to England soon and need more money before I start. I was given this address and an introduction.'

'I'd like to be helping, but we are not having as much opportunity as you might be thinking. Hundreds of people are coming to studio every day, hoping for opportunity. Some are getting a little work, but is mainly for Indians. Is not usual for western person to be getting work. But, you can still be trying.' He was an earnest young man, with his thin build and casual clothes, a stark contrast to his friend. 'Rahul is writing a book.'

'Where is it set?'

'I have centred it in the Dharavi slum, but it is also in Kerala, where my main character comes from,' Rahul told me in a more accomplished level of English.

'I've just been into a big slum near here. Is that the one you are writing about?'

'Yes.'

'Is there nowhere else for them to live? They are in such appalling conditions.'

'It is the biggest slum in the whole of India. Some say, the world,' Rahul answered. 'The people are coming from all over India. It is one giant melting pot of religions, languages and cultures and, most of the time, the people seem to get along very well. But there are always tensions that often flare into trouble. The biggest problems are disease, floods and fire.'

I can imagine a fire would spread very quickly,' I said.

There are regular outbreaks, some accidental others deliberate. More often than not, it is the majority Hindus attacking Moslem homes and mosques. Sometimes people are killed.'

'And what of disease?'

'As you have seen, the people are living so very close together and there is no proper sanitation. The toilets are shared by hundreds of people and most often are overflowing. When the rains come, everything floods into the lanes and the homes. There are regular outbreaks of typhoid and other diseases are widespread. It is a big headache for the authorities. They have been talking about redeveloping the area for years, but everyday people keep arriving in Bombay looking for work. They either go to the slum or sleep in the streets.'

'I suppose there is very little paid work.'

'That's true, but you would be surprised how many small industries there are in the slum, often employing others.'

'I've seen for myself how busy everyone is. Are there schools for the children?'

'Yes. Dharavi is a proper community. Even though the place is a slum, the people have great self-respect and want to educate their children and better themselves, although it can take a lifetime to do so. Surprisingly, there is a literacy level of over sixty percent.'

'And you, Ishaan. Tell me of your work. It must be very exciting.'

'We are having good days and we are having bad days. Most of the time, I am in studio with other musicians and we are recording the soundtracks for the films. I am not often seeing any glamour, although most of the stars are being very self-important.'

'I think you'll find that pomposity amongst many entertainers, although some are very modest about their abilities.'

'You like to hear Indian music?' Ishaan asked.

Ishaan picked up the pair of tabla drums he had resting on a table in the corner and made himself comfortable on the floor. Rahul joined him nearby, having left his repose on the bed and collected his teak carved harmonium. Squeezing the fan arrangement at the back of the instrument, Rahul's fingers started to play along the small keyboard, issuing a sound not unlike a harmonica, but a much richer timbre as air passed through the instrument's reeds.

As the tune became apparent, Ishaan joined in on the tablas, tapping his fingers and palms across the grubby skins. The sound was as enchanting as it was authentic in its distinctive Indian character. At one point, Rahul started to sing, his voice rising and falling with the enunciation of the words, further enhancing the performance. As they finished, I couldn't resist an applause.

'Tell me,' I asked, 'what was the song about?'

'It was a traditional folk song from Orissa,' Rahul said, 'about a man who loves two women and has to decide who he will marry. In the end, he loses both loves.'

I was immediately woken to my own plight. Could this be my fate, having now left Kamala behind in the mountains, while journeying to reunite with Belinda in England? I had not heard from her since writing in early September to explain the dichotomy I found myself in over my love for her and Kamala.

I knew at the time I would ultimately have to make a decision. It was now November and I was on my way back to Belinda, not knowing what her reaction had been to my letter.

'So, why don't you work for the films too, Rahul?' I asked, curious that his abilities weren't being fully employed.

'Sometimes, Ishaan brings me a little work, but my real love is writing. I get a regular income from the newspaper and I still have time to write my book. Look what I have written so far.' He reached onto a shelf where a pile of handwritten sheets sat in a cardboard box. 'Nearly two hundred pages so far, although I will eventually have to type it all out, before I can send it to a publisher.'

I ran my eyes across a couple of pages in which he beautifully described the canals of Kerala and something of life growing up in a family in that green, sun blessed paradise.

A clock on the table told me it was time to go.

It was the middle of the rush hour when I arrived at the station for the train back to Churchgate. The platform was full to bursting with people returning home from work and, as the train arrived at the platform, a vast surge carried me to the doors. Those wanting to leave were given no opportunity, other than to fight their way out, only to be replaced by the onward wave of bodies. I would find myself holding tightly to a handrail in the open doorway, whilst ensuring my bag was safe from pickpockets.

At each station, more souls scrambled to squeeze into an ever tightening space until, only a few stops from the end of the line, the train ground to a halt just outside a station. An announcement followed, informing us there had been a derailment and there would be a wait until it had been cleared.

The day had been hot and clammy, even for late November, intensified by now being trapped inside a metal box with hundreds of others, breathing and sweating profusely. As the minutes ticked by, I could feel my inner boiler building a head of steam.

How had I, in such a short time, come from the tranquility of the mountains to this living hell? To have left people I knew and one that I loved to the midst of a world where greed and blind ambition reigned supreme? Where the laughter and love I had forsaken had been replaced with selfishness and sadness? Closing my eyes, I could place myself back in that tranquility, breathing the fresh mountain air until a sudden jolt of the carriage an hour later signalled that we were on the move again.

At Churchgates, I was faced with the ordeal of finally leaving the train as people tried to board even before we had stopped. Shouting and screaming, arms waving furiously, in they swept in an unstoppable wave. There was no point in being polite, it was every man or woman for themselves. I pushed and heaved, shouldering my way forward an inch only to be repelled a foot, stopping for breath and starting again. This continued for what seemed an age with no capitulation on either side nor assistance from any railway employees.

I took another breath, stood as tall as my frame and circumstances would allow and shouted, 'Stop! Stop! Are you totally insane? Stand back and let us off first!' This seemed to freeze our section of the crowd and the pressure eased momentarily, but sufficiently, for those of us leaving to make one big surge, enabling us to burst through this human dam out onto the back of the less congested part of the platform.

Jen's Land Rover was not in the street when I arrived at the Salvation Army hostel, neither were she and Liam in their room. It was still early evening, so I wasn't particularly perturbed, although I was wondering if I would be able to sleep in the Rover again that night.

By eight o' clock, they still weren't back and alarm bells were ringing.

At the YMCA on the sea front, there were still no available rooms until the next day, but I persuaded the manager to let me sleep in the narrow foyer, rather than joining the thousands now resident on the streets.

It had been a rough night on a hard stone floor, when I woke next morning to seek out Jen and Liam again.

The Land Rover was still not in the street, but I went up to their hostel anyway. As I climbed the stairs and approached their door, I could hear sobbing from within. I knocked. The sobbing continued, wretched and distraught. I knocked again, but was totally unprepared for what I saw next.

The door opened slightly and, in between the narrow opening, Liam peered out, an angry red and purple bruise around his eye extending to his cheek and a cut and swollen lip.

'God, Liam. What's happened?' I exclaimed in total consternation.

'Hi Adam.' He replied, the words slurred by his injuries The door opened a little wider and I could see Jen lying on the bed trembling, a flannel held to her face and her torn blouse, its buttons missing, loosely covering her breasts.

'What the fuck has happened?' I shouted incredulously. 'What can I do?'

'Come in, Adam,' Jen called out, her voice quavering.

Liam pulled the door back and revealed the true horror of what lay in that room. Liam's face was bruised and swollen, dried blood still in his nostrils, his kameez torn and bloodied.

Jen had removed the flannel to reveal severe bruising to her face with her eyes displaying a disconcerting detachment. Her happy, confident countenance had disappeared to be replaced by this shuddering woman. Her joyous soul seemed to have been ripped out of her.

'Tell me, please. What happened? Do you want me to find a doctor?'

'Sit down, Adam.' Jen instructed me, recovering some of her mettle and pulling the remnants of her blouse more tightly across her body as she sat up.

I sat on the edge of one of the beds and noticed more bruises on Jen's arms and legs as Liam drew up a chair.

'You know we said we had to take the Land Rover in for a service,' Jen began, 'well, that wasn't strictly true.'

'So where is the Land Rover now?' I asked.

'We had to go to an address we'd been given up near the airport.'

'That seems a long way to go for a car service.'

'Let her finish, Adam,' Liam interjected.

Jen sniffled and blew her nose on a piece of toilet paper. 'This was not about a car service. You see, I had picked up some gold in Singapore and had smuggled it here with a view to making a profit.'

My eyes widened, willing her to continue.

'I had bought gold bars in Singapore, using money I had inherited from my Grandmother and had them hidden behind metal plates welded under the Land Rover. The seller had given me a contact in Bombay, where I was told there was a very high demand because restrictions had been put on gold imports. So far, so good.'

She went quiet and drew a few deep breaths. I caught Liam's eye and registered his concern for her.

'Are you sure you want to go on, Jen?' Liam asked.

Placing her hands on her lap, she composed herself, although still shaking, and continued.

'I had phoned a few days ago to make contact and confirm the meeting. When we arrived at the address and banged on a pair of large garage doors, they were waiting for us, The doors were opened and we drove in to a workshop, equipped with a ramp and mechanics' tools.

Four men surrounded us and one, who looked marginally more

intelligent than the others, asked where the gold was.

I told them how much we had smuggled in and wanted to know how much they were going to pay us.

It was then it started to turn nasty. The man slapped me across my face and asked again where the gold was hidden. Liam jumped forward and tried to whack the man for attacking me, but was quickly grabbed by the others, who proceeded to do to him what you see now.'

'Ah think Ah must have been unconscious for some time after they'd beaten ma face, head and body, kicking me on the ground.'

'It was so vicious,' Jen added. They shouted at me again and one of them pulled a knife, holding it to Liam's throat and running his finger across his own to suggest they would kill him if I didn't tell them. And, so I told them.'

'What happened next?' I asked, feeling almost as if I had overstepped a threshold by asking.

'They raped me.' Jen stopped and stared straight ahead of her, transfixed by the horrendous reality that had now clearly dawned on her consciousness.

'Of course, I blame myself,' she said hesitantly.

'You shouldn't say that, Jen,' I proffered as some meagre comfort. 'You weren't to know.'

'Of course it was my fault!' she screamed. Look at Liam, he's even got broken teeth. I've lost all my money and the Rover. What am I to do?' She broke down again, sobbing profusely, burying her already reddened and bruised eyes in her hands. 'And, I'm probably pregnant. I just want to go home, but I'm so embarrassed by it all. It was all down to my greed. Not being content with what I already had and now my life … is ruined.'

Liam rose slowly from his chair, wincing at the pain that tore through his body, and sat down beside her, carefully wrapping his arm around her.

'So where were you both last night?' I asked.

'They kept us both there, until they'd retrieved the gold and then threw us out into the street early this morning. We started walking until a kind taxi driver saw us and brought us back here.'

'What about the police? Aren't you going to report what happened?' I asked.

'We can't risk it.' Liam replied. 'Firstly, they're probably all in on it and, even if they're not, if we could find the address again, those men have probably all cleared out by now and melted into the city. If they ever found us again, they would certainly kill us. I'm sure of that.'

'So what's your next move. Are you still going to Kenya?'

'Fortunately, we left our passports, here in the safe, together with most of our money,' Liam replied. 'Jen's got her berth already booked and I'll go to the agent and get mine. The ship sails the day after tomorrow.'

'Well, at least there's some redemption, but I'm going to find a doctor for you both. You can't leave without a check up.'

At the reception, I explained that Jen and Liam had been mugged somewhere in the city by a gang of drunken hoodlums. Within an hour, a doctor was attending to them. While he was able to tend their surface wounds, there was little that could be done to address the trauma they had both experienced. That was going to take a lot longer and probably would never be healed.

There was much I wanted to see in the city, but now didn't have the heart for it. Instead, I took a solitary walk along the seafront, absorbed in an overwhelming sadness that the wonder of India had turned so sour. Of course, it would have been wrong to judge the whole of India on this incident, but there was a deep seated malaise that had seeped into the fabric of the country, tainting so much that was good. I could only think of the mountains, the innocence and Kamala.

I took some food up to Jen and Liam, but she had no appetite, instead preferring to curl up in bed, alive but distanced from the world around her.

'She needs to rest,' Liam whispered. 'Ah need to go out for ma ticket. Would you mind goin' with me?

He too had been traumatised by the event and needed the reassurance of some company.

'Is Jen going to be okay by herself? I asked, as we set off, passing the Gateway of India arch towards the agent's office by the docks.

'She must sleep for now. But, it's not goin' to go away. Ah didn't see it as Ah was unconscious but, when Ah came round, they'd clearly all had their way with her. She was lyin' there almost naked on a filthy blanket on the floor, cryin' and in obvious pain. Ah went to help dress her and they just laughed at us. If only Ah could get them, but it's pointless even thinkin' about it.

We strolled on slowly, with Liam still clearly in pain, past parades of run down shops and open doorways where young and often very beautiful girls of no more than fourteen or fifteen smiled and invited us to join them upstairs. Countless radios pumped out incessant film music enjoining us to empathise with unrequited and star-crossed love.

The shock of Liam's appearance on entering the shipping office was tangible, but he explained that he was travelling with Jen, spinning the line about being mugged, and he was soon walking out with a ticket and a cabin to boot.

'What time do you sail then,' I asked, as we walked back past the prostitutes and into the busy thoroughfare where a ceaseless barrage of beggars confronted us.

'High tide is at quarter to two in the afternoon and we sail soon after. We've got to be on board by one.'

As we walked alongside the cars and tongas, a young boy came speeding past us on a small trolley. I laughed at first to see him competing with the cars, only to be shamed on seeing that he had no legs.

My eyes continued to be opened to the realities of life in this huge city as we stepped over countless bodies, lying prone on the pavement or huddled across steps leading to one or other shop. These were not isolated individuals but often whole families with three or four children calling a few square feet of pavement home.

Would this suffering ever cease? I asked myself, *or is generation after generation destined to this living hell?*

Turning into the street towards the hostel, my attention was suddenly distracted. Looking across the road, I thought I saw something familiar.

'Hey, isn't that Jen's Land Rover?' I exclaimed.

Sure enough, parked in a space by the hostel, it was the same car, washed and bedecked with garlands of marigolds across the bonnet and roof rack. Two men were sitting in the front seats.

'Are those any of the men who attacked you?' I asked Liam.

'Ah don't recognise them.'

'What should we do? Why would they return the Rover and cover it with flowers? It doesn't make sense.'

We inched a little closer and suddenly the doors opened and the two men stepped out, turning to confront us.

'Oh shit,' Liam exclaimed.

The older of the two was just under six feet tall, thin with slightly greying hair and piercing almost black eyes. He must have been about forty years of age, well dressed with a not unkindly face. The other, shorter, plumper and younger seemed to defer to the elder.

The older man immediately acknowledged Liam and stretched out his hand. Liam took it reluctantly.

'Who are you?' Liam asked. 'Why have you got our car? How did you find me?'

The man spoke a few sentences before stopping to let the other translate into English.

'My name is Harjit Kalwar. I am here to offer my most humble apologies for what happened yesterday. I would like to talk to you and your memsahib.'

'Where are the bastards who did this?' Liam shouted, pointing at his face.

'I will tell you in due course,' came the reply

'Come with us,' Liam said as Kalwar reached into the car and brought out a black briefcase.

We led the two men to the hostel and climbed once more to the room where Jen was still sleeping.

The two men stood outside as Liam went and gently shook Jen to wake her.

'Jen, Jen. Wake up,' he whispered. 'We've got some visitors.'

She moaned a little as she came to and opened her eyes.

'Jen, We've got some visitors,' he repeated.

Rubbing her eyes, the bruising now much more swollen, she began to sit up.

'What is it, Liam?' she asked, sleepily.

'Two men have brought the Rover back. You should see it. It's all cleaned up and covered in marigolds.'

'Stop joking with me, Liam. You know I feel like shit.'

'Ah'm not joking, Jen. You should see it and the two men who returned it are just outside. They want to talk to you.'

'What are they, police?'

'I don't know. They're not in uniforms.'

'Bring them in then.'

I leant outside the door and beckoned the two men into the room.

Their consternation was palpable on first seeing Jen as they put their hands together and slightly bowed towards her, now sitting up in the bed.

The older man started to talk again before allowing his colleague to translate.

'Memsahib, my name is Harjit Kalwar, I wish to offer my most humble apologies for what was done to you and the sahib yesterday. I could not comprehend that such a terrible thing would have been done to a guest in our country.'

'Where are those men now?' Jen replied. 'And where's my gold?'

'I can assure you that they have been most severely dealt with.'

'Where are they?' Jen repeated, the tears of anxiety and those still very fresh memories once more occupying her mind with intense clarity.

'I can assure you they are now at the bottom of the ocean with most heavy weights around their necks. You will not be seeing them again.'

'You've killed them?'

'Of course. My honour had been violated and I wish to atone for what a most dreadful thing that was done to your good self and the sahib.'

He turned to his companion, who then laid the briefcase on the bed and unclicked the latches. He lifted the lid to reveal it stuffed with wadges of used hundred dollar bills.

'There is sixty thousand dollars there for you. It is your money, returned for the cost of your gold, your profit at fourteen percent and the rest is my compensation for your injuries.'

We were all totally incredulous that this should be happening after the overwhelming sense of desperation and loss that had been felt earlier in the day.

'Your car is even now waiting for you. Have a safe journey,' he concluded.

'Thank you, thank you,' both Jen and Liam chorused.

The two men then clasped their hands together, bowing again, before turning and leaving the room.

'Now, you can get your teeth fixed, Liam,' Jen said, somewhere on the brink of pain and joyous laughter as she ran her hands through the notes.

I'm going to turn in now,' I said, feeling I was now intruding in something of a special moment for them both. 'See you tomorrow on your last day.'

I was looking forward to curling up in my own bed at last, albeit sharing a dormitory with three Indians in the YMCA, when I bumped into the English and French girls I had met on that moonlit night many miles back at the Taj Mahal.

'Hello again.' Alison, the English girl, said, 'How are you? We're just going down to the seafront for a smoke. You want to come?'

Sitting on the solid sea wall just along from the Gateway of India, a joint passed between us as the water splashed gently against the wall; the myriad reflections from the lamps dancing like the Nereids, the fifty beautiful daughters of Nereus, who danced around their father in red coral crowns and white silk dresses trimmed with gold.

The girls' company lifted my temperament after recent events had conspired to disillusion my spirit and deplete my energy. Compensating for my sense of detachment at the Taj Mahal, I was now seeing the girls in a new light and soon we were all finding laughter in even the darkest incidents.

Six

I **HAD ALREADY DECIDED** that it was time to head north. I felt
that both my unsuccessful entry into the film world, together
with Jen and Liam's appalling experience were sufficient motivation to move on.

Jen and Liam stayed inside for most of their last day to further
nurse their wounds, while I now felt more inclined to enjoy myself.

Alison had spoken of taking a trip out to Elephanta Island and I
had agreed to join her for the day, while Maric, her French friend,
had packed her bags and left early to spend Christmas in Goa;
something I had considered for five seconds until I realised that
my limited funds were not going to allow it. I now had just over
one hundred rupees left and twenty pounds for the journey home.

I met Alison at the pier by the Gateway of India at nine next
morning and was stunned by her beauty, something I'd been
oblivious to when I first met her at the Taj Mahal. She was certainly
the same person, but my perceptions had been coloured by my
mood at the time, having so recently left Kamala. Her strong
jawline and well proportioned features were enhanced by clear
aquamarine eyes, full sultry lips and a flawless complexion, tanned
by the Indian sun.

The little boat chugged out into a calm, but misty sea, very
different to the last time I had taken a boat trip in the Greek
islands, months earlier. There, the water sparkled in the sunlight
with a clear view to the bottom. This day, it was a milky jade green,
murky and dense.

The journey took the better part of an hour in an oppressive heat with little breeze off the sea to bring relief.

We moored at the little wooden pier that stretched out from the tree covered island and walked ashore, passing hundreds of tiny crabs, seemingly stuck in the sand by the receding tide, each waving one claw in the air as if calling for help. On the other side of the pier, mangroves grew out of the salt saturated sand, their roots reaching for the stars as if the only way they could survive.

The small number of caves lay at the top of a long flight of stone steps. Being very exposed to the elements and the sea air, the degree of deterioration was far more evident than at either Ajanta or Ellora, not helped by water seepage, neglect and vandalism in an earlier time by the Portuguese.

Beneath the solid block of rock that merges into the hillside above, four grand pillars marked the entrance, leading into a vast temple precinct, celebrating the many manifestations of the Lord Shiva. Within a recess, at the back of the temple, the colossal, three faced head and shoulders of Sadashiva Trimurti emerged from the rock, representing the creator, the destroyer and, facing forward, the preserver. To his left, Shiva and his consort, Parvati, stood together bringing the River Ganges down from heaven. To his right, a fusion of Shiva and Parvati, symbolising the oneness that transcends all individuality in the all embracing universe.

At the heart of the temple rose an immense stone chamber with four doorways, each flanked by two gate guardians, housing a mighty phallic lingam and feminine yoni, symbolising the creative, energetic and regenerative nature of God and all existence.

What we saw was a powerful insight into the Hindu acknowledgement of our universal oneness and the many aspects of that whole that we, as living beings, are all a part of.

With still time until the return ferry left, Alison and I sat amongst the trees looking out across to smaller islands lost in the haze.

'What brought you to India?' I asked, as I offered her a beedi.

'Curiosity,' she replied, brushing back a thick swathe of blonde hair while I struck a match. 'I'd been living in Brighton and then some time in Amsterdam, where I met a lot of people interested in Indian religion, gurus and wanting to get out of the rat race.'

'I guess that's pretty much the motivation for most of us,' I replied. I then went on to tell her about the alternative underground scene in London, the nights at UFO, the bands, the drugs and the call to "find one's Self". 'I fell in love with a girl in London, but just had to satisfy this itch to come to India.'

'Are you still in touch with her?' Alison asked.

'I'm heading north tomorrow and will then make my way back overland. I last wrote to her in early September while I was living with Tibetans in the mountains and again last week, so I'm hoping she's still be there when I get back.'

'Everything and everyone seems so very distant from this reality,' she said. 'It's easy to forget what we were back there. I feel I've changed so much since being here, although it's been only four months now.'

'I know what you mean. Despite the crowds, the heat, the poverty, there is an indelible beauty and what I can only describe as magic, that seeps deep into your psyche. I wonder how much it will endure in years to come?' Did you come overland?'

'I took the Magic Bus from London until it broke down near Tehran. They had to send away for parts so I joined up with some of the others and we made our own way through Afghanistan and West Pakistan. That was in July. I've since been to Nepal, stayed in an ashram in Benares for six weeks, meditating and chanting and then to most of the touristy places. Now, I'm working my way down to the South for some winter sunshine and more temples.'

'I'd love to join you, but money's getting short and I've got to leave enough to get back for the new year. When are you planning to go back? Maybe you're not.'

I will eventually, probably in the spring, but who knows. My parents are in England, but I've got no other reason to go back, other than money.'

The ferry brought us back to the Gateway of India, where the postcard, nut and juice vendors and, of course, the inevitable snake charmers were all trying to make a living.

Walking across the wide plaza, we were both intrigued by one snake charmer, who was obviously creating a show for us. The snake didn't seem the slightest bit interested in rising out of its basket in response to the wailing pipe, until the charmer prodded it with a stick and it eventually deigned to rise up and hiss with its open hood. It was blatantly obvious that any connection between the pipe playing and the snake's response was purely coincidental.

He then pulled a mongoose out of a sack and set it to work taunting the snake. The lethargic and already injured snake was no match as the mongoose bit into its neck, hanging by its teeth when the snake was held up in the air.

I agreed to meet Alison for a farewell dinner, leaving me with the rest of the afternoon and one more chance of trying to make a bit of extra money.

As a western visitor, I'd picked up a couple of liquor permits as many Indian states are "dry" and the clamour for alcohol is rife.

Normally, if I'd had money to spare, I would have gone to Madras, where I'd been told I could probably have sold each for a hundred rupees. But, there was always the chance that the stories were apocryphal and that, with no buyers, I would have to change my plans for the journey home. The next best thing was to approach the numerous money changers that circled the Gateway of India like persistent flies. As with creatures with one track minds, they weren't interested in the permits, but only the liquor itself.

'You come with me,' one said, waving for another man and a young boy to come over. 'This man is wanting permit, we go in taxi, Sahib. Come.'

We all bundled in the back and the driver was ordered to go. With wheels spinning, we headed off to the north at great speed, following the main docks road. The dealer was attempting a negotiation with the other man as we screeched round corners, hit the kerb a couple times and narrowly missed people and animals along the way. It was really quite comedic seeing us all thrown about, unable to do anything other than hold on for dear life. Without warning the car drew to a halt, throwing us all forward and the boy and I were summarily cast out on the pavement with the dealer and the "buyer" speeding off with my permits. Moments later, a police car sped by in hot pursuit, its siren sounding. Clearly, I had been set up.

The boy quickly led me away, off through a squalid maze of back streets, where men skulked in doorways, kids played hop-scotch, a few stalls sold vegetables and hot food, while the beggars and prostitutes plied their business. A small group of boys and girls sat furtively in a dark space, sharing a cigarette and scattering as I approached.

Stopping by some young men, the boy, seemingly unaware that I'd just lost my permits, appeared to be discussing a possible sale. As with the money changers, they were only interested in having the real thing in their hands, notably a bottle of Scotch. One of them suggested I buy a bottle from a British ship in the docks and I could then sell it to them with a good profit. After Jen and Liam's experience the day before and the scam that had just been put over on me, I had no guarantees that I would walk away with the money in my hand instead of possibly a black eye or worse.

This idea did however sow a seed that, perhaps, I could work my passage back to England on a British ship. I even went as far as walking back to the docks and attempting to pass the security gates, where I was told by the officious guard that I needed a pass from a certain police station on the other side of the city.

These bureaucratic undertakings were increasingly becoming too much hard work and I quickly returned to my original plan, which was the overland journey.

I thought perhaps I might be able to persuade Jen and Liam to join Alison and I for dinner on their last night. Liam answered the door to their hotel room when I knocked a little later.

Hi Adam, Ah was hopin' you'd come,' he said, somewhat dejectedly. 'Can we go for a chai?'

It was clear that his injuries had had an impact on his overall health as he shuffled down to the Sunrise, wincing occasionally with the still very present pain. One of his eyes had almost closed over and the other looked more swollen than the previous day. As he took a seat, he began to pour out his concerns

'Ah hadn't anticipated hookin' up with Jen at the beginnin', but you know how these things happen. Ah like her a lot and think we could make somethin' of our lives in Africa. But, with what happened, she's changed. She's doesn't get out of bed, except to shower several times a day and she's scrubbin' her skin almost raw.'

'She must feel so defiled. It's bad enough being raped by one person, but four! I can't begin to imagine what she must be going through. You're going to get better and possibly have a few nightmares in your life but, for her, she's got the worry that she might be pregnant and then what does she do?'

'We've talked and she will more than likely get an abortion in Europe if she has to. It's against the law in Kenya with heavy prison terms. At least she has the money now to pay for a good clinic, but she's still in two minds about it. She had been usin' a cap but, if that hasn't worked, the other option is to go full term and put the baby up for adoption. The one certain thing is that there is no way she'll keep it.'

'So, she's had to consider so many scenarios in such a short time. It's knowing what's for the best. We can only hope she's not actually pregnant.

What about tomorrow? Is she going to be fit enough to get on the boat? I don't think she's going to be up to driving, even the short distance to the docks.'

'That's okay, Ah have ma US licence. Once we're on the boat, she's goin' to have two weeks of complete rest ahead of her, so she should look much better, even if she doesn't feel it.'

'I'd like to see her before you go and say goodbye. Would that be okay?'

'Come and see us in the mornin'. Ah'm hopin' she'll be feelin' better then, just because we're leavin' India and all of this behind.'

'But, what of your plans? You were going to London.'

'Ah still want to do that and we may have to go anyway to find a clinic.'

'So you think you'll settle in Kenya?'

'If Jen will still have me, Ah'd like to start ma own business, possibly graphic design. Ah trained in the States and worked for a few years before travellin' and Ah think there are still opportunities.'

I met Alison at a South Indian restaurant just back from the seafront and was flabbergasted as she strolled down the street in a long turquoise cheesecloth dress, silver sandals and hair flowing freely across her bare shoulders, like a girl from a fashion magazine. I hadn't expected she would have made such an effort on my behalf with me still dressed in the white top and jeans I'd been wearing all day.

Taking her hand, I led her to our table, my heart racing as I sat opposite and started the conversation.

'You're looking gorgeous. What a lovely dress.' It all sounded very corny, but I meant it as I looked into those eyes once again, mesmerised by her beauty, but knowing we were going our separate ways the next day and I still had to resolve my situation with Kamala and Belinda without complicating matters more.

'I want to thank you Adam for coming to Elephanta with me today. It was lovely being able to talk,' she said.

'It was for me too. I'm sorry I was so detached when I met you in Agra. You must have thought me quite rude. I had a lot on my mind at the time and didn't really feel like talking to anyone.'

'Not at all. In fact, I was quite curious, especially when we went into the Taj and you chose to meditate. What did you do after Marie and I went back to the hotel?'

'Oh, I rolled out my sleeping bag in the little temple on the edge of that terrace and, as the only person there, stood bathing myself in the moonlight and the very special atmosphere. I'll never forget it.'

'I so wish I'd stayed and could have been with you there. So, where are you off to tomorrow?' she asked, once we'd looked at the menu and ordered.

'I'll get a train out of town and find the road towards Benares, probably hitching. There's an English girl there I knew over the summer when I was living in the mountains. She went to stay with a boyfriend, so I want to meet up with her before I go to Bodh Gaya and Sarnath.'

'You'll love Sarnath. It's very tranquil, but Benares is something else. It's crazy town, where thousands of Hindus go to die and get cremated on the banks of the Ganges. I was fascinated by the burning ghats where the bodies are brought day and night, but found the whole experience too overwhelming. After that, I suppose that's when the journey really begins for you.'

'Yes, I've got to go to Delhi for visas and to collect my rucksack, which I left in storage. I've also got to get hold of some warm clothes and boots before I head for the Pakistani border. Then, who knows?'

'Are you planning to travel by yourself, Alison?' I asked tentatively.

'I was with Marie, the French girl, for quite a way, but I'm sure I'll hook up with someone before long.'

'I don't want to worry you, but you mustn't take any risks. I've had my fair share on the way and probably will take a few more on the way back, but there are some dangerous people about.' I then went on to tell her about Jen and Liam.

'Obviously, what they were doing was very risky, but look what happened to the guys who double crossed them. It's shows there are some very ruthless people about.'

'I've heard about this Harjit Kalwar guy,' Alison said. 'His name came up a couple of days ago when I was talking to some American sadhus in the Sunrise. It seems he's one of the main gang leaders in Bombay with quite a reputation for his ruthlessness but, it seems, he's also got a heart by the way he helped your friends.'

The meal drew to a close and it was as if we'd known each other for years, exchanging experiences and common ideas. She told me she'd grown up in Wimbledon, not far from where I had lived, just outside London. She'd even been to some of the same clubs I used to hang out in at weekends during those last three years of the sixties.

By the time we'd downed the last drop of chai, we were laughing at the futility of our lives and wondering how best to live them out.

'I just want to go back and paint,' I said, 'but that's probably not very realistic. I'll have to get some qualifications and then see. What about you?'

'I did a bit of modelling before coming here…'

'I knew it,' I interrupted, ' You're just so perfect,' I added. 'I'm sorry, but you are.'

She blushed but, by this time, her arm was already across the table as she walked her fingertips forward a little to touch mine. I hesitated momentarily, but my flesh was weak as I gently curled my fingers around hers, sending ripples of anticipation through my body.

'Alison, I can't. I've told you about my situation. It's too complicated. I like you, of course, but…' Catching sight of those blue eyes once again, I was stopped in my tracks, unable to continue, only to be consumed by an irrepressible force that I knew only too well.

I paid the bill and we stepped out into the street, the evening air still warm and a little stifling. She took my hand again and we walked silently past more restaurants and ice cream vendors, turning down to the sea wall and the inky waters beyond, where best intentions would be swallowed whole.

'Don't worry, I'm protected,' she said, wrapping her arms around my waist and nestling her body into mine. Her breasts felt firm against me as I now embraced her, sensing the warm nakedness beneath her dress and accepting what was now happening.

I've always loved women, generally preferring their company to that of men, whose crudity, macho affectations and competitiveness held no sway for me.

Women are the shelters from the storm. Beautiful, interesting, funny, creative, determined, sensitive, spiritual. So much to offer and so hard to choose between. Each has her own facets that have enriched my life and broken my heart. I had already lost through death and been torn apart, but I'd never lived with a woman long enough to experience what life would be like for years and years. To witness the tapestry of changing moods, the shedding of the old for the new, the disagreements and fear when perhaps I might be losing her.

What a wonder it must be to share a life with someone I really cared for. To bring joy to her face with little gifts and treats. Helping to heal when illness intervenes. To share in the joy of children.

At this time, I was on a carrousel of wonderment as each girl entered my life, presenting a new set of opportunities, challenges and experiences; guidelines for the future as fresh encounters were embarked upon. Often, there was nothing particularly sexual in the encounter, I was content to be in her company, to hear her story, to say, 'Good night, see you tomorrow.'

The bright morning light woke me early. Alison lay beside me still asleep, the sun through the window casting a warm glow across her face. She was indeed beautiful and had given herself freely and lovingly, but I knew I had to move on.

Her eyes opened and she raised her hand to shield them from the sunlight.

'Good morning,' I said. 'Thank you for last night.'

'Thank *you*,' she replied, smiling winsomely as I stretched across and kissed those lips, the faint aroma of patchouli still lingering on her skin.

'I've promised to see my friends before they leave this morning,' I said, 'and then I must go myself.'

I'd collected my bags from the hostel the night before and moved them to Alison's hotel where I now took a hasty morning shower.

'When are you heading out? I asked, as I dried myself and laid my things out on the bed to repack for the journey.

'I've got another night booked here and then I'll get a train tomorrow.'

'I've got your address in England, Alison. Who knows?'

'I'd like that. Write to me and keep safe on your journey. I don't like you having to go in the winter.'

'I'll be okay. I've got a guardian angel.'

I leant down and kissed her again, her arm wrapped around my neck.

'I've got to go. I'll see you again,' I said, as I pulled away, my hand running along her arm until it was just our fingers touching and then the warm air we'd left between us.

I shut her door, skipped down the stairs and outside into the melée of another Indian day.

Liam and Jen were packing and sticking labels on their bags when I arrived at their room. The door was ajar as I knocked and entered.

Despite their still miserable appearances, I asked, nevertheless, 'How are you both feeling?'

'All the better for leaving,' Jen replied.

With some effort, Liam stood straight and patted my arm in greeting.

Jen was wearing a pretty floral patterned dress, which I guessed she had on to hide some of her bruises.

'You're looking lovely in that dress. I don't think I've ever seen you out of shorts.'

'Thanks Adam. That's kind of you.'

'I noticed the black briefcase standing against the wall in one of the corners.

'Don't forget that,' I said, laughingly.

'We're leaving it behind,' Liam said.

'Empty, I presume.'

'Of course. We've had to sew it all into our bags in case we get stopped at customs for importing illegal currency. If you're wondering why we couldn't come out last night, that's the reason.'

Jen reached into her shoulder bag on the bed. 'Adam, we wanted to give you something for your journey, just so you don't have to work in Indian films to get home.' She pulled out two one hundred dollar bills and offered them to me. 'Here, take these. You've been good company and very kind to us,' Jen went on.

I was reluctant at first, being polite, but realised how the money would improve my chances of getting back safely.

'That's such a relief, Jen. You don't know what difference that's going to make. Thank you so much. That's very kind of you.'

When all was packed, I helped them take everything downstairs as they still weren't really up to it. 'You must ask for help when you need it. You could both have internal injuries that still need to heal.'

Breakfast was in the Sunrise, where the film guys were busy talking to a hippy guy and his chick. One of them looked up as we came in and strode over to our table.

'We need a few more people today and tomorrow,' he said, 'Are you interested?'

I glanced at Jen and Liam and chuckled ironically, before looking up at the man. 'Thank you for the offer, but we're all leaving today. Places to go.'

He was clearly disappointed, gave an empty smile and returned to his colleague.

When all was packed in the Land Rover, we gave each other a last hug, myself taking great care not to squeeze either of them too tightly.

'Now you must rest. Take in that sea air and get better.' I said in parting.

Liam sat in the driving seat and started the engine. He scrunched the gears, hopped a couple of times along the road before finding his clutch control and gliding away, hands waving from the windows and a few marigolds flying off in the breeze. A turn in the road and they were gone.

Seven

Victoria Terminus was the principal railway station in the city, built by the British in a fusion of Victorian Gothic and Mughal splendour, resembling something more like a palace than a railway station. Inside, I was overwhelmed by the floods of light pouring through the high windows, the columns supporting a vast vaulted ceiling and the distant apex of the central dome contained within a decorative octagonal gallery.

As to be expected, even in mid morning, the concourse was packed as I looked for information that would tell me which train to catch.

A suburban train, empty enough to give me a seat, took me out to Kalwa, a small station near the main Bombay to Agra highway, which would eventually branch off to Jalgaon, Nagpur and Benares.

At the Kalwa bus terminal, a crowd had gathered where a passenger had hit a driver, bringing all the drivers out on strike. The altercation became increasingly more hostile with angry shouting and pushing to the point that I didn't want to be around these people, instead opting for the chance of a lift.

It was the end of November and already the day was hot and stifling, lifting the acrid smell of the open drains that flanked the road. Naked children played games around the nearby mud and straw houses, where small groups of men squatted together over chai and a beedi, while the women pounded piles of clothes at the village taps or prepared an open fire.

Fat black and grey pigs wallowed in the drains to cool themselves or snorted around the open ground, scavenging for anything that might resemble food.

A young girl squatted alongside a goat, teasing its teats for a small bucket of milk. An old man squatted, emptying himself into the drains, further adding to the all pervading stench.

Nothing was stopping for me, except an endless line of taxis hustling for a fare, while the sun relentlessly drained my will to continue with yet still so far to go. On the point of fainting, I sought shade and sustenance in a roadside restaurant until, in the early afternoon, I crossed the road and was almost immediately picked up by a lorry that took me the few kilometres to a check point on the outskirts of Nashik.

The manager spoke good English and made every effort to see that I was comfortable in his office with a cup of chai while he made arrangements with a driver going in my direction.

An oil tanker drew up and, before I knew what was happening, my bags were being put in the cab with myself being invited to join the three man crew inside. The driver, a hulk of a man, made it very clear who was in charge, although I later saw his soft side. His companions were slight by comparison and certainly much quieter, one virtually saying nothing, while the other joked a little with the hulk and occasionally broke into song.

The road, being the main Bombay, Agra to Delhi highway, was, by English standards, merely a single track of uneven tarmac with a small strip of levelled ground for passing on either side. Although the distance to Dhulia, our next stop, was not much more than a hundred and thirty miles, the driving conditions took us through the night.

Some miles into the journey, we ran parallel to the wide Godavari River where tree covered islands divided the main stream into narrower rivulets. Here barges brought gravel to be carried to the shore by long lines of women balancing wide metal bowls on their heads.

We drove on through countless villages, the horn blaring incessantly to clear people and animals from our path. The rest stops were frequent as were the cups of chai bought for me by my hosts and, as the road turned north, darkness began to fall with the sun sinking over the vast banana plantations to the west.

At a filling station, a café provided food and the four of us sat down to eat. As well as buying my dinner, the driver also ordered a round of an alcoholic drink mixed with coke. It could have been rum, I didn't ask and I was too inexperienced in such things to know for myself. While it took the chill off the night air, it went straight to my head, despite drinking copious amounts of water in an attempt to dilute it some. I refused further offers, while the "hulk" continued to drink more.

It was just as well that the time had come for the drivers to change, the "hulk" lying across a pull down bed at the back as we drove on into the night for another hour or so until fatigue and the cold determined that we pull off to the side of the road. Our "songster" climbed into another bunk, the "mouse" lay across the driver's seat and the dashboard, while I wrapped in my sleeping bag across a side seat.

Despite the heavy snoring, I slept until just before dawn, leaving the cab to empty my bowels as a deep orange glow splashed across the top of the hills in the East, casting all else into silhouette. Other lorries had stopped nearby and their crews, wrapped in blankets, shivered around a blazing fire, the smoke curling into a chrome yellow sky, its northern and southern extremes by now a deep indigo glow.

Tea was made in a nearby hut and poured from a large aluminium pot into eagerly held enamel cups, serving to further warm our hands, until the sun was finally upon us and we were once more on our way.

It was another day and a half, with much waiting in between short lifts and a night in Jalgaon station waiting room, before I was eventually dropped on the Bhusawal by-pass.

I sat for most of the late morning with nothing passing save for a few lorries in the opposite direction and the slow passage of the occasional bullock cart, loaded with grass or maize, bells tinkling and the gold tips of their red painted horns glinting in the sunshine.

A group of young boys arrived at one point, speaking reasonable English and asking me neither where I'd come from nor where I was ultimately going. Having told them I was waiting for a lift onwards to Nagpur, they politely informed me that I was wasting my time as all the lorries pass through the town.

They led me along a dried river bed, up through a Moslem cemetery and into the town. It was a Moslem holiday and the streets filled with a procession of gaily dressed dancing women and children, adorned with jewellery, flowers and other ornamentation. The men dressed in traditional long tunics to their ankles and beautifully crocheted topis on their heads.

Yet more children waved balloons and coloured flags, while ornately dressed musicians swirled through the crowd banging traditional drums and blowing trumpets in what, for me, was a discordant racket.

I stopped for lunch near the town's centre where a man asked where I was going.

'I'm hoping to get to Nagpur in a lorry this afternoon,' I replied.

'Could I be making a suggestion?' he asked. 'If the sahib is going to the railway station and is saying that he has not much money, they may let you travel for nothing.'

I was a little surprised to hear this, but thanked him anyway and crossed to the station.

It was not unusual for me to walk straight onto a station platform and use the toilet in the waiting room. On this occasion, I went back outside to sit on a station bench and got talking to a local man about the procession.

'It is the celebration of Eid ul-Fitr, the last day of Ramadam when the Moslems can stop fasting.'

'I can see why they are so happy then.'

'Ticket, please, ticket!'

I was suddenly interrupted by a man in beige trousers, a white shirt and long brown serge waistcoat.

'I don't have a ticket,' I replied.

He was a thin greying man with a face that looked as if anger and bitterness had been etched at birth. His lips were thin and eyes bulging and bloodshot, encompassed by the profusion of lines that tracked his skin like a busy railway terminus.

'Where is your ticket? Where are you going?'

'I don't have a ticket. I'm not going anywhere.'

'Where is your platform ticket?' he persisted.

I couldn't believe that anyone would be asking for a platform ticket as I didn't know such things existed in India. The platforms are always crowded with people who, to my mind, could not afford train tickets, let alone a platform ticket.

'I'm sorry, but I don't have one,' I told him.

His tone of voice became threatening and malicious. 'You will come with me to be prosecuted then.'

'What!!?' I exclaimed, almost laughing at the absurdity of the suggestion.

'Come along to be prosecuted!!' he shouted this time.

The man I had been talking to was incredulous and merely shrugged his shoulders when I looked to him for an explanation.

I picked up my things, shaken by what was happening, and followed the man to the station master's office.

Coming from the bright sunlight, the office was dark even with its time worn cream walls, on which hung a large mahogany framed clock with Roman numerals, a large timetable and a calendar. A dominant fan throbbed with a repetitive hum on the high ceiling, beneath which a fat man in a white shirt and glasses sat behind a heavy wooden desk. Piles of ageing papers tied with string and stacked in serried columns lined one wall.

'Who is this?' the man behind the desk asked, spittle dribbling from fleshy lips and flabby jowels, wobbling as he spoke.

'Found him on the platform without a ticket,' my accuser replied.

'I don't know what's going on, but can you please tell me what I've done wrong?' I protested.

'Travelling on the railways without a ticket is a serious offence,' the station master said.

'But, I've only just come onto the platform to use the toilet. I arrived from Jalgaon by lorry this morning. Phone up the tourist office and the station master. I was there last night.'

'What are you, a hippy or a Beatle?' My accuser then asked, the intensity of his question, guided by his malice.

It took a few seconds for what had just been said to sink in.

'A What!!!?' I replied, startled. 'A hippy or a Beatle??' It was the first time I had been called that and I could see he was serious. 'What is a Beatle?' I asked, hoping to extract a ludicrous and possibly hilarious response, conjured by his obvious ignorance.

'You're a Fifth Columnist!' He said next, thwarting my plan, while further amusing me.

'A what!?' I replied, beginning to laugh a little.

'A spy from Mao-Tse-Tung,' he elaborated.

'Now, this is getting bloody ridiculous,' I exclaimed. 'First, you bring me in here for not having a platform ticket, now you're calling me a communist spy. I think you're getting a little stupid now.'

'Don't call me stupid,' he shouted. 'It is you who has been stupid, but we've caught you now. I'm from the CIA. Central Intelligence of America.'

'Then you're clearly not very intelligent and should be ashamed of yourself for being such an idiot,' I retorted. 'By the way, it's the Central Intelligence Agency,' I corrected him, much to his chagrin.

At this, the man lurched toward me, 'You're a spy from Peking!' he shouted. 'Did you know Montgomelly? I fought in Africa in the eighth army during the war.' By now, he was clearly exposing himself as a bigoted fool. 'What do you think of India?' he spurted out at the end of this bitter tirade.

'You're drunk,' I said and, although I couldn't smell anything on his breath, I was convinced he was either that or insane. I was beginning to get a little peeved, but now saw this show as something surreally humorous and was ready to play along and mislead his bizarre machinations.

'It is a very poor and dirty country. The people are lazy. Your government is corrupt and people are being murdered every day.'

He looked aghast at my analysis. 'What part of England do you come from?'

'London.'

'I should have known that. Only a lousy, fucking Londoner would say that about us. They were like that in the war and they're like that now. You fucking dirt!' he shouted with a contemptuous leer, echoing language he'd clearly assimilated during his time in the army.

'He's definitely from Peking. He's incriminated himself already,' the station master spluttered from behind his desk.

'I hate bloody Londoners,' my original accuser went on, his scorn now clearly unmistakable. 'Look what they did to our women.'

I had no answer to that, but, by this time, I had been in there for just under an hour, realising it wasn't a joke and they were more serious than ever.

'You will suffer for this,' my accuser said. 'Did you know Montgomelly?' he repeated. 'I hate Montgomelly.'

'Look, I don't know who or what you are, but I wasn't even born in the war, so don't take out your personal grievances on me. I'm not a hippy nor a communist spy. I have no interest in politics whatsoever. I'm an artist just touring India.'

'How can you be a tourist when you don't have a ticket?' His illogical mind continued to grind out more inanities.

'I don't have to have a ticket to prove that. Look, here's my passport. I'm a British subject and I want to see some sanity brought into this conversation.'

'You're talking too much. Shut up!'

So I did.

Several other railway employees had overheard the shouting and gathered in the room, assimilating the make believe story that I was a spy from Peking, who'd been travelling on the trains all over India for the previous six months without paying. All this had been manufactured because of the prejudice and bitterness of one man seeking a target.

'If I had done this in London, I would have been murdered,' my accuser said, with all conviction. 'Think yourself lucky you're in India.'

I laughed to myself and continued my silence.

Talks went on amongst the assembled men on the other side of the room, as they decided what they were going to do with me.

'What's your name?' the station master shouted.

'I can't talk to you by shouting in such an uncivilised way across the room,' I replied. 'Do you have a chair I can sit on, please,' I asked.

'Sit on the floor,' came the reply.

I carried on standing and maintained my silence, calming my oppressors a little, until they then decided that I should write a statement about my time in India.

On a sheet of foolscap, I sketched an account of what I had been doing, mentioning the beautiful sights that India had to offer, the kindness of its people and my interest in religion, although I didn't mention which to avoid causing further friction. They appeared surprised, becoming a little more respectful on reading this.

'You will pay a fine of twenty-eight rupees and ten paise. This is the train fare from Bombay.'

'That is an assumption I'm afraid I cannot contend with,' I replied. 'I have already told you that I caught a train from central Bombay to Kalwa and then hitched to here by lorries and cars. Here is my ticket,' I added, reaching into my pocket for the stub. 'If you want to make enquiries, you will find that whenever I have travelled by train, I have always paid. I am an artist,' I continued, 'travelling in India for inspiration. I have very little money now, only enough to see me to the West Pakistani border and then some travellers' cheques to see me back to England. Here is my sketch book.'

Opening it out on the desk, they turned the pages, revealing the sketches I had done of people, buildings and landscapes.

'These are very good,' the station master said. 'I am now having some sympathy towards you.'

'If you really had sympathy you would not have treated a visitor to your country in such a rude and inhospitable manner. I am unaware of Indian law, outside normal moral conduct. Instead of being so hostile, you should understand my situation and drop your accusations.'

'You still have to pay the fine,' my initial accuser said, regaining his hostility. 'If you fail to pay the fine, you will have to spend the night in the police station and then go to the magistrate tomorrow morning.'

'This is so stupid and unnecessary.' I looked at the clock again. 'Do you realise, I've now been here nearly four hours and that I have a right to contact my embassy.'

The station master said nothing, but my accuser persisted in his tirade of idiocy. 'You're a fucking nothing,' he said venomously, 'you're in India now and have no right to contact your embassy. It will cost you three hundred rupees for the right.'

I just looked at him for the idiot he was.

There was a further huddled mumble until they all filed out onto the platform to decide my fate, leaving me alone with my baggage and passport. It crossed my mind that I should make a run for it, being confident that I could outrun any of them. Then I considered that one of them might well have a gun and envisaged the parting of the crowd as I ran the length of the platform, my assailant taking careful aim to shoot me down for being a suspected communist spy, escaping whilst under interrogation. Such an escape would further convince them that I was a spy and would make it even worse for me should I be recaptured and end up in court. Although fazed by their fervour to prosecute in some way, I stayed still, calming my mind with the mantra given by my Tibetan teacher, until they all returned.

'Are you going to pay the fine?' my accuser asked.

'No,' I replied, 'not without further consideration of my case. I don't know who you are and cannot be sure the money wouldn't end up in your pocket.'

At this, every line on his face screwed and distorted into the embodiment of hate and anger as he lunged towards me and grabbed my nose.

'Where did you hear that? Who told you that? You *are* a spy!' he screamed in a manner that suggested I'd exposed a dark secret concealed within the depths of his distorted mind.

'It's common knowledge that corruption is endemic in India,' I said.

That's enough! You shall go to court.'

'Fair enough. I've got nothing to lose if all I do is tell the truth, something you're clearly not prepared to accept.'

'You come with us now,' he said, guiding me to the door with the station master in tow.

Darkness had now fallen across the station, save for the arc lights that lit the platforms, illuminating the masses assembled down their lengths. We climbed up and over a bridge that crossed the line to the next platform and, with no precautions in place to contain me and the endless ebb and flow of people, once again I considered a possible escape. While the station master kept to himself, my accuser continued with his tirade of abusive language. 'You fucking Londoner. You should be whipped and tortured like they do it in Asia.'

As we reached the bottom of the steps onto the platform that led to the street, I asked at the barrier, 'Where's the ticket collector?'

My persecutor glanced around fervently as if looking for the man in question.

'This man will be punished by not getting any promotion,' he replied, gleefully, as if pleased that maybe he could impose his hollow megalomania over someone else.

'I'm very surprised that, being so concerned about tickets, you have not ensured someone was on duty. It strikes me as a serious dereliction of duty by the station master,' I quipped.

The station master glanced at me, his anger betraying his vulnerability.

Seizing my chance at vindication, I saw a scrawny, elderly man dressed in a grubby dhoti slowly descending the steps with the aid of a gnarled wooden staff.

'Ask this man if he has a platform ticket,' I said.

'If he has a ticket, I will strike you,' my accuser bellowed, 'for suggesting that an Indian citizen would be travelling illegally.' He stopped the man and requested his ticket. Reaching into the creases of his dhoti, the old man pulled out a ticket. Fortunately, my reactions were swift enough to deflect the blow that immediately descended towards me.

We continued to the police station, just outside the station precincts, and up onto the brightly lit verandah, the insults still flying. As we arrived, a man in khaki shirt sleeves with a protruding gut overhanging his matching trousers came out to meet us. His English was excellent and he listened intently as the story was related, twirling his manicured moustache as if to focus his concentration while I defended myself.

He turned out to be the chief inspector of civil police, outranking my accuser. I was told that the charges had already been escalated up to a higher level, although I found that hard to believe, not having seen anyone in the station master's office make a phone call.

But, as I continued and began revealing the accusations and abuse that had been levelled at me, I witnessed contrition in my accusers' eyes as they were slowly being shamed before their superior. The inspector led the others out of hearing for a short discussion.

'The fine has now been dropped to a minimum of seventeen rupees and sixty paise,' the inspector informed me. 'If you pay it now, a receipt will be given and you can claim the money back at the UK embassy in Delhi.'

I doubted this but, by now, I was tired and keen to see an end to it . There was still the option of going to court in the morning, but I had no certainty that the judge would not have been bribed first.

'I am willing to forget this has happened if we all shake hands and you each give me the apology I deserve.' I said on hearing their compromise. 'This stupidity has wasted half a day for me and I now just want to sleep.'

To my great surprise, smiles appeared across their faces and each of the men outstretched his hand. The inspector handed me my receipt.

'Will this allow me to sleep in the waiting room tonight?' I asked. 'I should imagine this fine will give me a season ticket for life to sleep in any waiting room in India.'

A strained laughter pervaded the verandah and I returned to the station for the night.

CHAPTER
Eight

IT TOOK SIX MORE DAYS to reach Benares.
Since Bombay, I had been developing a chest cold due to the contrasting day temperature and the intense cold that prevailed once the setting sun had sucked the last hint of warmth from the sky.

Following the incident at Bhusawal station, I had lost my voice, being reduced to a relatively incoherent croak. My thin cotton trousers, jeans, a couple of tops and flip-flops were still my only clothes and, when not inside my sleeping bag, I only had a blanket and a towel to further warm myself.

On the first day, I was picked up by a work lorry carrying a contingent of women dressed in tattered saris, nose rings and copious amulets and anklets adorning their very dark skin. Each had a mattock and a large metal bowl.

The women were generally downcast and old before their time, wizened by the hot sun and beaten down by vigorous and relentless physical labour. Nevertheless, most managed a smile or just a curious look as I climbed up into the cab.

A few miles along the road, the lorry turned off and down to a mudbank rising from the trickle of a river near the road bridge. Other gangs of women were already carrying small rocks from the riverbed and creating piles by the shore. Our women had the task of filling their bowls with silt, one half of the gang filling the bowls then helping the others lift them onto their heads and take them to the lorry. All the while a warm wind blew, sending the dried mud up in whirlwinds around the women's wildly flapping saris.

When the lorry was full, they climbed back on top of the pile and we drove a few miles further until we left the road once more and all was unloaded.

Nearby, two men stood on a pile of corn, one filling an aluminium bowl for the other to gently shake the contents above his head, until the chaff flew away into the intense blue sky.

The terrain was generally parched extending flat for miles, only broken by occasional sharp pyramid like hills rising from the plain and often topped by a small white domed temple.

Another lorry took me further through this arid wilderness, wedged between the driver, his assistant and the gear lever. In another small town, where the two had gone for tea in their depot, I waited with a glass they had brought me, watching the eternal poor and unemployed, one squatting in the dirt, staring blankly as he made marks in the dust with a stick. The company coolies, barefoot in cotton vests and shorts bent beneath the weight of bulging sacks of flour, their bodies white with the dust, visibly winced as they heaved them onto the open side of another lorry.

Goats wandered around licking the dust for the odd unmilled grain, while frail and wide eyed children stood before me staring as if there was no better sport to occupy them. Some rolled hoops along the street, improvised from old bicycle wheels. Others with runny noses and bare feet coyly held out a battered bunch of bananas in the hope of a few paise.

We arrived in Akola after dark, driving in through the poorer backstreets, where people had lit small fires at the side of the road, around which they crouched, hands outstretched over the flames that cast a warm glow across their weathered and wretched faces. Small aluminium pots of food cooked amongst the embers.

I too welcomed a hot meal in one of the little restaurants that always gives life and light to the area around a station, where a whole community was focused on the comings and goings of trains and the people in them.

I took the precaution of buying a twenty paise platform ticket to enable unhindered passage to and from the waiting room, where I took a shower and unrolled my sleeping bag for another cold night. I was glad I had *learned my lesson* as, later in the night, I was woken to show my ticket. With my throat being as it was, I was in no condition for a protracted argument and glad that I could return to sleep with no further questioning.

The plan next day was to get to Nagpur, the half way point of this part of my journey. I felt miserable with the persistent cold that seemed to take longer to lift each day, the further north I travelled. A group of drivers were sat around a fire outside a chai shop. They waggled their heads to indicate that there would be no lorries going as far as Nagpur that day, but one told me to come back at six o' clock.

And so, with my plans for the day altered at a stroke, I set off to amuse myself for the day. Of course, the place was not really any different to any other town I had so far stopped in. It had a ruined Mughal fort where the British had fought and won a battle in 1803.

Directly up from the station, in the middle of the road, rose the five story clock tower in memory of Sundarabai Khandelwal, a local woman, whose celebrity escaped me, but nevertheless guarded by two painted stone lions. Built in 1942 in grey stone blocks as ugly as a breeze block, it had four balconies surrounding the tower, four clocks and a pointed roof, looking as if it started out intending to look like a Chinese pagoda, but ended up being very wide of the mark.

Already, the streets were teeming with rickshaws screaming for custom, car horns honking and the paraphernalia of daily business setting out its stall. The bigger shops were opening their frontages, unveiling beautiful cloth, kitchen equipment, shoes and electrical goods. In the street itself, a shoe repairer unfolded his few tools on an old tarpaulin and sat down for the day's work beneath a frayed and bent umbrella. A young boy swept out the previous day's dirt from one of the shops as another dampened down the rising dust with water splashed across the pavement from a shining copper container. Old men and women swept the dirt and litter along the road, to a point where it was collected and put in a battered metal dustbin on wheels.

A short walk brought me to the River Morna where, crossing to the middle of a wide bridge, I stopped to peer out and across the town. Whether it was the hot and humid weather that had, by this time, replaced the cold of night and begun to melt my brain, I couldn't be sure, but I was suddenly on Waterloo Bridge, staring into the cold River Thames, its dark and choppy waters reflecting fractured impressions of the sentinel lamps that lined the Embankment.

Then I was back in the light of day, my eyes fixed on the women and young girls walking amongst the mud islands where cows wandered freely and sewage gushed out from an open pipe. Here, they were collecting cow pats with their bare hands, crudely shaping it into bricks before depositing them on the shore to dry in the sun.

Further along the water's edge, people had built homes from driftwood and reeds, using hand flung and smoothed mud to glue the fabric of the constructions together. A man eased himself as predatory rats lurked nearby and buzzards circled in the clear sky above. All was poverty with a seemingly endless line of dirty and dilapidated buildings stretching the length of the waterfront, interspersed by the occasional temple; red flags flying to further poison the impressionable minds of those who placed so much store in the salvation of religion.

On the bridge itself were not bowler hatted city gents making their way from Waterloo Station to their banks and offices, nor mini skirted girls, red buses or mini-minors, but bedraggled men and women in white cotton dhotis, multi patterned lungis, bare feet and hollow cheeks. Those who could not stand, sat by the wall, dimmed eyes staring blankly with barely the strength to hold up one limp hand for alms.

Others were more conspicuous; women in fine cotton or silk saris and men in western style trousers and shirts, too busy and arrogant to acknowledge their less fortunate fellow human beings.

On the road, bicycles and rickshaws tangled in a conglomeration of spokes and furiously tinkling bells. Bullock carts rolled through the throng, laden with assorted loads of hay, wood and people, followed occasionally by a car, its driver incessantly blasting the horn, in the vain hope of clearing the way.

Over a glass of chai, I was told of a "park" where I could rest a little from the torrent of noise. A rickshaw took me to what turned out to be anything but the park of my imagination. No lush grass, shady trees and cooling duck pond. Instead, I was dropped at an open expanse of dusty ground with hardly a blade of green in sight. Numerous tatty tents had been pitched, together with several rough wooden and corrugated iron dwellings that were home to the people and cattle who milled about the site. Poverty and the stench once more prevailed and silence was far away.

It was time for an extended lunch to while more time away. Towards the end, as I sipped chai and fingered a sticky jalebi, a smart man in trousers and short sleeved shirt approached me carrying a briefcase.

Seeing the briefcase, I was reminded of Liam and Jen's sixty thousand dollars, which would by now be well on its way to Mombassa. I wondered if, perhaps, it was now my turn. In a way, the outcome turned out to be along similar lines.

'May I join you?' He asked politely in a refined Indian accent.

'Of course,' I replied, pulling out a chair for him.

'My name is Mohammed Merchant, I am curious to know what your impressions of India are,' he explained as he ordered a chai and pulled his chair into the table.

I told him of my overland journey and the four months I had spent in the mountains.

'Now, I'm travelling through Northern India, seeing as much as I can before I start back to England the same way I came.'

'That is very courageous of you to be travelling in such a way.'

'There have been a few close shaves, so to speak, but I believe I'm being looked after.'

'Have you been having any bad experiences?'

I immediately thought of Bhusawal and proceeded to tell the story.

'I cannot believe that you were treated in such way. How much is a platform ticket these days?'

'Twenty paise.'

'And they wanted to charge you the train ticket from Bombay.'

'I'm afraid so.'

He sipped his chai and fell silent for a few moments. 'I feel so embarrassed that my countrymen should behave in such a way. What can I do to make up for it?'

'It's all right. I have put it down to experience. It is only one experience out of many very beautiful ones, which I shall never forget.'

'I have to go now,' he said, finishing his chai, 'but I wish you all the very best luck for the rest of your journey.'

We rose to shake hands and I could see him reaching for his wallet, believing he was going to pay for the chai. At the same time, I was distracted by a dog that had come inside the restaurant.

'Thank you for your conversation,' he said as I waved him farewell. Returning to the table, I noticed my notebook had something sticking out of it. Inside, I found a twenty rupee note. I immediately ran to the street in an attempt to return it, but was only able to see him being driven away in his chauffeur driven Ambassador.

I ordered more chai and pondered what had happened. As with the mafia boss in Bombay, who wanted to right a wrong, this man, a complete stranger, had wanted to do the same. This generous act seemed out of place when so many other souls were, to my mind, much more deserving. I could only see it as a divine act of concordant action and reaction. While I felt some relief at having my fortunes restored, I could not detach my mind from the poverty that wandered the street only yards from where I sat.

'Was I indeed deserving and did I really need this money?'

I was reminded of a conversation months before in Delhi's Connaught Circus, where an elderly Indian poet had told me, 'Only if you can afford to and can provide for yourself, should you give to others.'

I arrived at the lorry drivers' bonfire in good time, only to be told that my lift had left at half past three, despite waiting for me.

Irritated that the arrangement I had made for six o' clock had been apparently ignored, I now suspected I could be delayed in this place for another twenty-four hours.

One man, very spruce in a red shirt, who had sensed my disappointment, stepped forward, speaking better English than the others.' If you can be coming to the office with me, I can be asking if there are other lorries going to Nagpur.'

I waited outside in the street while he made enquiries, emerging a few minutes later to tell me a lorry was leaving from the local dairy at eleven that evening.

'You come with me now,' he said, 'we go to dairy. My name is Samuel. I am Christian.' He clearly put great store in being a

Christian and this was evident in his beaming amiability and the sparkle to his eyes. He was probably in his mid thirties, perhaps a little podgy for his age, clean-shaven and with neatly combed short black hair. He disappeared down a side alley and emerged shortly after with two antiquated bicycles with rounded handlebars, hard leather saddles and the consolation of Sturmey-Archer three speed gears and dynamo lights.

I'd not ridden a bike for some time and wobbled a little as I balanced my things across my back and we set off through the crowded streets, weaving between cars, rickshaws and sacred cows. The cold night air was upon us as we left the lights behind and emerged into open countryside for the short distance to the dairy. In a clear sky, the stars shone in abundance and the moon, a bright waxing crescent, suspended in the heavens like a seesaw, cast its light over the fields.

At the dairy, men were loading milk churns into the back of a lorry, interspersed with blocks of ice. A short discussion between the drivers and the manager as to where I should travel determined that I would be in the back with the milk and ice. Not wishing to prolong my stay in Akola, whilst dreading the prospect of spending a night balanced on freezing milk churns, I reluctantly agreed.

I was asked to return at half past eight, and then cordially invited to join Samuel and his family for dinner. We rode back into town and down a dark gravel track to a larger than average newly whitewashed mud house, such as I'd so often seen on my travels.

Samuel was one of six brothers and three sisters, who had all been brought up in this humble place.

A charpoy took up much of the space inside the narrow verandah that led to the main door, its thatched roof and lintels supported by sky blue tree trunk columns. On another part of the verandah, beneath a suspended oil lamp, I was introduced to Samuel's mother and one of his three sisters, who were preparing food over a mud stove, its rich blend of spices immediately infusing my taste buds and sparking a yearning to eat.

Another sister brought a bowl of water and a towel to wash my hands before I removed my flip-flops and we entered the house. The solid whitewashed walls were both dry and warm, fingermarks still visible where adept hands had spread and smoothed the mud.

The house extended to three rooms and even a small bathroom with a basin, shower base and squat toilet. This was poverty by western standards, but luxury for the majority of Indians and those many thousands whose bedroom was under the stars.

In the main room, we sat on dhuris spread across the compacted mud floor, where the second sister brought a few home made nibbles and a glass of water. Small niches had been set into the walls for possessions to be stored and oil lamps to light the space. Pictures of Jesus and Mary and a small crucifix adorned one wall whereas, elsewhere on my travels, I had been so used to seeing Krishna, Parvati, and others amongst the Hindu gods.

'Where are your brothers and other sister" I asked.

'We are all drivers, except my youngest brother who is studying to be an engineer. My other sister is now being a nurse in the hospital in Nagpur. My father was driver too.'

'Is he coming to eat?'

Samuel looked despondently to the ground and slowly wobbled his head. 'Our father was killed in a road accident.'

'I'm so sorry,' I responded. 'The Indian roads are very dangerous and drivers take too many risks trying to overtake.'

'This is what happened to my father. Another lorry was overtaking and he couldn't turn away in time. We all miss him so much.'

Samuel's mother and sister brought the food in and served the two of us with a feast of rice, dhal, subji, mutton and chapatis.

Not having eaten meat since the Afghan desert, I wondered how best to respond. It had been cooked with love and given with kindness, perhaps depriving another member of the family. Not having created a direct demand and the possibility of causing an offence if I refused, I ate it.

The two women sat and watched us eat, declining for now as was the custom, but smiling at our enjoyment and ever thankful for any morsel of praise that might come their way.

As the meal came to an end, we washed the remnants from our fingers as chai was brought and the clock on the wall ticked closer to eight. A polite thank you and we were on our way back to the dairy, the lamps on our bikes lighting the road when clouds passed before the moon. Set back from the road, a torchlit procession of

Christian children, wove their way through a line of trees as part of the Christmas preparations.

At the dairy, my drivers were almost ready to leave as I thanked Samuel and climbed up into the cab, where I was allowed to sit as long as I didn't fall asleep. In ten minutes, we were out on the open road, speeding through the darkness that the clouds had now brought upon us.

The cab was warm and comfortable and, with very little English to exchange between us, I soon found it hard to keep my eyes open, feeling the occasional nudge from the co-driver. It was less than an hour into our drive that the lorry was brought to a halt and it was indicated that I must move to the back for the rest of the journey. They spread a tarpaulin across the top of the milk churns and, by strategically placing my body across the top, I managed to wriggle into my sleeping bag and find some semblance of comfort, falling asleep the closest I would probably ever get to sleeping on an iceberg.

I was woken at five next morning, shortly after pulling into the dairy in Nagpur, where the manager brought me chai and offered a space on the office floor to snatch another couple of hours' sleep.

A short stop in town for pouris and chai and I was out on the road again for what turned out to be my best day yet.

A jeep sped me about eleven miles, stopping on the way to join a crowd where a brick lorry had crashed off a bridge onto the riverbed below, crushing the cab like a tin can. There was no word to suggest the driver was either dead or alive.

I passed through the next small town, followed by a legion of children and older brothers, until I came to a gathering around a rickshaw rigged up with an amplifier and loudspeaker, blurting out political nonsense to the gullible assembly.

An India Oil tanker took me to the next village, where the runs, I had been dealing with over the previous few days, hit me again and I had to find a toilet.

I'd stopped in a small chai shop, where a young boy, understanding my call for a latrine, led me out of the back, though the colourful fruit and vegetable market to an undulating piece of waste ground just outside the village. Here, with the tin can full of water the boy had given me, I picked my way around the turds and bushes, apologising to those already easing themselves, and found a clear patch on which I relieve myself.

An open back public carrier was the next to stop. About twenty others were sat on hard wooden seats that formed a horseshoe around two sides and the space behind the cab. They moved along on one side to make space for me, where I sat and held on for the next forty miles on the way to Jabalpur.

Leaving the flat fields behind, the road continued more or less straight, but now fringed by an abundance of tropical trees and shrubs that exuded a rich palette of green. Large grey monkeys emerged from the trees, racing us along the road, pounding with all their strength on all fours, their long tails trailing behind, until they would suddenly swerve away and up a nearby tree to watch us disappear.

Having stopped for chai at another check point, I found another lorry going all the way to Jabalpur, eventually pulling in to its depot on the outskirts around ten in the evening. Stepping out into the street, the air was bitter and I still had another three miles to get to the centre, where I could get something to eat and find a bench in the station waiting room for the night.

Dressed in only a tee shirt, jeans and flip-flops with my blanket wrapped around me, I had to endure a painful rickshaw journey whereby, save for a thin sleeveless jumper and scarf, my driver was not much better dressed than I.

I arrived having lost all feeling in my hands and feet, imagining that frostbite was not too far away. Anticipating a really hot and substantial meal, all I could find was tepid rice and vegetable subji. Shivering, tired and despondent, I crossed over to the station, bought a platform ticket and found a space on the floor of the Second Class Waiting Room.

I was in no hurry to get up next morning, instead keeping myself zipped up inside my sleeping bag, whilst all around were packing up their thick bedrolls, using the washroom and organising children prior to the arrival of their trains.

Jabalpur, I had discovered, was the nearest town to Marble Rocks a natural marble gorge carved through time by the Narmada River. A rickshaw took me to the bus station, passing green public spaces, gently shaded by leafy trees and irrigated by a network of clear streams, looking nothing like the open drains I had seen elsewhere. Here and there, substantial private bungalows with verandahs were set back amongst trees and colourful flower gardens.

From the bus station, the only transport to the gorge was a three wheeled taxi, which had capacity for eight people, including the driver. I sat in the front and paid my one rupee fair for the hour's journey, while the back filled with what seemed an endless flow of corpulent beings, culminating in eight adults and three children.

The town opened out into a flat, cultivated landscape, peppered with numerous temples along the way; some painted pink, others white, sadhus outside drinking their first cup of chai. Two or three marshy lakes, edged by simple wood and straw dwellings and single domed temples followed. A long line of steps rose steeply up the side of a jagged mound of rock, topped by a whitewashed temple, its many domes and arches, gleaming in the morning sunlight, the ubiquitous red flags fluttering from long poles.

Arriving at the village near the river, earlier arrivals were making their way down to the water or inspecting statuettes of popular Hindu gods, carved from the local marble and now on sale in the many souvenir stalls.

Wide stone steps led past a small temple to the waterfront, where the river flowed almost imperceptibly. As the the water reached shallower parts, it tumbled in a ferment of cavorting waves, white foam and airborne droplets, eventually swirling in diminishing whirlpools, twists and eddies to a steady flow a little further downstream.

A number of brightly painted rowing boats bobbed on the shoreline, their owners calling out for customers, while other hawkers sold sticky sweets, pouris and samosas. A fat saddhu with long grey hair and beard sat on a platform beneath a tarpaulin, offering blessings to those who had delivered prayers to the river.

For a rupee, I joined a party in one of the boats and we set off upstream. Two men pulled the oars and, in the stern, a rudder man, deeply tanned against a shock of grey hair and bushy moustache, guided our passage. The little boat glided over the still waters, offering perfect reflections of the jagged marble and its subtly changing colour through blues, greys, pinks and white.

A tiny sky blue kingfisher perched in the shade of a small cleft in the rock, preening its yellow to orange chest.

On a small island, a saddhu had made his home. Near naked, save for a faded orange cloth around his groin and a rudraksha bead necklace around his neck. The intense whites of his eyes contrasted against the leathery weathered flesh, long grey beard and dreadlocks that had grown to his waist. Sitting amongst a few possessions, he blew curls of smoke from his morning chillum into the cloudless blue sky, as our oars dipped once more and pulled us away.

Drifting on, the rock rose sheer on either side, dazzling in the bright sunlight but, as we approached the end of the gorge, the roar of the water could be heard again, tumbling down from a higher level, at which point the boat was turned and we gently eased our way back to the waterfront.

On the waterfront steps, women were washing clothes and cleaning barley in large baskets submerged beneath the water. This was a perfect opportunity, before arriving in Benares, to wash what few clothes I had, using my towel to cover myself while they dried in the now hot sun. It was also time that I wrote to Kamala.

5th December 1970

My darling Kamala,
I'm sitting by the river at Marble Rocks near Jabalpur, my newly washed clothes drying beside me and a perfect reflection of the blue sky in the still waters before me.

It's now six days since I left Bombay and have been slowly making my way north, hoping to reach Benares the day after tomorrow.

There was no luck finding work in Bombay, so I'm resigned now to starting the main overland journey back to Europe before too long.

Thoughts of my time with Alison emerged, making it more difficult to continue writing with the conviction and integrity I should have had.

I knew that this spontaneous "fling" was a betrayal not just of Kamala, but also Belinda and now I wondered what I had learnt as a consequence of all those months in the mountains. I had already betrayed Belinda since leaving England and now I had done the same to Kamala.

Was this a sign of deep seated insecurity, the need for companionship and love? Was I myself indeed capable of true love? To be able to selflessly give of myself for another person without thought of personal gain or some other ulterior motive?

I believed my love was true and pure. That it came through my spirit, untainted by selfish desires. Was I merely a product of conditioning that, in the Christian culture in which I was born, entrusts one to another and, beyond that, it is seen as a sin? This was certainly true, but was it right?

We were living in a time where it was now far too easy to attain sexual fulfilment, perhaps without fully appreciating the emotional fallout that could ensue.

Certainly, within Kamala's Tibetan culture, polyandry was practised in remote regions. Quite how I would be able to deal with sharing Kamala with three or four other men and not knowing which one had fathered our child, is something I would find quite unbearable. So, flipping the situation back to a man being so flagrantly "shared" must surely cause great heartache, especially when it had not been socially approved by the community.

It seems an age since we parted amid all the laughter and cheers of the villagers and now I'm so far away, but could keep coming north until I had returned to the mountains and you.

But, we made an agreement. We must let time take its course and see how we feel then.

I will keep writing to you and you must write, if you still want, when I have returned to England.

Please send my very best wishes to your mother and please thank your father once again for teaching me as well as he did.

Sending you my love,

Adam x

I carefully folded the paper and put it in one of the last envelopes I still had, placing it carefully in my bag ready for posting. Despite this, I felt that the tie had already been cut and the decision made for me.

Getting back to Jabalpur was not as straightforward as I had hoped. The taxi driver was insistent that he would not leave until he had full capacity, in this case the legal limit was six people. A family of six climbed in the back, with myself in the front again, making seven, but the driver insisted that he would not leave until he had eight. The family, who were all overweight, got fed up with waiting and left to find another taxi, leaving me to wait for it to fill again. When we reached eight, he was still not happy and I was complaining that it was overcrowded and unsafe, much to the anger of the driver, who decided he didn't want to take me. But, standing firm, we eventually set off, the vehicle groaning under eight fat adults and four children in the back, myself and another pushed dangerously up against the gear lever and the exposed battery wires, while the final passenger balanced himself between one of the rear mudguards and the footplate, a total of sixteen.

The station waiting room was a welcome option as day gave way to night once again and the encroachment of the unrelenting cold. I felt I had made such good progress since Bombay and it had so far cost me nothing. I was nevertheless tired and, with the worsening cold and the runs to boot, I felt deserving of the train for once. I wanted to see the erotic carvings on the temples at Khajuraho and six rupees and fifty paise bought me a third class ticket to the nearest station at Satna, leaving at quarter to three in the morning.

I only slept for about an hour before packing up my things and venturing out onto that bitterly cold platform in preparation for the big sprint that would hopefully find me a small space in the corner of a carriage.

As the train pulled in, I was ready, running forward as I would have done in a rugby scrum, pushing in and under the crowd towards the carriage door. I'd grabbed the handrail and was just pulling myself up when, feeling one foot lost in the ensuing tangle of arms and baggage, a flip-fop slipped off and down onto the track. There was no going back as I continued to push forward, finally placing my bags down in what had become my usual place on the floor by the window and the toilet. *Now, my shoe?*

Retrieval was another story altogether, as I found myself pushing against the still prevailing tide, having to make quick bursts forward in order to achieve any progress. As I was just touching down on the platform, the unthinkable happened. My glasses were knocked off, causing me to instinctively thrust out my hand to save them from falling to the ground, but thereby finding myself fumbling in a young Indian girl's bra. Our emotions were palpable; hers that a physical affront had been made against her in a very sensitive part of her body, causing not only embarrassment, but obvious distress. For myself, I was not only embarrassed, but had to somehow convince her that I had no untoward intentions towards her. Holding my retrieved glasses before her, it was soon obvious what had happened and, together with my sincerest apologies, I was forgiven and allowed to get back on the train, having first climbed onto the track to retrieve my flip-flop. Catching her glances later during the journey, it was clear by her smile and the sparkle in her eyes that I was forgiven and she had seen the funny side.

We arrived at half past six with dawn barely breaking and the intense cold draughts passing through the cracks between the train doors. With head throbbing relentlessly, eyes watering with blocked sinuses and muscles exhausted with shivering, my first priority was a hot chai, before figuring out my next move.

Having missed the half past six bus to Khajuraho, I was on my way to find a lorry, when a young Indian, speaking good English, directed me back to the bus station where I was able to board a luxury bus going most of the way. With a seat to myself, I could set the two and a half rupee fare in perspective against the vast distance I had already travelled by hitching, still knowing I would just about manage to use up all my Indian rupees before reaching the West Pakistani border and having to change my sterling or the dollars that Jen had given me.

Our arrival at Panna was welcome relief as I was feeling the runs again and fairly desperate for a proper toilet. However, the best that could be offered were directions to another piece of waste land where a wooden platform, not unlike a scaffold, had been erected. Climbing the rickety steps to the top, there were no private cubicles, but four regularly spaced holes in the platform through which the open ground was visible below. Squatting, in the way I had become accustomed over these months, I did what I had to do, letting gravity take its course. A shadow and a loud bass grunt immediately became apparent and, looking down, the head of a hefty dark grey pig filled the space, effortlessly digesting what I had so recently excreted.

A second bus took me the last twenty five miles from Panna to Khajuraho, sitting three to a seat with many more squeezed together in the gangway, lurching from side to side while trying to keep their balance. With the loud churning of the engine and a regular crunching of gears, the old bus slowly lumbered out into a changing landscape, from the monotonous and seemingly endless flatness of the plains, to clear undulations and an abundance of trees and shrubs. Before too long, we arrived, at the edge of a steep escarpment, the discomfort of all within, apparent by the sullen faces and the prevailing heat that harboured a foul cocktail of bodily odours.

Prior to our descent through the trees to the bridge crossing the wide Ken River, the driver drew the bus to a halt alongside a small single domed shrine. Jumping out of the cab with a coconut in hand, he then proceeded to smash it to pieces with a small hammer, while pouring the milk over the lingam in the shrine. Returning to the bus, he passed the pieces down amongst the passengers as a symbol of the protection that had now been bestowed on us all.

Rising up the other side from the wide river, the bus trundled on passing small settlements and greater concentrations of houses and small businesses, occasionally slowed by a peacock, a deer or a half dozen cows wandering the road oblivious to any possible danger they might be in. A sharp turn off the main road took us into Khajuraho itself, stopping by the picturesque Shrivsagar Lake, stretching across to the western horizon and bounded by trees and the main temple complex on its northern shore.

A bed for the night was high on my mind as the sun was already sinking over the lake. The Circuit House lay on the village outskirts, where a bed was available for two and a half rupees, but the place was otherwise overrun by two coach loads of English boys and girls en route to Australia, all a little younger than myself, but such that I had absolutely nothing in common. Lounging on the grass or the odd chair on the spacious lawns, shouting in the inimitable way only the coarse, uncultured English can, a portable tape recorder, which I'd never seen before, further shattered the serenity of evensong with tinny renderings of Dionne Warwick and Cilla Black.

Fascinating as it was to hear music being reproduced in this way, I felt an immediate loathing for the whole scene and had to get away. Finding my way back into the town, I was directed to the Jain Temple where I was offered a room to myself for three rupees.

Being an obvious tourist attraction, Khajuraho was ripe for exploitation. Although the price for a bed had been reasonable, food was quite different. Whereas, I'd been used to generous portions of rice, dhal, subji and chapati for around one rupee, here, the price was two and a half rupees, the justification being that it was "special". In truth, there was nothing "special" about it, with the rice being cold and the quality and quantity of the rest being very poor. Why should it be the prerogative of proprietors around the world to put up prices to ridiculous levels when a tourist appears, often for an inferior product?

I was the first visitor into the temple grounds next morning after downing a hot cup of chai at a roadside stall. The nine sandstone temples in this complex stood peacefully in the midst of a verdant park of grass, trees and gravel paths, where pink, purple or yellow blossom exploded on the occasional tree or shrub.

The carvings, although only about three feet high at their largest, exceeded all expectations. Without any sign of prudery, the craftsmen had explored the many positions detailed in the Kama Sutra with intense observation, sensitivity and passion, whilst also depicting farmers, potters, musicians and much else that was common in people's lives at the time. I felt privileged to have seen them as many had been destroyed through time, particularly during Moslem rule, when figurative representation was forbidden. It had only been the fall into misuse and the encroachment of the jungle that had saved so many. In more recent times, even Ghandi had wanted them destroyed, but his wishes were never heeded.

Each temple had been built on a rectangular granite platform, upon which flights of steps led to an interior where a Hindu or Jain god or ceremonial lingam presided over the interior space and ornate outside balconies admitted light. Rising in ever diminishing tiers and small spires, these components formed the principal or multiple domes that dominated the buildings. Most of the figurative carvings could be seen from ground level, usually three tiers upon each other with carvings not much more than a foot high on the top tier. As I wandered the site, more carvings revealed themselves; those of elephants in battle, lions, copulating couples, ladies in their toilet surrounded by handmaidens, all immaculately preserved despite the ravages of weather and humanity over nine hundred years.

With my sinuses by now heavily congested, I left the temples catching the bus back to Satna, just as the coaches loaded with the English teenagers arrived.

Having had some lunch outside the station, I asked a local man the directions to the Benares road.

'Why are you not taking the train?' he replied a little taken aback by my question.

'I'm near the end of my time in India and need to economise,' I replied.

He immediately reached into his pocket and pulled out a ten rupee note, thrusting it into my hand.

'No, I cannot accept it,' I said, embarrassed by his generosity and that Providence should play into my hands in this way.

'You must certainly be taking the train,' he insisted.

I realised that I really did need the money now and the thought of yet more hours standing by the side of a dusty road was something I really did not want to consider for the foreseeable future.

'Thank you, so much, Sir,' I said, bringing a smile to his face, perhaps for having earned some good karma for himself.

There was a late afternoon train, arriving at a station just outside Benares at midnight and, as the sun began to sink on another day, I waited wrapped in my blanket, shivering and sniffling as the cold bit into every part of my body, resurrecting some of my rheumatic pains.

As usual, I found a spot down by the window at the end of the corridor, singing to myself in an attempt to take my mind off the cold. My thoughts drifted to home, arriving at Belinda's cottage snuggled down on the floor by her log fire, a hot cup of tea nearby, possibly a crumpet and jam or perhaps even some Christmas cake, as I told her of my adventures over the previous months.

Was this the reality I had ahead of me? How would the next few years transpire?

Nine

APPROACHING **A**LLAHABAD, an unfamiliar mist hung
eerily in the air. Then, as the familiar click-clack of the
wheels gave way to a hollow rickety-rattle, I realised we were on a
bridge, crossing a wide expanse of water, shimmering silver in the
half moon. I thought perhaps we had arrived at the sea, such was
the breadth of water, but realised quickly enough that this was impossible and I was in fact crossing the mighty Ganges. This was not
a mere trickle like the River Thames. I was in the vast subcontinent
of India, where such trivia was of no consequence. This was on a
scale far beyond my experience.

I had to change in Allahabad, eating a good dinner in the
station restaurant, before boarding a reservation carriage, where
I occupied a seat, unhindered by inspectors, until we arrived at
Mughalserai Junction at half past midnight.

There was still space on the waiting room floor, where I was very
soon asleep. A new and significant part of my journey lay in store
for the next day.

There was always good food to be had around a station precincts
and Mughalserai Junction, being a major hub, was no exception.
My constant shivering must have been using up a lot of energy
and this particular morning, hunger gnawed tenaciously. It took
two food stalls to sort me out, pourris and chick peas in one and
samosa and chai in another. A bus was waiting nearby to take me
the last few kilometres into the heart of Benares.

Driving first out into well irrigated countryside and then
sweeping in from the south to cross the Ganges once again, I was

able to see in the distance the famous waterfront with its many ghats, temples and legion of buildings, old and new, receding back into the city itself. Many more smaller temples lay interspersed with scrubland along the shore between the ghats and the bridge, while on the southern shore, from where we had just come, lay a wide expanse of mud and reeds, rising up into cultivated fields and trees.

Our arrival in the city was no different to any other. The universal bells, shouts and incessant horns of impatient drivers, forever thwarted by trundling bullock carts, rickshaws, wandering cows and pigs, pestering monkeys and the unabated flow of pedestrians, filled the clammy air. But, I sensed a different feeling here, the excitement of something that was quintessentially Indian.

Leaving the bus, I was besieged from all sides by rickshaw wallahs offering their services, but first I had to find someone who spoke English to be sure that I would be going where I wanted.

It never takes very long for someone to step forward and my man was soon before me, a young student keen to be of assistance to a bewildered Englishman. I showed him the address, which he then discussed with one of the keenest drivers and I was soon on my way through the packed streets to Sally's, hoping she had received my letter asking if I could stay a couple of days.

The ride was one of bustle, noise and a little menace, encountering a diverse sea of faces relentlessly pursuing their daily tasks, some animated by their mission, others bewildered and overwhelmed by what life has dealt them. The onslaught of bells, squeaking horns, wandering sadhus in orange robes, a sacred cow and flutes from a passing street band continued unabated as we wended our way through this colourful performance.

A simple turn in the road, immediately transformed the atmosphere, for I was now entering a Moslem area, where women wore tent-like black burkhas, their eyes just visible through a narrow slit. How they were able to breathe properly, when I was already struggling with my cold in the muggy heat, I knew not.

I imagined they would be harbouring stale air and germs as spittle built up on the material covering their mouths and noses. It made me feel quite claustrophobic and a little angry that this restriction had been imposed on them by their men. I really felt for the women, wondering whether this subjugation was something they accepted or were perhaps envious of their Hindu sisters, who walked and breathed freely in their colourful saris.

Each side of the road saw a tightly packed parade of chai shops and restaurants, with others stuffed to the ceilings with flat rolls of coloured cloth, pots and pans, shoes, books and posters, until the rickshaw drew to a halt and the driver helped me out of my seat.

I was in the area of the address I had been given, but still not certain of the exact location of Sally's house. I was just asking a man for directions, when Sally herself walked around the corner. She was as surprised as I was, a broad smile lighting her distinctive green eyes.

'Adam, you made it.'

'You got my letter then?' I asked, as we hugged each other. 'You're looking well.' She hadn't changed since I'd last seen her in the mountains in early November.

Her blonde hair with its ginger streaks was tied over her head, but still shimmered like a corn field in summer. She had caught the sun since being in the Plains and her rosy cheeks and freckles had been absorbed into a light tan.

'Like your pantaloons,' I said, pointing to the baggy, green paisley trousers that flared from her slim waist before narrowing at her ankles.

She gave me a twirl and laughed. 'Come, I want you to meet Mateo,' she said eagerly, grabbing my hand.

The house was only yards away from where we had been standing, set amongst another ten or so adobe type houses around a dusty courtyard with a solitary peepal tree at its centre.

Sally led me through the door, where stood the much talked about Mateo. He was tall, but chubbier than I had imagined and his thinning black hair made him look a lot older than he was.

'Hola Adam,' he said with a strong Spanish accent, 'ave you ad a good journey?'

'I've travelled up from Bombay over the last eight days, hitching most of the way.'

''itching! he exclaimed. 'That is so dangerous.'

'Well, I've had a few surprises, but been looked after most of the way.'

Mateo was Argentinian and although, at times, I found his accent hard to understand, I nevertheless warmed to him, seeing in his affection for Sally that he cared for her.

The whitewashed house comprised of two adequate rooms and a kitchen, with a small shower room and toilet.

'How much are you paying for this,' I asked, 'it's lovely,' taking in the cushions, the low bed with a colourful cover and the bookcase.

'Only fifty rupees a month,' Sally replied.

'That's very good, when you think I was paying thirty for that room in the mountains and I had no kitchen and we all shared that tiny shed with a hole in the floor, teetering on the hillside.'

It was still only nine o' clock as Sally re-heated some subji from the night before for breakfast.

'Mateo has a sitar lesson,' Sally said as she poured some chai, 'we can go down to the waterfront. It's very near.'

'That sounds like a good idea.'

From a couple of narrow alleys, stinking of urine and what I suspected to be raw sewage running across the paving stones, we emerged on the vast waterfront where a grassy bank stretched before us upstream and sadhus in orange loincloths shimmered against the bright green grass and the deep blue of the sky.

I'd never seen such a wide river, having only glimpsed its immensity on the train. Fast flowing at its centre, it was clear from the passage of the debris on the surface that the currents were both strong and dangerous.

Downstream, stretching as far as I could see, stretched the epitome of Hindu devotion. Tall houses, painted in weathered primary colours, palaces and spire topped temples, constructed in a diverse range of architectural styles, rose high above the steep lines of steps and terraces that emerged from the cloudy sacred waters of Mother Ganga, now glowing in the morning sunlight. This was the point of purification and redemption of sins for millions of India's Hindus.

Wide straw umbrellas, set in concrete platforms, sheltered a potpourri of half naked sadhus, each adorned with symbolic white markings and large red tilaks, finger smudged onto their foreheads. Those pilgrims who bowed before them and offered alms were rewarded with blessings and a sadhu endowed tilak over the third eye.

Hundred of people had already come to bathe, colonising the ghats in a colourful display of saris, loincloths and nakedness. Women stepped cautiously into the deep waters, their saris billowing with trapped air as they prepared to immerse themselves completely beneath the water. The men, often fat and mostly wearing the brahmin sacred thread, were usually stripped down to dhoti or baggy underwear, raising their joined hands in praise above their heads as they too submerged themselves.

For the most part, it was an opportunity for the young boys to just have fun, splashing and jumping naked from the steps or a nearby moored boat, of which hundreds bobbed along the shoreline.

As Sally and I made our way along the shore, boatmen, like rickshaw drivers, shouted out their daily chorus of, 'Boat, sahib,' 'Boat, sahib,' hoping to make a couple of rupees from rowing us along the waterfront.

'We'll walk,' Sally said, 'We'll see more.'

Where we stood, those not bathing, were beating clothes clean on flat stones, propped at an angle on bricks at the water's edge, where grey sand formed a small stony beach already strewn with a colourful patchwork of sun drying sheets and clothes. In between the worshippers, others were nonchalantly washing themselves, lathering soap across their skin, while others took the opportunity for a drink.

Climbing up one of the ghats, a gap between the houses led us through a narrow alley, where overhanging balconies, temples and devotional shrines, decked in marigolds, emitted invitations to participate in the ceremonies with bells, chanting and an emanation of sweet incense.

Women and children sat on doorsteps washing vegetables or picking nits from each other's hair. An old man crouched in the shadow of a wall, staring into emptiness. Cows and goats stood tethered with ropes or chains to weathered iron rings embedded in the wall, their dung collecting beneath them. In due course, it would be gathered up, mixed with straw, compacted into cakes and adhered to a wall while still moist, to be dried and eventually used as fuel for cooking or cremation.

Sally led me in a wide circle back to her house, stopping on the way for us to drink chai in a small stall at the end of her road. 'You see all these kids,' Sally said, pointing to the proprietor's two daughters and four sons, all under ten and helping their father with tasks around the stall. The youngest daughter, a pretty little thing, who must have been about three, stood entranced by our arrival, with her curly hair, wide eyes, snotty nose and thumb in mouth.

'Can you see how under nourished they all are? The father just isn't feeding them enough and they're wasting away.'

The little girl's thin body was clearly evident beneath her ragged dress and leggings, her little bare feet, dry and dirty on the mud floor. 'It breaks my heart, but what can I do? What can any of us do?'

We sat in silence, dumfounded by this impenetrable problem. Just one incidence in one quarter of one city in a vast country of intractable poverty.

I had had my fill, since leaving the mountains, in every town and village to Bombay, through the slums and pavements of that city and all the way back to this place. I felt so utterly helpless. Yet there were global charities that had been raising money for years and still the problem remained. Was it perhaps a consequence of corruption and greed, the poor, remaining poor, whilst the administrators filled their pockets?

I was pleased to rest for most of the day, lying on a charpoy outside the house, brushing flies away, while Sally wrote letters and prepared some food.

Late afternoon, we took a rickshaw further down the river, passing through more winding streets to a background cacophony of weaving looms producing the famous Benares brocade.

Within cramped spaces, open to the street, men with years of experience etched on their faces, sat before vintage wooden structures, fed by thousands of coloured yarns. Patiently and expertly, the operators passed shuttles and pulled levers that resulted in intricately patterned saris for those best able to afford such time consuming luxuries.

Elsewhere, shops were stacked to the ceiling with tins of coloured dyes or in a narrow alley yarns were being painstakingly prepared and dyed in readiness for the weavers. A boy passed pushing a bicycle with coils of golden yarn draped over the handlebars.

In the streets beyond, workshops and stalls sold soapstone incense holders, chillums, bowls of all sizes and complexity and small statuettes of elephants, buddhas and Hindu gods.

The craftsmanship and enterprise undertaken in often difficult conditions was extraordinary and prompted me to appraise what really is necessary when driven by a burning desire to achieve something. These people worked in hot, dirty and cramped environments, singularly minded to produce the finest and most beautiful items.

With all these distractions, there was still always time for a chai or a snack, ensconced in a street restaurant, where some sweet or spicy morsel went well with a gossip and a beedi.

At the waterfront, scores more holy men occupied the steps and terraces leading down to the water. The variety of shapes, colours and temperament blasted the senses. That so many men had relinquished former lives of family, profession and relative stability, to give their remaining years to the vagaries of devotion and the goodwill of others, was bewildering.

Some were fat and jolly, others emaciated by their sacrifice and extremes of self-punishment. Matted dreadlocks trailed down backs or were tied in coils above the heads. Beards to the chest and skin daubed in grey ash from funeral pyres were just some of the common elements of these men, most of whom wore the ubiquitous orange and yellow robes, the colour for those who have renounced the world.

At extreme levels, men could be seen with limbs contorted in incomprehensible yoga positions or had small spikes piercing their tongues, noses or ears. The smell of ganga emanating from large chillums, wafted through the warm air, mingling with the smell of food and street detritus.

Weaving amongst the holy men, dogs scavenged for scraps, cows moved imperiously as if conscious of their sacred designation and along the shoreline, a large number of western hippies lived in the brightly painted houseboats that floated at the river's edge.

As we stood absorbing this never ending fusion of noise and colour, a wedding procession arrived from one of the boats. A drummer and a shehnai player led the procession, the long wind instrument with its trumpet end, emitting a distinctive high pitched vibratory sound. As was the custom, the groom followed, dressed in tight grey cotton suit with a long jacket, slicked back hair and white winkle-picker shoes, swaggering up the steps as if looking for a fight rather than about to be married. A yellow silk scarf was tied to one wrist, trailing a few feet behind and attached to his bride's veil. She too was dressed in yellow, a colour believed to bring prosperity to the marriage. The opaque veil covered her entire head, requiring that she be safely guided up the steps by two female companions.

A procession of relatives, dressed in their best suits and saris followed close behind, together with yet more drummers and shehnai players, who danced informally alongside the entourage, until they all reached the top of the steps and disappeared through a gateway into a large courtyard for the ceremony.

Further along the shoreline, ancient temples that had been sinking into the thick, grey-green mud, were in the process of being excavated by teams of barefoot coolies. With so much disrepair throughout the city, still screaming for attention, such work could perhaps have been much further down the list of priorities.

Twilight was beginning to fall and lights switching on all along the waterfront. It was time to make our way back, returning to the market where vendors still sat in the midst of sacks of rice, pulses and nuts and wide baskets of fruit and vegetables laid out before them.

Beneath the lingering warm evening air, laden with the heavy smells of inadequate drains, we turned off into what became a maze of narrow streets. Every available space on each side seemed to be occupied by a small stall or temple, leaving only four or five feet in between to enable a two way flow of people. The streets glittered under the lights, highlighting the gaudy bracelets, necklaces, cheap metal statuettes and ornaments on display, alongside neatly stacked rows of sticky, multicoloured sweets. Outside the temples, vendors called out to passing devotees, offering garlands of flowers and incense to be taken inside as offerings.

A steady surge of people carried us along and those coming the other way, sometimes knocked us backwards. Then there were

the runaway bulls and cows, often forcing us into a doorway as
if we were on the Paloma bull run, their deadly horns sometimes
missing our flesh by inches, their urine splashing up off the paving
stones onto our feet.

Yet, as the sky grew darker, I suddenly shivered and the
debilitating cold intensified.

Arriving back at the house, as Sally cooked dinner, Mateo
practised his sitar, while I sat with my blanket wrapped tightly
around me and continued to shiver, my cold having worsened,
leaving me with a sore throat and a throbbing headache.

Sally felt my brow and confirmed I had a temperature, for which
all I could do was wrap myself in more blankets for the night and
try to sweat it out.

I wanted to see what all Hindus aspire to at the end of their lives
and, despite still feeling rotten the next morning, was determined
not to miss the opportunity.

Starting at the open river bank near to Sally's house, I began
my progress along the water's edge once again, taking in the
meditating sadhus, the clothes washers, those standing waist
deep in the murky water, pouring brass potfuls over themselves,
occasionally touching their foreheads with the sacred liquid and
sometimes even drinking it.

Further along, barefoot lines of coolies, both men and women,
were filling baskets with sand brought from the opposite bank
in flat bottomed sampans and carrying them on their heads to
waiting lorries higher up the bank.

On and on, the waterfront stretched as far as I could see, passing
the temples, private houses and palaces and the ramshackle huts
and tents of the very poor.

More gangs of coolies, unprotected by any safety measures, were
sinking concrete piles into the mud, chanting repetitively as they
hauled on ropes slung over pulleys on crude wooden rigs.

A few planks crossed over streams of sewage running out from
the city above and into the already murky river.

Beyond, columns of blue-grey smoke drifted up and across the
river in a hazy pall and I prepared myself for what might lie ahead.
A group of donkeys, their coats painted in orange and purple rings

and stripes, waited patiently for an unbearable load of sand to be set upon them. Water buffalo wallowed in the shallows where nearby women washed clothes and their children innocently splashed as children do on a hot day. On the water's edge, a dog was tugging at the bloated body of a baby.

Then, I was upon it, the famous Manikarnika ghat. The rising smoke had now revealed its source. There, on the muddy shore and a terrace above, burned seven funeral pyres in varying stages of progress. Some were only embers, the white flakes of charred wood and bone swirling in the breeze. Another had only recently been lit, the orange flames lapping at the cloths wrapped around the body, a few toes beginning to appear as the drapery fell away.

Bells rang out from the temple further up the steps and a fierce heat hit me as I gingerly moved closer, not really sure if I should be there watching such a personal ceremony, albeit within such a public arena. Imagining myself to be invisible, I sat on the nearby wall and watched transfixed as the ritual unfolded.

In a newly cleared space, a criss-cross of logs and straw had been prepared to a height of between three and four feet. To the repetitive chants of, 'Rama naam satya hain', God is Truth, a body, wrapped in a white shroud and strewn with marigold garlands on a bamboo stretcher, was carried on the shoulders of five male family members to the water's edge.

The men ceremoniously lowered the stretcher into the holy water for purification. Then, assisted by a priest, what appeared to be the eldest son, with shaven head and dressed in white dhoti and salwar, partially opened the shroud to pour ghee over the body and Ganges water over the face. With all their effort, the men lifted the corpse up and onto the pyre with more logs being piled on top. The priest continued his ceremony by scattering coloured dye over the body and uttering a few more prayers.

The son took hold of a burning sheaf of straw, given by one of the fire stokers, and began walking around the pyre.

A scream went up from where the women were standing, with one running down the steps, her arms waving in the air. Before anyone could say or do anything, she was climbing up onto the pyre, frantically pushing wood out of the way so she could lay across her husband's body, as she continued her wailing and screaming. The son, clearly flummoxed by this departure from the script, tried to console his mother while helping her down from the pyre, still clawing at the shroud.

In previous centuries, until the British banned the practise in 1829, a wife was expected to commit suttee by sacrificing herself on the already flaming pyre.

The other women came down to help the poor woman back up the steps to the viewing point reserved for them, allowing the son to regain his composure and continue his five circles around his father's pyre. Applying the burning torch to the straw, the flames leapt almost immediately, such was the readiness of the wood to burn, lapping at the edges of the shroud as the immolation began.

The stokers or Doms were of the Untouchable caste and, as such, received no respect for performing this essential service for many hours of a day under such extreme physical and psychological conditions. With damp turbans wrapped around their heads, and two or three coughing intermittently, they turned the logs with long bamboo poles, ensuring the flames were maintained and that body parts that had fallen free of the flames were tucked in again.

This was quite a well to do family as they must have paid extra for sandalwood to be mixed amongst the ordinary logs brought down from the slopes of the Himalayas. As the flames intensified, the sweet smell of this wood mingled with the cloying smell of burning flesh, the whole experience exacerbated by the sizzling and popping of the body.

The day was already hot, despite the time of year, and the sweat poured from me as I took it all in, my clothes and hair already covered by the floating ash. The shroud burned quickly, revealing blackening flesh, cracking and peeling under the heat until the charred bones were exposed. This would have continued for three to four hours until most of the body had been consumed by the flames.

Looking to some of the other pyres, young boys were scavenging through the cooling embers searching for gold teeth and jewellery, which could be salvaged and sold. From another, guts and bones, not consumed by the flames, were being cast into the river, immediately to be set upon by the congregated packs of dogs. At another, a priest threw a clay pot of water to smash on the embers as a final salutation to the deceased.

Despite the outpouring I'd witnessed from the distraught widow, the whole procedure appeared to be very precise and mechanical with little apparent emotion being expressed. Death was as much a part of life as life itself; the cycle that most Hindus recognised and was an event to be glorified, especially if the final destination could be within the waters of the Holy Mother Ganga. What I had been watching was a disposal factory to save souls from reincarnation and take them to paradise.

One last look across the river, where bloated, decomposing bodies floated downstream, perhaps a former prostitute, a pregnant woman, an unmarried girl or simply someone whose family could not afford the firewood or cow dung. I was told that bodies are usually weighted with stones but, in time, break free and float to the surface and drift to the shoreline, where the dogs, pigs and vultures do the job the flames had not been able to.

Seeing those bodies burn, provoked an intense sense of finality, emphasising how unimportant the body really is. But, even as a couple of crows picked at the face of a human carcass on the beach, I felt a certainty that this was not the end, but just a part of a much longer journey.

Unable to bear the heat and the stench any longer, I rose and left the pyres behind me, climbing steep steps that led back into the city, where stalls sold garlands of flowers, coloured dyes, clay pots and firewood was weighed out for upcoming funerals. Bodies, clad in golden shrouds were waiting in a queue at the top of the ghat, while more were being brought down even as I became enveloped by the ever narrowing streets.

Not knowing if it was the overbearing smell of death or the heat, my head felt heavy, throbbing with pain and nausea, as if I had absorbed sickness from the burning bodies. I had to stop and sit quietly for a few moments with my head in my hands, before staggering onwards through the narrow streets, past temples, more death orientated stalls and pitiful old men and women, crouched in the gutters, soon to be victims of the flames themselves. As with the rampaging cows the day before, I often had to duck into doorways and recesses as a steady stream of bodies was brought down on stretchers to join the queue to eternity.

For the first time, I felt overwhelmed by it all, sick and disgusted by what I was seeing and feeling. Everything was encrusted in dirt, the ancient walls, the artefacts for sale, the animals, the people, the foul open drains, the red splatters on the ground from chewed betel leaves. Barefoot and almost naked children stared from empty shells, stretching out their grimy hands and running after me in the filth beneath our feet.

Why was India still so poor and filthy? My only thought now, despite all the beautiful things I had seen and learned, was to leave this country and return to some cleanliness and hope, for here, there was none and I could not look at it any longer. The rot and the filth had got to me and I had to leave whilst I still could.

India held no more for me. The magic was gone. All I now saw was an ocean of sinking faces, which no longer brought pity, but anger at the simplicity and ignorance. Yet, there remained a deep intractable ambivalence. The country had brought about profound changes, including perhaps humility, a degree of compassion and above all gratitude for who I was and where I was from. But, I could no longer stay and further witness the suffering of its people on such a scale. They had to find their own destinies as I had to find mine.

My emotions were not greatly helped on realising that much of the pain I was experiencing was due to an emerging wisdom tooth.

Ten

MY WAKING FROM THE NIGHTMARE of the day before clearly marked the beginning of the end of my time in India.

A local herbal doctor gave me some tincture, which temporarily numbed the pain and energised me for one last plunge into the apparent wisdom that had lured me to India in the first place.

Sarnath was a mere half hour's bus journey from the centre of the city and the site of Gautama Buddha's first sermon some nine hundred years earlier, following his enlightenment in Bodh Gaya.

The bus drove out from the chaos of the city streets into green, sun soaked countryside, where orchards and fields full of crops surrounded walled private houses with large gateways on the outskirts of slumbering villages.

Sarnath itself was merely a village with a few chai shops and restaurants, serving the visitors who had come to see the various monasteries that lay the short distance beyond.

Taking the Ashok Road, north, I headed for the Tibetan monastery where Yeshe Thubten, one of the monks who had seen me off in McLeod Ganj, said he was hoping to be. Along the tree lined road, the sun filtering through the leaves, of all the monks making their way in both directions, the broad smiles and laughing eyes of the Tibetans stood out. My heart leapt to see these much loved faces after the wretchedness and desperation of the last month.

Two large Tibetan lion carvings stood as sentinels at the gates, beyond which a spacious courtyard with a mature Peepal tree was enclosed by dormitory blocks on two levels, set aside for monks and the occasional visitor.

The focal point was the unassuming temple, rectilinear in construction, its white walls and window surrounds with their distinctive red and black geometric edging. A portico leading into the temple itself had been richly decorated with four large and colourful tanka frescoes; two on either side of the doorway, depicting deities I had become familiar with during my studies.

Within the temple, a wide and polished parquet floor supported four central pillars, and transverse ceiling beams, all painted red and overpainted with the stylised cloud imagery so typical of tanka art.

Hundreds of tankas hung from the walls and large glass cabinets contained sacred texts and what appeared to be thousands of small Buddha like statuettes, probably representing the many Boddhisatvas, who had vowed not to enter Nirvana until all other beings had attained Enlightenment.

In a recess at the back, a dominant gold Buddha overshadowed the space, surrounded by more Boddhisatvas, deities and photographs of the Dalai Lama and Panchen Lama, Tibet's second most powerful senior monk.

In the centre of the floor, two lines of low tables and cushions faced each other as a single monk sat intoning the stack of sacred Tibetan texts before him, printed from hand carved wood blocks.

Both within this temple and outside in the courtyard a special kind of tranquility pervaded the space.

This was largely true of the remaining temples I visited, but not before ascertaining that Yeshe Thubten was not in the monastery but on a visit to Bodh Gaya. The absence of this last contact, further confirmed my break with Kamala and the Tibetan community.

My head pains re-emerged as I walked the few hundred yards to the Chinese temple, then a bowl of momos at the Tibetan food stall in a tent beneath the trees on the edge of the Deer Park.

On the wall of the nearby, Maha Bodhi Society was displayed a notice for a free dispensary. I was now down to just over ten rupees to get me to the border, without dipping into my traveller's cheques or my newly acquired two hundred dollars. I was determined to make the money last and, if possible, not touch the dollars until I'd got back to England and had been reunited with Belinda.

By completing a form and paying ten paisa, I was rewarded with a single dose pill, a small bottle of foul tasting liquid and eight pain killers. Whatever they were, there was an almost instantaneous reaction, prompting a recovery that gave the strength to visit the Indian temple.

Its magnificent reclining Buddha was set within a building that resembled a European church with spire and two belfries, but built in the commonplace Nagara architectural style seen on so many Hindu temples.

The Dear Park covered a wide area, laid to grass and surrounded between the excavated remains of former monasteries and the great stupa built by the Emperor Ashok, who had converted to Buddhism after being traumatised by the level of death he had witnessed in battle. Songbirds in the surrounding trees enhanced the ambiance and the suggestion that Buddha's spirit might still be present in this sacred space.

The noise of Benares was deafening as I stepped off the bus after a day of relative peace and clean air. Large cities the world over were not compulsory places to live and these experiences only confirmed that I should better value the tranquility that a small town or village had to offer, for the benefits to both health and spiritual equanimity.

This was to be my last night with Sally and Mateo and I tried to be the convivial guest over dinner, only to feel the exhaustion from the day and a yearning to sleep in readiness for the push onwards to Delhi the next day.

In bidding farewell to my hosts, I felt I was cutting the final cord of my time in India. After a filling plate of vegetable subji, a hug and promises to meet again in London, I was in a rickshaw, heading for the bus station where a bus would take me to the famous Grand Trunk Road.

This was part of the world's longest highway, running nearly thirteen thousand miles from Tokyo, through China, South-East Asia, East Pakistan, India, West Pakistan, Afghanistan, Iran, Turkey and the border of Bulgaria. This would be the road I should now be following most of the way to Europe.

Even at this early hour, my nerves had been frayed by the onslaught of people and most significantly the very poor. As I waited for the bus to leave, a young beggar so needled me, that I lost my cool and kicked him. I immediately, felt ashamed at what I had done and apologised in the best way I could with smiles and gestures, placing my hands together in atonement and offering the few spare paisa that I could afford to give.

The bus dropped me at the railway station right by the main road out of the city and, with a little walking, a lorry stopped and took me the one hundred and twenty miles to Allahabad, where the Ganges ended its journey from the mountains and merged with the Yamuna River, which I'd last seen coursing past the Taj Mahal.

We came in crossing the long road bridge that traversed the cultivated muddy flood plain of the Ganges, travelling at least three miles before reaching the other side, where my friendly driver had to leave me. With open fields and little villages before me, I started out in the direction my instincts guided me, only to shortly find that my instincts were not working particularly well that day. The main station, where I intended to spend the night, was another seven miles away, in the opposite direction.

It was late afternoon and I just couldn't face such a walk through busy streets, thus resorting to a rickshaw for one and a half rupees. I really felt for the man, straining in the cold air to carry me as far as he did, but I now had less than eight rupees and just couldn't afford to give him more.

Putting my thoughts to my current situation, there I was in the middle of India with no guarantees of getting any further, yet I trusted that I would be looked after and eventually find myself in West Pakistan where I knew I could at least afford to eat properly everyday.

On this occasion, I didn't buy a platform ticket, instead going straight to the Second Class Waiting Room where I rolled out my sleeping bag as per usual in a space on the floor. With no money with which to eat, I read a little before turning in for an early night. My calm was very soon disturbed by a little man in uniform, who thought it appropriate to ask for my platform ticket.

'Fucking Hell,' I said, under my breath.

'Are you hearing that?' He said, turning to the audience in the room, temporarily distracted from his original purpose. 'He was saying, "fucking"'.

Incredulity crept across their faces at the utterance of this word, which they clearly disapproved of, whilst gathering in a huddle with the inspector to discuss the matter. While they spoke in their native Hindi, every so often, someone would utter, "fucking"; a word so censured but, nevertheless, here a grand opportunity to say as often as they liked, to the obvious disgust of the ladies present.

'You will have to go to the Station Master for permission to sleep here,' the inspector said in his disapproving and authoritative manner.

Collecting my bags, I sloped off down the platform to the office, knocking on the door before entering.

The room was not unlike the office in which I had passed so many hours in Bhusawal. The high ceiling, rotating fan, forms and more forms, an antique wall clock and a chubby man sitting behind a desk with neatly parted hair and features lost in folds of skin.

Fortunately, he was less officious than his predecessor and had no problem with me sleeping in the waiting room. Returning to my space on the floor, the inspector, sensing his power evaporating, insisted I had the permission in writing. The station master for one reason or another, was not prepared to write anything down, insisting the inspector would just have to take my word for it.

When he didn't, I merely ignored his protestations, too tired to argue, and promptly slipped into my sleeping bag and watched him leave, a dejected man.

I was glad to take an albeit cold shower the next morning to wash off some of the previous day's dust, before a hot cup of chai and puris. I then had to orientate myself for the road towards the next big city of Kanpur.

My first lift was a mixed blessing. A lorry drew up with the driver telling me I had to stand up at the back. It wasn't until he'd dropped me some miles outside Allahabad, that I realised I was speckled with coal dust, causing me to have another wash and make some effort to brush down my clothes.

Only a short time later, a green wood framed station wagon

pulled up going all the way to Kanpur, another 160 miles.

My hosts were a lawyer and his wife, naturally speaking fluent English and curious about my time in India.

I made myself comfortable in the back and, for the first fifty miles or so, I recounted my adventures to date, before the conversation tailed off and I was left to my thoughts.

Rather than contemplating the rigours of what lay ahead for the next few thousand miles, I was transported to the late summer of the previous year which, following our reconciliation, I had spent with Belinda in her cottage near Cambridge. Lazy days spent dipping our feet into the cool streams running off the meadows, a picnic laid out before us beneath the dappled light of a willow canopy.

Despite her overdose and all the trouble that ensued from that, I had fallen in love with her. She had been my first love and subsequently I'd felt a deep bonding with her. What had emerged following her hospitalisation was a woman of great strength and integrity, who had truly inspired my future path. I had deviated from that path with my burning need to come to India, but that was coming to an end and I was at last going home - to her.

Then I remembered Alison, whose bed I had shared only two weeks before in Bombay, succumbing to her beauty and the opportunity of comfort for one blessed night.

Before that, the one night spent with Kamala, whose innocence I had no right to exploit for my own selfish ends. Yet, I had come to know Kamala over several months and been moved by not only her unique beauty, but the resonance of her personal story and the sufferings she had endured crossing the Himalayas with her parents to escape the marauding Chinese. Hers was a love of which I knew no precedent and would always remain in my heart.

By mid-day, we were pulling into Kanpur, crossing the Ganges again and into what appeared to be a strong military and industrial centre, where my hosts insisted on taking me to lunch. Over the biggest meal I had eaten for days, the couple told me more about themselves.

'I trained at Bombay University, but now work for a law firm in Benares,' Manish told me. He was in his late twenties, but had an air of confidence and determination about him. 'I met Samiha at

University.'

'Are you a lawyer too?' I asked her.

'No, an English professor at Benares University,' she replied with an air of pride and a little swagger. 'I completed my PhD last year and was very pleased to get this position.'

They were clearly very ambitious, but their kindness to myself absolved them of any pretensions.

After we had gone our separate ways, they to stay with family for the weekend and myself out to the Delhi road, I came across an old single deck English bus parked on the main road, emblazoned with a large Union Jack on the back. Loitering on the sidewalk, a number of boys and girls in their late teens and early twenties were chatting amongst themselves.

'Hi,' I said, as I approached, 'are you coming or going?' A small group of them gathered around me in curiosity and an Australian boy piped up, 'We're on our way to Kathmandu, but the van we're with has broken down,' he said, pointing to a Bedford van further up the road, not unlike the one my old headmaster drove the football team to away matches in the 1950s. 'It's not the first time this has happened,' he continued.

An English girl took up the conversation. 'We all paid fifty quid for this "all in" trip from London, but it's just been a terrible con.'

The Australian continued. 'We first broke down in Gravesend and were there for a week, then again in Dover, before we'd even left the country.'

'My God, that's terrible. I'm surprised you've all stuck with it,' I said.

There was a clamouring of voices as several others tried to join in the conversation, but the English girl won out,

'We're the survivors,' she said, smiling triumphantly and raising her fist in the air. I could see there were now only enough of them to fill about half the bus.

'We've had trouble most of the trip and, because of all the unplanned stops, we've spent much more than we anticipated. Quite a few have left along the way and we're now just debating whether we should quit now. We've asked about compensation, but the drivers aren't interested.'

'Where have you been sleeping?' I asked.

'We occasionally stop at a cheap hotel for a shower, she continued, 'but, most of the time, we sleep on the bus and it looks like we're going to be stuck in this dump for a few days.'

Looking around, the street housed leather workshops, where saddles and bags had been made since the British presence, following the Mutiny in 1837. But, most disturbing was the putrid smell of rotting flesh and the pall of steam and smoke that hung across most of the city, emanating from the many tanneries preparing the leather. Indeed, the unpleasantness was sufficient to drive me out of the city of my own volition.

By this time, a large crowd of curious onlookers had gathered, pressing ever forward to both see and hear what was going on amongst us. Even a decamp to a chai stall could not shake them off as they lingered outside while we drank and talked.

With the best of the day over and the sun well on its way to the horizon, it was too late to get on the road. Some of my new acquaintances were getting cold, but couldn't get their things from the bus as it had been locked.

When I thought of all the places I had seen and the people encountered since leaving England, it struck me that, for such a potentially mind changing trip, these people had very little freedom to explore and gain a rich diversity of experience. Even more so, as they all tended to stick together, leaving little opportunity for those unforgettable and very meaningful one to one encounters.

Nevertheless, I strung along with them for something to eat, but more so for the company.

The two drivers were at the bus on our return, peeved that they had been kept waiting. Julian, the older of the two, thick set in his thirties with a heavily pockmarked face, gave the appearance of a rough diamond who perhaps could not be entirely trusted. Martin, the other, in his twenties, tall and thin with a pinched nose, small eyes set close together and long greasy hair to his loose cotton kurta. Julian announced that we would be driving to the outskirts of the city for the night. The two or three that I had got to know better, invited me to join them.

As I boarded, my way was blocked by Julian.

'Where do you think you're going, mate?' he asked with an educated, but somewhat aggressive tone.

'I was invited to join you all for the night. I'm on my way back to England overland, so don't worry, I'm not muscling in on a free ride. I'll be gone tomorrow.'

He hesitated a little, not sure whether to exert his authority, but drew back to let me on.

Mercifully, the engine started first time, but sounded laboured as we passed through the tight mesh of streets, until turning into the grounds of a former British colonial bungalow with wide covered veranda on three sides, a large entrance porch and the ubiquitous red corrugated iron roof. Set amongst trees, well tended borders and sweeping paths, it probably wasn't much more than fifty years old, but had aged well through the heat and rains and had taken on a timeless identity.

We were all greeted by the owner of the house, an elegant Indian lady, beautifully dressed in a red sari, her greying hair gathered behind her head and trailing down her back, her hands together in a namaste.

'Welcome to my home. I cannot offer you beds, but there is plenty of room on my lawn and I have a toilet and washbasin around the side of the house, which you can use, ' she concluded, turning a little sheepishly to point out the direction.

It wasn't quite what I was expecting, but gave an insight into what my new friends had been enduring on their journey. I'm sure I would have been amongst those who left on the first day, but then I would never have signed up for such a trip in the first place, depriving myself of the freedom I had so far enjoyed, despite sometimes fraught encounters.

The large piece of plastic I'd used to keep me dry on such outdoor occasions had long since disintegrated, but one of the boys lent me a spare groundsheet. I'd still not completely got over my cold and was already feeling the evening chill.

'Here, have this jumper,' an Irish girl said, pulling it from her rucksack. It's a spare and I'm not going to be wanting it now.'

'Wow, thanks. That's just what I've been looking for,' I exclaimed with real joy, taking the light blue woollen polo neck and slipping it over my head. It was a little tight, but a gift horse not to be sneered at.

There was conviviality in this group and perhaps something

I missed a little as I had largely been on my own these past few weeks. I sensed that the encounters I'd had with the many travellers on the outward journey the previous spring would be few and far between during the winter return.

A heavy dew woke most of us early and there was much yawning and stretching as some of us rolled up our sleeping bags and wandered to the toilet before a long queue had formed. Some meandered around the wide lawn and fringe of trees, while I sat on the veranda with one of the guys and smoked a beedi.

'Where are you off to today?' Simon, a blond haired boy about my age asked.

'I'll get onto the Delhi road and hope to be there by tonight.'

'Do you actually hitch rides, by yourself?

'Well, yes. The past few weeks, apart from a couple of train rides, I've hitched all the way to Bombay and back to here. From Delhi, it will be a mix of train, buses and whatever lifts I can get. I've got to make the money last.'

'I'm thinking of quitting today and going on to Kathmandu by myself,' Simon said. 'Do you think I should?'

'I can't answer for you, only say what I would do. I would want to get back to England with stories to tell and would imagine your trip, to date, has been somewhat two dimensional. If you hitch or take a train this last bit, and it's not too far now, you will surely meet new people and have experiences you wouldn't have had going onwards with the bus. Does the fifty quid you paid just take you to Kathmandu?'

'Yes, but I'm going on to Oz. I've got family in Perth, who went out on a ten pound transit in '63. I might even stay. I think some of the others are planning to do the same.'

I'd definitely leave today then. You'll meet up with the others in Nepal. You might even get there first.'

'I like a challenge. Can I join you when you go?'

'Sure, but once we hit the Delhi road, we'll be going in opposite directions.

Have you got much stuff?'

'Just a rucksack and sleeping bag.'

I pulled out my map and unfolded it on the wicker table before us.

'If you trace your way back through Kanpur, you can go to Benares.' Here, I took out my book of hostels and flicked through the pages. 'Here it is. You got a bit of paper? Write these down,' I said, pointing to a couple of addresses in Benares. 'It's worth spending a couple of days there, to really see what India is all about.'

'Thanks Adam.'

Returning to the map, I traced my finger out of Benares. 'Then head for Patna and it's just a straight road north to Kathmandu. I've been sleeping in station waiting rooms where you can generally get a shower as well, but make sure you buy a platform ticket. Go for it!'

Simon was overjoyed that he now had the confidence to take control of his life and he beamed with excitement and anticipation of what might lie ahead for him.

'One other tip,' I added. 'When you settle down to sleep, tie your rucksack to your wrist. It's not foolproof, but it might just wake you if someone tries to get into it.'

A bell rang nearby where Julian and Martin had set up a trestle table with a large aluminium teapot and terracotta cups, such as I'd often seen in railway stations. A queue was already forming for a hot cup of chai. On another table, the lady was dishing out bowls of subji from a large cooking pot, delivering warm-hearted smiles for each of her guests.

As we sat on a low wall eating our breakfast, Simon glanced at my feet, still in flip-flops.

'Are those the only shoes you have?'

'I'm hoping to find something better in Delhi.'

He pulled over his rucksack and rummaged inside.

'Here, will these do, you're about my size? he said, handing over a pair of desert boots.

I couldn't believe my good fortune as they were in excellent condition and exactly my size. Simon was already wearing a substantial pair of boots, more appropriate for the weather and terrain he was going to.

'Being over cautious, I brought two pairs of boots, so you can have them.'

'That's so kind of you. Thank you. Do you want my flip-flops? I won't be needing them anymore where I'm going.'

He was happy to receive them, stuffing them down into his rucksack, while another boy, witnessing the conversation, pulled out a pair of thick socks as another gift.

Dressed in my new clothes, I felt ready for the next stage, only needing a coat, but already I was feeling warmer.

Not long after, we both waved a farewell to the others and set off, reaching the Delhi road sooner than I had anticipated with no time to talk more.

I wished him well as he crossed to the other side and we each stood with thumbs out to the passing traffic. Within minutes, a lorry had stopped for Simon and I could see the sheer joy and leap of excitement as he gathered his things, running to catch his first lift. A brief wave and he was gone.

Moments later, an army jeep drew up, driven by a sergeant with an impressive Lord Kitchener moustache, trimmed and waxed. He was going to Agra, half way to Delhi, and seemed beyond the law judging by the speed he drove. There was little conversation other than asking where I had been and where I was going, reacting with little concern on hearing that I would be travelling on my chosen route at the coldest time of the year.

'We will be going to the mountains before long for winter manoeuvres. It is essential training because we are having trouble with China again,' he told me with the certainty that anything China might do, the Indian army would be more than ready for.

He dropped me on the outskirts of Agra, from where a lorry took me a few more miles, dropping me outside a small restaurant where I had to concede for the first time that I didn't have enough money to eat. My stomach rumbled and I was certain that it had already begun to shrink. With chai being all I could afford, I sat alone at a table only for a bowl of rice and dahl to be placed in front of me. Despite gesturing that I couldn't pay, the manager waved his hands and smiled. Providence had held my hand once again.

It was already mid-afternoon, as I waited once again for the last hop to Delhi. The day was still warm as the curious and sheer annoying formed an alliance with the host of flies that unceasingly swirled and touched down upon my face. The next lift came as much a relief as an onward step in the journey.

The green and yellow lorry, overpainted with psychedelic swirls and patterns carried a cargo of bulging sacks, but an open box-like space above the cab was where I was directed. Climbing a fixed ladder on one side, I hauled myself and my things up and we set off.

Watchful of low hanging branches and the occasional stray insect, I had a three hundred and sixty degree view of the flat countryside, once again taking in the whitewashed village houses set amongst clumps of trees, the bustle at the village ponds, the buffalos, exuberant children and garlanded temples.

As the sun slowly disappeared into the mist on the horizon, we drew in at a restaurant, where my driver proudly displayed his English cargo and bought me a much appreciated meal.

In faltering English, he told me he expected to arrive in Delhi in the early morning so, back in my nest on the roof, I rolled out my sleeping bag and pulled some empty sacks over to keep out the worst of the cold night air.

Miraculously, I managed to get some sleep, although I was woken by the lights of the city outskirts and the uneven road surface as we rolled into Old Delhi around five o' clock, pulling into a dingy yard where coolies slept on crates and sacks in anticipation of work later in the day.

I was on my own again, setting off past firmly shuttered shops, as men wrapped in blankets, suffused in an orange glow, huddled around small fires burning on the rubbish strewn streets. It was akin to a post-apocalyptic scene, whereby all had been destroyed and the survivors were making do as best they could.

Elsewhere, save for the occasional sleeping body in a doorway, the streets were deserted. Cows slept in spaces on the edge of the road, while the dogs seemed to be on constant alert, one eye half open, ready for action at a moment's notice.

Turning off, here and there, I followed the train whistles somewhere in the near distance, hoping they would lead me to a station. A few more streets and I was looking across the tracks of a goods yard towards the lights of a small station. Picking my way over the lines, I was up onto the platform, where I was told I could catch a train into New Delhi.

As I waited, a pale grey light, tinged with orange began to spread across the sky and I was comforted by a hot cup of chai and a piece of delicate honey cake infused with coconut and cardamon, brought by the station master.

This early in the morning, there were seats for the taking all the way to the station where, the usual shower facilities were waiting and an opportunity to oil and bandage my feet, much dried, split and quite sore from the months of exposure and neglect in flip-flops. Perhaps, now that I had a pair of proper boots, they would have a chance to heal.

The short walk to Connaught Circus brought me back to familiar territory, where poetry and transvestitism had once collided. The city was well and truly awake with an underlying background roar, highlighted by the ubiquitous horns, bells and human interaction. The chai shops and restaurants were already serving and I imagined that, with the long list of things I needed to do that day, it would be good to fortify myself at this stage and once again chance to luck later in the day. It was therefore a plate of rice, dahl, two different vegetable dishes and chapatis, leaving me with just over four rupees to see me to the border.

Eleven

FOLLOWING ON FROM the incident at Bhusawal, I was curious to see if I could get some redemption on the fine I had paid and if perhaps there was any chance of getting hold of some more warm clothes before setting off.

A bus took me to the embassy colony, passing close by the sprawling government buildings designed by Edward Lutyens for the closing years of the British Raj.

Wandering the tree lined avenues, I stumbled on the Portuguese Embassy, the Swiss, the French, American, the Australian and finally, tucked away, the British High Commission, looking not unlike an exhibition centre at Expo, reflecting the bright sunlight from the many blue tinted glass panels.

A clerk at reception, following a decorous "Namaste," was then besieged by my catalogue of questions.

'Where can I get my cholera and typhoid certificate?' 'Do you have a fund that could help me buy some warm clothes?' "I have this fine ….?'

To the second question, I was told quite emphatically that there were no funds available.

'Then, I would like to see someone with more authority, please.'

As I waited in the foyer, the noticeboard was warning travellers, like myself, not to take hashish and other drugs through Middle Eastern countries. *"Since the beginning of this year, 50 people have already been executed by firing squad in Iran,"* one notice warned.

A very English young man in suit and tie, fair wavy hair and glasses, came out and invited me into his office, where he sat at his desk, the obligatory portrait of the queen hanging from the wall behind him.

'What can I do for you?' he asked politely after a little diverse chit chat.

Repeating the three questions, he thought for a moment before declaring,

'I'm afraid the incident at Bhusawal was just a farce,' he started, his clipped words running into each other in the way that the privileged English often speak.' He looked down at the receipt in his hands, 'I'm afraid this was just an excuse to get rid of you.'

'I did think as much and what about clothes?'

'There are some Christian churches in the city where you might be able to pick up a coat, but we really don't have any money we can forward to you.

Your vaccinations can be certified at the main town hall. I'm sorry I couldn't have been more positive.'

'Well, it was worth a try. It was nice talking to an Englishman again,' to which he was clearly embarrassed for the sake of the Indian clerk, who had stayed in attendance.

Next stop, the Pakistani Embassy, where I needed a road permit to cross the country. Set amidst spacious lawns, this was a much more imposing building, with a central dome, decorated with tiny ultramarine blue tiles and a pair of mock minarets at the end of each wing. A few hippies were lying on the grass as I entered and requested the permit. A completed form and a forty minute wait later, I was on my way again with the permit, issued free.

The town hall was less obliging. I'd last had a booster in Dharamsala the previous month but omitted to get my certificate stamped at the time. Despite much pleading and the assertion that there was no reason to lie about it, for who would want to get a vaccine twice, this was the only way I could get a stamp on my certificate.

The day had quickly passed into late afternoon by the time I arrived at Cox and Kings to collect my rucksack. I had forgotten how heavy it was and asked if it could be shipped back to England only to be told they wouldn't accept cash on delivery. I was tempted to exchange one of my hundred dollar bills, but realised that I would end up with a surplus of rupees, which I couldn't take out of the country and would receive a bad exchange rate for any other currency.

Slinging it over my shoulder, I set off to find somewhere for the night that would cost me nothing. As I trudged out of Connaught Circus, the rucksack felt as if it was filled with bricks, rubbing painfully into my shoulders, already painful from the booster vaccines I'd had earlier in the day. *What was in it that was so important?*

Stopping for a chai, a young Sikh, his beard whispy and sparse, pointed me towards a Gurdwara Sikh temple where I could find accommodation and something to eat. The light was already fading, street lights on, but my arrival at the temple was only met with disappointment as the entire premises were undergoing renovation. I fared no better at the YMCA, who wanted an extortionate sixteen rupees a day for a bed and three meals. Another Gurdwara, I was told, was a little further away, but that eluded me.

By this time, I was becoming quite desperate, wishing that perhaps it would have been better to bypass Delhi altogether.

The poverty was becoming more apparent as darkness fell and the shadows more sinister. At a row of private houses, the idea came that if I knocked on the pretext of asking directions, someone might just take pity and invite me in. But, even with my hair only just growing back after having it shaved off in the mountains, I still looked like a filthy hippy on their doorstep.

One man, a little irritated that I had knocked on his door, directed me to another Gurdwara, where again no accommodation was available, but I was taken to the kitchen and given a bowl of dahl and a couple of chapatis. By chance or destiny, an Indian, a little younger than myself had overheard the conversation and clearly observed my state of dejection.

'If you would like to be coming with me, I can be giving you somewhere to sleep.'

I was too exhausted to ignore him and, although wary and not knowing what to expect, willing to take the chance and follow him nevertheless.

'My name is Maanish,' he told me as I plodded after him, cursing the rucksack that now bore down on me. 'I am in the third year of my B.A. studies in Politics. I am having three sisters and two brothers and I welcome you to my home.' It was apparent that no one else was in as we crossed the threshold into a dimly lit room of a ground floor apartment. Beyond this, a small square room with three single beds, no window and an equally dim light.

'Here are sleeping my brother-in-law, who is having eight children, my brother and myself. My brother-in-law is working as a sweeper in the Defence district and my brother is typing the letters for people. You will be having my brother-in-law's bed and he will be sharing with me.'

Too tired to argue the offer, I climbed into the designated bed, oblivious to any issues of hygiene. The radio still on, left me to drift off to Dylan's, *Lay, Lady, Lay*.

Maanish was the hospitable host, bringing me hot tea first thing in the morning, before walking me the few streets to catch a bus to a transport area, from where lorries regularly went to the border at Ferozepore.

It was difficult to be sure, but I believed it to be the same area I had been dropped the previous night. The offices of numerous transport companies lined the street, their shutters now wide open. The previously sleeping cows and dogs wandered freely along the street, where sacks and boxes were being loaded and unloaded, while fat proprietors shouted instructions from their open frontages. It would now be a process of elimination until I found someone willing to take me.

A familiar story emerged when told a lorry leaving for Ferozepore would take me, but not until the evening. Elsewhere, enquiries only brought, 'Yes, but we're only going as far as Amritsar.'

The day passed slowly, writing, sleeping, drifting through the streets, spending a few of my dwindling paisa on chai and a bowl of rice and dahl, drawing children, tolerating inane questions and even conversations with those whose English was passable.

By five, I was back in the transport office with the lorry not arriving until about eight and not leaving until nine or ten. Another long sleepless night lay ahead of me, but I would be on my way.

Between cups of chai and more food brought by the people in the office, I contemplated why my view of India had changed so dramatically.

What had started so long ago as an improbable dream, nascent in divine revelations on LSD, countless hashish infused discussions in Notting Hill pads, the influences of music, books and films had culminated in the overriding belief that the answer lay within the borders of Mother India. So much had been said about gurus and holy men who had attained enlightenment and achieved wondrous skills through meditation and devotion.

Fired by these stories, the firmament of my imagination and tales from overland travellers, I determined to make the journey myself.

India was a conjectural concept. A place where the highest expectations lay, but without the specifics of a precise destination. When I walked across the border that hot June afternoon and a young boy pedalled his rickshaw down the eucalyptus lined avenue, speckled with the flit and trill of exotically coloured birds, I felt magic in the air. I had arrived after months of heat and dust, ready to seek out those wise men, while only hoping that they too were not an illusion to be swallowed amongst yet more poverty and unbearable sights.

I always remember the phrase, 'when the student is ready, the teacher appears.' For me, this couldn't have been more true. It was a chance, or possibly, destined encounter with two Dutch guys in Lahore, who told me about the exiled Tibetan communities in India. The most significant was in the Himalayan foothills at an old British hill station named Dharamsala.

My knowledge of Tibetans was sketchy to say the least but, when told of their gentleness, kindness, suffering and the enduring mystery of the country itself, I was fired with an unquenchable excitement that I might be able to meet some of these people.

By way of one conversation, it was as if the whole of India, the object of my odyssey, had been discarded for a small band of refugees in a remote hill station. There I would find what I was looking for.

And, in many respects, I did, together with one of the greatest loves of my life, Kamala. Her love had sustained me for much of my time in the community yet, ultimately, we both realised that our cultures were so disparate that somewhere along the line the differences would divide us, whether I stayed with her in India or she came with me to England.

I had since travelled many miles, to Bombay, Varanasi, now Delhi, rubbing shoulders with ordinary Indian people, but no other opportunities or teachers had manifested themselves. Despite my karma and all the good things that had emerged from my interactions Indians and westerners, no calling had emerged.

In many respects, I suspected I had found the light already and that my journey back to Europe would be a journey into darkness; a repudiation of all I had learned, to be swallowed in the pursuit of mammon. Yet, I was driven onwards into that dark.

As the clock ticked towards nine-thirty, I was told to collect my things and follow one of the drivers. The street was by then lined on both sides with fully laden lorries, waiting to start their respective journeys.

At our lorry, my expectations of riding in warmth and comfort up in the cab were immediately dashed when the driver pointed to the back amongst the sacks. I would not be alone as I had a companion in a coolie, hunched in a corner wrapped from head to foot in a blanket.

Although still without a coat, I made the best of things, dressed in my newly acquired jumper, boots and socks, wrapping my own blanket around my shoulders and settling down by my companion as the engine started and we were away through the buzzing streets and out into the countryside.

Under a clear, star speckled sky, the icy wind relentlessly whipped around the sacks, digging its darting fingers into my face and numbing my hands but, somehow, between a few beedis and gestures about the cold, which my companion acknowledged with a smile and waggle of his head, I managed to fall asleep.

It was gone midnight when we pulled into a yard, some distance from Delhi, where more loading was to take place. My companion came into his own, jumping off the lorry and heading towards a pile of bulging sacks. I was invited to place my luggage in the box above the cab, before being ushered into the office. A coal burner glowed in one corner, two clerks, one quite elderly, sat at their desks, bent diligently over the forms before them, while an unidentified man lay on a charpoy, snoring beneath a blanket. For myself, I took advantage of the chair by the fire, stretching out and dozing from time to time.

Hours passed, the lorry had been loaded and the driver stretched out asleep in the cab. His assistant had gone top to toe on the charpoy with the other man, while another bed was brought in for the older of the two clerks. This left the younger clerk maintaining a steady pace with the forms, mumbling the details under his breath.

Another hour or so passed, the heavy snoring and the clerk's mumbling, forcing me out into the crisp night air. By now, I was used to an improvised bed above the cab, but there was a pervasive damp, exemplified by the droplets of heavy dew on the metalwork reflecting the waning moon high above. I seemed to have got over the worst of my cold and could only see these conditions beneficial in building my resistance to any further infections.

The engine started again and I was now the only passenger.

Several hours later, I lifted my head to be met by the darts of early morning sunlight breaking over the horizon in the East. We were heading north towards Chandigarh, beyond which I could just make out those mysterious green uplands that ultimately led to the mighty Himalayas.

For most of the journey I rested or slept, oblivious to much of the passing countryside. I had seen it all before, the ox carts, temples and the passage of village life. Now it was an unremarkable blur.

Continuing on that trajectory for most of the day, we stopped occasionally for the driver to tinker under the bonnet and for a bite to eat, kindly bought for me. Towards mid-afternoon, we had turned West into the setting sun, stopping on the outskirts of Ludhiana to offload some crates and then onwards into the second night.

By morning, we had pulled in to another town and I'd slept on until woken by the driver.

'Ferozepore,' he shouted up to me as I stretched and rubbed my eyes. As my feet hit the ground, he beckoned me over to join him for chai and a sweet bun.

Thanking him, I set off with my last two rupees, taking a rickshaw to the bus station, from where a bus took me to the border.

I recognised the road I had taken in the other direction, six months earlier to the day. The old railway line that died with the coming of partition, the rusting girder bridges, the canals and sluice gates to irrigate the dry landscape and make the perilous growth of food possible where, for centuries, drought and famine had held their evil grip.

At the border, even as I set foot off the bus, a small band of chai wallers, shouted and pulled at my clothes until, realising I still had fifty paisa left, I sat down to my very last Indian chai and samosa.

Then, once again, the formalities of passing from one country to another. The same fat Sikh guard I had met on my arrival was on duty, still sporting his vest and voluminous underpants, his long hair tied in a bun on top of his head. The official departure stamp thudded down on a page in my passport, I assured him I was not exporting any illegal substances and he waved me through.

One last look down that tree lined avenue leading to India and all I had marvelled at, those I had met, those I had loved, the haunting spectres of omnipresent poverty and destitution, and the clinging question of whether I had really fulfilled the whole purpose of my journey. But, it was now all behind me, except in thoughts and those would churn and manifest I knew not how as the months and years advanced beside me.

Twelve

I WAVED TO THE SIKH and walked over the border into West Pakistan.

This time, it held no excitement for me, it was just another place to pass through. So, with very little emotion, I had my passport stamped and completed the currency declaration, a far cry from my arrival at Indian customs when I was concealing nearly a thousand black market rupees in my underpants.

After all this bureaucracy, and while waiting for the bus to Lahore, I was ready for my first Pakistani chai, in reality, no different to the Indian.

Having been with Hindus for so long, I had forgotten just how different the Moslems were. I was back in a land where most women cover their heads and often their faces, where domed mosques and calling towers dominate the city skylines and most men wear skull caps and beards, often dyed orange with henna. Even the bus journey to Lahore was enlivened by a goat in the corridor, nibbling at a pile of grass and leaves supplied by its owner.

The General Election had recently taken place and there was a feeling of disquiet in the streets. That day, provincial elections had occurred and it looked like they would echo the unpopular outcome of the General Election.

The majority Awami league had won virtually all the seats in East Pakistan and an overall majority for Pakistan as a whole. Unfortunately, the people in the Western divide did not want to be ruled by a government based in the East. The leader of the Awami party had declared that no one could stop the formation of a new country called Bangladesh. So soon after the turmoil of partition in 1947, disruption was breaking out again, which could lead to a civil war between the two Moslem factions.

A public holiday was in full swing but, with the banks closed, I couldn't change any money, even on the Black Market, and would be unable to buy a train ticket for Peshawar on the North West Frontier that evening. With five Pakistani rupees left from the outward journey, there was sufficient to buy me a room for the night in the same hotel I'd stayed before. The manager recognised me and showed me to a small room on the roof.

And what a room!

From the tiny cell-like space with its single wooden charpoy and ceiling fan, I could walk out across the roof into a panoramic vista of the city. The sun was by then a hazy late afternoon yellow ball, just managing to hold its own within the orange mist of pollution that defined the city. Through this, emerged the diffuse dark orange silhouettes of the Badshahi mosque's onion domes, encircled by the swirl and squark of city crows. I had no energy to wend my way through the crowded streets to see it up close, but this ethereal light lent something to its reputation as being one of the most beautiful mosques in all Islam.

Having washed off the grime accumulated over the previous few days, I collected the one rupee and few paisa I had left to enjoy a good meal and even an orange and a few nuts.

I'd not slept in a bed since leaving Alison in Bombay. The night air was cold again, but this night I had the benefit of heavy bed covers, under which I pulled myself into a foetal position and breathed my own warm air until an all encompassing warmth pervaded the space and I drifted off to sleep.

With no money left, I had to fall back on the goodwill of my hotel hosts for a cup of chai in the morning, assuring them I would repay on my return from the American Express.

Since my last visit, a special tourist rate had been introduced to beat off the Black Market. Changing my last twenty pound travellers' cheque into two pound denominations, I was able to save the problem of ending up at the Afghan border with too many rupees. With an exchange rate of twenty-one rupees and thirty-two paise to the pound as opposed to the illegal rate of eighteen, I was glad I'd not been able to find a buyer the day before.

The early morning streets of Lahore didn't appear to have so many people rolling up bedrolls and preparing for another day of begging, such as I'd so often seen in India. Instead, shops and stalls were opening and people making their way to work in offices and whatever other occupations the city could offer.

A tonga wallah, stripped to the waist, was washing down his magnificent white steed, clearly loving the attention that was temporarily ridding him of flies and other insects.

An ox cart pulled a precarious hand painted hoarding, advertising *Heer Ranjha*, a tragic Punjabi love story showing at the local cinema. The larger than life painting depicted a wistful hero with pencil moustache standing in front of a perturbed looking heroine adorned with bangles, nose ring and head jewellery. Perhaps she was concerned about the smaller depictions in the frame of a jealous uncle and the other man she is forced to marry.

Chai wallahs boiled their kettles, sweet shops laid out their sticky, colourful attractions prepared in deep pans of sizzling oil or puffy pouris to be eaten with plates of subji or meat. Goat, chicken and beef were commonplace and asking for a vegetarian dish was met with puzzlement, unlike the expressions of joy from the average Indian.

With money in hand, I was able to buy my train ticket for the evening departure, returning to the hotel to write letters.

With no return address for her reply, I'd obviously not heard from Belinda since writing over a month before and, with weeks to go before I would be able to see her again, I was beginning to wonder if perhaps karma might be planning to play a cruel trick on me as payback for my philandering.

Lahore
18th December 1970.

My Darling Belinda,
This may be the last you'll hear from me for a while.
I am now sitting on a flat hotel roof in Lahore, gazing out across the hazy skyline of this hectic city.
I crossed the border from India yesterday and will be catching the

train tonight to Peshawar on the North West Frontier.

From thereon, I'll be back over the Khyber Pass to Afghanistan, using buses and any means I can to confront the rigours of winter on the road back to Europe.

I want you to know that, despite all that has happened since I left you so many months ago, I love you and am so excited about finally getting back to you and Harry and trying to pick up where we left off.

Of course, I realise things will be different. I know I have changed in many ways; such has been the influence of several months on the road, but I sincerely believe that it is all for the better and thank you for encouraging me to make the trip.

It looks like I'll be spending Christmas in Afghanistan, so I imagine I'll find one or two surprises there.

I suppose, if I had left the mountains earlier and not gone to Bombay, I could be almost home by now, but it is not to be and I can only wish you and Harry a Very Happy Christmas.

With all my love,
Adam xxx

P.S: Save some mince pies for January!

By five o' clock, I was collecting my things together and making my way through the streets towards the station. A good meal was a priority as I didn't want to rely on station wallahs with whom I would inevitably be eating a variety of snacks at different times on the journey.

It was particularly hard to separate the meat from the vegetables on this occasion, leading me to succumb to the tender mutton prominent on my plate. It was the first time for months that I had relented to the pressure of meat and finding myself actually enjoying it, with no repulsion or inclination to be sick.

The station, built by the British at a time of great political unrest shortly after the Indian Mutiny in 1857, resembled more of a fortress than a railway terminus with castellations and positions for cannon and riflemen. The relative tranquillity inside, belied the terror and bloodshed of Partition, when trains would arrive from India full of massacred Moslems and their families.

This day, apart from the indecipherable voice of a woman

announcing arrivals and departures over a tannoy, the platforms, spanned by a succession of high Victorian Gothic arches, were clean and orderly with a discernible absence of beggars and rough sleepers.

When my train drew in at 7.30 pm, I was immediately aware of the civilised manner in which the far fewer passengers, than for an average Indian train, slowly moved forward towards their carriages, almost comparable to the mannered surge one might see on an English platform. I had the added advantage of a young Pakistani boy, with whom I had been talking, who graciously went before me, found a seat and then returned to help me on with my luggage.

My companions were a Pakistani man with his wife and teenage daughter, who appeared more liberated than some. The mother was dressed in a long sleeved dress in a pretty turquoise brocade with a loosely draped mauve hijab around her head and the daughter in a fashionable three quarter length burgundy skirt and paisley blouse, her hair, long and black, framing her subtly made up features.

They came across as well educated, talking in a characteristic Pakistani accent, whilst defining their English words beautifully.

As I had become well used, we talked about my travels, my life in England and hopes for the future, giving me little opportunity to enquire about their own lives. Whilst they handed out copious amounts of nuts for hour after hour, I did manage to deduce that the head of the family was a wholesale grain supplier in Rawalpindi and his daughter attending a very good school in the same city. Of course she was going to be a doctor as so many young Indians and Pakistanis aspired to be.

In due course, the conversation waned, and I settled to my book about Buddhism, taking care to conceal the title, lest it upset Moslem sensibilities.

The train sped on into the night, progressing further West with every clackety mile, the air becoming perceptibly colder, consistent with what looked like snow on higher ground, luminous in the moonlight against the dark countryside.

With my blanket wrapped around me, I sat upright on the hard wooden bench seat, snatching snippets of sleep in between our arrival at the many stations on the way, where hot cups of chai were passed through the windows by the platform hawkers to be eagerly received by those of us shivering inside.

My companions eventually left at Rawalpindi and the number of passengers dwindled form thereon, enabling me to stretch out on a seat to myself until the breaking of dawn and our slow entry into Peshawar, a heavy frost hanging on the trees and across the fields.

It was welcome relief to leave that wooden seat behind, despite the obvious change in temperature. As with my outward journey, I had ventured little into Pakistan, only tasting the delights of the two peripheral cities, Peshawar and Lahore. I wondered how different my journey might have been had Partition not happened and this part of the world was still defined as India, where so much collective history remained.

There was now clearly more Islamic influence, as evidenced by the propensity of mosques and minarets, but then there was the all pervading legacy of two hundred years of British rule scattered across the sub-continent. The railways, government buildings, roads, bridges, military cantonments and houses. In most places could be seen some legacy of the Raj.

A quick wash with cold water in the first class waiting room and I was out in the street, my blanket shielding me from the icy breeze that brutally cut into my face, numbing my nose and ears.

In the main street, remembered so well from six months earlier, the clip-clop of horse drawn tongas and jingling bells awakened memories of my arrival with Feathers, an English guy with whom I'd travelled most of the way from Mashad. Some of the horses had then stood tired, bedraggled and steaming in the heavy rain as we checked into a small hotel, where the manager brought chai and hashish to our room and lizards watched motionless from the tangle of electric cables.

The bus to Kabul would not be leaving until seven in the morning, but the hotel manager welcomed me back with a big handshake and a smile as broad as the Khyber, lifting his waxed moustache high upon his cheeks. On this occasion, the hashish was not forthcoming, but the chai was a welcome antidote to the winter air.

I had yet to get my Afghan visa before morning and a short

taxi ride took me to the embassy, where a small crowd of Indians, Pakistanis and a couple of German hippies were waiting outside. Three forms and three photographs later, I was asked to return after lunch.

The streets themselves had not changed much. The plethora of street stalls, now piled with oranges and winter vegetables. The stacks of ornately decorated copper and aluminium cookware sparkled in the low midday sun and even the Bata shoe company was still going strong. The pervasive aroma of spicy food lingered on every corner as the many restaurants were beginning to serve lunch from the large aluminium pots facing the streets.

The people were preparing for a Khyber winter with scarves, overcoats and boots, not the life giving monsoon that had been slowly brewing from the stifling summer heat. Meanwhile, the very poor remained in the same cotton clothes, hunched and shivering in empty doorways, some even barefoot.

It was good to see the few hardened and diverse Afghan faces amongst the crowds, reminding me of these embattled people and the centuries old melting pot of cultures that made Afghanistan so unique.

My Afghan visa had been stamped in my passport, costing me nothing, compared to the eight rupees I would have been charged in Delhi, leaving me free to wander the streets a little before settling for an early night.

A street stall displayed an unruly jumble of clothes, discarded by westerners making their way east earlier in the year. Shoes, trousers, jackets and pullovers in a multitude of colours and sizes drew my attention and I immediately homed in on a warm looking pullover. It certainly hadn't been washed since leaving its previous owner but, despite all my attempts at bargaining, the vendor wouldn't let it go for less than the equivalent of seventeen shillings, whereas I would probably have got it for sixpence on the Portobello Road. Not wanting to buy any more rupees, I thought better of it and trusted that chance might find me something better across the border.

Back in the hotel, I was rudely awakened to my previous life in London. Reaching the top of the stairs, one of the doors was open and, glancing in, I saw what I believed to be a familiar face.

'Hi! Haven't I seen you somewhere before?' I asked.

A thin, bearded man, pale and unkempt in a torn Afghan coat with tangled hair to his shoulders was sitting on his bed shuffling through a leather bag. He looked up, squinting with his unusually pale, but lifeless, grey eyes.

'Yeh, I re-mem-ber you,' he stuttered. 'You sold p-posters on the P-P-Portobello.'

'That's right. I think I scored off you once or twice. You lived in Colville Terrace.' I immediately pictured the five story Victorian terrace in one of the most run down parts of Notting Hill and his room in what was a notorious doss house.

'Yeh, man. You got a good m-memory. Whatcha doin' here th-th-then?'

'I'm on my way back to England. I was in India for six months.'

'I-I-I'm on my way t-t-to G-Goa. You're goin' t' find it fuckin' cold from now on. There's thick s-s-snow in Afghanistan.'

I heard the door creak and sensed that someone else was in the room. Looking round, my eyes fell upon one of the German hippies I'd seen earlier at the Afghan Embassy.

Without acknowledging me, he spoke to the Englishman.

''Ave you got my stuff?' he asked, somewhat agitated.

There was something disturbing about him, something I felt in my gut I didn't like, an ominous aggressiveness as he took a small packet from the Englishman, sat on the bed and brought out the paraphernalia for a fix.

I wasn't sure if it was heroin or speed, but I'd seen this scenario of wilful self harm too many times before and didn't need another replay.

I had two nights of sleep to cram into one and was only too glad to find my bed and the sanctuary of the few blankets provided.

At six-thirty next morning, a small crowd was waiting in the bus yard, wrapped in blankets, stamping feet and breathing out clouds of warm air. The passengers were mainly Afghanis with a smattering of Pakistanis and Iranians. The rest were principally Europeans; A German and an Indonesian returning to Dusseldorf University, Hugo, an archetypical long haired French hippy and Gary originally from England, but now a Canadian resident.

Seven o' clock arrived and the minutes ticked on until just after half past, when the driver and the conductor finally arrived to direct the loading and lashing of baggage onto the roof. By quarter past, the engine had spluttered into life and we were pulling out into the main street.

Gary and I sat together with much to talk about as we progressed across the flat plain that led to the lower slopes of the Khyber.

He was a mild mannered guy, with a maturity about him, expressed in his calm voice and actions. Probably about five foot, ten, his shoulder length, light brown hair was already receding, but compensated for by a bushy moustache and about three days stubble on his face.

'I left England about ten years ago,' he told me. 'I went with my parents on one of the ten pound voyages to Australia.'

'You must have been quite young.'

'About seven or eight. It was all very exciting, going up onto this great big ship, hearing the horn booming as we sailed out of Tilbury, nearly frightening me to death. I can remember everyone crowded onto the deck as we passed along the Thames Estuary, waving goodbye to England. I didn't really understand what it was all about then, just enjoying all the things we could do on board and the great food.

I remember how the light changed as we approached the Mediterranean. Everything was brighter and more colourful under the blue sky.'

'It obviously made a deep impression.'

'It did. Coming from grey Surbiton in Surrey…'

'Surbiton? I lived just along the river.'

'Small world, isn't it? But, at that age, the world seemed vast. To see camels and palm trees along the Suez Canal and people dressed in strange clothes. Arriving in Colombo, where the smell of spicy foods wafted across from the town and elephants were pulling loads in the harbour, opened my eyes to so many possibilities.

'So, how did you end up in Canada?'

'I never really took to Oz. I got most of my education there but, by the time I was eighteen, I was ready for a change. My parents had settled in Melbourne, but, when I left school, I moved to Sydney for a few months, which was great with the beaches and open air life. Then a friend was going to Canada and asked me to go along with him. I felt that, being near the States, I'd have more opportunities. I settled in Vancouver, British Columbia, where I've completed my Civil Engineering degree and now only have one more year to go before I get Canadian citizenship.'

The bus rolled on across the flat rural landscape, where the morning frost still clung to clods of ploughed earth. Small villages of mud walled houses lay strung between sleeping outcrops of rock, left behind when massive glaciers formed the valley.

Beyond rose the lower slopes and bends of the Khyber Pass, where formidable bare ochre rock drew us into this mythical no-man's land. Here, Pathan tribal law ruled across the border into Afghanistan, while Pakistan was slowly disappearing behind us into the winter mist.

The gears crunched and engine screamed as the old bus, resplendent in its green, red and silver livery, its coloured tassels jumping wildly as it snaked up the narrow half made road. Outside the villages, notices, in the local language and English, warned travellers not to take photos of the women; an infringement possibly attracting a death sentence.

As we passed through muddy streets flanked by a motley collection of shops, traffic squeezed past going the other way. Buses, stuffed with tribal passengers - women in burqas pressed together inside like shrouded living corpses, while the men, in assorted coloured kameez, hand wound turbans and blankets, sat on the roof or hung onto the ladders at the back, rifles slung over their shoulders.

Some of the shops maintained a steady trade of miscellaneous rifles and pistols; some antique flintlocks and others, more modern, made in local foundries to precise specifications, further reminding us of the gun's significance in this frontier land.

Unwieldy Bedford lorries with heavy winter tyres, were commonplace all along the Pass, so laden with cargos of goods and people, they seemed ready to overturn at any moment, their distinctive multi coloured panels and Islamic imagery resonant against the dark rock faces.

Up we climbed, in diminishing loops, passing abandoned forts and look-out towers, so strategic in the British efforts to maintain a tenuous semblance of power.

The weak mid-day sun glinted on the fretwork of steel girders and concrete pillars, soaring from the valley floor to carry the Khyber railway across river beds and wide chasms all the way from Peshawar to Landi Kotal near the Afghan border. It was hard to imagine that it had only been open a mere forty-five years since 1925, at first carrying British troops and supplies and now a once a day passenger service.

Groaning under the weight, the bus reached the highest point, where the massive Ali Masjid Fort spread across a pinnacle of barren rock. Far below lay Afghanistan, for me now tainted by memories of deception, treachery and death, which I knew my return to Kabul would surely reawaken.

At the border, everyone had to leave the bus for passport stamping and currency declarations.

Time for a last milk and sugar laden chai in the chai-khana at Torkham, where Feathers and I had sheltered from a thunderstorm on our passage out. Then we were back on the bus, the barrier raised and we were in Afghanistan, driving on the right side of the road.

The bite of winter was tightening its grip and I was conscious of every little draught passing through badly fitted windows or seeping along the floor from the rattling door. Blankets were a vital accessory and it seemed everyone had one to curl up in.

Winter rain had swollen the rivers, tumbling icily over boulders in the Kabul River, which here served to irrigate the multitude of fields laid out across the flood plain, where red faced peasants tilled their plots in the hope of some fruitful return. A broad expanse of water reflecting turquoise against the sky bulged out behind a gleaming new dam in the river.

Beyond the river banks, where villages clung sufficiently elevated to escape the high water, the land was barren and empty, rising gently into low lying hills, around the outskirts of Jalalabad and later the mighty crags of the Kabul Gorge.

Our little bus now faced a far greater challenge, requiring the skill of the driver and the prayers of the occupants to see it up the looping road that soon towered above the river far below. The light was fading as we were still doubling back on ourselves, negotiating blind bends, tunnels and bridges, where recent rockfalls had narrowed the passage on the already much broken road, steering us ever closer to the precipitous edge.

I was still haunted by Feather's story of the defeated British legation being given safe passage from Kabul back to India, one hundred and twenty-eight years earlier, but betrayed and set upon by the Afghan ruler's forces. The outcome was a complete massacre save for a few women and sepoys and a surgeon, who was allowed to ride on to Jalalabad to tell the grim news.

The highest point passed and, as we descended toward flatter terrain, the sun was departing in a blaze of pink and vivid orange streaks. This was the cue for the bus to stop and all the men to empty out, placing their blankets in a long line on the dusty ground in the direction of Mecca. With hands washed using water from a thermos flask, prayers, bowing and prostrating continued for about ten minutes, completing the evening salah. Blankets were retrieved, shaken and folded as they all returned to the bus and we set off again for the last few miles to the capital.

A red light shines every night from the highest mountain just outside Kabul and this night was no different. On the approaches, we passed the lines of lamp posts that edged empty plots which would one day become apartments and shops.

Somewhere along here, on one of the lamp posts, I had seen the slumped body of Galina, a beautiful Russian woman, who had been at the centre of a drug running ring and had unwittingly upset her Afghan hosts.

I had first met her in Istanbul and had almost become embroiled in a dope smuggling bust, which had seen two English acquaintances arrested and thrown into a Turkish jail.

There were few people on the streets at this time as we encroached closer to the centre, the dim street lighting casting a feint orange tint upon the passing tongas and their horses. A few more turns and we were passing the Khyber Restaurant, a three story building that looked as if it had been lifted from an English new town shopping centre and was now the hub for many of the travellers going East, where clean water and a western style lavatory could be found. On this day, just outside the main entrance, the lights of a line of Christmas trees sparkled in the night air.

Thirteen

W HEN WE WERE finally dropped near the bazaar, there was no snow as reported, but I could feel it wasn't far off and we needed to find somewhere for the night.

The onslaught of hustlers for taxis and hotels was overwhelming and it was a blessed relief to see the smiling face of Edris from the Najeep Hotel.

'Hello again, Mr Sahib, you are wanting very good room,' he asked, his hair neatly combed, moustache trimmed and dressed in a brown suit with an orange and brown striped tie. 'We are having hot water, bedding and fire in room. All is only twenty afghanis.'

Doing a quick calculation, I realised it was about one and thrupence each. Not something to quibble over.

Retrieving our bags from the pile waiting on the pavement, Edris led us to a taxi, paid for by the hotel. Within minutes, we were stretching out on our beds in the same dormitory room I had shared on the way out. In the heat of summer, there had been no free beds, but now it was just the three of us. The boiler stood as a focal point in the middle of the room, a chimney pipe rising through the ceiling and an old man feeding more wood in through the boiler's door.

The windows in the restaurant over the road were steamed up as we opened the door from the desolate street and headed straight for the boiler to warm our hands. After India and Pakistan, it was good to be able to eat in a restaurant with some protection from the elements.

We were of course the centre of attention as the men looked up from their plates to take in the sight of these three motley dressed westerners.

Finding space on the floor, we sat on cushions covered in squares of carpet with a red cloth laid out on the floor before us. We were brought steaming rice, meat and a small bowl of spinach each, which we hungrily ploughed into with our fingers, making small balls of rice or collecting mouthfuls of meat and spinach with pieces of the crispy naan bread.

From one of the shelves behind the counter, the waiter lifted three prettily patterned tea pots, which he duly filled with green tea, topped up with steaming hot water from the copper samovar in the corner. At tuppence a pot, the three glasses it contained was the best way to quench one's thirst.

I'd not had a chance to talk with Hugo since leaving Peshawar in the morning and, with my school French and his broken English, we managed some dialogue.

'Porquoi vas tu en France maintenant?' I asked.

'I am not 'aving much monnai et je veux rentrer chez moi.'

'Combien de temps es-tu en Inde?'

'Depuis J'étais là pendant trois mois. J'étais in ze south.'

'I've only been as far as Bombay. Did you go to Goa?' I asked, anticipating he would be gushing with tales from that epicentre of hippy life in India.

'I was zere pour trois semaines. I stay on ze plage.'

'Beaucoups des filles et dope?' I asked, thinking of Alison who would probably have arrived there by now and would be perhaps on the same beach puffing at a big chillum. I didn't want to think of her with another man. As the weeks had gone by, I had thought more of her and wished that perhaps I'd been able to get to know her better.

There was no hot water on our return, but a boiler in the washroom was throwing out warm air, sufficient to take the chill off, while enabling me to strip wash in cold water.

We were all exhausted and not up for conversation, preferring instead to slip beneath the blankets and sleep.

It would be two more days before we were ready to catch the bus for the onward journey to Kandahar and Herat.

Apart from eating at every opportunity, we had to equip ourselves with some warmer clothes, while I still had to get my visa for Iran.

Hugo and Gary had already got theirs in Delhi but, with omelette, naan and tea inside us, they agreed to accompany me to the Iranian embassy.

Needing directions, we stopped a group of girls. Dressed in maxi coats, tights, shiny patent leather shoes, knee length boots, fashionable hair styles and make-up, we assumed at first they were from Europe, only to be astounded to find they were Afghan. Their clothes and manner oozed confidence and liberation, exceeding any parallels I might have seen in India. To boot, they spoke excellent English, albeit with an unfathomable accent.

Purdah had been banned by the government in 1959, despite the *phantoms* in burqas still mingling in the bazaars and elsewhere. Nevertheless, the girls told us that they too would go under the shroud when they married.

The people in the Iranian embassy were not forthcoming.

'I have to go to the airport shortly to collect someone and you need a photo,' a surly official told me. 'Come back tomorrow.'

As in West Pakistan, the black market appeared to have collapsed, with the bank now offering two-hundred and two afghanis to the pound, encouraging me to change sufficient to cross the country and buy more warm clothes.

Flakes of snow were falling steadily as we negotiated the narrow suspension bridge that crossed the river towards the bazaar. Plates of ice had formed on the fringes where, in the summer, children had frolicked in the water and women had been washing clothes. Where the snow was now settling, only a solitary bird was pecking for what crumbs could be found.

The bustle of the bazaar had not diminished much. People's gait seemed more brisk, with an enhanced sense of purpose as they moved from stall to stall, eager to do their business and return to the warmth of their homes.

Mounds of dried apricots and nuts tempted the palate as the turban headed shopkeepers squatted by their wares waving us toward them. As in India, there was a miscellany of dark, mud walled shops, shadowed by groaning, damp and torn awnings, now weighing heavier with the falling snow.

Song birds perched within rusting cages, too depressed to sing. The shoe mender was still there, crouched inside his makeshift shelter made from discarded packing cases, his frozen fingers too enfeebled to comfortably pass a needle through a piece of leather. Young boys, a little older now, scurried around us with their trays of cigarettes and trinkets, their education forgotten and futures uncertain.

In one of the many clothes shops, I found warm socks, a scarf and balaclava, but a good coat was not so easily come by. Most were in the region of one thousand afghanis, far more than I could afford.

Gary and Hugo were happy to spend time in one shop, while I went off by myself to find something else.

It was then that, in plain view before me, appeared another link in the chain of events that had brought about the Russian woman's demise.

At the entrance to an alley, now empty save for a couple of copulating dogs, I was reminded of the crowd that had gathered around the dead body of an Englishman named Ralph.

He was an attaché in the British Embassy, who had wound up embroiled in a drug smuggling cartel and had been so compromised that he came to this alley and shot himself. I could almost see his panama still lying in the ditch where it had rolled. He was also the father of Caroline, my deceased girlfriend, murdered by the same crooked London policeman who had been blackmailing Ralph. But, that's another story.

Turning away from this place, I felt disconcerted once again; a feeling that I had not entertained since the night of the shooting. Then, I seemed to be going onwards to the light whereas, here, in the snow with night encroaching on what was the shortest and darkest day of the year, I felt myself falling irrevocably into the blackness of my soul and the shadows I had left behind in England.

Further down the street, past a spectrum of spices spilling from large round baskets, more coat shops appeared, each having a smiling assistant beckoning me to join him for chai. My curiosity drew me to one, where I was invited to try on an array of coats. These symbols of hippy chic in London's King's Road and Portobello were the real thing, selling for a fraction of the huge mark ups seen in London.

Nevertheless, even the cheaper ones would be testing my funds, but I had to consider that money wouldn't keep me warm and I still had my two hundred dollars. The journey had become something of a challenge. With probably three to four weeks before I would arrive back in England, I was treating my passage as if the dollars did not exist, knowing they would be needed on my return until I could find work.

One inferior quality coat actually fitted me, with others being stiff and tight around the shoulders. With the shopkeeper wanting eight hundred afghanis, I had to resort to my bargaining skills that had already won me an excellent deal with the Kabul money changers in the summer.

With a solemn to and fro, reducing the price in increments, I managed to beat him down to six hundred with a pair of gloves thrown in.

There was no question of packing it as I finished my chai and secured the eye fasteners in the front, feeling the warmth of the sheepskin immediately embrace me.

It was dark as I stepped back into the street, the oil lamps now alive in the shops, providing a glimmer of pre-Christmas cheer.

With the need to return to the Iranian embassy the following day, I remembered a small photographic shop near the river, where I might get the photo I needed for the visa.

Near the barber shop where I had had my long hair finally cut, still stood the shop displaying an ancient box camera, decorated like an Afghan bus.

The window, filled with soft focus shots of young liberated Afghan girls, told me I would be likely to get my passport photo taken there.

Within the dim interior, I was met by the photographer, a little man with a full head of hair, heavy black eyebrows and a zapata moustache, casually dressed in the ubiquitous brown trousers and stripy green pullover. The room was set up with a Rolleiflex on a tripod, a white pull-down backdrop and several lamps on adjustable stands.

'I need photos for my visa. Can I collect in the morning?' I asked, not sure he would be able to understand me.

'Of course. Will you please take a seat,' he replied in good English, directing me to a stool in front of the screen.

Turning on a couple of lamps, he directed them to achieve a balanced light and stood behind his camera. With a few clicks, the job was done and I promised to see him again in the morning.

As I trudged back to the hotel, the snow's rapid descent seemingly intensified against the glow of the street lights, I passed a huddle of phantom women, their shapes giving no indication of their ages and looks or even if they were women. Two police paced on a street corner, their baggy, ill-fitting khaki uniforms and flat hats offering little protection from the ever more inhospitable elements settling on their clothes.

Gary and Hugo had returned to the hotel earlier and were reading in bed, their new coats spread out across their beds.

'You managed to buy one then,' I said, warming my back and hands against the boiler. 'It's absolutely bitter out there now. I hope we're going to get through this and don't get stuck somewhere for days because of the weather.'

'It's a strong possibility, but this is nothing so far compared with what we get in Canada,' Gary said. 'I'm in Vancouver on the Pacific, so we don't see much snow, but go over the Rockies to Alberta and it's normal to get minus twenty-two degrees.'

'I can't imagine how cold that must be.'

'It's cold, but remember, we have the right clothes, our houses are well insulated with proper heating systems and even our cars are well heated. It's also a dry air there, so it never seems as cold as it is.'

'I'm just wondering how those old buses we have here are going to manage in sub-zero.'

After so many days on the road, it felt sublime to stand under a hot shower, just letting that warmth run over my head and down my body. Unbelievably, it was my first wash in hot water since I'd had an impromptu "Turkish" bath in old oil drums at the back of the main restaurant in Bamian, where I had gone to see the Great Buddhas.

After eggs, naan and chai, next morning, I collected my photos, surprised to see the first photo of myself with short hair, since school days. Eventually, I would get to see the developed photo of my shaven head.

It was then back to the embassy where, once more, I was told to return the next day. This was the last straw and I wasn't prepared to lose any more time. With the weather worsening by the hour, I opted to take my chances at the Herat consulate.

With tickets bought for the Kandahar bus next morning, we decided to celebrate our last evening in Kabul.

A small, single room restaurant was our choice for dinner, adorned with hand coloured photos of Russian or, more to the point, Soviet heroes. Of course, there was Lenin and Uncle Jo Stalin, Khrushchev and Yuri Gagarin, the first man in space. The remaining photos were of men and women, most in military uniform heavily adorned with medals, of whom I knew nothing.

The air was warm with the heat from the boiler and the breath of a small crowd of Afghans, eating kebabs while still dressed in thick overcoats and karakul hats.

We took our seats at a table at the back of the room where, as we ate our food, we found ourselves being enticed to join two loud Russians already drunk on whiskey.

Gary and I kept quiet, knowing better of it, while Hugo, in his good natured, over friendly manner, seemed blissfully unaware of the possible consequences of getting involved. But involved, he became, passing his glass over for a shot, while Gary and I merely shook our heads with a smile, blew out our cheeks and rubbed our tummies.

With many potential weapons readily on hand, such as pointed kebab skewers, I could see a nasty scene evolving either if we joined them or if we left. If we stayed, I could see it going on into the early hours and, thereafter, who knows what? Leaving was considered the best option. Finishing our food and paying the bill, we stood up, politely smiled again, made our apologies and sidled out with Hugo firmly in tow.

A pink and orange glow on the mountains around the city heralded the rising sun as we left the hotel at six o' clock, carrying our things through the grey slush to find a taxi. We were dropped at the bus pick-up point alongside the river, having to argue with the taxi driver over the price as he became increasingly enraged, throwing our bags out and across the road in response, until we settled with him.

Once again, the bus had not arrived by seven and, watching all the Afghan passengers wandering off towards a small restaurant, we joined them for chai and greasy pouris. By quarter to eight, the bus finally drew in and luggage loaded, but the driver continued to wait until two latecomers eventually turned up just before nine.

By this time, I was edgy and moody, not prepared to tolerate the stupid little incidents that were now so much part of a typical day. I just wanted to move onwards and had become quite judgemental.

With nearly two hours wasted, waiting for two people to arrive, the engine started and the bus pulled out on the road towards Kandahar.

We were soon out in open country with Kabul behind us. Snow from a fall two or three days earlier still covered the mountains on either side, while the white barren landscape stretched away, only broken by small communities of square windowless mud houses, spirals of white smoke rising from their meagre chimneys.

As the miles rolled on, I became increasingly conscious of the icy air filtering in through the bus, despite my new clothes and a blanket.

It was therefore only a few miles further that I was awakened to the true reality of the intense cold on seeing an old man shuffling slowly along the roadside ahead of us. The bus stopped and he was hauled in, collapsing in a heap at our feet unable to move.

Dressed in a worn overcoat, a scarf protecting his head and ears, his thin cotton trousers tucked into black leather boots, possibly left over from his army days, he was clearly in great pain as he looked quizzically at his bare reddened and seemingly paralysed hands. Tears streamed from the slits that contained his eyes, mingling with the runs from his nose and eventually coalescing in his beard, where icicles dangled like Christmas decorations.

I could almost feel his pain as my mind drifted back to the countless times, as a schoolboy, coming in from the football field to embrace the hot water pipes in the changing room, crying for feeling and warmth to stream back into my body.

I lent the man my gloves, but he could only falteringly slip his bent fists into the top halves and pray for deliverance from his suffering, his tear-filled eyes pleading for more. I wrapped my blanket around his frail body, only to watch helplessly as he merely shivered uncontrollably.

Arriving at a small village, my gloves were returned and he was reluctantly delivered to the mercy of the elements. Incomprehension of life's potential to be cruel came over him when he realised that he was to be torn from his short lived comfort and would once again be pitting himself against the onslaught of an Afghan winter. We could only hope that he either lived in the village or that someone would be kind enough to take him in.

Yet more miles slipped behind us until the bus drew in where a number of lorries were parked. In the nearby mud constructed restaurant, where more Japanese teapots filled the shelves and a huge brass samovar steamed in the corner, the distraction of food took our minds off our own discomfort offering a warm welcome from the bus.

The interior was built on three levels, receding back into a labyrinth of long rooms, their compacted mud floors enriched with dusty and worn patterned carpets.

Blazing logs threw out an agreeable heat from the stoves in the centre of each room where, sat around the walls, dark bearded men of all shapes were manoeuvring meat and rice between fingers and naan bread, before popping it in their mouths.

Dressed mostly in white shirts and loose kameez, they appeared as a hybrid between their own culture and that of the west as most wore dark suit jackets, while their beaded skull caps were encircled by loosely wound turbans. All wore thick socks encased in black shoes or sandals made from old car tyres.

A small opening cut through the wall led to another room where others were still eating, while some drank green chai or smoked hashish through a large hookah, passing the mouthpiece from one to the other.

In another room, it was time for prayers and amid the muttered prayers, prostrating and bowing, one elderly, white bearded man, his eyes closed, knelt motionless within a shaft of bright sunlight, piercing the darkened room through a small skylight in the roof.

The sun was almost gone as we drew into Kandahar, the orange, crimson and pink sky silhouetting the hills behind the city and catching the few wispy clouds that bestowed magic on the dying day.

Gary had developed a fever on the journey and simply wanted to be warm and quiet, so it was doing him no favours when Hugo took on the hotel hawkers on our arrival and was about to lead us off, when a kindly local man, seeing Gary's distress introduced himself.

'I am Karam. I see you are tired. I give you very nice warm room. You come. Is only fifteen afghanis.'

At just less than a shilling each, it was cheaper than Kabul and quickly and unanimously agreed upon.

The Pamier hotel was welcoming enough as was its manager, Tarek, a man in his forties, his beard and hair showing flecks of grey, his long straight nose as a mast and sail to his broad boat like grin.

He personally lit the stove in our room as we got Gary to bed, piling the blankets and his new afghan coat on top. While discussing the possibilities of food, Tarek had been out and returned with antibiotics and lozenges bought in the local pharmacy.

Hugo and I found an upstairs eating house, packed with Afghans, greedily tucking into kebabs, other varieties of meat, rice and small dishes of vegetables. Choosing the same, we ate in silence as we savoured every mouthful of this sublime comfort food.

As I looked around at the people, the stove belting out its heat, a picture of Mohammad on the wall, I could have sworn I saw a nearby photo of Hitler and Eva Braun, but it could well have been an Afghan and his wife who had a close resemblance.

Afghanistan was officially neutral during the war, but had leanings towards the Axis until Germany invaded Russia and the country suddenly found itself surrounded by British allies.

Much as I warmed to Hugo for the most part, he irritated me profoundly with his constant bartering for everything he bought from a coat to a meal. There are some occasions when the line is drawn and bartering for dinner was one of them.

Due to his inexperience and naivety, he seemed to lack respect for anyone, often being very rude. Deep down, his intentions were probably good, but he did tend to have a *bull in a china shop* approach to so many things, which is not only irritating for everyone else, but must surely have taken a toll on his own inner well-being. He told me he had been studying for the previous four years to be an accountant. Perhaps the confines of an office had been the catalyst that had prompted his diverse behaviour.

Gary was in some distress on our return, his condition having worsened with an intense headache and every indication of a higher temperature. He wasn't helped by the presence of two Danish freaks, who had come into our room for the warmth of the fire, ignoring Gary's plight by loud talking and cacophonous flute playing. We too were worn down by the long day's events to show any enthusiasm for their impromptu party, instead insisting that they leave.

CHAPTER

Fourteen

NEXT MORNING WAS Christmas Eve and Gary had slept
well, sweating out much of the fever, but still not well
enough to travel.

Tarek gave us assurances that he would be well looked after as
we left our Christmas wishes and the hope that we would meet up
again the next day in Herat.

I was convinced Hugo, given the choice, would live on bread
alone. On this morning, he had already eaten half a yard of naan
and a glass of chai, before we could run down the road to catch
the bus, for which we had bought tickets the previous evening. It
was still only quarter to seven and the glow of another day spewed
across the clear sky in diffuse orange tones. The tongas were out,
horses trotting on the compacted and frozen dirt road, their breath
metamorphosing into nebulous clouds against the chill air.

Men were setting up street stalls of fruit and vegetables, while
others tightened their blankets around their shoulders and
shuffled purposefully through the streets, pausing momentarily to
stare. Even young children were out on errands for their parents,
collecting some fruit or milk; some carrying younger siblings,
their European features, dark hair and rosy cheeks giving certainty
to their Alexandrian origins.

Hugo and I were the only Europeans on the bus, which turned
out to offer little of the luxury the ticket vendor had claimed. The
seats had metal frames and little upholstery and, with both Hugo
and myself being tall, we had little option but to scrunch our legs
with feet resting on the bulging sacks, which appeared to cover the

entire floor.

The bus was wildly decorated outside, as we had so often seen, but with the extra dimension of interior paintings above the windows featuring the Kaaba in Mecca, portraits of the prophets Mohammed and Ali, together with gaudily coloured images of mosques, oases and military tanks. With a good nine to ten hours ahead of us, we would be confined in the midst of much turban, beards, gurgling and spitting.

For the first few miles, the concrete road, built only a few years earlier by the Russians, was lined on both sides by sapling fir trees. Suddenly, we burst out into open desert, its barren sandy soil stretching out across dried river beds into an empty wilderness, eventually rising on both sides into a formidable line of mountains, the line of sight broken only occasionally by a small skeletal shrub, quivering in the bitter breeze.

The mountains were at times more than spectacular, as the crevices and crannies, twisted and turned, playing with the imagination to form majestic animals and humans, even a horizontal Hanuman, the Hindu monkey god.

Sunlight played on passing objects. A spectre of white sheep being driven across the bright concrete road, appeared at first in black silhouette until they passed before a dark outcrop of rock and resumed their original colour. Was it the same flock I had seen crossing the road in the summer?

The journey passed slowly, hypnotised by the bumps between the concrete slabs in the road and the visual tricks of the mind.

Some way off, nomads' black canvas tents fluttered vigorously in the desert wind. Camels swerved off across the sand at the approach of our chugging engine, their long stick-like legs seeming frail and unwieldy beneath top heavy bodies and swaying humps.

Eating at the chai-khana, that had welcomed us with carpets spread beneath the trees in the summer, was now confined to the inside of the mud walled building; everyone now sitting on cushions scattered around low tables.

A wood burner glowed in the middle of the room as dishes of mutton, boiled potatoes, spinach and rice were brought to our table, accompanied by Hugo's favourite bread.

This now all seemed so routine to me as the sparkle of novelty had long since departed and I was more than ready to consign it all to memory.

Hours more passed, swallowed by the desert's history of conquest and tyranny, stretching back to Alexander the Great, who brought his great army across this land as far as India to drive out the Persians, who had preceded him.

Few witnesses remained within this vast wilderness, save for the mountains, enveloped in a purple shroud, and the sun in all its unchanging splendour, stretching its evening light like all encompassing arms to mark the closing of another day in eternity.

As the sun sank behind a whiff of muddied orange cloud, the silhouette of pious men prostrating in gratitude for safe deliverance from their problems, purification from sins and spiritual nourishment, made Hugo and myself seem quite Philistine, despite the experiences of India.

However, this apparent piety was shattered as we entered the line of poplars marking the outskirts off Herat, where the wind had intensified whistling through the skeletal branches.

A fine display of tribal temperament followed as the bus suddenly drew to a halt. An Afghan youth, possibly a shepherd or cowherd, had been hailing the bus for a lift into the centre of town, whereupon the driver set upon him, dragging the poor boy into a gap between the trees, repeatedly beating and punching him with an intensity that seemed disproportionate to any misdemeanour short of murder. This went on for several minutes with the boy on one occasion even managing to knock the driver down, prompting roars of laughter from all of us on the bus.

When he had satisfied his anger, the driver merely returned to the bus, restarted the engine and drove on, leaving the boy where he had found him, looking less injured than shocked and dismayed.

Flurries of snow were beginning again as we drew into the dimly lit streets of Herat, where our things were unloaded and Hugo and myself sought somewhere to spend the remains of Christmas Eve and pass into Christmas Day.

"Upgrading" of rooms had taken place in two of the hotels I remembered from the summer, as had the prices. With both of us needing to conserve what funds we had remaining, we concluded that, whilst still cheap, the rooms were more than we could afford.

It looked like there would be "no room at the inn", until I remembered where I had first stayed at the far end of town, where darkness prevailed almost entirely save for a few hurricane lamps. In sight of the remnants of Alexander's fort, the little one story hotel still perched on a mound within a mud walled courtyard. A man, just visible at the bottom of the steps, dozing in the light of a lamp, was woken by our arrival, jumping up with a smile ready to lead us to a room.

Changes had been made here too with wood burners having been installed in each room, but with an overnight price of twenty-five afghanis, no different to what I'd previously paid.

Our host attended to the stove, whilst Hugo and I completed the day with pilau, spinach and potato in a nearby restaurant, returning to a warm room and what was to be my first Christmas away from home.

I woke to a muffled 'Joyeux Noël', from Hugo, conscious of the lack of glitter and anticipation that pervaded the one day of the year that had always been differentiated from the rest. I was, instead, not only away from home but, not even in a Christian land, where the majority of the population had possibly not even heard of Christmas. Nevertheless, we had to make the best of it.

The snow flurries of the previous evening had not come to anything, so it was not to be a white Christmas, despite the freezing air, numbing both nose, ears and fingertips.

We took refuge in a café just down from the main crossroads. The ubiquitous wood burner glowed in the centre of the room, drawing us in to thaw our extremities. Christmas breakfast consisted of hard boiled eggs, naan and chai, a far cry from ham, orange juice and croissants.

In the corner squatted a boy of ten or eleven, dressed as one of his uncles might in white kameez, turban and western suit jacket. Before him sat a huge plate of cut meat, from which he was methodically placing pieces onto wooden skewers.

On the other side of the room, a wide-eyed Afghan puffed at his hash filled water pipe, the smoke curling up to the darkened tree trunks that supported the next floor.

The street itself was more akin to Christmas with numerous open stalls, brimming with a variety of dried fruit from apricots to figs, raisins and nuts, supplemented by fresh oranges, apples and grapes.

Horse drawn tongas raced up and down the hard tarmac street, the bells around their heads and bodies attached by coloured ribbons, jangling in time to their hoof beats. Behind them, the red enamel paint on the wheels glistened in the morning sun, sending out sparkles of light as the wheels turned.

I had only requested a week's visa for Afghanistan and was sure we couldn't have reached Herat any faster than we had, but it would be running out the next day. I still needed to get an Iranian visa and ensure I could get to the border next day before the Afghan one expired.

The Iranian embassy was close to the crossroads but, to my surprise, it was closed, despite being a Saturday and the beginning of the working week. The Afghan guards at the gate, rifles over shoulders were only too keen to tell me that I should return at nine in the morning.

Hugo had taken out a longer visa, so was not suffering the same anxiety as myself, but there was little I could do to remedy the situation, instead suggesting that he come with me to see the city's mosque, which I'd visited in the summer.

Retracing my steps, the route firmly embedded in my memory, we walked the short distance along the tree lined main street, passing children at play with tops and hoops, their mothers nearby entombed in their ghostly burqas. Owning a horse was something of a status symbol and men were proudly riding down the street, some with a couple of children and a phantom wife up behind.

Turning down a side street we passed chai shops, fur traders with camel pelts laid out before them, antique shops selling a plethora of curios from flintlock rifles to copper kettles.

At the end, the high walls and minarets of the mosque stood before us. Strong brick piers, some eight feet apart, not only strengthened the walls, but formed the sides of pointed arches, embellished with tiles, rising to between eighteen and twenty feet high. Central to these, a rectangular doorway, framed by an arch and rectangular panels, rose to the top of the wall, embedded with mosaic of predominantly white and blue tiles, forming stylised plant designs and Islamic script.

The doorway led to a dark tunnel and ultimately the mosque's main square, where we removed our shoes and marvelled at the expanse of the square, akin to a football pitch. Embellished by yet more blue, white, red and yellow mosaic, expressing an unbounded devotion and love for Allah and the Prophet, Muhammad.

Although reflecting brightly off the tiles, the sun was nowhere near as hot as it had been on my first visit, when it was almost torture to stand with bare feet for more than a few seconds. In a broad recess, a large carpet, perhaps made by some of the desert nomads, had been laid across the tiles, upon which four men were performing their next salah of the day.

In a large side room, an old man in plain kameez, turban and waistcoat, welcomed us with a warm smile behind his long beard. Beckoning us into the room, he led us across richly coloured, deep pile carpets to show us a cupboard full of cloth covered Korans, not unlike the sacred texts that Tibetans would wrap in consecrated cloths.

Several arches and cloistered corridors led on from the main square until we came to a door at the foot of a minaret. Finding it unlocked, we pushed against it, feeling resistance from accumulated debris inside. The door bent and scraped against what lay behind it, until the opening was wide enough for us to squeeze through into the space draped with years of cobwebs and dust.

Treading over the rubble, we cautiously inched our way up the narrow spiral staircase. Darkness lay ahead as we climbed higher, until nothing could be seen and we had to trust to the worn surface of the stone wall to lead us nearer the top. Eventually, we were at the tail end of a shaft of light that revealed its source as, at a turn in the spiral, a window came into view and clear vision returned.

A narrow door opened onto a balcony from where a panoramic view opened out over the precincts of the mosque to the city beyond. I had only known the small area beyond the crossroads and was therefore astonished at the extent of mud houses, stretching to the middle distance and appearing almost invisible, as they blended with the terrain from which they had emerged.

As I looked down upon the square, a woman entered and started to walk across towards the men still praying on the carpet, taking the logical shortest route. Immediately, a man, sweeping the tiles nearby, sprang at her with angry abuse, flailing his arms and hitting out at her with his broom, indicating for her to take the long way around the perimeter. Such was the level of disrespect some Afghan men had for their women. It was apparent that the mosque was the preserve of men and that women were only welcome under sufferance.

That craftsmen, inspired by their love of God, could construct a building of such intricate and overwhelming beauty, yet show such disrespect for the women who are the mothers of all men, was quite beyond me.

Leaving the mosque, we threaded our way through a bazaar dominated by second-hand western clothes until we had retuned to the main street.

Christmas lunch was a mere formality full of expectation but infused with a dull reality. Ten afghans or one shilling bought a plate of pilau rice, spinach and potato, not forgetting a large naan and a pot of chai, sufficient to fill a gap, but hardly Christmas fayre.

Hugo was more intent on passing the afternoon in the pursuit of unnecessary tat to take home, haggling down to every last cent, while I was happy to catch up on sleep in a warm bed until it would be time to meet Gary arriving from Kandahar.

His bus was due in at six but, after an hour waiting by the fire in the bus company's office, he still hadn't arrived and I could do nothing else but return to the hotel. Familiar voices were emanating from our room as I approached down the hallway, Hugo's, for certain, and I was sure the other could only be one other person.

Having a good old chin wag, Gary was stretched out on my bed as I squeezed through the narrow gap between the two beds and joined him.

'I thought I'd missed you. I've been waiting in the bus company office. Anyway, Happy Christmas.'

'Same to you. Sorry about that,' Gary replied. 'I came with a different company and got in a little earlier, going round town asking after you guys.' His voice was still a little strained and he coughed occasionally, evidence that whatever he had was deep down on his chest.

'How are you feeling now?' I asked.

'I'm exhausted. Some of those heads in the hotel decided to have a Christmas Eve party in my room. I was feeling so rough after you'd gone and slept a little through the day until three guys and two chicks came in for the warmth, playing guitar, singing and filling the room with hash smoke. That went on until I was getting up at half five this morning to catch the bus. I slept a little on the bus, but not a lot. I didn't realise the desert stretched so far across the country. It's so vast and empty.'

'I went up to the Bamian valley in the summer,' I said, 'to see the giant Buddhas and it's a little greener there. Tumbling mountain rivers, irrigated fields and fruit trees. Quite different.'

'I wish I'd seen those. Perhaps another time.'

'Did you manage to get a bed here?'

'Yes, I'm just next door. Hugo was just telling me about the mosque here and the way some woman was beaten.'

'We couldn't believe how vicious some of the men are. Hugo, did you tell Gary about the boy who was beaten up on the way in here?'

'Oui, ve vere just talking about it.'

'Well. I don't know about you two, but I'm hungry. We only had something quite light for lunch. Not really food for Christmas day. Let's see if we can find something better.'

Returning to the same place we'd been for lunch, the logs were burning bright in the wood burner and there were only a couple of tables free, such was the press of men eating and passing the evening with convivial chatter and laughter.

Whether by coincidence or not, chicken was on the menu and we each had virtually half a chicken each with potatoes and spinach for fifteen afghanis. Nuts, raisins and chai were the perfect complement to finish before stepping out into the bitter wind blowing up the street.

By nine o' clock, I was under my blankets, grateful for the wood crackling away in the burner as I drifted off into that comfortable netherworld that lies on the way to sleep.

I thought of Belinda, to whom I was returning, and what she and Harry, her son, might be doing at this moment for their Christmas in England, where it would have been early evening. I now yearned to be with her, having long realised that there had been something very special between us.

Her spiritual "awakening", following her near death as a result of a heroin overdose, had coincided with the drug induced experience I had gone through during an LSD trip. To cease seeing myself as an individual person amongst the billions who inhabited the Earth, instead fully comprehending that I was all embracing spirit that had always been and always would be, one with all entities and the greater universe, was mind-blowing to say the least. Until my body mind had tried to hold and own the experience, I was pure light without form and thought. There was nothing beyond or within the light, yet it embraced everything.

Since that time, I had tried several times, whilst in London, to regain it with more acid trips, but to no avail. A heightened awareness, yes, but more often nausea, muscle cramps and after images of passing objects like birds flying by. This failure to recapture something I knew to be so real and true was the principal motivation for my trip to India, as it had been for so many others.

I had been resolutely drawn to the Tibetans to secure a meaningful method that would enable me to re-enter that blissful state without resort to drugs. The ceremony and meditation technique I had been taught and had practised for the short time I had been in the mountains had helped to calm my mind, but nothing of the white light had been regained.

I was beginning to guess that perhaps there was no doorway to enter and no place to go. That, having realised irrefutably that I was not just person, but pure spirit having a human experience, was perhaps the secret.

The white light had been my *opening of the wisdom eye,* to quote the Dalai Lama, and it was sufficient to know unquestionably that, like the blending of all primary light colours to produce white light, the phenomenon of all things being one was in itself white light, but was not always readily apparent. The visual experience was in itself immaterial and it was sufficient to just wallow in being infinitesimal spirit.

The next morning was my last chance to secure my Iranian visa, so I was down at the consulate early as the bus to the border would be leaving at ten.

The officials were both friendly and efficient, rushing through the stamp in my passport in ten minutes. But, there was a hitch.

The stamp had to be signed by the consul who had not yet arrived at his office. I was therefore asked to take a seat, imagining his arrival would not be long. One hour, two hours passed, all the while conscious that I would have missed the bus and would have to catch the others up somewhere in Iran.

Meanwhile, the neatly dressed and fastidious elderly official, in whose office I was, sat at his desk filling in books and stuffing envelopes, gently puffing at a cigarette, ensuring not to drop ash anywhere other than in the ash tray before him. For him, every accessory had to be utilised from a silver letter opener to a wetted sponge pad for stamps. As he worked, he would occasionally stop to brush or pick off a piece of dust or stray ash from his suit.

A clerk brought in a silver tray, balancing a silver teapot and two small glasses held in silver trellis holders.

'This is our own special Persian tea, grown in our tea gardens in Iran,' the official told me.

The clerk, a young man dressed in suit and tie, poured into each glass the dark, coppery coloured liquid, infused with cardamon and served without milk but with two sugar lumps placed on the glass saucer. Also on the tray was a plate of traditional sweet crunchy biscuits, embedded with pistachios and almonds.

'You like the sweets?' the official asked, as I cupped my hand under my chin to catch the crumbs. 'These are very typical in our homes.'

About half past eleven, the consul's car finally drew up outside. The official rang his small brass bell, calling in the clerk who took my passport in to the consul, retuning a few minutes later with the stamp duly signed.

Thanking the official for his hospitality, I hotfooted it back to the hotel, surprised to find that Hugo and Gary were still there with bags packed ready to leave.

'I thought you would have gone,' I said, 'I had to wait for the consul to turn up. Why didn't you take the bus?'

'We thought you would have been held up and asked the manager when the next bus would be leaving. We've got to be quick now, but he's arranged for a mini bus leaving at noon, which will take us to Taybad on the Iranian side of the border,' Gary replied.

The manager had just finished his lunch and led us out into the street towards where the bus would be leaving. It then transpired that the drivers were still having lunch and wouldn't be leaving until one o' clock.

The one hour wait saw us entranced by metal workers beating out sheets of shiny tin, which were transformed into travelling trunks. It was indeed a production line from the beaters to the boy in the street who worked on six at a time, decorating the surfaces with a series of coloured squiggles. First all the red lines, then the green, yellow and so on until a recognisable design had emerged.

Joining the drivers in our last Afghan chai shop, we watched the final minutes tick by until we were summoned to the bus, where we joined ten Afghans, who were probably on their way to Iran for work.

With limited leg room and overall comfort, we set off out of the city, once more passing lines of trees before emerging into the desert. The road had a good tarmac surface and we felt at ease with our smiling companions as the dust swirled in an amorphous vortex, masking the Afghan desert stretching away behind us.

By half past four, we were at Islam-Qala on the Afghan side of the border, where passports were inspected by a young Afghan whose eyes were far too close together, his slight undernourished frame buried in an oversized blue serge uniform and a peaked hat that sat just above his brows. I wondered if he had any idea what he was looking for as he flicked through the pages that revealed such a varied collection of stamps.

A bus load of Afghans had to have their baggage cleared before us, further delaying our departure but, as the sun was fading ahead of us, we were finally crossing the four miles of empty no-man's land to Iran.

Fifteen

ENTRY WAS BY NO MEANS straightforward, stopping first at a small single story building to have our cholera and typhoid stamps checked, then on again to another checkpoint for entry stamps in passports.

Just as we thought all was finished, we were driven on to Taybad where, at the customs house, we were met by the same hostile officials I had encountered on the way out. The uniforms, boots and guns were all designed to intimidate, ensuring that everyone did as they were told, when told.

Almost immediately, one of our Afghan passengers was dragged off into a corner where he was violently stripped of his three coats and his baggage strewn across the floor. The man looked terrified as he pleaded with the two men for some kind of mercy. I had no idea what they were looking for but, in the light of the warning I had read in the British Embassy in Delhi, I suspected that drugs were high on the list.

When it came to my turn, I was asked the inevitable question, 'Do you have hashish?' Of course, when faced with that kind of question, despite being innocent, I was always conscious of not knowing quite where to look. Looking away, possibly suggested guilt, whilst looking them in the eye suggests that you are trying too hard to look innocent.

Looking the officer in the eye, I foolhardily asked, 'Do you think I want to get shot?' An impertinent statement, but one I couldn't resist. I felt impervious and believed that being a little impertinent and even a tad caustic, might ironically lower the temperature and even raise a smile. But, I was only met with sullen indifference.

By the time my rucksack had been half emptied and he'd unwrapped a few gifts I had bought for my return, a weariness overcame my inquisitor as he ultimately stuck his hand in for a cursory rummage of what remained. The same followed for Gary and Hugo, before we were allowed to repack and go on our way.

With the clocks turned back an hour to five o' clock, we were in good time to change some money and catch the bus leaving for Mashhad at six.

The word, *bus*, was something of a disservice to the luxury coach that we came to board. Soft seats with headrests, lights with dimmers, music, a toilet and washbasin with absolutely no sacks on the floor or goats in the aisle.

Most of the Afghanis, who sat with us, had probably never seen anything like it and did look very out of place as they played with the lights and seat recliners.

Although scheduled to leave at six, the ticket collector was still easing his way along the aisle with men behaving like excited school kids, unable to settle and still getting on and off until we eventually drew away fifty minutes later. Then, just as we thought we were underway, we were flagged down by a military patrol for another baggage check. Over zealous soldiers overwhelmed the coach, shouting at and pushing defenceless Afghans, while pulling their bags off the racks for another rummage. Ultimately, we weren't on our way until gone nine; half an hour before we were supposed to have arrived.

As we took the road north, the mellifluous voices of popular Iranian singers wafting through the speakers, so the snow encroached upon the road. In Kabul, it had largely been in the mountains with just a few flurries in the city, but here it was deep and stretching far into the darkness.

As we stepped off the coach in Mashhad, some time after midnight, we were immediately enveloped by the intense cold, such as we had so far not known. Despite my new clothes, Afghan coat and the exotic Tibetan fur hat I had bought in Dharamsala, the cold still managed to find a way in, biting at my senses as we waited for our things to be handed down from the roof of the bus.

A taxi took us to the centre, passing through wide, empty streets and the Imam Reza mosque, where Feathers and I had been roughly ejected by two very large mosque guards, merely for being infidels.

We were dropped at an hotel, where we found the door to be locked and had to ring the bell several times to wake the stubble faced proprietor, who cautiously opened the door to us, wrapped inside a splendid silk dressing gown.

At fifty rials or three shillings, it wasn't cheap but, in that cold and at nearly one in the morning, none of us cared, only glad to be shown a room where a boiler was already alight and we could temporarily escape the invasive elements for a few hours.

I had wanted to be out on the road early to catch a lift towards Tehran, but we didn't wake until eleven when Gary announced that he was staying on for a couple of days to see something of the city.

After swapping addresses, by midday, Hugo and I were walking out of town, followed by a crowd of kids and two educated students, with whom I found myself discussing the pros and cons of purdah.

'One's wife should not be exposed to the view of all and sundry,' the one with the better command of English started. 'If she goes about the streets in mini-skirts and so on, she will promote sexual thoughts amongst the other men, so leading to sex crimes and perversion.'

'I can't completely agree with you on that,' I replied. 'Men think about sex anyway. I've found on my travels, through the Middle East and India, where a relationship is not free and natural, dictated by the will of parents and not their own desires, men have become incredibly hung up about the subject. I've been asked countless times how many girl friends I've had. When I start to tell them, their eyes widen and the inevitable question follows, "Have you made love with a girl?" It seems to be the one obsession that dominates their lives, when it should be a natural thing, which every man should experience.'

'That is true. We would all like to make love, but our society is very strict and we have to follow these rules,' the boy replied, a little disheartened by what I had just said.

'Of course,' I continued, 'I don't know if this true, but I was told by an Iranian man, such is the deprivation of women in this part of the world, making love to one is like making love to Hitler. An extreme simile no doubt, but illustrating that many are cold, tense, unemotional and afraid; all things that hinder sexual enjoyment. For most women, sex is a necessary function to endure in order to reproduce. Whereas, women in the West have free access to the contraceptive pill to enable enjoyable sex, I presume that would be unheard of here?'

We had reached the outskirts of town and, whilst we were still talking, a bus came along and stopped, the driver beckoning us to come in. With a hurried farewell to our two companions, Hugo and I eagerly boarded the bus. The driver wouldn't accept money, instead guiding us to two vacant double seats.

We had at first imagined the bus going all the way to Tehran, but the capital was over five hundred and fifty miles away and this bus, visiting all the small villages, clearly wasn't going that far. Nevertheless, we drove for some four hours through flat, fertile country, contrasting strongly with the terrain we'd found in Afghanistan.

The snow had disappeared after Mashhad, despite the continuing intense cold, but the sun managed to put in an appearance, throwing some warmth through the large windows, and casting a magical orange light across the cultivated terrain.

As the sun began to set, we drove into Bojnūrd, a fair sized town, passing a large grassy roundabout decorated with flowerbeds, an artificial lake and the obligatory statue of the Shah of Persia; a sight to be found at each end of any Iranian town. With modern glass fronted shops, far removed from the ubiquitous fly covered Indian stalls, the town had a history dating back to the 13th century, but, in more recent times, had suffered serious earthquakes and had needed to be rebuilt.

A steady fall of snow had started as we pulled into an open yard from where, with the help of a couple of young Iranians, we booked into a local hotel, where the beds were covered with thick eiderdowns such as I had only seen before in Switzerland.

Whilst my appetite remained unassuaged by locality, climate or funds, Hugo continued to sustain himself on bread and dried fruit, shunning the warming and very nutritious Deezy that was so common in Iran.

I remember the first time I'd had this in Tehran, being shown the method of eating. The mutton, beans, potatoes, chick peas, tomatoes and mild spices are brought to the table in a small aluminium pot together with a pestle and unleavened bread. In season, it would be accompanied by iced water, radishes and wild rocket, but now I was lucky to see a sprig of coriander.

Some of the sauce is poured off into a bowl and a piece of bread soaked in it for a few minutes. The combination of gravy and vegetables hits the palette in an explosion of flavour, leaving a thin fatty film on the roof of the mouth.

The remainder in the pot is then crushed to make a paste, which is then eaten with the rest of the bread. It is warming, sustaining and a formula for a good night's sleep.

Hot soup started the next day, but its warmth soon forgotten as we set out early in the hope of a lift to Tehran. The sparse traffic was nearly all local, passing backwards and forwards to local villages.

Driving snow had set in for the day, the cold sapping our will until, by eleven, we had given up and returned to the town to catch a bus. The fare was two hundred rials, over a pound, and far more than I could really afford, but I knew there really was little alternative.

With the bus due to leave at twelve, there was just time for more hot soup, but we needn't have hurried as it was predictably late. By half past three, the clerk in the office was telling us that we should stay another night and catch the six o' clock departure, when a bus rolled in and Gary stepped off.

'What are you doing here?' I asked after I'd rushed outside to greet him. 'We thought you were staying on in Mashhad to have a look around?'

'It was too cold for sight seeing and I was sent packing at the mosque. I'm now on my way to Tehran with this bus and we've stopped off here to eat.'

'Hugo and I managed to hitch this far and we're waiting for a bus to arrive now, but it's way overdue.'

'I saw a bus, overturned on our way. That wouldn't be yours would it?'

'Could well be.' I was by this time feeling quite deflated by the delays and the cold. 'Is there any room on your bus?' I asked in anticipation that Hugo's and my troubles could be solved at a stroke.

'It absolutely chocker,' Gary replied.

Guess we'll have to catch up with you in Tehran, but first you must have some lunch.'

No sooner had I said this than a bus rolled down the road and stopped beside us.

'Tehran?' I shouted to the driver as the door opened.

He nodded and I waved furiously to Hugo, who was queuing at a bread stall.

All the seats were full, but we were allowed to sit on our rucksacks in the gangway, the objects of fidgeting and grunting as the men rose in their seats to inspect us more closely. The few women, imprisoned in their burqas, remained detached from our presence although I could only speculate what was going on in their minds.

There was little to see as, within an hour of our departure, darkness had fallen and we continued for another seven hours, stopping only once at a restaurant, too expensive for either of us to afford little more than chai. As the hours rolled by, so my eyes grew heavier and I occasionally found myself rolling over onto my neighbour's leg, jumping back into consciousness and signalling an apology.

By midnight, we had drawn into a small town just before Gorgān, the regional capital of Golestan province, where we were given the option of a few hours sleep in an hotel before the bus set off again in the early morning.

At half four, we were woken by banging on the door and the shouts of the hotel boy telling us that the bus would be leaving in half an hour.

Too tired to care, we merely buried ourselves deeper into the bedclothes, listening to the banging and shouts until the engine started and the bus pulled out.

It was at times like this that I thought of Kamala and how different things would now be had I decided to stay and make a life with her. Was I already having regrets? Anticipating my arrival back in England and my reconciliation with Belinda, there was no certainty there either, yet I had made a decision that would determine the whole course of my life and I was now a mere speck in this vast frozen snowscape, perhaps out of mind to both of them.

It would be another four and a half hours before I finally pulled myself from the covers and made my way out to the bus office to ask when the next one would be leaving.

My hopes were raised on hearing one would be leaving in less than half an hour but, on showing my ticket for the earlier bus, I was told in broken English and Pharsee that it was no longer valid for another bus. We were still only half way to Tehran and had already spent far more than the direct Mashhad to Tehran fare would have cost.

At this point, all my practised calm in the eye of the storm deserted me and I began to hurl angry abuse at the people in the office, who just stood bemused by my reaction, merely shaking their heads.

In the midst of an argument that was going nowhere, I heard a voice in very bad American English. 'Can I be helping you, sir?'

I turned to find a spivy looking Iranian with piercing dark eyes and well trimmed pencil moustache, dressed in tight black trousers, an oversized leather jacket, winkle-picker shoes and sunglasses perched on top of his greasy head. My first reaction was to dismiss him causing my irritation to increase even more.

'Can I help you?' he repeated.

Relenting to his question, I explained what had happened and visibly watched his concern for our plight define his expression.

'I am Ervin, soldier in the Iranian army. Let me make enquiries for you.'

Turning to the office clerks, he asked a few questions in Pharsee.

'There is a bus arriving here at half one and you can use the same ticket. But, for now, come with me.'

By this time, Hugo had joined us and Ervin led us downstairs to the office entrance where he spoke to a soldier in uniform. 'This man will help you get on the bus and ensure your ticket is okay. Now, you come to my house and we eat together.'

He lived in one room with two other soldiers and, despite his good intentions, which I deeply appreciated, I couldn't help but be amused by his retro tastes, like a dance hall spiv of the late fifties.

Colour photos of various naked European beauties adorned the walls, while a guitar was propped by one of the beds.

'Here, I show you my photos,' pulling out a photo album with a mottled green cover and a tassle on the spine. There were photos of him in his uniform with his comrades in arms. Others of him in his leather jacket, sunglasses, legs apart and thumbs thrust in his belt.

'This one is in my room in my parents' house.'

He was sprawled on the floor, a record player beside him, sunglasses firmly in place.

On a small table, the same record player took pride of place as he set the arm down on a black vinyl single. John Lennon's harmonica rang out the first few bars of *Love Me Do* as Ervin took to the floor turning and twisting his arms and torso to the music.

His limited collection of contemporary music was more than made up for by his food. In a small kitchen adjacent to the room, he produced the best meal either of us had eaten for a very long time. Rice, kebabs and flat bread filled our plates.

Our time together passed quickly, leaving little time to digest our meal before rushing to catch the bus. Once again, we needn't have bothered as it wasn't there when we arrived at the departure point.

Seeking warmth in the nearby army quarters by the bus office, it soon became apparent that some hostility had arisen between the Iranian army and the bus company officials. As the minutes ticked by, a couple of soldiers regularly went to the office demanding to know when the bus would be arriving. Each time, voices were raised, but nothing was resolved.

Two unshaven civilian prisoners, their bruised faces testimony to their crime, sat on the floor handcuffed together, their differences resolved as they chatted and shared a cigarette, uncertain as to what their fate might be.

By mid afternoon, we had almost given up hope when a minibus arrived and we were ushered on. It soon became apparent that it wasn't going all the way to Tehran, but to Gorgan, the regional capital, still some six hours distant from our destination.

The recent weather had coloured the landscape with a white blanket across the line of soaring mountains and deep valleys to the south, where thick deciduous and pine forests dominated the lower slopes, their branches heavy with fallen snow.

To the north, rich farmland stretched away towards the not so distant Caspian Sea, peppered with well built barns and farm houses and where tractors now replaced oxen to pull the ploughs.

Our arrival in Gorgan was met with the same unfriendly reaction from the people in the bus company office, still refusing to accept our tickets for the onward journey to the capital, instead insisting we pay a further one hundred rials to secure a seat.

Hugo was prepared to pay, but I was thoroughly pissed off and just wanted to get on the road again, determined not to spend another penny to reach Tehran.

Over a warming chai, I gave Hugo the option to either stay and catch the bus or to take his chances with me on the road.

Dragging him away from another bread shop, we walked off down the long main road to the outskirts of town, where a man in a Mercedes stopped, promising to take us some eighty miles to Sari.

All was well as we settled back into the worn and grubby leather seats until, some miles on, he asked us for money. Despite making it clear we didn't have any, he stopped abruptly and ushered us out.

It was a lonely prospect seeing that car speed off into the distance, leaving us with the cold wind blasting down from the mountains, darkness beginning to fall and not even a box of matches between us. But to lose heart at this time would have spelt the end. We had to keep our spirits up and promptly burst into song with a very untuneful rendering of Dylan's, *Like a Rolling Stone*, picking each other up on forgotten words.

Within the time taken to finish the song, an open backed van stopped, going as far as Behshahr, the next big town. With no room at the front, we were consigned to the open cargo space behind, huddled in the two corners behind the cab, trying to find as much protection as possible from the fierce wind that cut into us from the road. With my balaclava and Afghan coat, I was well insulated as I lay back and watched the multitude of stars, thankful that we were once more on the move again.

The journey was over all too quickly as we were dropped at a roadside restaurant just outside the town. It was a timely opportunity to eat, not having had anything since Ervin's meal the night before.

It was still only seven o' clock and we were the only customers and of sufficient interest for the moustachioed proprietor, his plump wife and an older man to sit beside us and watch. There was no common language other than a portable radio playing Cream's, *Badge* and the expressions of delight as we cleared our plates.

We felt we were now on a roll and wasted no time in getting back on the road, where two educated young Iranians in another Mercedes stopped for us.

Speaking French and a little English, we could at last communicate a little more meaningfully, not having to sit for miles like dumb mummies. Being young men though, the subject inevitably wound round to women and sex, leaving us no option but to answer their banal questions with a helping of hyperbole to both amuse ourselves and quell their excitement.

The short journey to the centre of Behshahr saw us receiving handshakes and an orange each as apparent gratitude for the "enlightenment" we had provided.

Stepping out of a warm car onto a cold street momentarily prompted the idea of the night in an hotel, but I was already fired up to continue as we engaged in conversation with some young boys, who led us on the road out of town where a lorry stopped going as far as Sari.

With one leg forcibly wedged between the two gear sticks, I cared little for the discomfort now as Hugo and I, sandwiched between two burly men, were well compensated by the warmth of the cab and the progress forward.

Arriving in Sari, luck was still with us as a policeman, blowing his whistle and shouting at the passing traffic, led us up the middle of the road towards an hotel, where four men were sitting in a parked taxi, their curiosity aroused by our arrival. On hearing that we were hell bent on getting to Tehran, they drove us out of town, keeping us seated until they had flagged down two lorries and arranged for each to take us to Tehran.

So, here, Hugo and I split up, he to one lorry and myself to the other, unsure whether we would meet again.

With my rucksack securely tied to the top of the load, I climbed up into the spacious cab, knowing that finally I had secured the essential ride that would end this part of the journey.

CHAPTER

CHAPTER
Sixteen

D ARA WAS MY DRIVER and the salt of the earth. Save for
the language issue, he was like any lorry driver you might
encounter in any country. In his case, he was middle aged, a little
overweight, strong and well in command of his vehicle. We soon
became friends, driving into the darkness, singing at the tops of
our voices all manner of English and American pop songs, which
he'd been able to hear on the radio.

By eleven, we had pulled into a roadside café, where a lorry
laden with gas cylinders had driven too far into the mud and was
at the point of tipping over. Dara immediately jumped out to help,
attaching a steel rope to our lorry, before using all his skill, judicious
use of the gears, creaking, cracking and heaving to gradually ease
the other lorry free to the applause of the bystanders. He was the
hero of the hour with much backslapping from the others as we all
went inside to eat.

I had thought we would be on our way again, once the food had
been washed down with chai, but the café interior soon put me in
mind of my school gym, which had been used for lunches before
reverting to a gym in the afternoon. Here, once the tables had been
cleared, fold-up beds were brought out and those drivers who had
pulled in for the night settled down to sleep. I merely retrieved my
rucksack from the roof and rolled out my sleeping bag on the floor,
ensuring the odd bits of dropped food had been brushed aside.

By six next morning, the darkness still obscured most of the
parked lorries and a heavy frost sparkled in the light of the café
window. My new companion wished me a good morning in very

broken English and handed me a glass of green chai, before we climbed back in the cab and set off on the near empty road that led towards a distant range of snow capped mountains.

For the next two hours, we wound up a well made road, still fringed with compacted snow, until Dara pulled in to a small chai house. It was time for breakfast. Huddled around the wood burner, we and a few others scoffed the traditional Iranian start to the day of fresh baked flatbread, wrapped around feta cheese, drizzled with a little honey, naturally accompanied by sweetened chai.

Dara paid for this, as he did at several stops during the course of the day as we slowly wound our way up the mountain road, gears frequently grinding to keep our momentum and the weight of our load firmly on track.

The road became increasingly more mountainous, sometimes rising to a high ridge before winding down again until the next long climb.

We followed the line of a river most of the way, its volume roaring and swashing white torrents up, over and round the huge boulders which had tumbled down the steep ravine that soared to the icy peaks above.

Small communities eked a living where patches of fertile soil rested on a valley shelf, sufficient for a few cattle and crops.

A dark shadow appeared to stain the road and, as we drew closer, it was clear that several wolves had tried to cross the road in search of food only to have been hit by an oncoming lorry, scattering their battered corpses across our path.

Dara drove on regardless, still climbing the narrow, precarious road that wound steeply to the highest pass, where we could look back and see giant lorries, like ours, dwarfed far below by the majesty of nature.

Having passed through in the heat of summer and now in the mid-winter chill, I wondered how anyone could contemplate building such a road under such extreme conditions.

Below lay the long valley that would lead us through the lower foothills to Tehran, its snowy landscape glistening in a moment of morning sunshine,.

As we approached the capital, I could see ski slopes, equipped with chair lifts, hotels and car parks, at this time heavily patronised by the city's elite who, after a short drive, could escape the city for some winter recreation.

The snow passed away behind us and the mountains became lost in the clouds as the terrain turned to flat, dusty soil supporting little agriculture and flanked only by a few gently rising hills.

Advertising signs now blotted the view on both sides of the road, quickly followed by suburban factories, shops, traffic, paved sidewalks and people. It was all too much for me as Dara dropped me on a main road inside the city, where he indicated for me to wait until Hugo's lorry arrived.

Even at this point, we were not even half way from Delhi to London, only having covered around fifteen hundred of the almost five thousand total, so I was eager to move on as quickly as possible.

Once again, I gave Hugo the opportunity to decide what he wanted to do and, as before, he chose to carry on hitching with me.

I still had the map of the city I'd picked up on the way out in the summer and could see we were on an east west trajectory for which we needed three buses before we could realistically find ourselves on the road to Tabriz, another three hundred and sixty miles away.

It was mid week and the streets were busy with the glass fronted car showrooms and clothes shops, displaying their contents with flair and sophistication. This only served to emphasise what a modern city Tehran was, starkly contrasting with anything I had seen in India.

Along the pavements, young women in make-up, maxi coats and western hairstyles were strolling, talking with friends in a manner no different to what I might see on a London street. But, as I had already learned, this was a social veneer and sadly the women had been shown their place in society, having little status other than that offered by an arranged marriage; a costly enterprise for many Iranian men.

Even after leaving the last bus, it was a long walk with our heavy packs out along the tree lined road, still busy with modern shops and the ever present minarets from where the mullahs called the faithful to prayer - reminders that we were still far from home.

An elderly man in an equally worn Citroen 2CV stopped and

took us to the main Tabriz road, ash falling from the cigarette held between his fingers on the steering wheel. He had lived for six years in Toulouse and now fluent in French, a great boost for Hugo's morale as I knew he struggled to speak English for any length of time. We were dropped in a perfect place to catch the onward traffic and within five minutes were sitting in a comfortable car speeding on towards Qazvin, a third of the way to Tabriz.

The mutual ignorance of each other's language found us sitting in virtual silence for a hundred miles, save for the occasional observation from Hugo or myself. Instead, we listened to a medley of Iranian pop and western middle of the road music on the radio, watching the miles of coastal mountain to the north, the flat plain across which we were driving and the low undulations to the south-west. As the day wore on, the sun began to set behind the hills in a splash of deep spectral colours until the night had come down revealing the slither of light that was the new moon.

It was only half six when our lift put us down, but we were both exhausted and opted for a cheap hotel where we imagined we could catch up on lost sleep.

The next few hours were to change all that.

It didn't take long, before we met up with three long haired freaks staying in the same hotel, who were on their way east.

Two Germans, one of whom spoke English like a native, and a Yugoslavian had been driving a VW van until one of them had turned it over on the icy road and were now awaiting the verdict from a local garage as to whether it could be repaired or not.

So we found ourselves being drawn into their misfortune, eating dried apricots and bread in their room, listening to sounds on a portable cassette player and talking of the changes Europe had seen over the previous nine months.

Joints started to be passed around, which made me more than a little nervous in view of the warning in the Delhi Embassy, regarding the fifty something westerners who had already been shot this year for possession.

The Yugoslav, was probably about my age, quiet and enigmatic, whereas I had already sensed that the two Germans, both a little older, were not awake to anything remotely spiritual, instead intent on the pursuit of more drugs and, ultimately, chicks on arrival in

Goa.

As the evening wore on and I was nicely stoned, despite my apprehension, the thinner of the Germans looked up between the long, lank hair that framed his face and directed a question to Hugo and myself.

'We have some acid. You wanna tab?'

I knew instantly that I should have made my apologies and left at that point, sensing a bad scene and a lot of trouble, but my curiosity got the better of me.

'What acid is it? What's it cut with?' I asked.

'It's pure acid.' came the reply - one that I'd heard so many times before.

He passed one of the tiny purple tabs over and I sensed that at least it would be cut with some speed and, more than likely, some strychnine thrown in for good measure.

Once again, my instincts told me to leave. I was tired and the scene was not conducive to a good trip. The room was untidy, they were agitated and excitable, insisting on playing Deep Purple, Led Zeppelin and more as loud as the little cassette player with its tinny speakers could manage.

The other German was jigging about, his long curly blond hair swaying from one side to the other as he exclaimed, 'You know I have taken over one hundred trips, man and they have all been, *far out.*'

I immediately considered that if they had all been cut with speed and strychnine, they would have taken him no further than a bottle of arsenic. Judging by his speech and overall disquiet, I could tell that he had never been lucky enough to have been exposed to the real stuff during the early days when it was a colourless, tasteless liquid that opened up a broadened spiritual consciousness almost every time. Without that experience, I know I would never have made my way to India and sought answers to my spiritual conundrums.

The situation was made even more fraught when we were joined by two Iranian men for a smoke, either of whom could have grassed on us.

But, I was up for a challenge.

With my own acid experiences and the training I had received with Geshe Kundun, I saw the opportunity as like entering the Bardo Thodol; the stages one passes from death to rebirth, encountering deities both benign and wrathful on the way, who can tempt you off the true path of enlightenment.

I saw the chaos around me and wanted to see how I could best deal with whatever was thrown at me. Perhaps this was a reckless proposition.

So, we dropped.

Hugo had never tripped and, anticipating the possible effect a bad trip might have on him in this environment, I advised him not to. Advice he was thankfully happy to take, sitting quietly as he waited for ours to seep into the system.

And so it did.

From the beginning, I felt the speed in my blood, but still I persevered and tried very hard to get into what little acid was there and use it to advantage. But, after two or three rushes of hope, the energy died away and I had to content myself with at least another seven or eight hours of sleeplessness, wind in my system, pulsations and aching all over my body.

Realising I was going nowhere, I settled into a mental merging with the music and, to be fair to the others, could see that they had been working hard to get us all there. As we all agreed, when the light was turned on and we'd all sighed deeply, our efforts were in vain and it was ultimately yet another speed trip.

I took my leave at around five thirty and returned to our room, where I tried to get a little sleep, but the speed was still far too active, leaving my mind awake and alert. Instead, I lay beneath the warm covers, whilst Hugo and two other Iranians snored away the night and reflected on what a complete waste of time and energy drugs are. Perversely, I felt it had been a good thing to have had this experience before returning to England and finding myself under possible peer pressure again. The outcome was a resolution never to take any drugs again that were of a regressive or harmful nature.

As daylight broke, reflecting the shadow of the window bars onto the opposite wall, I couldn't help thinking that Hugo, with his lack of drug experience, was far more admirable than myself. He consistently showed far more kindness and lack of thought for himself, being even less well off than myself, yet still offered to share what little he had.

I also had a much greater worry, as the Germans had also given a tab to one of the Iranians who, after he dropped it, insisted that he had to sleep in order to be in the office by eight o' clock.

Knowing he had never experienced anything like it before and that one is totally unable to sleep could have freaked him, not to mention the pains and awareness of mind. It worried me that he might have panicked and called a doctor and subsequently the police. The prospect of the doors being kicked open and being dragged away to an Iranian jail with the possibility of being shot was not one I wanted to linger on for too long.

Catching sight once more of the window bars on the wall, I woke Hugo and told him to get his things together as we were leaving.

Bidding our farewells to the Germans, surprised at our early departure, we had time for hot soup in a small café before hitting the road. As the speed weakened in my system, so my eyes grew heavier and I was falling asleep where I stood, until a van stopped going a forty minute ride to the small town of Takestan.

Save for a few houses, a couple of shops and a police station, there was little to hold us as the road passed on through and out into the bleak desert beyond.

No one wanted to stop. Cars passed by empty, lorry drivers waved and bus drivers just put their feet down further on the accelerators.

The hours passed, kicking stones across the road, shivering with the ever encroaching cold and feeling thoroughly dispirited.

Time eventually came for me to declare that we should finally split up in order to improve our chances. I picked up my rucksack to walk further along the road to thus give Hugo a better chance, but he became forceful and insistent that he walk ahead.

We bid our farewells and I stayed. Not long after, some local kids, speaking a little English, suggested I go and ask for help in the police station. Following the night before, it was ironic that I should be doing this, but took up their suggestion nevertheless.

A young officer, who spoke good English, ordered another policeman to stand out in the road with me and flag down vehicles. Several refusals later, a minibus driver agreed to take me a hundred miles or so to somewhere beyond in the great white wilderness. Hugo was not anywhere to be seen along the road, so I assumed he'd got a lift while I was in the police station.

The snow had indeed returned and I watched for miles a monotonous flat landscape passing on either side while the sun was a dim hazy ball in the mist. The temperature was plummeting all the time and I suspected that quite likely there would be worse to come.

The bus pulled into a yard just of the main street, where a bowl of deezy was hastily eaten before I was out hitching again.

It was another lorry that stopped soon after where, yet again, my driver and I were silenced by lack of common language.

I managed to break the ice by giving him an English lesson, pointing out landmarks as we passed. 'River, trees, mountains, water, snow, road, lorry …' supporting the words with hand gestures to better illustrate their meaning. It wasn't much, but it seemed to make him happy and was something of payment for my lift.

But, as we drove deeper into the wilderness and darkness began to fall, his mood changed with him, becoming inquisitive about my passport and money.

I saw him churning the thoughts over in his mind as he stared ahead onto the empty road, convincing me that he was about to rob me or worse.

My rucksack was in the cab with me and I pretended to rummage as if looking for something. I pulled a few things out as if to enable me to better see within, amongst those things was my sheath knife, which I made sure he could see.

Returning to the English lesson and the reassurance that he knew I could protect myself, the atmosphere calmed as the final few miles through the slush were covered.

He dropped me in Tabriz at around seven, leaving me somewhere in the city, cold and tired and not knowing where I would be sleeping that night.

It was New Year's Eve and all I wanted was an hotel and sleep. They were all far more than I could afford until I was able to negotiate a bed for thirty rials. In a long narrow room, where four beds had been crammed together with barely a two foot gap in between. My bed was up against the window, looking out on the snow covered street below, but it was of no concern as I wedged my things underneath and quickly crawled beneath the covers, my breath misting in the cold air.

As I drifted into sleep, I thought back on the year that was passing. From my last sight of Belinda, making silly faces at each other through the window as the bus pulled away to my friends waving me off at Victoria station. The many people I encountered as I hitched down through France and Italy, crossing by boat to Greece and the islands. Hours spent on hot dusty roads waiting for a lift until I finally reached Istanbul and my meeting with Galina, the beautiful Russian drug dealer.

Here I was now, months later, sheltering from the intense cold in the very places where the debilitating heat had sapped my energy and the road had led me to mysterious and exotic places, where the exhilarating and sometimes menacing often happened.

Ultimately, that road had led me to a small English hill station in the Himalayan foothills, where my meeting and falling in love with Kamala had created the greatest emotional conflict of my life.

Seventeen

T**HE FIRST OF JANUARY, 1971,** brought sunshine on the busy street below my window. Three others now occupied the other beds, still snoring and farting as I collected my bags and squeezed my way out of the room.

I had to find my way to the Turkish border just beyond Maku but could find no one speaking any English to get me on the right road, until a school of motoring car picked me up, the young learner driver jolting and crawling until we reached the main road out of the city.

As I waited, a car drew up on the other side and out stepped an English guy, his blond hair cut short like mine and dressed in a thin Indian cotton shirt, jacket and jeans. He was on his way back to England from Australia via India and had been waiting further up the road. Understandably, he'd found it far too cold in his current wardrobe and had decided to return to Tabriz to catch a bus to the border. I was almost tempted to join him, seeing him walking back towards the bus station, but stuck it out for a further five minutes.

Out of the morning sunshine, as if a gift from heaven, emerged a battered blue and white Volkwagen campervan, blue smoke swirling from its exhaust.

'Where are you heading?' a young Pakistani man asked as he leant out of the window.

'Maku and the border,' I replied.

'Are you not going any further?'

'England!'

'We're driving across Turkey and up to Germany. Come and join us.'

I couldn't believe my luck. One lift nearly all the way. I threw my things in the back and joined the man on the bench seat in the front, together with the driver, another Pakistani.

I'm Masood,' the younger man said, 'and this is my older brother, Latif.'

'Hi,' Latif replied in a faux American accent.

'Hi, I'm Adam.'

Hi, Adam,' they both replied in unison.

They appeared to be well educated and financially sound. Masood was just a little older than myself at twenty-one, while Latif was twenty-six. I had an immediate liking for Masood, who was tall, thin, clean shaven, quiet and considered in his speaking, while Latif, resembling a fat sultan with jowls and a big belly, had me puzzled. He effused an air of superiority, whilst proving to be kind hearted and jovial, but somewhat narcissistic.

As Latif put the old machine into gear and we rolled forward, I could see the road ahead appearing increasingly more perilous, stretching to a lost horizon. A heavy white mist hung from the sky to the ground as hard packed snow encroached across the road. Strangely, I felt very cold, even inside the cab.

'I have to tell you,' Masood started, 'the heater is broken.'

Despite sitting close together on the bench seat, swathed in coats, scarves, gloves and an accumulating body heat, it was our feet that suffered. While Masood and I could stamp up and down on the floor to mitigate the clawing cold, Latif had to keep going, occasionally taking his feet off the pedals for a quick stamp.

We reached the border as the light was fading, completing the Iranian formalities very quickly and moving on past the machine gun toting border guards towards the open Turkish gates. Peering ahead, it was clear that our route was going to be even colder and whiter.

All the lights were out in the customs house and the officials straining their eyes by the windows as they stamped our passports and checked vaccination certificates. One guard indicated for the van to be opened up, but didn't bother checking the contents; such a demand would have jeopardised everyone's well being.

Waving us through, we were soon driving out into open country, just able to see Mount Ararat through the darkening mist.

With ice increasing by the minute, we agreed it would be too dangerous to attempt driving at night and risking a breakdown in the middle of nowhere.

Arriving in the first town, we booked into a small hotel, taking a room at the back of the large tea room, where several elderly Turks, in flat caps and overcoats, sipped tea and chatted around the boiler in the middle.

My new companions bought me dinner in a restaurant across the narrow street, the tarmac obliterated by hard ridges of muddy, frozen snow.

Besides the beans, rice and bread, I had my first exposure to what would become a regular occurrence for the remainder of my time with the two Pakistanis. The nightly bottle of vodka.

I never had been a great drinker, preferring the occasional pint of beer, but both Masood and Latif enjoyed more than the periodic glass. Whilst Masood seemed to apply some moderation to his consumption, Latif, with the help of a couple of Turks, consumed the whole bottle without apparent ill effect. So, kicking the slush beneath our feet, we crossed back to our room, warmed by vodka and the hotel boiler.

The air was cold on my breath as I walked out into the near empty street early next morning, leaving Masood and Latif still snoring in the narrow chilled room. There was little joy to be found in this snow draped village, save for some dried fruit, a bag of which I bought to share on the journey.

I waited huddled around the boiler with a cup of chai until my new friends eventually emerged, yawning and dishevelled, informing me that they had to send a telegram before we could start out, leaving me to wait a further hour until they were ready to go.

Mount Arafat, the Biblical landing of Noah's Ark after the flood, rose into the snow laden sky, still some distance away, whilst, in the street, horse drawn Ottoman carriages rumbled over the tarmac and through the slush.

Children on their way to school, wrapped in varying coats, boots and gloves, stopped to speak their few words of English and pass on their way.

I'd judged by the smoke billowing out of the van's engine the day before, that it was not in the best of health so, on the Pakistanis' return, the several attempts to start the ignition inevitably proved pointless. A crowd of passers-by had gathered, who were roped in to propelling the van down the street until, after a couple of shudders and an explosion of smoke, the engine kicked into life.

With Masood at the wheel, Latif and I jumped in, waving to the crowd as we drove out of the town towards Agri.

With the heater dead, there was no warm air to prevent the ice build up on the windscreen. Masood struggled to see the road ahead as he constantly scraped the glass with a piece of card, whilst struggling to keep the circulation going in his feet.

Our progress was further slowed as each in turn stopped to spend time in the back of the van removing shoes and socks and wrap their feet in towels to restore some circulation.

As we slowly rolled into Agri, I recognised the bridge I had slept by with my travelling companions so many months before and the hotel we almost stayed in until we discovered the damp mattresses.

Little seemed to have changed as we passed on into open country where, amid the stretches of open fields, the occasional tree sparkled and drooped under the weight of the white crystals now rapidly descending from a heavy grey sky.

The road began to climb and us with it, zigzagging towards high reaches of jagged rock, their nooks and crannies catching the windswept snow. Despite everything, the road was surprisingly clear, save for a few clods of frozen slush. The tyres gripped well and, for the present, there was no need to get the snow chains out.

Reaching the top of the pass, I could almost feel the relief being expressed by the tired engine as we gently freewheeled down the black road that wound its way through gentle virgin white slopes, dazzling in the afternoon sun.

Darkness crept upon us for a second night, as we arrived at a small town just before Erzurum, driving slowly down the narrow main street, peering through the icy haze on the windscreen for indications of an hotel.

A sudden knocking on the side window startled us all, but it was only a young man pointing the way to an hotel and leading us the few extra yards until we arrived at a splash of yellow light cast out upon the frozen snow.

He led us through a double set of doors to a large room filled with the drifting smoke of burnt tobacco, accumulated during the long days where little work is done outside. As the night before, men sat at tables chatting, playing cards and drinking tea. A silence prevailed amid a sea of curious stares as we were led through to a bedroom with its own boiler and thick covers on the beds. In a small outhouse, a cold tap provided water for our ablutions. Splashing it over my face seemed to freeze the brain and cause an intense ache behind the eyes whilst the stone splash back and the floor beneath the sink had taken on an ever thickening film of clear ice.

At dinner, Latif acquired another bottle of vodka, most of which he downed himself until overcome by a state of indecorous vulgarity and incoherence.

With the light of a new day barely visible in the mist, the van's engine once again refused to start, necessitating another round up of villagers from school children, young men and a few old timers. As some put their shoulders into the back end, others pushing with bare hands on the frozen bodywork, a disorderly funeral procession passed by carrying aloft a green coffin constantly lurching like a small boat in a heavy sea. The motley group of mourners followed the route to the cemetery; those closest to the coffin with heads bowed, while the rest shuffled behind with hands thrust deep into their pockets.

Seeing them turn off further down the street, it was all hands back to the van, heaving the heavy metal box along the road as our feet gave way on the compacted ice. A few kicks and false starts and we had to admit defeat, glad to be able to hold numbed fingers to our mouths and blow some warmth back into them. A mechanic revealed himself from the crowd, peering into the tightly packed engine in the rear, screwing and unscrewing until he signalled for us all to have another go. Pushing until we had almost run out of the slope on the street, the engine finally kicked into life, sending up its now familiar cloud of blue-grey smoke into the chilled air, followed by the cheers of all those who'd lent a hand and the few intrigued bystanders.

As the engine gently turned over by the side of the road, a horse drawn sleigh came into sight, bells jingling, as its four heavily clad passengers waved, one with a white beard, red coat and boots. Was he perhaps late for Christmas?

Latif was still snoring in all his drunken immensity as Masood shook him to some semblance of wakefulness and dragged him out to the van, the engine still mercifully ticking over.

A crystal frost hung from the tree branches on the road out towards Erzurum, the empty fields testimony to the smoke filled cafés.

Some miles on, we encountered a small gathering of men dancing arm in arm on the edge of the road accompanied by a big drum and a queasy flute. They were part of a wedding party making its way to Erzurum in a flotilla of cars, stopping every so often to dance.

Onwards we drove, the mountains flattening out into vast plains of desolate emptiness, where the occasional plume of smoke from an isolated house broke the stillness the snow had cast across the landscape.

The wedding procession caught us up, stopping once again to celebrate the joy of a winter wedding, banging the drum and dancing joyously in a fog of condensing hot breath.

Passing along Erzurum's peripheral road, we continued westward, where we passed Gary sauntering along followed by a crowd of schoolchildren. I could only presume he was killing time before catching the night train to Istanbul. In some ways, I wished I was joining him, but then remembered how cramped the compartment had been on the way out. Six of us and all our bags, taking turns to sleep in the luggage rack, stretching out for an hour or so as remission from the confines of the seats.

From hereon, I was covering new territory, that which had previously only been seen from the train window.

Following a valley, for the most part, flanked by high mountains, the road ran parallel to a fast flowing river in which large chunks of compacted snow and ice tumbled along the turbulent spaces between the shores and the myriad of boulders protruding above the water's surface.

The engine chugged us onwards, occasionally backfiring; a

regular reminder that all was not well under the bonnet. As we hit yet more snow, the van started to produce a grating noise from underneath increasing in intensity until we were forced to stop.

Compacted ice had accumulated within the wheel arches, causing the tyres to scrape a smooth groove that made it virtually impossible for the wheels to turn freely. Half an hour with the snow shovel broke most of it up, but it remained a warning that there might be worse to come and it would need all our ingenuity to keep the van going.

The road climbed a couple of times during the day, before flattening out as the river entered a broad plain, the fog thickening as we passed into Erzincan for the night. This modern town with its banks, apartment blocks and shops threw up an hotel not unlike those we had stayed in before, but costing another shilling; money that could well have been spent on a plate of beans and a hunk of bread.

Masood and myself were hungry, whilst Latif was eager to get his legs under the table with another bottle of vodka. In a comparatively upmarket restaurant with smart waiters and the local clite, I felt even more shabby in my now quite dirty secondhand clothes which had been cobbled together from a collection of passing travellers. As Latif downed one glass after another, he stopped mid swig and put his glass down, leaning over in my direction. In a soft vodka laden voice, he breathed his words over me.

'You are wanting to know why we are making this journey?'

'No, Latif, but tell me,' I replied knowing I was being sarcastic.

'Our van is being a very valuable van.'

At first I wondered who would put a premium on a rusty heap of metal that needed to be pushed every morning to start the engine. Then my focus sharpened and I looked him straight in the face, then at Masood, who was sitting back in his chair, a self-satisfied grin on his face.

Latif's eyes sparkled through the alcoholic haze.

'We have hidden several kilos of the very best Afghan hashish. If you are wanting, you can be helping us to sell it in England.'

I knew that I was barely a third of the way across Turkey to Istanbul, where I would be on the proverbial crossroads of Europe and better able to make my way north to England. I could not lose the trust of these two and find myself abandoned in this winter bound landscape.

Masood had drawn his chair closer to hear my reply.

'You've been very lucky to get it through Iran. They've been shooting smugglers this year.'

'We heard,' Masood said, 'but they don't shoot people in England.'

'Maybe, but there are some dangerous cartels there, no less amongst the police.'

I wanted to tell of my experiences in London. The intimidation, the murder of Caroline, my girlfriend, by Helsdon, the bent copper. Of the scars he had inflicted on my face and body with his cut-throat razor and my final encounter with him on the Westway flyover on a wet November night and how he fell to his death, his foot caught in a carelessly placed rope. But, I knew that Latif and even Masood were not people I could truly confide in.

'Have you got contacts there to distribute the stuff?' I asked.

'Yes, but it is *your* country. You will be knowing who to see and where to go.'

'It's not that simple. People are murdered for stepping on toes.'

'What are you meaning, stepping on toes?' Latif asked.

'I mean. If you go where you should not go, there can be big trouble. Especially if you are a stranger. My advice would be to go to your contact and get the best price you can, but don't be greedy. It will be a cash transaction and you have to watch your backs.'

Latif finished his glass and poured another. Silence prevailed between the two of them and I could sense there was some discomfort at what I had to tell them.

'But, people are wanting to buy hashish?' Latif eventually asked.

'Yes, but this is a huge international business. I got into trouble for trying to sell small amounts. Really small amounts - one pound deals. Compare that with trying to sell kilos. Then you could also be double crossed by the police and arrested. With yourselves coming into the market, you're cutting someone else out and that means trouble.'

Latif continued sipping and Masood reached for the bottle.

'Fortunately, you will not have lost too much money on what you have bought, but taking it any further than Istanbul is a big risk,' I added.

We finished our meals in silence and left the restaurant, Latif belching then stopping under a street lamp to piss into the undefiled snow.

Latif went straight to bed, while Masood joined me around the wood burner in the dining room for chai.

'I really appreciate what you have told us, tonight, Adam,' he started. 'We thought it was going to be easy to sell. Now we have ten kilos hidden in the hollows of the van and don't know what to do with it.'

'I had an acquaintance in Istanbul, who arranged to buy some dope there,' I said. 'He had it all planned to take back to England in a friend's car. At the last minute, when they went to collect the dope, they were arrested and presumably lost all their money. They're probably still in a Turkish jail with little hope of being released any time soon.'

Masood sat passively sipping his chai, staring into the middle distance. He looked so disillusioned as if the whole purpose of their journey had been irretrievably stolen from them.

'I'm so sorry, Masood. I wish I could bring you better news. Are you still going on to Europe?'

'Yes, we have family in Germany.'

'Perhaps if you stay there for a while, you can keep your ears to the ground and maybe find a way of getting rid of it there a little bit at a time without drawing too much attention to yourselves. But, don't think about England.'

'Thank you,' he said, managing a strained smile and reaching out to put his hand on my shoulder.

It was eleven o' clock when Latif finally came round with all of us having a hot meal before setting off for Sivas, the halfway mark across Turkey.

We had hoped this stretch of the route would take us over the last high mountains before reaching Europe, but the flat plain soon fell away behind us with the road climbing through gaps and high passes until we found ourselves on the other side looking down along the course of a river that wended its way along an intensely green and fertile valley.

The snow here had melted, leaving everything very wet.

Pollarded willows stood like sentries along the river bank, tractors and donkeys alike pulled ploughs, churning over the deep brown fertile soil. In the villages, the children came out in their school smocks to greet us, waving and laughing, banging on the windows and optimistically asking for lifts. The tall oblong stones of a Moslem graveyard protruded from the uncut grass around them.

Then, just as we thought we had passed the worst of the mountains, we were climbing once again in amongst icy crags now being bathed in the orange light of the sinking sun.

Rounding a particularly sharp corner, not far from the summit, the wheels locked again with no traction on the steep icy rise to the top. Having knocked away most of the ice stuck in the wheel arches and with Masood at the wheel, it fell on Latif and I to give some push from behind. Latif, despite his weight, contributed little to the effort, huffing and puffing for breath at every heave.

Miraculously, a slushy patch gave the wheels much needed contact with the road and the van suddenly pulled away, continuing onwards in a cloud of smoke to the top. I ran ahead, leaving Latif to shuffle in his own time to join Masood and myself. I was indeed shocked to see someone of his age so incapacitated by years of gluttony and insufficient exercise.

In Sivas, the hotel was even more expensive than the night before and, knowing my financial dilemma, Masood kindly slipped me five liras to help towards the eight lira bill. This was only six shillings, but having changed my last two pound travellers' cheque the day before, I now had precious little to see me the rest of the way home.

Of course, I still had the two hundred dollars Jen had given me in Bombay, but this would have to be my absolute last resort, knowing I would have to change a one hundred dollar note into an irrelevant currency, successively losing out on exchange rates as I moved north through Europe. I now had just over fifty-six liras left and was determined to make it last.

Another confrontation arose over dinner in a local restaurant where, once again, I persevered with politeness and diplomacy, suffering another evening of the slow descent into drunkenness and boorish behaviour from Latif.

As his words began to slur, Latif swept his elbows across the table, his head nodding erratically in my direction. 'Why don't you drink?' he slurred accusingly, breathing out the foul fumes of coarse Turkish vodka.

'People find happiness in different ways,' I replied, 'and I don't find mine in a bottle, but don't let that stop you if you believe a bottle of Vodka every night will bring you happiness, then who am I to suggest otherwise. I'm afraid I cannot empathise with your methods and philosophy.'

He turned away before I had finished and in his roaring voice began a conversation with a drunken Turk who had just joined us at our table.

'You are my brother,' he said very loudly as he linked his two index fingers together and raised his glass to the bemused Turk. He lowered his voice slightly and curled his lip in disgust as he took another gulp of vodka. 'We sons of the Prophet must show solidarity,' he said, 'Peace and Blessings be upon him. A curse be upon those damned, sons of a bitch, fucking Hindus.' Looking back towards me, he continued, 'How many years did we put up with those British in our country, bowing and scraping and being humiliated by their orders.'

I could see he was fishing for an argument, a political showdown in which he could declare himself superior to the nation that had occupied and transformed his country over nearly two hundred years.

I had learned by now that Latif was a Jekyll and Hyde, transforming himself into Mr Hyde after the first few swigs; a character that had to be dealt with carefully. I suspected underneath his jovial facade he was a very sad, unfulfilled man as every morning he would come round unable to remember the previous evening and apologising profusely for whatever embarrassment and duress he might have caused everyone else.

At this moment, he was capable of anything, so tact and diplomacy were essential pre-requisites to best avoid a sudden spike in his behaviour. He had a passion for violence, especially when it came to any talk of Hindus or an affront to national pride.

'Look at my strength,' he would say, puffing himself up before sinking back exhausted into his chair. 'I am the son of my great father and grandfather in the line of the Sultan Emperor, who the

British humiliated. He was equal to ten men and would have given his life to Allah. In battle he had to kill two hundred men. Any less and he would not be a man.'

I pitied him his lack of self-worth.

The hours ticked by until we were the only ones left in the restaurant, my eyes growing heavy as I would sink into sleep and suddenly start awake until I heard the chairs screeching back against the wooden floor and we rose to leave. Latif and the Turk staggered across the floor arm in arm, hardly able to support the leaden weight of each other until Masood helped them to the door.

Out in the street, they targeted a street trader innocently plying his floor brushes, snatching them away with boorish ridicule and attempting to clean the pavement, until the poor man managed to retrieve them and make a hasty getaway.

Why do people degrade themselves and others so? It has always been so, but what aspect of their humanity is lacking and what brings it about?

In the hotel room, an unbearable silence prevailed. I could tell Latif despised me for not joining his little party and for indicating my disapproval through my silence.

I continued to ignore him as I climbed into bed, Masood to his, leaving Latif to bang his way noisily down the corridor to be violently sick, before staggering back, slamming the door and turning off the light as he fell into bed snoring for Pakistan.

Surprisingly, Latif was not in his bed when I awoke, leaving Masood and I to merely surmise where he might have gone. *Surely, he'd not gone for more vodka?* was the thought that ran through my bleary mind.

'I've never seen him as bad as this,' Masood volunteered. 'You know that alcohol is forbidden for us Moslems, but Latif had been drinking in private before we left Pakistan and now we are seeing this. I can only apologise for his behaviour.'

In the dining room, while we were having some coffee and something to eat, Latif wandered in looking spruce in clean clothes and having a rare smile on his face.

'Where have you been?' Masood asked.

'There's a great Turkish bath here. You should have one,' he replied.

I would like to have taken up the offer as I was now very conscious that I was probably smelling quite rank by now.

'It's getting late and we've got to get on,' Masood reminded us.

On the journey out, although constantly hot, I had been able to wash clothes and keep myself clean, but now this was virtually impossible and I only hoped that a day would soon come when I could feel as clean as Latif.

I still sensed some resentment and a tad hostility from him, but I had by now recognised that he was no better than me, despite his boastings, and I was learning to exercise an air of indifference and generally ignore his exhibitionism. This was sufficient to quell most of his tactics designed to belittle others for his own ends.

I was of course grateful that I was still getting this lift, for that is what it was. I was a hitch-hiker, a stranger, who the two of them had seen fit to help on his way. I had no right to criticise and condemn and I made sure that, when appropriate, I pulled my weight, helping to make the journey unfold as smoothly as possible.

What was to unfold in the next few hours was sent to try the mettle of all of us.

Eighteen

THE ROAD WAS at first reasonably flat, passing by newly ploughed fields and the green tinge of freshly sprouting crops. Occasionally, the land would gently rise and fall and it was on one such stretch in the late morning that Masood stopped the van for Latif to take over. As he turned the key to start again, there was no response from the engine other than a weak chugging sound.

Masood and I got out to start pushing as we'd now become accustomed, but as soon as we'd picked up some momentum and Latif lifted the clutch, the engine seemed to just lock and the tyres scraped to a stop.

Masood looked resigned to something far worse than anything we had been experiencing to date. Opening the engine cover, his worst fears were realised.

He muttered something in Urdu, probably the same as I would have said in English.

The engine was dripping with hot oil.

'I can't be sure, but I think something is jammed. We'll need a mechanic.'

Latif had by now joined us outside and the three of us just looked at each other and surveyed the empty landscape that stretched far beyond us in all directions. According to the map, we were miles from the last town and yet more miles until the next. As we waited for anyone to come along and go for help, we could only be grateful that it had happened where it did and not in the debilitating cold of the mountains. On this day at least, the land was clear of snow and an evasive sun, largely hidden behind scudding clouds, was providing a tinge of warmth.

A van appeared not long after, going back towards where we had just come and we had to wave him on.

Minutes later, as we were commiserating about our bad luck, a lorry appeared over the horizon going our way. Hailing him to a stop and without a word of Turkish between us, we managed to get him to understand what had happened and persuade him to tow us to Yozgat, the next town of any significance.

The driver and the six Turks accompanying him took five minutes for a consultation before confronting us.

In very broken English, the driver indicated that they would load the van onto the back of the lorry and take us to a garage. The sting followed. For two hundred and fifty liras or just over six pounds sterling.

Masood and Latif knew that there would then follow the repair costs, extra nights at an hotel and everything else besides, but there was no choice.

For myself, I had already spent more during this lift than if I had joined Gary and caught the train, whereby I would already be in Istanbul and possibly beyond. But my choices were now limited and I had to see this through.

Nevertheless, Latif tried the old "Turkey, Pakistan, brother" thing, linking his fingers in solidarity, but to no effect. Reluctantly, he handed over the money and the men set to work.

The lorry was backed up against a convenient grassy bank and the back flap lowered to form a ramp. We then had to push the van off the road into a muddy field and, with all the manpower available, rock and push it up onto the back of the lorry.

The back flap was locked shut, handbrake on and rocks put under the wheels. The three of us then had to squeeze through the partially opened door space into the van for the duration of the journey as those men, who couldn't fit in the lorry cab, stood beside us peering through the windows as if we were rare animals in a cage.

An hour later, the lorry was driving down an unmade road on the outskirts of Yozgat, where the driver stopped within a huddle of brick built houses, a restaurant and motor workshops all linked by an unpleasant sea of mud.

Two mechanics were brought over, climbing up onto the lorry and inspecting the engine before quoting five hundred liras, cheap by English standards. But, it was expensive enough for Masood and Latif, who ultimately got them to agree on three hundred and fifty.

It seems the cam belt had gone, rendering the engine useless for now until spare parts could be brought from Ankara, a two and a half hour drive away.

The two brothers discussed the situation resulting in Masood, who knew more about mechanics, opting to go, leaving me to contend with Latif.

It was still only early afternoon and Masood wouldn't be leaving until the bus departed for Ankara in the evening, giving us time to eat and for me to settle to my book in the inconceivably clean restaurant with its shiny plate glass windows, formica topped tables and soft red vinyl seats.

I was turfed out at closing time at seven, wandering back to the van now ensconced just outside the garage workshop. There, in the dim overhead light, I found Latif sat at the small pull-out table inside the van, a middle aged Turk opposite him, looking with anticipation at the newly opened bottle of vodka between them. It had been agreed that I would be sleeping across the front seat but, despite being very tired, I had no idea how much sleep I might get with Latif holding forth in the back for much of the night without Masood's restraining hand.

I had to get away from the two men, their energy troubled me and, much as I tried to be tolerant and not let Latif's behaviour affect me, something deep inside made me feel disquiet in his presence.

Remembering I had seen a restaurant on the road into the town, I walked out into the night along the empty road, killing two to three hours eating a full meal and drinking chai until I thought it might be prudent to return.

I was glad to find that the "party" was winding up, Masood had not yet left and was settling his brother down to sleep before catching the bus at ten.

Grateful for Latif's unusually calm disposition, I rolled my things out on the front seat and settled for the night, my legs bent due to the lack of stretch room, but sleep overcame discomfort.

The cold night air crept into the cabin in the early hours, affecting my bladder and causing me to creep outside no less than four times while Latif continued to snore throughout.

As first light broke around seven, with a few wispy clouds concealing the sun, I knew I wouldn't be sleeping anymore and decided to move across to the restaurant, where I made my base for the day, reading, writing, drinking chai and snacking on bean soup, bread and rice pudding.

Occasionally, I would be interrupted by one of the staff or a curious customer or two coming over to take a look at my map, dumfounded by the idea that I had travelled all this way since leaving India.

Looking up between my thoughts at around mid-day, I caught sight of Latif precariously picking his way across the muddy street, immaculately dressed in a dark suit, white shirt and matching striped tie and handkerchief poking out of his top pocket.

His shiny shoes now looked a little worse for the mud but, against the shabbily dressed Turks around me in the restaurant and those making their way along the street, hunched shoulders and caps pulled down over their ears, he was a picture of foolishness.

'I'm off to see the town,' he told me as he poked his head around the door and dropped the van keys into my hand. Turning on his heels, he bounced off down the street, doubtless to show that the Pakistanis were now in town.

The rest of the day passed quickly and, by seven, I was dropping off over my book and ready to return to the van, where I settled for a very early night.

There was no sign of Latif but, by nine, I was woken by a tap on the window. It was Masood, who had returned with the parts. The mechanics had removed the engine from the van the day before and were now completely dismantling it ready to rebuild it anew.

'They're telling me it should be ready by tomorrow afternoon,' Masood told me optimistically,

Latif was feeling worse for wear the next day with a cold, cough and sore throat, so I joined Masood on the back of a truck going into town. He was getting medicine and I was heading for the

Hamami, Turkish bath.

A young boy with shaven head and a thin jacket over his shirt led me to the brick building with its narrow arched windows and overhanging roof, where I felt an immediate change in temperature from the icy air outside.

I was charged 1.75 Turkish Lira about one shilling and threepence in English money, a bargain I thought in view of how much dirt needed to come off.

An elderly attendant, thin and muscular with close cropped grey hair and a large protrusive nose that cast his mouth into shadow, led me downstairs to a changing room. I exchanged my clothes for a clean white cotton towel, hanging my things on one of the hooks attached to the wall, which immediately fell to the floor. Remaining positive, I kept my hopes high that there would actually be hot water, something I had been dreaming of since showering in Kabul.

I was not disappointed, as the door opened and I entered a large octagonal room, entirely veneered with marble, into which recesses had been built and a raised octagonal dias formed a focal point in the middle. In every other wall, a door led off into small rectangular ante-chambers, in which one could sit for a little more privacy. Small marble basins with hot and cold brass taps protruded from the walls, around which several men of all ages, shapes and sizes sat using small copper dishes to occasionally pour water over themselves.

In one of the side rooms, I sat for some minutes feeling the hot steam whirl around my body, bringing beads of perspiration to the surface until I reached for the hot tap and poured dishes of the welcome liquid over myself. It had been a long time. Even in India, I had only washed in cold water. As I began to wash more vigorously, the dirt fell away as if I had lost a second skin that appeared to render me some pounds lighter.

Time came to leave, facing the prospect of reuniting with the filthy *living* clothes I had been wearing for so many weeks.

Back at the garage, swift progress had been made, with the new parts having been fitted and the remainder of the engine being reconstructed around them.

By early evening, the work was still not complete as we sat by a wood-burner in the workshop, its flames occasionally being fed with drops of oil poured into the hole in the top. As the engine took shape from a number of assorted bits, I could not help but marvel how these mechanics, in the sticks of Turkey, were able to reconstruct a Volkswagen engine they had never worked on before.

Masood joined me in the restaurant for breakfast the next morning.

'They've started the engine. It sounds beautiful,' he gleefully told me. 'They've got to run it for a couple of hours to let it settle in, but we'll be going today after lunch and should be in Ankara tonight.'

This was the news I had been waiting for as this was now the eighth day since we had entered Turkey and my frustration at still being so far behind, where I might otherwise have been had I taken the train, was beginning to get to me.

'That's great news. We're on the move again. Thank God and Allah,' I said.

Masood smiled at my acknowledgement of the Prophet and returned to the garage, leaving me to continue with my writing.

As lunchtime approached, I looked up from my notebook and a sudden feeling of desolation and abandonment ran through my body. The van was moving up the muddy track and away down the road. I froze in my seat, overwhelmed by a thousand thoughts as I watched it slowly disappearing - without me!

Had I upset Latif so much that he had persuaded Masood to abandon me in this desolate place?

My reason told me that they couldn't possibly have gone without me, but my mind continued with its tricks, speculating on what might be.

A lump rose in my throat as I considered that they may have left me behind, taking all my things except the filthy clothes I was wearing, a pen, notebook and a map of the Middle East.

In the workshop, the mechanics indicated that they had merely gone up the road for more petrol and would be back. In a way, I felt foolish exposing my fears to these men, who had seen me over the last couple of days as part of the Pakistani *team*.

But, I still wasn't absolutely sure as terrible feelings of loss, failure, despair and even anger, welled within me accompanied by a few tears as I contemplated the very real possibility of getting out on the road and having to hitch from hereon.

As the veil of depression dropped further upon me, the familiar, but now much healthier, sound of the engine came into earshot and the van appeared rolling down the track towards the garage.

Concealing my elation borne from despair, my blood began to flow more readily and joyfully as they came to a stop. All seemed well between us as Masood opened the door and let me in.

'She's going like a dream,' he said. Even Latif was grinning as he sat behind the wheel, occasionally pressing his foot on the accelerator to let me hear the thunder in the engine.

The road to the capital was fast but monotonous with very few communities.

However, as darkness fell and we approached the outskirts of Ankara, the reality of city life was soon upon us. Signposts marked Ankara as being ten kilometres distant, while suburban houses and industrial units lined the road into the foreseeable distance and, as the sun disappeared, they were replaced by thousands of sparkling little lights on the city's hilltops.

Like torches they created a fairytale spectacle, which quickly disappeared as we drove deeper into the city and the source of the lights became all too apparent, emanating from tall apartment blocks and office buildings now rising all around us. Traffic lights flashed on the long road ahead as sleek American cars cruised past and the multicoloured fluorescent lights, emanating from the many shops and restaurants, cast distorted reflections on the gleaming chrome and enamel.

Girls walked arm in arm with their boyfriends, their maxi coats skimming the wide pavements that edged the dual carriageway running through the city centre. The flashing neon of BOAC, Pan Am, SAS and Lufthansa lit the sky, flashing promises of faraway places that might bring happiness and escape from the turmoil of the metropolis.

For me, they meant that sometime a plane would be leaving for London without me, arriving in only a matter of hours.

The distinctive profile of Ataturk, the father of modern Turkey, following the fall of the Ottoman Empire, flashed before us in a huge replica made from hundreds of light bulbs.

Policemen and soldiers mingled amongst the pressing evening crowd, while traffic poured in from every direction, brakes screeching, horns blaring and fists waving as errors of judgement and loss of patience prevailed.

With the centre behind us, we were soon on the road out of the city, stopping for loaves of crusty bread to accompany a spicy one pot wonder that Latif was to make on the small stove in the van.

By nine next morning, we were on the road again but, not towards Istanbul, as I had hoped, but back into Ankara. In a fracas at one of the Iranian borders, Latif had had some ink poured onto one of the pages in his passport with part of the page torn out. Now, as we were on the brink of entering Europe, he was worried that the passport might not be accepted, unless a new endorsement for entry into Iran was entered. After much driving about in search of the Iranian embassy, he was told that the endorsement would take several days to obtain.

By this time, I was totally pissed off with Latif and what I had thought would be the dream lift.

So keen was I to get to Istanbul that I told Latif the customs people probably wouldn't even notice or care, after all, notihng had been said at the Turkish border. This convinced him and by half eleven, we were speeding out on the road that skirted the Black Sea and would take us to Izmit on the Sea of Marmara.

A brief stop for an egg and coffee brunch and to wash the previous night's dishes in a freezing mountain stream tumbling through a craggy gorge and out through vast snow tipped pine forests. As Masood put the gears into neutral and we free wheeled down towards flatter terrain and small villages, the trees were still autumnal with the fluttering yellow leaves of tall poplars.

Dropping closer to sea level, a fog descended, limiting visibility and challenging Masood and Latif's driving skills to the point that, when darkness enveloped us, a halt was called on the day's journeying, as we pulled off the road and into the forecourt of a service station. Heavy rain had turned the dusty forecourt into a swamp and I resigned myself to another cramped night in the van.

I was glad to leave the cab next morning and seek refuge in the nearby café, where a few Turks had huddled around the wood-burner, eagerly checking the lottery numbers and quite oblivious to my arrival.

Masood had filled the van with petrol and I found him in the sales office where the attendant had apparently been slagging off Americans and British,

'This is our friend, Adam, he's German,' Masood said, as I walked in.

The attendant spoke no German and we were speaking in English anyway, until a friend of his came in.

'Ah, Omer. You speak German. This young man is German.'

'Du sprichst Deutche? Gut. Gut,' the man proffered.

'Jawohl,' I replied shyly and with a very un-German accent. Clearly exposing my true origin, I sidled out through the door.

The fog was still hanging over the countryside as we set out again with visibility only a slight improvement on the previous evening.

Passing through a small town just before Izmit, we had to slow down as a brick lorry had careered off the road. A crowd of poor peasant folk had gathered around a crumpled white sheet that partially covered the body of a young child. As we slowly passed, it was possible to witness the shock and disbelief on distraught faces now just coming to terms with the sudden loss of one of their own.

The cemetery lay up the hill ahead of us, where the family and friends would be entering in a day or so, causing me to ponder what it had been in the child's karma that took its life so soon and in what form its spirit would be reborn.

By two o' clock we were driving into Izmit and the sparkling sea beyond.

While Latif and Masood went for a Turkish bath, I stayed in the van watching people go by, noticing those with blue eyes, possible descendants of Alexander and other European invaders, who now confirmed just how close we were to the European frontier.

The last hundred miles along the coast road leading to Istanbul, became increasingly more built up and industrialised. Rows of dreary grey suburban houses with red or grey roofs, smoke belching factories and, in the weak winter sunshine, the aluminium pipes, and cylinders of oil refineries and storage tanks glistened as, from occasional chimneys, a flame of burning gas would colour the grey misty sky.

Rain began to smatter on the windscreen as the road widened to dual-carriageway, undulating in a straight line over the low hills leading to the city.

Rising from the last few ploughed fields that intermittently reminded us of the natural world, huge hoardings advertised everything from cars to breakfast cereals, distractions from our real mission on earth to realise our true selves.

As the rain beat down harder, sending relentless shots of water back up off the road, a line of runners passed down the central reservation in shorts and vests.

But, Istanbul was upon us as we followed the signs down narrow winding streets that led to the car ferry. An assortment of quite different traditional buildings in Ottoman style lined our route as people hurried along the wet pavements to escape the rain. The east seemed to be well and truly behind us as pedestrians scurried under coloured umbrellas, dressed in hats and macintoshes, just as most others would in a European country.

At the dock, queues of cars and lorries lined up before the waiting ferries, the distant shore with its mosques and minarets was almost lost in the mist hanging over the Bosporus. A balloon man in little more than rain soaked trousers and jacket, plied his wares at every open driver's window with little result. With tickets in hand, Masood drove the van up the ramp onto our ferry, being guided to the front where we would be amongst the first off on the European shore.

As the boat chugged away into the murky light, the land I had known for eight months as Asia was itself being lost in the evening gloom and diffused lights on the shore.

Masood and Latif, now bathed and dressed in clean shirts and suits, had earlier given me the impression that they would be visiting relatives in the city, but I felt sure that they would not want me and neither would I want to be with them in my filthy and highly offensive ragged clothes hanging from my thin and very tired frame. I felt and probably looked like a tramp and was beginning to worry where I might be spending the night.

Driving off the ferry, circling around numerous crowded backstreets that rose exponentially up from the shore, the rain had started again and night had fallen.

In the highly westernised sector, distorted coloured lights from elegant shop windows, hotels and bars were being reflected on the wet paving stones and tarmac.

After about ten minutes, it soon became apparent that the boys were not going to their relatives, but instead looking for somewhere to park for the night. Turning my mind back eight months, I took stock of our present surroundings and six or seven minutes later, had directed us to Sultan Ahmed Square and the Blue Mosque.

Parking in the square, I led them to the Pudding Shop, still fresh in my memory after all this time. Here, coffee, Turkish pastries and contemporary music continued to be offered to travellers making their ways back and forth to the east.

Here too, I was reminded of the last time I saw two English travellers who had fallen into a honey trap with Galina, a beautiful Russian woman, seducing them into buying a quantity of hashish before double crossing them on the night I was leaving for the east. I had no knowledge whether or not they were still in jail, although I knew too well of Galina's fate; tied to a lamp post and shot in Kabul.

To the crashing cymbals and Simon and Garfunkel's harmony on *The Boxer*, we walked out across the square to the Sultan Ahmed hotel, a cheap hostel where I had stayed on the way out. While Masood and Latif booked into a room, I retained my quarters in the van for the night, but not before another incident centred around Latif's drunkeness.

We joined a young English couple with their seven year old daughter and a German couple for dinner in a nearby restaurant. The evening progressed with wine being passed around the table, while Latif got stuck into his bottle of vodka. Our guests were all on their way east and curious to know as much as possible about my experiences.

'Of course, I've come this far through the worst of the winter and from the Turkish border to here thanks to Masood and Latif,' I told them. 'It was very different in the summer. Many more going east at the same time and it was the hottest time of the year. Did I perhaps get my timing wrong?' I quipped.

I told them of the train across Turkey, to take care when trying to enter the mosque in Mashaad, not to be lured into buying turquoise there, of the buses across the desert in Afghanistan, the

Buddhas of Bamiyan and so much more about India itself.'

As the evening wore on, Dieter, the somewhat overweight, but jovial German, turned to Latif, who was sitting next to him and already slurring what words he was contributing to the conversation.

'And you, Latif, are you a Hindu or a Moslem?

It took a few moments for the question to fully sink in to Latif's adled brain, before he turned on the poor man, grabbing him aggressively by the throat.

'You called me a Hindu! A filthy cow licking Hindu! How dare you call me that!' he shouted, his face contorted with anger. Squeezing the startled and bewildered German even tighter to the point that his eyes began to bulge and he choked out the food still in his mouth.

'I am a Moslem and you call me a Hindu. You dare to call me that!' he continued, raising his fist as if about to hit the German in the face.

It was clear that Latif was well out of control, causing Masood and myself to lunge forward just in time to restrain him. Latif mustered all the strength he still had to break free and lunge forward towards the German, picking up a knife off his plate on the way. The women screamed at what might transpire until we once again pulled him back to his seat.

'Are you totally mad, Latif?' I shouted. 'Can't you see how futile and hurtful your prejudice is. You're no better than anyone else. Hindu, Moslem, Christian, Jew, whatever.'

David, the Englishman looked harshly at the now partially subdued Pakistani.

'His father,' he said, pointing at the German, 'could have killed mine during the war, as mine could have killed his, but does that mean that I should now take this man and kill him. We accept each other for what we are and not by what our predecessors did in the past. You're full of false pride man and that's your weakness. Learn to live peacefully with all people.'

But the Pakistani merely shrugged at the words being offered him. Words of love and reconciliation had no place for him as he merely scraped his chair back and stormed out into the street. We all watched in astonishment as we saw him pacing up and down the road, his hand occasionally lifting to his brow as if seriously contemplating what he had just heard. Then, just as suddenly as he had left, he turned on his heels and returned to his seat at the table. A silence hung over him as he bowed his head in one hand and he started to shudder and sob.

'I'm so sorry,' he eventually said as he lifted his head, tears running down his cheeks, and stretched out his hand to the German. 'Please forgive me.'

Dieter rose from his seat and strode towards Latif and, as the Pakistani stood up, the German wrapped his arms around him.

'I forgive you,' he said.

There was the usual time wasting next morning as Latif recovered from the scene he had created the evening before. He wanted to sell a diamond and asked me to guide him into the bazaar. My memory of the whole place was sketchy and certainly did not extend to diamond merchants, but I took Masood and Latif nevertheless, knowing it might possibly be my last opportunity to visit for some time.

The main hall of the Grand Bazaar was probably everything that Latif could dream of. The bling capital of the world hosted countless stalls beneath the ancient stone arches and colonnades.

Here could be found every conceivable piece of tourist tat, where neon tubes cast a vulgar light on unreal looking gold jewellery and faux gem stones - necklaces, bangles, brooches and much more.

Latif was like a kid in a sweet shop and couldn't resist handling the false idols that lay before him, running them through his hands like erotic fetish toys.

No one would buy his diamond, but he left the Bazaar with a bag full of worthless junk.

It rained heavily that afternoon, most of which was spent eating cakes and drinking chai in the Pudding Shop, where I was pleased to find the young Turk who had sold me my false student card.

'Hello again, my friend. You are back then?'

'Yes, on my way to England now.'

How was the card for you?'

'Brilliant! I saved so much money, particularly on the Indian railways. No one even questioned it. It was perfect. How are things with you?'

'I've had a good year. Lots of people coming through here and soon I'm about to get married. My final call-up papers for the army come through shortly, so we're planning to leave Turkey and go to Germany. They're looking for workers and the money is good. We can make a new life for our children.'

I was pleased for him as I could imagine the fake student card business would not last for ever, but glad that I had been able to benefit from having had one.

Latif had clearly learnt nothing from the previous evening and was suitably equipped with a new bottle when I knocked on the Pakistanis' door later that evening. A young Turk had joined them and ensconsed himself in the only chair, playing exquisite Turkish folk music on his guitar, not too different to the bouzouki music I had so often heard in the Greek islands earlier in the year.

William and Ronnie, an American couple, had come in from the next room but, on hearing that I was on my way home from India, were more interested in gleaning as much information from me as they could before they started their own journey east the next day. It seemed like only the day before that I had been in the same position. Excited, but a little nervous of what I was embarking on, happy to talk with anyone who could give me some insights into what lay ahead.

As the hours ticked by, the level of vodka in the bottle steadily dropped until Latif decided he wanted to go for a walk. The rest of us were happy to stay and listen to the musician and talk of our motives for this journey and what would lie at the end of it all.

For myself, I had reached a destination of sorts and satisfied some of the questions I had been asking before I set out. But, I realised that my journey was by no means over and would not be, even when I reached the shores of England. There were pieces to pick up and new avenues to explore. Ultimately, I suspected that, despite the insights into my true being and the training I had received, there was more that needed to be revealed or perhaps just confirmed more substantially.

The Americans had rolled a couple of joints and we were nicely stoned, when we heard shouting in the street below, drawing us to the balcony to look down.

Latif was confronting two Turks, swinging his arms at them and shouting.

'Moslems are the bravest men on Earth,' he shouted, before tripping on a cobble stone and falling over. The Turks just laughed at his foolery, giving him another opportunity to stand up and repeat his boasts.

It was not long, before our drunken friend, rose once more to his feet and fled into the hotel, not wasting any time to climb the stairs and burst through the door.

He was clearly terrified and as white as any Pakistani can look as he stood before us breathless and sweating. 'They're after me. They've got a knife. Quick, call the police and the embassy,' he shouted, panic exuding from every pore of his body.

Having seen what had actually happened, we could only humour him.

'The telephone here is out of order,' William said, ' I tried to use it earlier and had to go to a shop up the road.'

As none of us were prepared to succumb to Latif's paranoia, we left him to sit shaking on the bed, terrified of an imaginary enemy.

The party began to break up and I descended to the street to spend another night in the van, leaving without wishing Latif a goodnight, such was my continuing disgust at his ongoing behaviour. The streets were wet and empty, save for a few taxis, their tyres making a swishing sound against the road. No threatening men with knives were anywhere to be seen.

I sensed my time with my Pakistani friends was nearing its natural end.

The next day, Latif was angry and deeply offended by my not having wished him a good night.

'Everyone was offended by your behaviour,' I told him, not at all concerned that I was doubtless jeopardising my lift. Nevertheless, once again, he dug deep to find some remorse, until the next time, shaking my hand in the process.

Meanwhile, sitting on Latif's unmade bed, a girl in her late teens, scrawny, barefoot save for a pair of much repaired sandals, but pretty with her shoulder length chestnut hair, blue eyes and full lips.

'This is Scarlett,' Masood said, 'she's going to join us tomorrow.'

I was little taken aback but, seeing Latif's leering eyes, knew full-well why she had been so willingly taken on board.

'Hi,' I proffered. 'Where have you travelled from?'

'New Zealand,' she replied with a very pronounced *down-under* accent.

'How long have you been without proper shoes?' I asked looking at her grimed and blistered feet.

'A long way. Since India probably. I've been kind of attached to these sandals since I left home. I haven't really thought of replacing them.'

We must find something for you then. It's been bad so far in Turkey, but we all have Europe ahead of us and it's still only January. I'm going to the bazaar again this afternoon, we can find something there.'

Like me, when I had set out, she had very few warm clothes to her name, save for her jeans, a jumper and a pair of knitted gloves with holes in the fingertips. All the travellers going both ways at this time were in need of whatever warm clothes they had, so our only option was to search the bazaar.

'Where are you heading?' I asked as we passed into the Grand Hall.

'Oh, I've got an aunt in England near Canterbury, so I'm going to stay with her for a while an' look for work. I'd like to stay, but we'll see.'

As before, the Grand Hall offered very little other than bling and a multitude of leather goods and carpets, so I led her into the old bazaar where, in the narrow cobbled alleyways, the many deformed, blind and abandoned members of society eked out a living.

Little had changed since I had first passed this way earlier in the summer, following my English acquaintance to a rendezvous in a dark and dismal building to do a hashish deal. Within twenty-four hours, he and his English friend had been arrested, betrayed by the beautiful but wily Galina, making my return to these bedevilled streets not one of fond memories.

As Scarlett and I wandered past workshops where the all pervading cacophony of the metal beaters dominated the area, woodworkers planed planks of wood, standing ankle deep in shavings and we were met with the persistent calls to buy hashish, carpets and dubiously hygienic food and drinks.

Turning a corner, we found ourselves in a street heaving with textiles and leather, where Scarlett instantly fell in love with a woven shawl, which she immediately wrapped around her frail body.

'How much?' I asked the surprised vendor, perched on a raised platform above the cobbles. Leaving his cigarette dangling from his lips, he raised five grubby nicotine stained fingers.

I returned the gesture with two fingers, displayed the way Churchill would have done.

He replied with three.

'Are you sure you want it?' I asked Scarlett.

'Mmmm. It's so warm,' she said, her smile almost reaching her twinkling eyes.

'It won't keep you dry,' I ventured.

'I've got a plastic sheet in my rucksack.'

'You've done well to hang on to that. Mine went missing a long time ago,' I said.

I gave the man the money and noticed a pair of socks on his stall, offering another lira from my pocket.

'Now, we've just got to find you shoes,' I said, handing her the socks.

We had to pass along another couple of streets before anything vaguely suitable became apparent, when Scarlett picked out a pair of second-hand fur-lined boots under a pile of other used shoes.

'These'll do,' she said, a broad smile across her face as she looked inside to confirm they were her size. 'I can pay for these. You've spent too much. I've just about got enough to get me to England.'

She washed her feet in a nearby trough, drying them on her shawl before putting on her new socks and boots.

'Wow, you're quite the lady about town now,' I said, as she gave me a twirl.

As we left the bazaar for the busy streets once more, I realised that from this point on, there would be no more bazaars, bargaining and beggars. These would be left far behind as I moved deeper into Europe with its cities, industry and spiritually empty cultures. *Would I ever return to this tragic, magic part of the globe?*

CHAPTER
Nineteen

I SHARED THE van with Scarlett for the last night in Istanbul, she on the pull-out bed at the back and myself on the front seat again.

We had talked into the night, she telling me of her arduous journey from India, travelling at times by herself and occasionally with others, highlighting the harrowing train journey she had had across Turkey, stuffed into a compartment with five Turks, who would take turns to touch her every time the lights went out, as they frequently did.

'I was spared that this time, although I've now been with Masood and Latif for the last twelve days and that's been something of an ordeal,' I told her. 'What with the breakdown in the middle of nowhere and Latif's drinking every night, I've just about had enough. I would think twice about staying with them after we reach Greece. But, you might be lucky and could get all the way to Frankfurt in three or four days.'

Streams of condensation ran down the windows when we woke next morning with everything being cold and damp. When we finally hit the road around lunchtime and headed west towards the Greek border, Scarlett was firmly ensconced between Masood and Latif in the front, while I was relegated to the seat in the back.

It was not that I minded as I finally had room to spread out and better see the passing countryside, but it made clear exactly where Latif's intentions lay.

Four hours passed before we reached the river crossing at Ipsala that marked not only the border between Turkey and Greece, but also our arrival in Europe.

Passports were duly inspected in the small border posts on each side and a small amount of lira bought enough drachmas for food.

Little, other than their uniforms, distinguished the Turks from the Greeks with their swarthy complexions, deep set eyes and black bushy moustaches.

As we travelled deeper into the country, eventually arriving at Komitini, a half way point on our journey, several Moslem calling towers rose into the evening sky, reminding me that so much of this part of Europe and beyond to the gates of Vienna had once been Moslem occupied.

Komitini had no less than nine mosques, built over time since the fourteenth century and now used by the still substantial but much maligned Moslem population.

Pretty street lights gave a friendly glow to the main square as we arrived, dominated by the impressive nineteenth century Turkish clock tower and the slim rocket like minaret adjacent to the nearby mosque. It was time for dinner and once again the delights of a Greek menu, discovered by a tour of the kitchen and inspection of the large cooking pots.

Scarlett looked happier than I had seen her so far as we sat down to a convivial meal in the sanctuary of the warm restaurant below the hotel where Masood and Latif had booked a room. The hearty owner welcomed us, personally bringing a succession of fabulous Greek dishes, demonstrating in the process that his fulfilment was clearly derived from the pleasure his food brought to others.

All went well until Latif's glass was repeatedly emptied and he reverted to the debauched Neanderthal that he so often became.

On this occasion, he had Scarlett to focus his attention on, heightening his licentious inclinations and, as the evening wore on, I could see him inspecting her as if she was some prize cow he had just bought.

Seeing her as one of his possessions, with which he could do what he wanted, he eventually left his seat and shuffled across to the other side of the table, drink in hand, Drawing up a chair beside her, he wrapped one arm around her and messily kissed her on the cheek, his fat, rubbery lips spreading out across her delicate skin.

Scarlett reeled in horror, pushing him away. 'Get off me!'

'But, I love you,' he said, surprised at the rejection.

'Latif, stop!' I shouted, 'You can't behave like this. Scarlett is your guest. You should be ashamed of yourself.'

Latif slumped back in the chair and immediately started crying. I helped Scarlett to her feet and paid for the meal.

'It's time for bed, ' I said. 'May we have the keys?' I asked Masood.

'Latif has them,' he replied.

'Latif, can we please have the keys?' I said, asking what looked like an impossible question to a man on the cusp of violent assault and childish histrionics.

'The keys please, Latif. Scarlett and I are tired.'

The slob just continued to slump in his chair, smugly grinning as if to emphasise what little power he had over us.

'Give them the keys, Latif,' Masood intervened.

He knew he was now outnumbered and as the grin left his face, it was replaced by resentment and anger. Kicking back the table, he knocked over the remains of our wine bottle, showing himself as the spoilt brat he was. Rising slowly to his feet, he attempted to reach into his trouser pockets, his hands missing the openings each time, until, Masood stepped forward, taking his brother by the arm and fumbled for the keys himself. Pulling them out, he passed them over to me. 'Sleep well,' he said, as he helped his brother upstairs to their room.

Scarlett was visibly shaking as we left the restaurant and crossed the square to the van.

'That's it. I'm off. I'm not putting up with it any more,' I said. 'I don't know about you, Scarlett, but when we reach Thessaloniki tomorrow, I'm going it alone. You're welcome to join me, if you wish, but that slob has gone too far tonight.'

'I half expected it,' she said, 'but never thought Latif would behave like that. You did warn me though. I'd like to come with you, if that's ok.'

We settled down to sleep in the cold, damp van, with Scarlett in the back and myself on the front seat again, until we heard shuffling outside and the side door was suddenly pulled back. Scarlett gave out a scream and I looked up over the top of the seats. It was Latif, looking in through the open door.

'What do you want, Latif?' I shouted.

'I came to see you two together.'

'Well' I'm sorry to have disappointed you. Now, go back to bed!'

He slid the door shut and we heard him shuffling off, unable to fathom the extent of his jealousy and what thoughts must have been churning inside his mind.

We sat in relative silence next morning as we covered the last two hundred odd miles to Thessaloniki, this time with Scarlett sitting with me in the back.

On the way out, much of the journey from Thessaloniki had been in darkness, but now I could take in the precarious hairpin bends that gave rise to wide vistas of open fields and tiny villages that stretched far away to the distant Adriatic sea, where mythological heroics had been acted out in another age.

Then we were upon the coastal strip where the deep blue sea broke in small waves upon long stretches of an undulating dune backed shoreline and fishing shacks nestled as they had for centuries amongst the tufted windblown grass.

Beyond lay Mount Athos and the sacred peninsular that remained a sanctuary for Christian monks, before skirting the deep and vast Lake Volvi, edged by woodlands, fields and a deep red landscape.

The atmosphere in the van had become heavy with resentment with Scarlett and I only too pleased to see the outer approaches of the city, where I finally broached the subject of our departure.

'Masood and Latif, I think you must know what I'm going to say. We have been together for two weeks now and I really do appreciate you stopping for me. We've had some adventures together but, I believe, for reasons you must surely understand, this must now be the parting of the ways. Latif, your behaviour towards Scarlett last night was totally unacceptable.

Virtually every night on this journey, you have lost control of your faculties and your manners and you don't seem to be making any effort to take hold of the demons that are possessing you.

Life has so much more to offer than glittering prizes and the need to so excessively subject your body and mind to the distractions of alcohol. I can only point out what a destructive path you are now on. What fork in the road you take from hereon is up to you. We are both grateful for the lift and we wish you both every success on the rest of your travels.'

There was a moment's silence, before Masood responded.

'Thank you, Adam. It's been fun and I do understand why you would want to leave, but won't you reconsider?'

'No. We've talked it over and think it best that we go our separate ways. Do you have an apology for Scarlett, Latif?'

He sat silently with his eyes fixed on the road, unable to swallow his immense pride.

'If you can drop us at the station, that would be great. Thank you.'

Signs for the central station began to appear as we approached the city centre with Latif weaving from one lane to another as he searched for our destination.

From the large car park, the station stood before us, its rectilinear modernist edifice barely ten years old..

Taking our bags, we all stood together outside the van, none of us knowing quite what the protocol for farewell was under such circumstances. In the end, I stepped forward and put my arms around Masood.

'Thank you, Masood, for all your kindness and be careful with that dope.'

Then, with a slight hesitation, I turned to Latif, placing my arms around him too.

'Thank you Latif. I'm sorry it had to end like this. I wish you all the very best for the rest of your life.'

He smiled, a little shamefaced as tears welled above his podgy pockmarked cheeks.

'Thank you too, Adam, for being so honest with me. I know what I have to do.'

Scarlett hugged Masood and gave a timid wave to Latif as we turned and walked into the station precinct.

This was the first railway station I'd been in since Lahore and wondered if perhaps Scarlett and I could sleep in the waiting room. Despite its modernity, traditional benches were still available that we could stretch out on for at least a few hours.

'Last time I was here, I sold blood,' I told Scarlett. 'We've still got time today to go to the hospital and try. I just need a bit more money to get me home and four hundred drachs, that's just over four pounds and ten shillings, will make all the difference. Are you coming?'

'I'm not too keen on needles at the best of times,' she replied, 'but I'll come with you, just in case I change my mind.'

A forty minute bus journey took us along the city's shoreline, where well laid out parks and squares provided relaxation space and blissful shade from the sun, which on this day was not much more than 10 degrees Fahrenheit.

My blood was tested, but I was told to come back the next day after a good night's sleep and a good meal. It was evidently not good enough to take as my iron levels were too low, such had been the toll on my body from these many days of travelling. The story was the same for Scarlett.

We looked at each other, eyes wide, big smiles on our faces and, in unison, exclaimed, 'Foood!!'

With what little money we each had left, we returned to the station and a nearby restaurant, caring little for food ethics as we chose meat filled moussaka, lamb kebabs and lots of vegetables in an attempt to boost our haemoglobin levels and have our blood accepted the next day.

The station seats were sufficiently comfortable to enable us to get several hours sleep followed by scrambled eggs in the restaurant before catching the bus back to the hospital next morning.

As was the case before, blood would only be taken if a patient needed it and payment was made directly by the relatives. Scarlett didn't have to wait too long as a young man, who had lost a lot of blood in a street fight, was already waiting for a transfusion and her blood was a perfect match. Having met the parents and heard that he had survived, she was paid her money.

'I think I'll go back to the station Adam,' she said, as she stuffed the notes into her pouch. 'I'll see you there,' She kissed me on the cheek, turned and disappeared down the corridor.

I had to wait another three hours before I heard that a woman had been rushed in following a road accident and may have to have her leg amputated. The surgeons wanted to be sure they had enough blood in case there was too much bleeding.

Whilst I waited to be paid by the relatives, I was relieved to hear that she had survived, her leg intact.

It was already early afternoon by the time I got back to the station, where Scarlett was nowhere to be seen. I searched in all the waiting rooms, the restaurant and all the platforms, in particular the one from where the trains north to Europe departed. She was nowhere to be seen. I felt forlorn, having travelled with her for a couple of days already and begun getting to know her. I had thought we would be hitching north together and perhaps, selfishly, thinking in the back of my mind that having a female companion might make people more inclined to stop. But, she had gone.

The train fare was more than I was prepared to spend, perhaps putting me at risk of being short of food again, so I caught a bus to the outskirts, where I waited on the main road for Yugoslavia.

Twenty

A s I STOOD WAITING, I wondered if Masood and Latif had already journeyed this way and perhaps even Scarlett. Would I perhaps by chance see them again as I passed through some European town or city?

As a cold wind from the north blew down along the road, a car drew up alongside me. In a German accent, but in good English, a man shouted out through the passenger window, 'Where are you going?'

'Back to England. How far can you take me?'

'I'm going to Bonn. Get in.'

Putting my things on the back seat, I joined him in the front. Unlike the Volkswagen van, his Mercedes was both warm and comfortable and Hans, my new host, was friendly and full of conversation.

A man in his early forties, he wanted to know about my travels, where I had been, who I had met and something of my adventures over the previous few months.

'Travelling like this was not possible for me,' he said. 'I was growing up in the thirties when Hitler was rising to power. Life was not easy. Everything had been so expensive and he did at least put a stop to all that, but then the war came. Of course, I knew nothing of what was happening with the Jews and gypsies. The camps and …'

He stopped momentarily as he gathered his thoughts.

'Most of us knew nothing about what the Nazis were doing until it was all over. Towards the end, I had been conscripted into the

Hitler youth, but it was hopeless as the Russians and Americans drew closer on both sides. Of course, when it was all over, we had to rebuild what had become a divided country. Even now, I cry every time I see someone trying to escape to the West and being shot by the GDR guards. If they're caught, they are tortured. I have never understood communism. Where is the equality of status and opportunity in a society that oppresses and tortures its citizens?

But then, in the West, we are debt slaves to the elite minority. We go to school, university, marriage, children, career, a semblance of retirement, then death, all under the umbrella of being forever in debt. Of course, the joke is, we do all this under an illusion of freedom?'

The miles passed through a landscape of mountains and cultivated valley floors in a country ruled by Tito, another communist dictator. To the untrained eye, the country and its people seemed like anywhere else, where poorly dressed men and women, still mostly dependent on horse drawn carts and ploughs in the most remote parts, eked out a living.

But this poverty was compensated for by the rich choice of food in those restaurants we stopped to eat in. The Ottoman occupation over three centuries had left a strong legacy of dishes. Cabbage stuffed with minced pork, sauerkraut and rice regularly appeared on the menu, as did many platters containing goats' cheese, peppers, chillis and eggs, but my favourite was the filling Prebanac, made from beans and onions baked in the oven. With the *blood* money I had received in Thessaloniki, I was able to pay my way, but Hans was more than generous most of the time.

As the first day drew to a close, Hans stopped the car in a small town, where we were able to eat and then catch a few hours sleep in the car, before setting off next day in the early hours. The air was already cold and the snow beginning to appear once more as we drew closer to the mountains that heralded the Austrian border.

By early evening, we had crossed the frontier where passport inspections seemed to be of little importance compared with the need to clear the roads of the ever encroaching snow. The onion topped churches and wood framed houses with their wide, overhanging roofs, now covered by a good helping of snow, had become scenes akin to the most archetypical Christmas cards.

Despite the slower pace brought on by the snow, Hans pushed on to Klagenfurt, where he drew in at an hotel, beckoning me in to join him. Here, he booked a double room for us to share for the night.

'It is too cold for the car tonight,' he said. 'and besides I am very, very tired.'

It was an unprecedented arrangement for me, sharing what turned out to be a double bed with a man I hardly knew, but I was only too glad of a hot shower and to slip under pristine white sheets for a night where any sort of encounter was peripheral to my need for sleep.

I knew that next morning the rest of the journey could only be another two or three days at the most, so prising on those dirt engrained clothes once more did not seem to be such an imposition.

By lunch, we had passed through Salzburg, crossed into Germany and had arrived in Munich. Some Munich sausage and sauerkraut and we were speeding up the Autobahn to Nuremberg, Frankfurt and, by early evening, with rain in the air, passing into the suburbs of Bonn.

'My home is in a small village on the other side of the city,' Hans told me, 'but I will drop you on the road to Cologne, where you can easily get a lift on to Brussels and England.'

It was raining heavily by the time he had dropped me and I was aware all too quickly of my unpreparedness for such weather. I had my Afghan coat, which offered some protection and a woollen balaclava which I wore as a simple hat pulled over my ears, but the rain was beyond wet, it was freezing. Heavy traffic sped by in both directions, front and rear lights reflected in the spray, reminding me how I had started my journey at the beginning of April the previous year, trying to get a lift in similar conditions in Northern France and wondering if I was completely mad.

By the time a lorry stopped, I was well saturated and, in the warmth of the cab, both my driver and myself screwed our faces with wry smiles as we both acknowledged the smell emanating from my coat.

He was indeed brave to take me as far as Aachen on the Belgian border, where I snatched a few hours sleep in a bus shelter.

Long before dawn had broken, I was on the road again, walking out towards the border post. The rain had lifted, but a mist hung over the road as the first car to stop belonged to the local police, asking where I was going whilst inspecting my passport.

'You have been to India, I see,' one of the officers observed, 'and now you are coming back home, yah?'

It crossed my mind that a mere twenty-seven years earlier, had I been stopped in the same place, I would have been arrested and interned as a prisoner of war or even a spy. How things had changed and I was thankful for the freedom that I now had to roam comparatively freely without too much hindrance.

As they drove off and I walked nonchalantly with my thumb out to the traffic, a Land Rover drew up with a right hand drive. My first thoughts were of Jen and Liam, whom I had waved goodbye to in Bombay, but a second look revealed a man a little older than myself. Winding the window down, he yelled, 'Going to England, mate?'

'Too right, I am,' I replied.

'Hop in. I'm going to London. Is that okay for you?'

'That's perfect. Thanks. I'm Adam,' I said, stretching across to shake his hand.

'Pleased to meet you, Adam. I'm Roger. Looks like you've come a long way.'

'Yes, India. It's been a long way and a long story.' Thus, the conversation was set for much of the journey.

On the dashboard, lay a collection of the new music cassettes that were beginning to replace vinyl records, among them, the Beatles', *Revolver*. It was odd to see the familiar black and white cover artwork condensed from a substantial twelve inch square to a dismally small square set within the rectangular cover that the plastic box dictated.

'I haven't heard this for a while,' I said.

Roger, removed the cassette from the box and slid it into the player and soon we were immersed in *Taxman* and *Eleanor Rigby*, the latter bringing back memories of the empty English church and the overgrown gravestones, lost in the woods of McLeod Ganj, where I had waved farewell to Kamala.

This was the first time I had thought of her for days. So much had happened since we had agreed to part and yet her beautiful, compassionate smile was etched into my memory as clear as if she was sitting in that jeep beside me.

By the time the last *seagull* strains of *Tomorrow Never Knows* had faded, we were approaching Maastricht and only hours from the Channel.

The flat landscape of Belgium and Northern France was as desolate as when I had last passed through it. The empty villages that straddled the road, the lines of skeletal poplar trees and the clusters of white crosses enclosed in walled enclosures, while the ploughed fields beyond disappeared into the winter mist.

The road to the port in Calais remained a desolate reminder of the destruction inflicted on the town by the war and gave us no cause to linger before boarding the ferry. As Roger's passenger, I was able to board without any further payment, finding myself relieved in some way to be finally on a British ship with a British crew, speaking in my own tongue.

As the ship pulled out of its berth into open sea, I stepped out on deck to watch the continental shoreline disappear, taking with it the hundreds of people I had encountered over the previous nine months, wondering what lay in store for them in the years ahead, while even now beginning to focus on my own future and the prospect of seeing Belinda within a few days.

END OF

Part One

Part Two

CHAPTER

Twenty-one

ROGER DROPPED ME at Piccadilly Circus in the early hours, leaving me to wait for the tube to open at five o' clock.

Although tired, I was fired up about seeing my family again and whiled away the time wandering around familiar haunts.

Eros, the ever youthful mythical god of Love, still stood on his fountain aiming his bow at those who passed before him, bestowing Love upon whoever received an arrow. Perhaps it was fitting that I should be spending time in his company, remembering the *Summer of Love* of 1967 and my first meeting with Belinda that had been at the heart of my whole adventure.

I had not heard from Belinda for months now and could only imagine how I would feel when very soon she would be opening her door to me again.

There were very few passengers on the first train out on the Piccadilly Line to Hounslow West. As I watched the solemn figures coming and going along the journey, belted and braced for a lifetime of compliance to a system that cared little for them, other than as cogs in a ruthless economic machine, I felt somehow I did not belong. I began to question the purpose of my return.

Yes, I wanted to reacquaint myself with Belinda but, beyond that, I had no idea what I would be doing in this society of manners and defined traditions. I had no qualifications to speak of and no inclination to obtain any. The prospect of years in college to become *something* was beyond my comprehension.

Once again, I drifted back to the hills above the Punjab, where a simple, uncomplicated life with Kamala might still be possible.

But, what of money?

As the train came out into the open, I wondered if the grime of Gloucester Road, Earl's Court and Hammersmith was any different to that of Delhi and Bombay. There, the poverty was out in the open within the great slums, whereas my own experience of bleak bedsits in the many Victorian tenements that backed onto the railway, told me that fundamentally things were not much different.

Passing out through Stamford Brook and Turnham Green, I was then reminded of the endless roads of Victorian terraces and 1920s identikit semi-detached houses with their neat gardens and lifetime mortgages. An occasional park with a football pitch, swings and a roundabout, provided vent for people's frustrations. But, they were of little consolation for the cyclic lives of birth, education, work and death, punctuated by a few precious moments in the relentless drudge to the grave. Was it then surprising that violence was carried out behind closed doors?

The red 237 bus took me from Hounslow bus station to my parents' home some miles out by the River Thames, the Indian conductor dispensing tickets and authority that seemed to bely his origins. As I moved further out of London, the stares and disapproval of my presence became more obvious, until I reached my stop and got off as I had done so many times before. Now, it was all in plain sight. The suburbia that had so horrified me at a distance from the train was now all around me. The fluttering curtains, the hard tarmac and pavements, the clipped hedges, permeated with the smell of dog shit; evidence that all was not quite so perfect.

There was the newsagent, set into the ground floor of a thirties terrace where, as a boy, I would be sent on a Sunday to buy a block of ice cream for Sunday lunch. There was the 1960s estate built on the fields behind my house, where I used to crawl through our hedge to explore and play, now yet more suburban boxes with trimmed communal frontages and car ports.

Throwing my rucksack over my back with my sleeping bag, rolled and tied around the old walking stick I'd found in the mountains, I walked the couple of hundred yards up to the main road and the detached thirties house set back from the road with its gravel drive and front garden. My father's Ford Anglia and mother's Prefect were standing in their places. They'd not yet left for work.

A lump came to my throat as I picked my way across the gravel, my footsteps announcing my arrival. I felt myself regressing to the young boy, worried about his parents' approval. Seeing me now in my dirty and weatherworn state, how could they approve?

The rat-a-tat on the knocker confirmed my arrival and I could hear my mother's footsteps in the hall. I'd not written or phoned to tell them when I might be arriving, so being on the doorstep at quarter past seven on a Tuesday morning was something she was totally unprepared for.

As the door opened, her eyes widened in surprise. 'You're home!'

'Yes, I arrived in London early this morning.'

'Have you eaten?' she asked with some concern.

'No, but the first thing I want is a hot bath and clean clothes.'

My father was still eating breakfast and came out to the hall, wiping his mouth with a napkin. We shook hands and half hugged.

Food was left in the kitchen as they left for work, leaving me to that bath. Despite the cold lino and condensation running down the frosted window panes, it was pure bliss to sink into the hot water and doze as the heat lifted the dirt and stress from my body. I lay there until the water had gone cold, thinking of the ordinariness of this day compared with what had been transpiring on a daily basis over the last few months. It was good to be safe and still, not having to worry about where I might be sleeping of a night and whether I would have enough money for food, but this was all part of the illusion that had been spun by the powers that be. Just enough rope as long as you do as you're told and pull your weight.

I was already feeling restless and making plans for my journey to see Belinda. Only three and a half years earlier, I had shared a joint with her in this very bath. It seemed too extraordinary to be true, but I knew it was.

With clean clothes and food inside me, it was with keen delight that I took my filthy clothes into the garden and set a match to them. I couldn't quite bring myself to include the Afghan coat but, seeing its wrinkled and reeking skin, knew it wouldn't be too far behind.

I was woken from a deep sleep by my mother's return from work as the front door shut on her arrival.

The conversation was light and peripheral until my father's return and I could begin recounting some of my adventures. As I spoke, I was seeing these events as mere echoes of something that had been so real and profound. Worse still was the realisation that it was over and the routine that lay in store for me was unbearable.

Two days later, I packed a bag, returned to London and caught a train from King's Cross to Cambridge.

It was the same rickety bus that had previously taken me out to the village, its tired engine churning along the narrow lanes that wound across the flat ploughed landscape, where lines of pollarded trees defined the river course. Nothing seemed to have changed as I alighted at the pub by the ancient oak tree and made my way towards Belinda's cottage.

There was little evidence of the colourful flowers that had enchanted me on my first visit two summers before. Instead, the foliage looked tired and overgrown and the windows dusty and neglected.

I knocked, my heart throbbing with anticipation.

An unfamiliar shuffling approached the door from inside and slowly it was opened, revealing an old lady, possibly in her eighties.

'Yes?' her thin voice enquired.

'I've come to see Belinda,' I replied. 'Is she in?'

'She's not here,' she replied quite sternly. 'Don't you know?'

'Know what?' I replied, some panic in my voice.

'The terrible fire at the Vicarage…' She stared at me momentarily, as if wondering whether to say more. 'Won't you come in?'

She beckoned me across the threshold, wrapping her burgundy cardigan across her cream blouse fastened at the neck with a ruby brooch. Her slippered feet turned and she led me to the sitting room, where once I had chanted mantras with Belinda and shown my proposed route to India on the map. Most of Belinda's furniture was still there as the lady offered me a seat on the sofa. Patting the grey bun of hair at the back of her head, she sat in a nearby armchair.

'I was telling you of the fire. It was towards the end of September that the village was woken in the early hours by a huge bang. It was like a bomb going off. I should know, I lived in London during the Blitz. Not long after, we heard the fire engines arriving and word soon got round that the Vicarage was on fire.'

I was already sensing the worst as it was in the Vicarage that Belinda's parents, the local doctor and his wife, lived.

'Many of us put on whatever clothes we could find,' she continued, 'most in dressing gowns and slippers and gathered as near as we were allowed. It was an inferno engulfing the entire house and all the while we were all asking the question, "Did they get out?"

Sadly, they didn't. It was a dreadful shock for the whole village…'

'Where were Belinda and Harry, her son?' I interrupted.

They had joined us in the crowd outside, thank God, but it was devastating for poor Belinda. She was screaming hysterically and the police had to hold her back from running into the flames. She was a broken woman after that.'

'So, where is she now?'

'I'm afraid I don't know, dear. A taxi came soon after and took her and the boy away. She was such a lovely girl and taking after her poor father with her herbal healing.'

I sat dazed and overwhelmed with remorse that I had gone to India leaving her alone. *How could I even start to find her now?* I thought.

There was no-one else I knew in the village who could help me. Caroline, who had been murdered so brutally, lay in the graveyard, while her diplomat father had shot himself in Kabul and her mother had been arrested as a Russian spy. I had no idea where her younger brother might be, having only recently completed his degree.

'I expect you'll be going back to London now. Let me make you some tea,' the lady said.

While she was in the kitchen, I breathed in the air as if trying to capture something of Belinda's essence in the vain hope I might make contact with her spirit and receive some guidance. Nothing was apparent, except a very faint whiff of her favourite incense still embedded in the corners. I felt so utterly helpless and empty as if my whole purpose had been torn from my soul.

The lady returned to explain that she had been living with her sister at the time of the fire but, when Belinda left, there was the opportunity to move into the cottage.

I was only half conscious of her voice, thinking how my return to Belinda had been the linchpin of my journey, my *excuse* for leaving Kamala. Now, I had neither. I could not go running back to Kamala with her knowing she was second choice and I was left with the ongoing emptiness of not knowing what had become of Belinda.

I remembered the letter I had written at the beginning of September, re-affirming my love for Belinda, whilst telling how I had met Kamala. Maybe, she had received the letter and was about to reply when the tragedy at the Vicarage took place or she was hurt by my mention of Kamala and did not want to reply.

Then there was the letter from Lahore, written just before Christmas.

'Has there been any post received here for Belinda, since you've been here?'

'Oh, I almost forgot,' she said, as she reached over to the mantelpiece. 'This arrived quite recently,' handing me a familiar envelope.

I recognised my hand written address and the Pakistani stamp on the front but, of course, it hadn't been opened.

I thanked the lady for the tea and her help and walked further down the road to see what remained of the Vicarage. Little now stood, but charred and heat damaged walls, some of which had already collapsed. No one could have survived the intensity of such a fire and I only prayed that Belinda's parents had died of smoke inhalation in their sleep and not been trapped by encroaching flames. My imagination brought about a shudder of horror as I immediately thought of the seventeenth century *witches* who had suffered under the Cromwellian persecutions.

In the village shop, I asked if anyone knew of Belinda's whereabouts, but was met by the same blank replies. Further depressed by the response, I bought ten cigarettes and a box of matches, hoping for some solace in the tobacco, but it only gave me a cough and a headache.

Half an hour passed as I sat by Caroline's grave in the little churchyard, pulling away the weeds that had encroached on her stone while talking of the futility of her untimely death and the events that had now overtaken my own life. Yet, her spirit was with me, willing me on to a new beginning, despite feeling utterly sick and dejected. I had no choice but to return to London.

I had last seen my old friends, Alex and Teresa, when they waved me off from Victoria Station at the start of my journey east. They were still living in Powis Square in the heart of Notting Hill and, once again, I saw fit to pick up the pieces from our time together when I had lived nearby.

They were pleased to see me, but something had changed. As I spoke of my time with a Tibetan master, they listened politely, but I sensed they were merely humouring me. They were no longer keen to follow my footsteps to India as we had all once aspired to do back in the heady days of the *Summer of Love*. Instead, they now spoke of their devotion to Guru Maharaj ji, a boy guru from India, who claimed to be the Perfect Master and living incarnation of God, currently attracting a large following of hippies and others.

As advocates, they were contributing hard earned money to the Divine Light movement, yet this guru was apparently staying at top hotels and being chauffeur driven in a Rolls Royce. This was not how I saw my spiritual path and I could see a chasm of differences opening up between us.

Teresa was still the blonde maternal figure she had always been, although a little more plump than when I had last seen her. Alex's long hair was now tied in a bun on his head, better exposing his bearded face to scrutiny. He had always had issues with his health, being asthmatic, and lines of stress and weariness were now present. Nevertheless, they remained kind, feeding me that evening and letting me stay the night, but I realised that the common ground we once knew had shifted irreversibly.

Next day, keen to re-establish my links with the Tibetans, I had heard of a newly founded Tibetan Society somewhere in Pimlico and thought that, following my time in McLeod Ganj and my audience with His Holiness, I would perhaps be able to make some connection in order to further my studies.

My idea couldn't have been further from the reality that confronted me. Although a few Tibetans were present, the place was dominated by grey, frumpy, middle class English women, whose pompous and condescending attitude spoke of a control agenda. It was of no interest to them that I had lived for those magical months in a Tibetan community and their haughtiness only served to repel me from wanting any further involvement. The atmosphere felt devoid of the spirit of laughter and joy that had so attracted me in India, replaced instead by a cold detached authoritarianism, reminding me of everything I hated about the English establishment from school to offices of state. I knew little of politics, but this infiltration suggested something dark that I could not put my finger on.

I took the opportunity to exchange the two hundred dollars that Jen had given me in Bombay, receiving just over eighty pounds sterling, enough to set me up for a couple of months, although I knew I had to find work.

This wasn't long coming.

On the strength of the posters I had designed and sold in London prior to leaving, I was given a full time illustration job working on a catalogue promoting office and drawing equipment; a stark contrast to the psychedelic contents of my portfolio.

Using a pen and ink stippling technique, my days were taken up drawing compasses, drawing tables and any sort of device that might be found in an office. The work was repetitive and a little mindless, but a kind of meditation, as I sat in a warm room with windows out to the countryside, carefully placing dots to simulate light and dark and three dimensionality. I was left to myself for most of the day, occasionally asking one of the girls in the office to provide a piece of type to be pasted into a page layout or stopping to share sandwiches and a chat at lunch.

My life was taking a very different direction now that living with Belinda was no longer an option for the time being. Instead, having established a much more manageable relationship with my parents, some of which I believed had been gained through the success of my overland journey, I chose to pay them rent and save what I had left.

As the weeks and months progressed into the summer, I enjoyed the ten minute cycle ride to work, having time to develop my portfolio of drawings, to paint and even take part in local amateur dramatics. There was a restful *normality* about it all that enabled me to reassess where I had been and where I might be going. I valued being able to ease myself into each day without being pressured by anything too demanding to impinge upon my space.

As summer melted into autumn and the bike ride became more of a challenge against the deteriorating weather, I managed to pass my driving test, despite doing an unscheduled and bungled emergency stop for a pigeon as I was driving into the test centre at the end. With my savings, I bought my first car, a Morris Traveller Estate with its characteristic ash wood framework. Suddenly, I had freedom to go where I wanted; to work, out of an evening and even into London.

At the same time, a friend of my mother introduced me to a local woman who practised psychometry; the ability to hold a personal possession and intuitively tell something about the owner.

She had nothing of the gypsy that I had imagined with dark curly hair, golden hooped earings and a face that spoke of sexuality, intrigue and even a little subterfuge.

As I sat in her very ordinary suburban living room with its beige velvet three piece suite and buttoned cushions, spindle legged coffee table, orange pile carpet, colour television and Lowry prints around the walls, I wondered what this woman could tell me. With her coiffed greying hair, mauve wing-tipped glasses, pearl earrings and necklace, a sensible calf length skirt and ribbed turtle neck top, to all intents she was an extension of her surroundings.

'Sit yourself down,' she said, pointing to the sofa. 'What I want to do is hold something that is personal to you. I will sense a vibration in that object which has been subject to your unique energy. I believe that all experiences are recorded in what you might call a cosmic aura and can be recalled at will. It's like a giant cosmic tape machine.'

If I had heard a hippy in Notting Hill talking like this, I would have easily accepted it, but this woman? It all seemed so out of place, yet, why should she be excluded from perceiving things that were beyond most people's normal understanding?

'Now, I can assure you that Elaine, your mother's friend, has said nothing about you, so this is all totally new to me and I know nothing of your background.'

'I've got my watch,' I replied, 'but I've only had it just over six months since my twenty-first birthday. Is that okay?'

'That'll be just fine,' she said, taking it from me and holding it in her cupped hands as she closed her eyes and concentrated for some moments, her facial muscles moving involuntarily as if driven by images and thoughts.

'I see you on a long journey,' she began. 'I see mountains. It is misty. I see men in long red robes…' she paused for a while, her face intensifying in concentration. 'I believe you have a guide watching over you. Could he be Tibetan?'

I kept my silence.

'Yes, he is Tibetan. He is telling me that you are being looked after and that you have a long life ahead of you.'

'Should I take this literally' I asked myself, *'or perhaps exercise a little scepticism, despite her identifying my Tibetan connections?'*

'I can see you being academic, possibly writing. Books, maybe? I also see you teaching. You are in front of a group of people talking.'

Now it was becoming implausible. *'True, I had taught English, of a fashion, to a couple of Tibetan monks and quite enjoyed the experience. But, formally teaching? No! After all, I saw myself as an artist. How was I currently earning my living?'*

'I definitely see you as a teacher.' she reiterated. 'I think you might move to another part of the country. I see the sea and a river for certain. Now, it's going misty again…' She paused for a few seconds, perhaps willing another image to appear. 'No, I can't see anything else,' with which she opened her eyes, unfolded her hands and returned my watch.

On my return home, I told my parents of what had been said, my mother immediately jumping on the idea. She'd always seen me as a doctor or even, implausibly, an actor, due to my performances in school plays, but now she had something tangible to grasp onto.

'How wonderful,' she said with glee, 'you'd make a great teacher.'

'Mum, you know that's the last thing I would want to be. I hated school and was even expelled, as you keep reminding me.'

'Yes, but think of the holidays. You could do your painting.'

'I don't want to be a teacher and that's an end to it.'

But, she had sown a seed and, by Christmas, I was sending off my application form to a teacher training college in Bristol.

Even as I drove down the M4 to the interview, I couldn't quite grasp what I was doing. I had applied as a mature student with art as my principal subject, seeing this as the best way to continue my own work, while being in the maelstrom of the creative world through student ideas, immersion in galleries and discussion.

My portfolio of posters and current work served to convince the panel of my creative abilities and I had only to talk of bringing experience beyond that of school to enrich my teaching. Most applicants came straight from school after A levels and, to my mind, were mostly lacking in confidence, while ill equipped to stimulate and pass on information with the authority that kids little younger than themselves would be looking for.

The acceptance letter followed a week later and I had the better part of nine months ahead of me to continue in my job and save for the following three years.

CHAPTER
Twenty-two

BY THE TIME I ARRIVED IN BRISTOL for the start of the
September term, I had saved enough to find a room in
Clifton and continue running my car. On top of that, I had a full
grant, which cushioned me from being the archetypical impoverished student.

My room, in one of the grand Victorian houses on the edge
of Clifton Village, had a high ceiling and huge bay windows.
Compared to some of the bedsits I had lived in whilst in London,
it was a palace. It became even more so when I salvaged wooden
planks from the docks, which were in the process of being
gentrified, and built a platform, high enough to walk under and
wide enough for a double mattress. The only disappointment was
the shared bathroom with its well worn bath and mushrooms that
grew from the gaps between the bath and walls.

I remembered how I had used the public baths in Hotwells
the last time I had lived in Bristol at the end of the sixties, such
were the conditions in the house I was in. I wondered if perhaps I
should be doing the same now but, having made an effort to clean
it up a little, I continued to brave it, whilst taking care not to let my
clean feet touch the floor.

College started well enough. Although I had little interest in the
younger students, I soon made friends with Eric, another mature
student, whose principal subject was English. Like me, he saw
teaching as a stepping stone to his own creativity. Being an ardent
follower of Samuel Beckett, he saw writing as his true vocation. He
was a Yorkshireman and lived nearby with his girlfriend, Emily, a

midwife at the local maternity hospital.

At the time, I was reading Herman Hesse, having first been introduced to him with *Steppenwolf,* prior to going to India. Now, I was catching up with every book of his I could find from, *Siddhartha*, a fiction built around the life of the Buddha to the dichotomy of *Narziss and Goldmund* and the baffling, *Glass Bead Game.*

Eric and I would convene most days for lunch at his flat, where we would discuss literary ideas and philosophy, a secondary subject that both of us were studying at college. On occasion, we would spend the whole lunch time playing chess, a game I had dabbled in at school which, nevertheless, Eric won most of the time.

Together, we had a rapport which served to stimulate us both as we bounced intellectual ideas off each other, delving into metaphysics and politics.

I can remember in an open forum at the beginning of the course, when the philosophy lecturer was recruiting students for her classes, she asked the question, 'What do we need?'

Of course, hands went up as she surveyed the hall. eliciting replies in quick succession, 'Fridge.' 'Car.' 'Money.' 'Job.' until she came to me and I nonchalantly answered, 'Air, water, food, shelter.'

'Yes. It's what we *need*, not what we *want.*'

This was a precursor to an enduring interest in philosophical exploration and finding my metier in writing essays that took me beyond the narrow confines of religious dogma.

My art module was like being at art college, having free reign to express myself as I wished, taking brush to canvas, whereby many of the philosophical conundrums I was exploring manifested themselves in paint.

In a way I had not expected, I was being stretched intellectually and creatively and I loved it.

There was a range of subject modules, not consistent with our main area of study, which we were all expected to pass. I merely paid lip service to these with the exception of English.

Ultimately, came what the whole course was preparing us for - teaching a class of children. For this, we had teaching practises in each term, where we were farmed out to local schools.

I had opted for the junior/secondary age group and spent some of my practises before a class of eight or nine year olds for a number of weeks. I would be teaching the same class the full gamut of subjects from English to geography, history, maths, art to outdoor games. My only exclusion was music, for which I knew I would never have any aptitude.

But, there I was, as predicted, before a group of children, passing on my knowledge with enthusiasm and joy. Preparing interesting and stimulating lessons became part of my life, rewarded by the smiles and looks of satisfaction as one child after another solved a problem or assimilated some information they had not known before.

All the while, I had made friends outside college life, who were on a different trajectory.

Mark and Stephanie rented a cottage outside the city and I would often visit for the weekend, smoking a little dope, listening to new music and hearing Mark's endless joy at being able to have sex every night.

This reminded me once more of what I had lost in Belinda; not just the sex, but the companionship and journeying into life together.

As the year wore on, a restlessness invaded my soul so, when Mark told me he had got a job in Germany for the summer and that there would be one for me, I was thrown off course and decided to join him and Stephanie.

When the summer term drew to a close and everyone departed until the autumn, I was driving to Dover for the ferry back to France where I had last been eighteen months earlier in the last stages of my journey back from India.

Now, I was driving myself through Belgium and on into Germany, where I met up with my friends in a small mediaeval town near Dortmund.

There was a spare bed in the flat they had rented and on my first Monday morning, Mark took me into the job I was to find myself doing. The drahtwerkes, put me in mind of something akin to *Arbeit Macht Frei*, with its austere iron gates and pre-war factory containing the machines that had been turning out wire fencing since 1830.

A machine was found for me and, after a short training, I was let loose.

It didn't take long to get the hang of it to the point that by the end of the second week, I was regularly being told, 'Langsam! Langsam!'

The older Germans, who were largely veterans of Hitler's failed invasion of Russia, were peeved by the speed I was producing my metres of fencing, showing how much faster the job could be done and upsetting the unions.

As the weeks passed and I settled into life in the town, drinking beer and eating wurst and chips, I began to consider quitting college and travelling back to India, where I might be lucky enough to ingratiate myself with Kamala.

I had written to her since my return and she'd replied, but the correspondence was a superficial description of what we were both doing with neither of us venturing into our feelings for each other.

While I considered these possibilities, Sofia arrived on the scene.

One evening, we'd decided to try out a new bar that had just opened and she was there serving customers out on the pavement terrace. As she returned to the tables with trays of drinks, I couldn't take my eyes off her, so much so that she would catch me gawping.

From time to time, she would smile across the tables until, by the end of the evening, instead of going home, she came back with us to the flat, where, with her good English, we talked into the early hours until I eventually walked her back to the bar where she had a room.

She was Greek, blonde with prominent dark roots and legs accentuated by short skirts and a pair of red platform shoes.

Over the ensuing weeks, we got to know each other better as she told me of her wish to visit England.

One afternoon, we drove out to the rebuilt Möhne dam, one of the Royal Air Force targets during the famous 1943 *Dam Busters* raid that breached the dam and damaged several others. It had a devastating effect on the German industrial war effort and the lives of the many thousands of civilians and war prisoners who found themselves downstream of the ensuing torrent of water.

Sofia was a little older than myself and with a very different experience of post-war Europe.

As we lay on the little beach that skirted the huge lake beyond the dark circle of pine trees, she told me of the hardships her parents had suffered under the Nazi occupation of Greece.

'My parents lived in the port of Kalamata on the Peloponnese peninsula, when the war started, although they hadn't yet met. My father was only seventeen and hoping to become a doctor.

All those dreams ended when much of the country was occupied by the Italians. Then, as our army started to push them back, the Nazis arrived to dominate the country completely. My father was still too young to join the army, but instead joined ELAS, the communist resistance, carrying out raids against German supplies. Every time something like that happened, innocent people were rounded up and shot. It was brutal, but it didn't stop them fighting even harder to free their country.

My parents didn't want to talk about it much but, I have since heard horrible stories of the Germans retaliating, even for the death of a single German soldier. There are so many accounts of how the Germans would move into a village, killing anything living.

The people were already emaciated by starvation but, still, they would rape all the girls and women before bayonetting them and mutilating their bodies. The babies and infants either had their throats cut or were bayonetted. Even the animals weren't spared. Then they would round up all the men and boys over the age of twelve and shoot or hang them. Often, people were set ablaze in their homes. I cry thinking about it.

I believe there is a lot more we've not been told as people are always trying to apologise for the German atrocities.

You can understand why the Germans were so hated and still are. Nothing can exonerate their barbarity, which they perpetrated wherever they went.

My mother managed to escape with her mother and younger sister into the mountains, where they lived with others moving from one cave to another, constantly short of food and warmth.

My father's unit had retreated to the mountains after a raid and by chance he met my mother as she was collecting water. She was only a year younger and my mother tells me they fell in love straightaway. My mother couldn't bear to see my father leaving and decided to join him in the resistance.

For the rest of the war, until the Germans were thrown out in 1944, they lived from hand to mouth, carrying out raids and were lucky to survive until the end.

The Germans left behind a power vacuum which resulted in a civil war between the Communists and the Democratic Army of Greece, who eventually won.'

'So where do the Generals come from that you have now. I got caught up in one of their Sunday meetings on my way to India in 1970. It seemed very frightening. I was also told of the numbers of political prisoners being held in island prisons away from the mainland.'

'The hard line right wing has always been there, despite the Nazi massacres, and the divisions have never healed with the communists, bitterly opposing the government we now have.

During the war, so much of our industry and infrastructure was destroyed. The Germans have not offered reparations for the killing and damage they were responsible for and, consequently, we've never fully recovered, depending, as we do, so much on tourism to keep the country going. I'm glad to be out of it for now.'

'So, what of your parents?

'My father eventually qualified as a doctor in Athens and still has his practise in Kalamata. My mother became a lawyer and is always busy. I think they both want to retire and enjoy life on one of the islands, but they work so hard. I can't see it happening. They will always find an excuse not to.'

'After what you've told me, I really don't know what I'm doing in Germany. I feel an intense evil here, deep in the soil. The whole country is swilling in blood.'

The summer wore on and I saved a good pot from the work in the wire factory. As September approached, I had to make a decision; go back to India or to England. It was a painful decision but, ultimately, I told myself that I had to finish something. So often, I had started a course or a job, only to abandon it. This time, I knew deep down that teaching would probably be my last chance to get a qualification that would stand me in good stead, wherever I was.

I told Sofia of my decision and, at the end of August, we set off together in the Morris bound for the English Channel and England.

It was somewhat bizarre to be repeating what amounted to the last few miles of my journey back from India, driving my own car with this attractive woman as my companion. Much as I wanted to sleep with Sofia, ultimately, we had become friends and it didn't seem right that we should. We drove through the night after the ferry, Sofia curling up to sleep on the back seat until we arrived back in Bristol on a cold autumn morning.

I had kept my room on through the summer, so it was only right that I should invite Sofia in to sleep a few hours, but she was eager to find somewhere to live and chose to start her search straight away. We saw each other once or twice after that but, ultimately, went our separate ways.

And so it was back to college for two more years, growing in confidence as I faced more children in their classrooms, further developed my interest in Philosophy and enhanced my painting abilities.

Girlfriends came and went, some in a very unrequited manner.

There was Caterina, one of the younger students of Italian descent. Typically, she was dark, curvaceous and perfect for some of the characters in a set of illustrations I was preparing at the time for a book of Indian Love Poems.

I had tried working from photographs to get what I wanted, until I finally bit the bullet and asked her if she would come to my room and model for me.

It was a corny chat up line, but I really did want to draw her and, to my surprise, she agreed.

I wanted her in a woodland setting looking out towards a mythical Indian palace in the distance and, for this, I needed a view of her naked back. She was quite happy to take off her top and get into pose, leaving me to see her flawless back and the under curve of her left breast.

So happy was she with the outcome, that she volunteered to be my queen on the peacock throne, Yasmin, the village girl who spent one night with a warrior from Kabul and the princess deserted by her lover as the paling stars withdrew.

But, despite the romantic overtones of the poems, nothing came of the experience save for a set of drawings.

Then, there was Rosa, a northern girl, whom I had often seen coming and going from the house opposite, as I stood working on a canvas in my big bay window.

One day, she was curious enough to ask what I did all day long, a cue to invite her in for a cup of tea.

Over succeeding days and several cups of tea later, we finally crawled into bed for a relationship that burnt itself out a few weeks later.

I always remember her telling me that her father had taught her to drive, ensuring she knew her way around the dashboard even in the dark. He had been a navigator on Lancasters during the war and, to him, flying in the dark was quite normal.

As I had got to know more people during my time in Bristol, so I was invited to parties. With my course over and the qualification in my pocket, Rosa and I went to one such party at a house in Clifton.

As the evening wore on with drinks coalescing with marijuana, low red lights enveloped everyone in a soporific inertia, whereby couples had mostly settled to beds, sofas and spaces on the floor.

Still standing in a small cluster in the middle of the room, *Big Susie*, the star attraction, held sway. As her name suggested, she was big in many ways. Not unpleasantly so, just tall, blonde, long legs, high heels and black dress with a more than ample cleavage.

On this night, she was the *prize*, should any of the guys be so lucky.

Towards the end of the evening, I needed a pee, leaving Rosa on a couch in the sitting room. On the way back, I was distracted for a while, talking to some people who had heard about my Indian trip. When I eventually returned to the sitting room, Rosa was cuddled up with a guy who had been sniffing around her all evening. Not really certain where our own relationship had been heading, I left her to it and, seeing Susie momentarily unaccompanied, I asked her to dance. It was a smooch and we were very soon cheek to cheek, shuffling slowly around the room.

The warmth of her body, the faint whiff of perfume and the softness of her breasts against my shirt were enough to rouse me towards only one destination.

Rosa was lost elsewhere, when Susie suggested we leave.

Grabbing my jacket, she took my hand and led me out into the chilled night air.

We walked the short distance to her flat. Tiptoeing up the flight of stairs to her door on the middle floor. She reached down to turn on the gas fire.

'Would you like a coffee?' she whispered from the small kitchenette. 'Sit yourself down and get warm.'

She joined me soon after on the floor by the fireplace, scrunching her knees up to her chin on the carpet space between the two armchairs. We stared ahead, mesmerised by the flickering blue flames.

'What brought you to Bristol?' she eventually asked.

'I'd been down here at the end of the sixties, working on a hippy shop in Hotwells."

'I remember that. The one with the big painted dragon in the window?'

'Yes. I painted that.'

'Really, I'd often wondered who'd done it. It had become something of a local icon. The shop was very busy for a while, being the only place in Bristol where you could buy Indian clothes and things. Then, suddenly, it was no more. All closed up. The dragon stayed in the window for a while, then it was empty. And so it remains. They keep talking about developing all the shops and houses along there, but it's all derelict still.'

'I had fun working there, but fell out with some of the people involved. It all seems like another lifetime. So much has changed from those days of love and peace and thoughts of changing the world. We've only just seen the end of the Vietnam war and for what? All those deaths only for the South to be ultimately overrun by the communists.

The world seems to be in more chaos than ever before. We've had the three day week and people coming out on strike all over the country. Even most of the music now is crap. Something has definitely been lost. I feel like a piece of paper being blown in the wind at the moment, not really knowing where I'm going to land or even if I want to.

I had all that time in India, but now that I'm back here, I don't know anything anymore.'

'I think I know what you mean,' she replied, taking a sip from her coffee. 'I do wonder sometimes where it's all going. I thought my career was all mapped out. I'm a researcher at the BBC in Whiteladies Road. The job has it's moments, when I get an interesting radio programme to gather information for, but I can't see me doing that forever.'

'I thought I was beginning to grasp something of what this is all about when I was in India. The assurance that all is One and that everything lives forever is fine and I do feel that I'm more than just my body. But, that's hard to reconcile with many people I encounter and living within the constraints of our very superficial social structure. It's all so empty.'

We drank our coffee and stared once more at the fire.

'I suppose we'd better go to bed,' Susie eventually said at three o' clock in the morning, an inviting smile on her face and a sparkle in her eyes.

We were both tired and our coupling was merely an obligation fulfilled, before sleep encompassed us both.

CHAPTER
Twenty-three

WITH MY COURSE OVER, I had to decide where next. Despite my success, I didn't want to go into a teaching job just yet. I was now twenty-five, yet could not countenance the idea of a daily routine that might well take me toward the end of my days.

It was nearly four years since I had last seen Kamala and once again, the idea of returning to India seemed appealing. I was going to London more often, attempting to raise ghosts from the past; those places and people that had been so motivational during the last few years of the sixties.

But, just as I had found my dear friends, Alex and Teresa, *lost* in the hype of a young guru, so too had places changed, with familiar shops having become something else and people either having left for other pastures or settled to jobs and family.

Even the pub in Rathbone Place in the shadow of the Post Office tower, where my story had started, had lost all that was familiar; the dwarf behind the bar, the dog that hoovered the slops from the floor, the menacing edge that prevailed alongside the jangling bells of the 1967 *flower children.*

Should I perhaps be following the example of others? Putting away *childish* things and *growing up*?

It was late October, I'd been for an interview with an animation company in Soho Square. They'd been amiable enough and liked my drawings, but didn't have the resources to offer me a work experience, whereby I could learn the techniques, instead suggesting I apply for a college course.

Having been fired by the creative possibilities within animation, I was obviously despondent and wandered the streets for a couple of hours, conscious that another avenue had effectively been shut. Going back to college was not an option, it would be costly and another three years would probably put me at a disadvantage against younger students arriving on the market when I had eventually qualified.

I'd been staying at Alex and Teresa's and was on my way back to see them in Notting Hill, descending the first escalator at Warren Street station. I was in one of those detached states, where all around was unreal, dreamlike. I was not my body, but a more expanded essence. Suddenly, a girl's voice called my name.

'Adam! Adam!'

I was jolted back to a state of reality and looked around, seeing a girl waving at me as she was going up the other side. She was blonde, pretty, in fact stunning, and somehow familiar.

'It's me, Alison,' she shouted above the rumble of the escalator.

In that moment, I was back in Bombay, my fingertips just leaving hers as I bade farewell and set out on my journey north.

Without any hesitation, I turned to the narrow space where people were hurriedly running down and, with a succession of, 'Excuse me', pushed my way upwards against the downward momentum, tripping a couple of times as my footing missed the moving steps. After much dodging and squeezing, I reached the top, passing across to the ascending escalator as Alison stepped off.

We fell into each other's arms and kissed. A cheer went up from those who had seen the drama, as if a scene from a Hollywood movie.

'Alison. God, I missed you!'

'Me, you. You got back safely then.'

'Yes, I'll tell you about it. What're you doing now?'

'I'm on my way to work, but I've got time for a cuppa.'

I took her hand and led her out into the autumn sunlight.

'This is a long way from Bombay,' I said. 'Did you go on to Goa for that Christmas?'

'Yes, I caught the ferry that runs down the coast from Bombay. It was fabulous, following the coastline down for twenty-four hours, sleeping on the deck and eating fresh fish. I loved it and met so many people on the way. People played guitars and sang late into the night and we shared whatever we had. It was like one big family having an extended party.'

I felt a lump in my throat when she mentioned others she had met and I wondered if she had slept with any of them as casually as she had slept with me. But, then, who was I to talk?

We walked the two hundred yards down Warren Street to the Fitzroy Café that hadn't changed much since it had opened in the late Victorian era. With chipped and rusting enamel signs for cigarettes, tobacco and cold drinks in the window, its interior contained small tables with red and white check cloths and dark stained bent-back chairs. A counter ran down the back wall with a doorway leading to the kitchen where the smell of hot food was wafting out.

'We've got twenty minutes. I've got to be at work at quarter to one and it'll take me ten minutes to walk there and get changed,' Alison said.

'What're you doing?'

'Nursing.'

'You're not modelling any more?' I asked, taking in the beauty I had first appreciated when we took the boat out to Elephanta Island for the day. Those deep mystically blue eyes, the flawless complexion and the lips I had already touched this day.

It was now autumn in England and gone was the cheesecloth dress and sandals to be replaced by a long grey linen dress, boots, a loose polo neck and camel coat. A blue velvet hat sat roundly over her head. She took it off, shaking her blonde hair free, although now drastically cut to only reach her shoulders.

I caught the proprietor's eye and asked for two teas.

'There's no time to eat is there?'

'No, I'll get something at work. Thanks.'

'So where are you working?'

'UCH - University College Hospital.'

My heart stopped, as I remembered the journey with Belinda in an ambulance after she had overdosed on heroin in Middle Earth, the night Arthur Brown, the *God of Hellfire* was due to play. How we had arrived at the steps of this daunting red brick Victorian building and I had followed Belinda on a stretcher into its bowels.

Alison could sense my distress.

'What's the matter, Adam? You've gone very pale.'

'The hospital is the same one where the girl I was telling you about was taken after she overdosed.'

'I'm so sorry.'

I feigned a short laugh. 'It's not your fault. Just a weird coincidence.'

'Did you find her again when you got back?'

'No, I went to her home near Cambridge, only to find there had been a terrible tragedy when her parents' house in the same village had burnt down taking them with it. I was told that Belinda disappeared soon after. I've no idea where she might be.'

Alison reached across and held my hand and I felt her warmth and loving energy.

I raised my head and looked into her eyes. The minutes were ticking by as the teas were brought to the table and I knew I wouldn't have much longer with her.

'So…' we both started at the same time.

'I'm sorry,' I said, 'after you.'

So, where are you living now?' she continued.

'I'm in Bristol. I've just finished a teaching course and contemplating what to do next. I had thought of going back to India, but now that I've found you…' I looked at her, willing a response that would seal our fate.

She held my hand more firmly.

'I'd love to come and see you in Bristol. I've heard it's a lovely place to live.'

'You're welcome any time.'

She looked at her watch and sipped down the rest of her tea.

'I've got to go. Walk with me.'

I paid for the teas and we stepped out into the street, retracing our steps back to the tube station, taking a right turn into Tottenham Court Road before a left into Grafton Way and finally the enormity of the red brick University College Hospital with its five floors of joyless windows, black railings, fire escapes and grey pyramidal towers.

As we arrived, I scribbled my address on a piece of paper and gave it to her.

'Come any time, Alison,' I said.

'I will,' at which, she kissed me on the lips and turned to go up the steps that had led to so much of my own apprehension and disquiet.

Christmas came and went as did the New Year into 1976 and I had heard nothing from Alison.

I continued with my painting, entering for exhibitions only to be rejected for the *disturbing* subject matter of my work.

I had started to get small free-lance illustration jobs, mainly for advertising but, despite the money, I found them soulless exercises designed to sell products I had no interest in.

This continued into early spring when, one Friday afternoon, my bell rang.

Thinking it must be the neighbour complaining about my music, I opened the main door somewhat abruptly.

'Hi. It's me.'

Me was, much to my surprise and delight, Alison.

She was the light I had craved all Winter and she had at last come, stepping inside lugging behind her a large, battered suitcase.

'Here, let me help you. Did you come on the train?'

'Yes, then a very kind man at the station, seeing me a bit lost, offered me a lift up here.'

I led her into my room, where paints were out on the table and my newly washed laundry was spread out on the sofa.

'Excuse the mess. I wasn't expecting visitors.

I remember the first time I came to Bristol. It was a freezing cold day and I had no idea where I was, following some vague instructions on a piece of paper and having to traipse through the old docks until I found where I was staying.

This is one of the nicer parts of the city. I'll take you to Clifton Village, the Georgian area near the Suspension Bridge.'

'Aren't you going to kiss me?' she asked, teasingly, as she wrapped her arms around my neck, pulling me to her mouth.'

Now a little older, having succumbed to some of the pressures of work and life, she had perhaps lost a little of the sparkle I had first seen in India. But, she remained beautiful in both soul and body. I adored her presence, her soft touch, her comforting voice, her confident being.

'This isn't strictly my first time in Bristol,' she said.

'Oh.'

I came down just after Christmas for a job interview at the Bristol General. I start Monday. I've been working my notice. When you told me how lovely Bristol was, I had been looking for a way out of London anyway and this opportunity came up. I knew you were here and thought we could possibly make a go of it together.'

'That was hell of a risk, leaving your job. Supposing I'd moved or died or just didn't like you anymore?'

She giggled. 'I know. I can be a bit impetuous.'

This came as a bolt from the blue, but one I had no argument with.

'Good thing I've got a big room, but you won't like the bathroom.'

'I'm sure we can do something with that, besides we can look for something better between us.'

She had it all worked out and, despite the sudden invasion of my solitude, I could only agree that it was a good idea.

'What made you decide? It's been nearly five years since I left you in Bombay and the last time I saw you was October. Are you sure this is what you want?'

'I'd never forgotten you. The day on Elephanta, our dinner together and that one night. You left me alone next morning, worrying if you were going to be alright on that mad journey home in the middle of Winter.'

'I thought of you too in my darkest days. I only wish I had found you earlier. I tried writing to you at your parents' home in Wimbledon.'

'I'm sorry, but they moved soon after I got back to England and I didn't have an address for you.'

'I realised that later. So foolish of me. But, that's in the past, now, we're together. We've got a lot of catching up to do.'

We drove to Clifton Village that evening, walking across Brunel's bridge lit up with its host of white light bulbs as a cold breeze came up the river from the sea. On the other side, we surveyed the city spread out beneath us that would now be our home.

We had chicken in a basket in a local pub and Alison insisted I tell her something of my journey home from India. This dominated the conversation for most of the evening until I finally got to ask her when she had decided to become a nurse.

'It was definitely in India,' she replied, 'in fact, it was specifically, Bombay. Like you, I had been to the slum and wandered the streets, finding the poverty and suffering unbearable. I felt I had to do something to help. I started my training at UCH, living in the nurses' home for the first year, until I shared a flat with three others for the second and third.

I found it tough though, especially after all the glamour of modelling but, as I got to know my way around, I realised how much I cared for ordinary people here in England. I just love talking with patients and hearing their stories, although I have to keep an eye open for sister or matron,' she chuckled.

'So, when did you finish training?'

'Summer, seventy-four.'

'You must be a pretty good nurse by now then?'

'I do my best.'

'It looks like we've got some thinking to do.'

Over the weekend, I drove Alison around the city, down to the Bristol General, near the old docks, where she would be working.

It was then up the steep hill that was Park Street, along Whiteladies Road and Blackboy Hill, home to some of the most interesting shops, before opening out onto the wide green expanse that was the Bristol Downs. There, people exercised their dogs, played football and breathed the fresh air blown in from the Bristol Channel.

We slept together for the first time since Bombay and realised that nothing had been lost in our passion for each other.

Sunday evening came and Alison wanted to prepare for her first day in her new job, asking me to run a bath for her. Dutifully, I went to tiny room that just about contained the bath, only to find fresh scum and black hairs lining the tub.

Two Iranians lived in the back room behind ours and I could smell the trail of aromatic soap wafting all the way to their door. I knocked and one of the young men, bearded and with receding mid length hair, answered, his torso bare and a bath towel wrapped around his middle.

'Hi, I started, a little nervously, 'I wonder, have you just had a bath?'

He looked at me blankly, knowing this question was a mere formality, based on his state of dress.

'Could I ask you to please clean the bath after you? My girlfriend wants to have a bath now.'

His eyes popped with rage as he lunged toward me, backing me up against the hall wall.

'I will stick a knife in your belly,' he seethed. 'I have killed one man. I will kill another,' he continued earnestly.

This was not the reply I had anticipated.

'I only asked you to clean the bath after you. Is that too much to ask?' I retorted.

He looked menacingly into my eyes, stepped back into his room and slammed the door.

'Bit of bother over the bathroom,' I said to Alison as I returned to our room to grab a bottle of Jif and a cloth.

I thought of all the people I had encountered in Iran, yet I had to return to England to have my life threatened over a matter that was so fundamentally trivial.

Next morning arrived and I drove Alison to work for the seven o' clock shift. I felt so proud of her in her stiff uniform, her cape and the ornate shiny silver buckle on her belt that marked her out as a Registered Nurse.

For me, it was back to our room to start a new illustration commission.

This became our pattern for the next few months into the summer. Every four weeks, Alison would be on night shift, making it difficult for me to work and her to sleep whilst both in the same room. Something had to change and it prompted us to find a proper home between us.

Alison was by now earning just over three thousand pounds a year, myself about two thirds of that but, between us, it was sufficient to take out a mortgage on a house.

Clifton Wood was becoming a popular destination for people

like ourselves, where lines of Victorian terraced houses clung to the steep slopes overlooking the river, the docks and the open countryside beyond.

We found a broker who, with some smoke and mirrors, concocted a more substantial combined mortgage and we were very soon holding the keys to our first house.

With an attic, two bedrooms, bathroom, two rooms and a kitchen downstairs, we had the basis for a home, but it was far from what we wanted. In fact, it was a wreck, requiring a new roof, floorboards, bathroom, kitchen and then furniture.

Our mortgage had included a bit more for renovation work and we managed to get a small grant towards the roof.

As Christmas drew nearer the main work had been completed and we could say goodbye to the builders. Now, it was up to us in our spare time to finish the project. Sanding floors, painting and tiling were largely new skills and mistakes were made, but they were our mistakes and each one prompted a memory which we learned to live with and sometimes laugh at.

One afternoon, Alison was at work and I decided to finish installing new sash cords in one of the main windows looking out to the street. I had bought a couple of cast iron weights from a scrap yard to replace the originals which had been lost and fitted the cords for the upper window, pushing it back into place, nailing the beading and locking the two halves together while I had my bath.

Returning, with just a towel wrapped around me, to further check the window was running smoothly, I undid the lock that held the two windows together. Before I knew it, the upper half slammed down, the frame trapping both my hands in the gap between the two windows, leaving me *crucified* of a manner with the towel loosening around my waist by the minute.

It would be almost an hour before Alison was due home and the towel had already fallen to the floor in the first five minutes. The lights were on, the curtains drawn back and it was dark outside. I was there facing the street like a bizarre Christmas decoration.

Alison couldn't stop laughing when she finally arrived, doing her best to tickle my naked body before eventually responding to my distress and lifting the lower window to free my hands.

Daisy and Graham were a couple about our age, who lived nearly opposite. He worked as a laboratory analyst in Bristol's main hospital, conducting essential tests and diagnoses. Daisy was another nurse, whom Alison had met and befriended at work.

'I've asked Daisy and Graham for dinner on Saturday. Is that okay?' Alison pronounced the following week.

'Fine,' I replied.

Saturday came and we had been preparing food for most of the day, applying our curry making skills to a host of different dishes, leaving just enough time to bath and dress before their arrival.

Alison looked particularly lovely, indeed sexy, with a loose rose print skirt and low cut v-neck jumper that showed off her firm breasts and just enough cleavage to catch the eye.

Graham was quite *straight* with short cut hair, a slight paunch and dressed in a white shirt, cavalry twills and black shoes as if he had just left the office. Daisy, slight with dark permed hair, perhaps a little Spanish, arrived in tight black trousers, a flowery cotton blouse and an embroidered waistcoat. She had a curious sparkle in her eyes when I welcomed her and she kissed me on the cheek.

The meal went well with compliments flying about our cooking, with Alison and I telling of the rich variety of food to be found in India.

'You both met out there, didn't you?' Graham said, as if to confirm the authenticity of the food. 'It must have been quite an experience. I missed out on all that as I went straight from A levels to University. Daisy did a bit of travelling though.'

'Not quite in the same league as Adam and Alison, I'm afraid,' she said.

'But, it was pretty damned important.' Graham added.

'I went out to Turkey after the 1971 earthquake that killed about a thousand and injured many more,' Daisy started. 'It was May and all over the papers. They were calling for volunteers to help and I was given special leave from work. Along with other nurses, doctors, specialist disaster rescuers and others, we flew out to this remote part of eastern Turkey, where it was how I would have imagined a place to look after it had been bombed.'

'I must have just missed it,' I said. 'I was going through in early January and a little further north. If I had been there, I think I would have seen some damage.'

You can't imagine how bad it was. Everything of any worth had collapsed. Despite the rescuers with trained dogs searching and pulling people out of the rubble they couldn't rescue everyone. The crying went on for days, day and night, until it was no more. Then, we had to deal with the injuries, broken bones, breathing difficulties because of the dust, cuts and bruises and the trauma. Mothers were screaming in the streets for their lost children. I'll never forget it.'

'How long were you there?' I asked.

'A couple of weeks to clean up the worst of it, but others stayed on much longer. They were needed.'

'Looks like we've all had a calling of some sort. Alison and I were certainly influenced by India and the need to do something to help people. What about you, Graham?'

'Oh, I just liked science at school and it looked like an interesting area to get into. The money's not bad either.'

'I was much the same,' Daisy said. 'My Mum was a nurse, so I just got inspired by her.'

The meal over, we went into our new sitting room with coffee and another bottle of wine. Then, out of the blue, Daisy spoke up as she took another gulp from her glass.

'Have you recovered from your ordeal at the window, Adam? You've got quite a specimen there.'

'You didn't see me, did you?'

'How could I miss it?'

Weren't you at work with Alison?'

No, we had different shifts that day. I couldn't believe what I was seeing, all lit up there. I was very impressed.'

'You've gone all red, Adam,' Alison piped in. 'It was so funny though, you poor darling. But then, you are bit of a show-off.'

She winked and took an in-take of breath that lifted her breasts, with Graham clearly captivated by what he was seeing.

Alison looked as if she was up for something more daring, but she looked at me again, took another sip of wine and relaxed into the sofa.

CHAPTER
Twenty-four

W E WENT TO Alison's parents for Christmas. They had moved to a cottage in Kent, backing onto fields with oast houses, apple orchards and hops.

Her older brother, Chris, worked in the City and I took an instant dislike to him. He was one of those exceptionally good looking, almost pretty boys, with no rough edges. Clean shaven, no spots, neatly parted hair and a feint whiff of after-shave.

His casual trousers were sharply pressed, complemented by a red and white striped shirt, such as he might have worn with a tie at work, now open at the neck with a pink V-neck pullover. Even his casual shoes were shiny leather slip-ons.

He talked about his deals and his Christmas bonus, evidenced by the Aston-Martin sitting outside in the drive. Beyond work, he had little conversation, although he did mention a girl from Ruislip he had met in a bar.

Alison's father, Bill, was ex-army, a major or something, Alison had told me, who had taken early retirement.

'Father dabbles a bit in the market,' Chris told us. 'That's how he got this place, although I did give him a tip-off.'

'Now, now, Christopher,' Bill chastised his son.

'Dad always calls him Christopher when he's out of order,' Alison said.

Her mother, Audrey, had been beautiful in her younger days. She still had good poise and *bone structure*, although she must have gained a little weight in recent years. She spoke impeccably and was clearly Alison's gene pool.

Over lunch, as we ate our turkey and sprouts, our heads adorned with paper hats, Chris couldn't resist having a go at Alison and me.

'So, you're a hippy, Adam, like my sister. Into Peace and Free Love no doubt.'

'Adam is a very talented artist and has a teaching qualification,' Alison piped up in my support. 'Besides, what's wrong with Peace and Love. You lot in the City could do with a bit of that.'

'That's enough of that, my girl,' Bill said. 'It's Christmas day. We don't want any arguing. You two always start when you get together.'

'He's such a prick,' Alison retorted.

'Alison!' her mother snapped.

The afternoon went well enough, exchanging some presents, eating Christmas cake and answering Audrey's questions about our relationship.

'When are you two going to get married? I want to see some grandchildren before I pop off.'

'Mum, don't start now. We're happy as we are.'

'You've got your house. Now you need to fill it, like most people.'

'Yes, but we're not *most* people.'

'Come on, Adam, aren't you going to make an honest woman of her? She's been *scrubbing around* for far too long.' Chris intervened.

'What do you mean scrubbing around?' Alison shouted back at him.

' You know, you've been here and there for years - scrubbing around. You're not exactly the Virgin Mary.'

Alison whipped round and slapped his face, leaving a red weal across his cheek.

I wondered how Chris had derived such a low opinion of his sister.

Life carried on much the same into the new year, the one defining moment being when we eventually did decide to get married.

We had been living together for barely a year and were lying together one April afternoon, having spontaneously made love on the sofa.

'We've been very blessed,' I said, 'having each other, our house, our health. We might as well get married.'

She leant over and kissed me. 'That would be lovely, darling. Let's do it!'

'I'll go to the registry office tomorrow and make arrangements.'

'My parents will hate the idea of the registry office,' she said. 'They've always imagined me in a white dress in church with hundreds of guests.'

'Is that what you want?'

'Certainly not. Besides, it would cost a fortune. We could spend that on a trip.'

In the event, the trip became more important than the wedding, with us making plans to go to Ireland for a couple of weeks. Putting the cart before the horse, we did the trip first, arriving on the ferry at Rosslare on a bright May afternoon.

We found a bed and breakfast in the town with Alison wearing the ring I had bought her to get by the Irish morality test on reception. It was then fish and chips and down to the pub, where a whisky tasting was in progress.

With several tots and a couple of pints of Guinness inside us, we rolled into bed to pass the first night of our Irish adventure.

We had brought a small tent with us, but had planned to spend some nights in the Traveller as the budget couldn't extend to bed and breakfast every night, except for the second night in Cork.

We arrived late with rain spitting on the windscreen, so we agreed to spend the money on a proper bed. While the idea was good enough, the reality was something else. Driving along the North side of the River Lee, we spotted a sign and drew up outside.

'Wait here. I'll go and investigate.'

Set in a long terrace of four storey buildings, I knocked on the door.

'Good evenin', sir. Are yer wantin' a room, then?' the scruffily dressed woman on the threshold asked.

'Yes, for my wife and I.'

'Well, yer better be comin' t' have a look.'

She turned and led me along the dark hallway and up the steep flight of stairs that took us to the top of the building. Removing a bunch of keys from her apron pocket, she fumbled to find the right one and opened the door to a room at the back of the house.

A high double bed lay before us, a washbasin in the corner and a window looking out to a yard and the backs of more dreary houses beyond.

'It'll be three pounds wit' the breakfast between seven and half past nine.'

It was not exactly what I had wanted, but the rain was by now beating on the window and it was getting dark.

'Okay, we'll have it.'

I followed her downstairs and she handed me the keys.

'This one is for the front door. I'll be lockin' up at half past ten.'

It was already gone nine and we hadn't eaten. I took our bags back to the room and we drove off into the city.

'Look, Adam,' Alison exclaimed, 'there's an Afghan restaurant.'

'You're kidding!'

No, really.'

Finding a parking place, we ran in under an umbrella, shaking ourselves dry before sitting down at one of the scrubbed tables.

An Afghan flag, a gaudy mural of what looked like the countryside along the Bamiyan valley and a few discoloured photographs of village life in cheap frames hung on the wall. A huge iron cowl over a bed of burning charcoal occupied the far corner, from where waiters in coloured kameez carried trays of food to the customers.

The menu was limited and any notions of re-capturing something of the desert restaurants beneath the stars, which had been so much a part of our Indian adventures, were soon shattered. Plates of tough and greasy barbecued meat, rice and raisins, a small serving of cauliflower and stale flat bread were brought to our table. It was edible, but a wet evening in Cork did not quite substitute for the myriad stars and the warm night air of the desert.

With five minutes to spare we had returned to the lodgings and climbed to our room ready to sink into bed together. Pulling back the covers, we realised the sheets had not been changed for some time and that the room itself was altogether grubby. It was a stark reminder of our travels, where such places were taken in their stride. Not knowing which door to knock on to complain, all I could do was return to the car and bring up our sleeping bags for the night, placing them side by side on the bed.

Next morning, we surmised that, if the bed was in the state it was, what sort of condition was the kitchen. As we had not paid, we tip-toed down the stairs at six o' clock, glancing in the kitchen on the way, where preparations were being made for breakfast, only to confirm our suspicions. Quietly closing the main door behind us, we got in the car and drove off.

Our two weeks passed quickly, with us sleeping in the presence of a prehistoric stone circle, on towering cliff tops and harbours facing the wild Atlantic, where the next stop was America, the destination of so many impoverished and persecuted Irish before us.

Being amongst the wild honesty of this beautiful country with its uncompromising seashores, its verdant trees and hills, tumbling rivers and a history lost in the myths of fairies and leprechauns, served only to cement the love between Alison and myself.

Our return home, as with our individual returns from India some time before, only served to clarify how pedestrian our lives had become and might continue to be.

Both of us were still not yet thirty with at least as much again ahead of us. We could not keep grabbing at the next material fix to sustain our sanity over this time, whether it be a new house, a car, sofa, meal out or a tryst with friends.

The wedding went ahead with families and a few friends gathering in the former mediaeval friary in the centre of Bristol.

The two families had never met with tentative rivalry between parents at first, principally between the two mothers who initially compared outfits and hats from afar, until after the ceremony when they could finally relax.

Alison recaptured something of the cheesecloth and sandals she had worn in Bombay for our evening together. On a beautiful June day, she was indeed the bride to whom all others looked.

In a flowing delicately embroidered cream dress, gathered at the waist with a plunging neckline and long billowing sleeves, she was a fairy tale princess. A turquoise necklace decorated her slender neck and a garland of white roses and daisies crowned her head.

She was the beauty I had always thought I would never find, such was my long held lack of confidence in my own gifts, drummed in somewhat by my mother's constant comparisons of myself with other's achievements and qualities.

The ceremony was formal and brief with Graham acting as best man, before we all relocated in a flotilla of cars to the Avon Gorge Hotel where we assembled on the terrace overlooking the bridge for the reception.

The sun continued to grace us all as friends and family circulated with drinks and banter. Even the two mothers had found each other and were engaged in what looked like convivial conversation.

All went well until we were sitting inside to eat and time came for the best man's speech. Drawing on anecdotes supplied by Alison, Alex, Teresa and others about myself, he raised a few laughs until he thought it would be amusing to describe in graphic detail, no doubt derived from Daisy, my humiliation at our window when all was displayed to the world.

There was a gasp, some embarrassed titters and a prevailing silence until Daisy pulled him back into his seat.

That August, Elvis died and a little bit of me went with him. It had been hearing *Heartbreak Hotel* that had projected me at the age of seven into a trajectory of enquiry and rebellion.

Twenty-five

ALISON WAS EVENTUALLY promoted to sister and with that came not only more money, but also more responsibilities. She had stopped taking the pill some time before, as we had thought perhaps her mother was right and we should try for a baby. The weeks and months progressed with us committed to the idea and making every effort for a conception. But, it just did not happen.

Alison had been complaining of painful and heavy periods, feeling sick, constipation and diarrhoea. Even making love was painful. Above all, she had no energy for life. Everything had become such an effort, waking each morning after a fitful night, hating the thought of another day. She often snapped at me for little reason. Eventually, we both went for tests. While my sperm count was considered good, Alison's condition was more problematic and mysterious.

The doctor said she had something called Endometriosis where, apparently, pieces of the womb lining start growing where they shouldn't and, in Alison's case, around the fallopian tubes.

They put her on pain killers at first, but the problems persisted and an operation was suggested to remove some or all of the growth around her tubes. The operation was successful and, after a month off work, we tried to return to some sort of normality. She'd been told that the operation might improve her chances of getting pregnant, but there were no promises.

We were well into 1980 when she returned to the doctor to seek a more permanent solution. The bleeding had increased and so had the pain. It was intolerable for her and it was ripping us apart. She was often off sick, putting more pressure on me to supply the income.

The country had seen the dying days of a Labour government with rubbish piling up in the streets, the dead unburied and, it seemed, an endless cycle of strikes.

In the General Election of 1979, the Conservatives were elected, led by Britain's first woman Prime Minister, Margaret Thatcher. By November of that year, interest rates had risen to seventeen percent and we still had a mortgage to pay.

My illustration work no longer brought in enough, although I had had some success with a limited edition of prints with a London publisher but, after the initial advance, the royalties were only a trickle. I worked through one winter as a postman, getting up at five each morning, sorting my letters and completing my *walk* as quickly as possible in order to get home to look after Alison and get on with whatever commissions I was managing to get.

Eventually, I realised that I had to do something more substantial and found myself dusting off my teaching certificate.

I eased myself back in as a supply teacher, constantly having a *bag of tricks* ready for a phone call at a moment's notice to go to one school or another.

Sometimes, I would find myself with a class of junior children for a week or two, teaching most subjects throughout each day. Alternatively, I might be in the turmoil of a secondary school where, as in many of those in Bristol, you took your life in your hands. Most of the time, I would be teaching art and, if I wasn't supervising an on-going project set by the teacher who was off sick, I would be able to set my own. However, there were many a time I would be facing a class of teenagers, whose attention span and interest in Geography, History or English was limited to say the least.

There was one day, I went in with a winter cold, having been constantly blowing my nose. During a Geography class, I blew it once too often and was shocked to find my handkerchief suddenly saturated with blood from a profuse nosebleed. Despite my efforts to stem the flow, it persisted and I ended the class with paper tissue stuck up my nostril.

It caused much mirth and indeed a little sympathy from a couple of the girls.

Meanwhile, Alison could not get pregnant and her pain had worsened.

There followed months of visits to the doctor for drugs and treatments with homeopaths and even an acupuncturist, whose needles helped alleviate the pain, but not the condition.

Eventually, we both concluded that Alison's well-being was more important than a baby. The doctors recommended a hysterectomy and an operation was fixed for February 1981.

Christmas was a dismal affair. Alison wanted to be with her parents. She had lost a lot of weight and her complexion was pallid. The life seemed to have gone out of her with pain permanently etched on her face. Her parents were caring and considerate over the couple of days we were there with her brother not once bothering to provoke his sister.

To add to our misery, John Lennon had been shot dead in New York, just as his new album, *Double Fantasy,* was being released. Alison gave it to me for Christmas and, as I looked at the black and white cover of John and Yoko, I cried for what we had all lost and for what Alison and I were about to lose.

A firework display in Bristol docks saw in the New Year and Alison, wrapped in jumpers, scarf and a warm coat, managed to feign the occasional smile as the clusters of coloured light burst over the water.

Alison had her small case packed for the days she would be in hospital and, on a cold, February evening with the street lamps barely visible through the fog, I drove her down to the hospital in readiness for the surgery the following day at three in the afternoon. They needed to completely relax her and ensure she had no food or drink for at least eight hours beforehand.

I returned the next day to be near during the surgery and was allowed to see her before she went in.

'I'm frightened,' were her first words as she lay in the bed, her beautiful blonde hair already lank on the pillow.

'Don't worry, my darling,' I whispered. 'They'll make sure you're okay. You've met the surgeon and he's answered all your questions. I'll be here when you wake up and remember, I love you. Come on, give me one of your smiles.'

Her cheeks twitched a little in response as she tried to allay her fear, but it still showed in her tearful blue eyes.

'I won't be able to give you children after this. It's all my fault,' she sobbed.

'What do you mean? It's nobody's *fault*,' I replied as I dabbed her cheeks with my handkerchief.

'I liked sex too much. I'm sure that's what caused it.'

'I don't think the doctors really know what causes it.'

'I wanted it to be so good for us. I'm so sorry, I've not been able to be close to you. It's been too painful for me.'

'I didn't want to impose on you either, knowing you were in pain.'

'It must have been so frustrating.'

'At times. Don't worry, darling, we can still cuddle.'

I kissed her gently on the lips and forehead before I was eventually ushered out by the nurse.

There was time spent preparing her before the anaesthetic and then I waited. I'd brought a book to read, my third attempt at Herman Hesse's, *Glass Bead Game*, but couldn't concentrate, instead pacing the waiting room, drinking vile coffee from a vending machine and staring out at the buildings and the street below. Matchstick people were pursuing their lives. Who knew what problems rested on their shoulders? Were their dilemmas any worse than mine or just different?

The clock on the wall ticked steadily round to four o' clock, half past and five. I'd been told the operation would last between one and two hours.

'What were they doing?'

The road below caught my attention again as a siren pierced the air and I saw an ambulance speeding through the traffic and turning into the hospital admissions, doubtless containing some poor soul, the victim of a traffic accident, heart attack, burst appendix or a thousand other reasons.

'Mr Busk? Mr Busk?' a gentle disembodied voice behind me enquired.

I turned to face a young nurse, a replica of Alison in many ways in her uniform.

'It's all over. We've brought your wife back to the ward. She's a little groggy as to be expected. Would you like to see her?'

I nodded and smiled on hearing she was all right, then followed her through the corridors to the ward.

'It was a bit more complicated than we first thought,' she said. 'She's going to need a lot of rest.'

The surgeon, a tall thin man with greying hair and grey complexion, his habit betrayed by the nicotine on his fingers, was with Alison when we arrived at her bed. She lay motionless with eyes shut, her face drained, but more peaceful than I had seen her for some time.

'Mr Busk?' the surgeon enquired.

'Pleased to meet you,' I replied stretching out my hand to meet his. 'How is she? Is she going to be all right?'

'It was complicated and she lost some blood, but she's pulled through. She's still young and strong. We'll be keeping her in for a week or so to keep an eye on her. How are things at home? Will she be able to rest?'

'I can assure you, she's going to get the very best care.'

He smiled and nodded his head in approval.

'A nurse will visit for the first few days at home to inspect the wound, check for abnormal bleeding and advise on exercising. Your wife will have to wear special stockings for a while to prevent blood clots. The nurse will be able to answer any questions and we're always here if you're at all worried. She'll also tell you about the follow ups over the next few years.'

'Few years?'

'Yes, it's up to five years. We have to be sure all is well.'

I looked at Alison again, so still under the covers and thought of that thin line between life and death and how easily it could have gone the other way.

I sat by her side for an hour or two, waiting for her to open her eyes. The nurse brought me a cup of tea and a couple of biscuits, but her eyes remained closed until it was suggested I go home for the night and come back in the morning.

I kissed her forehead, now a little cold and damp, praying she would awaken before I left, but she was lost in another world to which I had no access.

I shivered as I opened the front door to our house and turned on the light, sensing its silence and emptiness. Normally, at this time of the evening, we would be cooking dinner with some music playing, perhaps a glass of wine on the go and chatting about our days or something we were planning to do.

Now, she was lying in a hospital bed, forlorn that something so central to her being, her womanhood, had gone for ever. It would never come back and we would continue living together the best we could with this great emptiness in our lives.

Somehow, we would get through it, finding happiness where we could.

I heated some cauliflower cheese that had been left over from the night before and sat alone at the table. Repressed tears brought a lump to my throat. I was not even able to put on any music, such was the hollow inside and my overwhelming need to swallow the sadness in silence.

I left the half eaten food on the table and went to bed, my tears eventually being assuaged by the deep overwhelming exhaustion that had been consuming me.

A bunch of sweet smelling freesias were little compensation for what had happened when I went to see Alison the next day.

She was awake and sitting up, her eyes red from crying as she stared into nothingness. I had to hold her hand to bring her focus back. 'Hello, darling. How are you?'

Her face started to scrunch as more tears welled up at the realisation of what had been done to her. She seemed to have aged overnight, such was the distress now showing in every line of her face.

'Are you still in pain?' I asked.

Her mouth turned down and she nodded.

'What have they given you today? Are you allowed to eat anything yet?'

I asked these futile questions, while trying to comprehend how she felt. To get under her skin and transfer the pain from her to myself.

'I bet I look wretched. Don't I?' she eventually said. 'They've put me in this awful gown that doesn't even cover my bum, I've got bandages over the cut in my belly, a drain tube hanging out and

I'm on a catheter with a piss bag.'

We both laughed.

'Can you drink water?'

'Yes, but I'd love a glass of wine.'

'You shall have it, when I get you home.'

'My mother phoned today. She wants me to go there for a couple of weeks.'

'Is that what you want?'

'Our bedroom is still a mess.'

'I'll take you if you want and work on the bedroom next, but I'm not sure if you'll be well enough to travel all the way to Kent and what about the nurse visits?'

'I've already asked and they said they would liaise with the Kent health authorities and send a nurse to my parents' home.'

'I just want to see you well again, darling. I'll do whatever's best.'

In the end, they kept her in for eight days, exercising her daily to ensure she could walk unaided and to reduce the possibility of blood clots..

I took her home for the first night, cooking spaghetti bolognese with a salad.

'I got your favourite wine,' I said, as I gently helped her to sit at the table and poured a glass.

'Welcome home, Ali,' I said, as I chinked my glass on hers. 'Here's to a speedy recovery.'

'The therapist came to see me yesterday,' she said, 'and told me we can have sex in a few weeks, when all this bleeding and discharge stops. She said that many women report having even better sex after the op.'

'That's good news, but there's no hurry. We can always cuddle.'

That night, we fell asleep spooned together in a loving embrace. She woke a few times feeling sore around her wound, peeing and turning frequently to make herself more comfortable. Having her home was the greatest gift and I thanked God for bringing her through it.

It was normally a seven hour drive from Bristol to her parents' village half way between Canterbury and Dover but, allowing for several pee stops and for Alison to stretch her legs, we knew this journey would be much longer. It was a long time for her to sit and I was all too conscious of the possibility of the blood clots we had been warned about, although we listened to the advice to take sufficient drinking water.

The rain had started even before we'd left Bristol and, by the time we reached the straight stretch of road on the A4 between Avebury and Marlborough, it was torrential with the wipers barely able to clear the water from the windscreen quickly enough.

With little warning, the car suddenly jolted, slowed and ground to an ignominious halt. We had plenty of petrol and there had been no untoward noise to suggest something too serious. We looked at each other in despair. I had no option but to brave the wet with my jacket over my head and look under the bonnet.

Before we had left for Ireland, I had replaced the cylinder head gasket, straining my chest in removing the head to the extent that I woke in the middle of the night, thinking I was having a heart attack. On seeing the doctor next morning, he assured me my heart was perfectly okay and that I had merely pulled muscles in my chest. In the process of doing this job, I'd got to know a fair bit of what went on under the bonnet.

My first instinct, putting the rain into the equation, was that it was something electrical, but where? As the rain drove into the engine space, I was desperately trying to keep everything dry, throwing our picnic blanket over the bonnet like a curtain to keep the worst of it off. I cleaned and dried all the spark plugs and their connections, then removed the distributor cap. It was wet inside. With a bit of sandpaper, I burnished the points, dried them as best I could and replaced the cap.

Hopping back inside, I turned the ignition and, with a little hesitation, the engine burst into life.

'You're soaked, Adam. You can't go on like that,' a concerned Alison said.

We stopped for coffee in tea rooms in Marlborough, where a roaring fire took the edge off my sorry state. As we set off again with our heater blowing warm air, I told Alison of my journey through Turkey with Masood and Latif in the VW with the broken heater.

Our eventual arrival was met by lots of fussing and I could see Alison shrinking straightaway at the thought of two weeks with her mother. I had dried a little, but was still offered some of Bill's clothes, while mine dried completely over the AGA.

I stayed the night and Alison was grilled over dinner about her condition and assured as to how Audrey, with the very best intentions, was going to look after her.

As I left next morning for the long drive back, I was concerned.

'If there are any problems, you must ring me. The nurse will be with you later, so you mustn't worry about a thing,' I said, holding her close and kissing her.

I'd promised to finish the bedroom before Alison returned, working on an illustration by day and the bedroom by evening into the early hours. Over the first four days, one day was *lost* as I had a day's supply teaching and had to work into the night to make up my hours to finish the illustration by the following morning. But, for most of the time, I worked into the early hours to complete all the paintwork and paper the walls before I received a phone call on the afternoon of my fifth day alone.

'Hello,' I said on picking up the phone.

'Can you come and collect me, Darling? I can't stand it here a moment longer.'

It was Alison and I could tell she was distressed.

The next day was Wednesday and I had to turn down three days' teaching in order to make the journey back to Kent and home again.

I had suspected that the problem might have been between Alison and her mother and my arrival only confirmed my suspicions.

Alison had been waiting at the window and rushed out to me as I drove in.

'Oh, Adam, it's been dreadful,' she said, tearfully. 'She's been going on at me about not having grandchildren for her and how they paid for our wedding and this was how I had rewarded her. She's such a selfish bitch.'

Audrey was shamefaced as I went into the house, acting as if nothing had been said and fawning over me with a cup of tea and a huge slice of Victoria sponge.

'Alison has told me what you've been saying to her. That's really not fair, is it?' I said, not caring if I was being polite our not. This was not a time for standing on ceremony. 'Do you really think she wanted this? We had been trying for a baby for some time, until we went to the doctor and heard the worst. I don't think you appreciate what this has done to Alison and all you can think about is how it's upset *your* tidy little world. Well, I'm sorry, but you'll just have to learn to live with it as we are having to.'

She sat down at the table, burying her chin in her hand and dabbing her eyes with the handkerchief she kept in her cardigan sleeve.

'It was so unexpected. I had such hopes,' she sobbed.

'You'd better start hoping for something else then. Firstly, that Alison is well again. She's been through hell the last few months. Have you ever considered that? Probably not!'

'Now, now, old chap,' Bill piped in.

'I'm sorry, Bill, but I don't think you have any more idea about this than Audrey. We thank you for the wedding but, as John Lennon said, "Life is what happens when you're busy making other plans." Come on, darling, let's get you home.'

The traffic was light with only a few roadworks to slow us down as we drove through the evening and, after a few pee stops and take-away fish and chips, got home just before one in the morning.

Alison was exhausted, but too wired to sleep, instead wanting to open a bottle of wine and unwind, eventually agreeing to bed at just gone three. I helped her upstairs and into bed, but she was too distraught to notice my work on the bedroom.

Twenty-six

THE DAYS TURNED into weeks and months and slowly Alison came to terms with her condition. She became stronger and more often than not had a smile on her face, although I would witness her sadness when we were out and saw mothers with children, shopping or playing in the park.

We often talked about adoption, but she was sure she could never give the same love to a child that was not her own.

She returned to work, diverting her love and compassion into caring for her patients, just as she had always intended when she first became a nurse.

We had bad days as do most people. For us, it was being reminded of what might have been. Friends, of course, had children and we always heard of their progress, although most were sensitive enough not to dwell too long on the subject unless Alison specifically asked.

Her brother, Chris, eventually married. Not the girl from Ruislip but, Celia, a girl from Reigate, whom he had met at work. They eventually had a boy and a girl, who Alison adored and always made sure they had lovely presents for Christmas and birthdays.

For myself, after several teaching positions during the eighties, I eventually got a job as a lecturer in a local college where, as well as teaching a range of art and design skills, I became a specialist with the fledgling Apple computers, having had the opportunity to be one of the first in the country to use one of the machines with a nine inch black and white screen and 400 kilobyte floppy disk.

My first exposure to computers had been watching someone

poring over a BBC machine, entering tedious code in order to draw a red circle. This was definitely not for me as I returned to my drawing board with compasses, brushes and gouache.

But the Apple-Macintosh, as it was better known, with its aptly named mouse to guide an arrow on the screen and execute commands was a game changer. At first, I was using simple black and white drawing and paint programs as well as what was commonly called Desk Top Publishing to create page layouts for magazines and news-sheets.

As time went on, I heard about something called Photoshop and other programs that enabled page layouts, animation, video editing and, with the advent of the internet, web design. I was completely hooked into the creative possibilities, so much so that my interest and use of fundamental drawing and painting diminished.

I too threw myself into my work, often coming home to sit up late learning a new program so that I could better teach it.

As we grew older, so my love for Alison grew stronger. Our sex life had seen a marked improvement as the issues with her operation diminished and, to all intents and purposes, she was her old self most of the time, having regained her strength and vitality. But, most of the time, I just wanted to care and nourish her, much as I might have indulged a child, had we had one.

She had passed the age when she could have had children and had mostly put that behind her, save for the occasional lapse into despondency and silent tears.

Nevertheless, as pressures of work increased, the gulf between us widened with her often staying out late at a wine bar, leaving me to get on with my work.

Our lives were led as fully as we were able, taking holidays, meeting friends, watching the passage of history take its course; The Falklands War, The Miners' Strike, Live Aid, Roger Waters leaving Pink Floyd, the first Gulf war, Nelson Mandala's release from prison, the fall of the Berlin Wall, the coming of the internet, genocide in Rwanda and Bosnia and then my own brush with death.

It was the mid nineties. autumn of 1995 to be precise. The trees had almost shed their leaves into damp piles on the ground. The smell of rotting and death hung in the air as the days shortened and Britain descended into cold wet days and prolonged darkness, only broken by the occasional flash of sunshine, through rain drenched clouds.

Pain is a funny old thing. Like an aspect of polite social behaviour, we instinctively know when we should or should not publicly display our distress.

Alison's brother, Chris, wife, Celia and their two fully fledged teenagers, were staying for the weekend. We'd had a long but pleasant Saturday touring the sights of Bristol, before returning home to pizzas, salad and a good bottle of red.

Like the early rumblings of a shift in the earth's crust, a dull pain crept up within the deepest recesses of my stomach. At first, I put it down to indigestion and wind, but it intensified as the evening wore on, leaving me increasingly more detached from what was going on. Pulling my knees up to my chest, I rocked a little from one side to the other in the armchair.

'Are you all right?' Celia asked.

'Just a bit of stomach pain,' I replied. 'It'll go in a while.'

But, in a while, it hadn't and I excused myself for the toilet, hoping for some relief that never came. Not returning to the others, I first lay on the floor in the hallway, but it made little difference as I groaned and rolled from one side to the other.

I had no true understanding of what was going on inside my body and needed to know where I stood. So I groaned a little more before hauling myself slowly up the stairs to stretch my naked stomach on the cool bed cover or roll from one side to another in vain attempts to sooth the pain. As the minutes ticked by, any palliative effects soon wore off and the pain intensified. I'd never known anything like it, lying in a state of semi-oblivion, only really conscious of my own sweating and shaking.

I don't know how long it was before Alison came up to see how I was. By this time, I was writhing across the bed totally unable to allay the pain for even a moment. For some bizarre reason, she initially found this funny, her laughter increasing incrementally with my groans, until she finally realised I wasn't joking.

'Adam,' she called, coming over to touch my brow, by then brimming with hot sweat. 'You're not well, are you? Do you want me to call the doctor?'

'Yes! Fucking Yes!' I screamed.

It seemed like an age, after she'd called and returned to mop my brow with a damp flannel, before the doorbell rang and she went down to answer the door. There was some muffled conversation as feet were scraped on the mat and Alison led the doctor upstairs. He seemed huge from the perspective of the bed, arriving around the door, his hair streaming raindrops over his face and onto the shoulders of his damp raincoat.

Amidst the rustle of gaberdine and the occasional involuntary splash, the doctor found me rolling on the bed in a foetal position, the pose that seemed to be the most beneficial. Being the doctor I had known and trusted for years, he immediately put me at my ease, making the obligatory temperature check, a call to cough and probing with the cold end of his stethoscope and agile fingers that made me wince.

'I think I can safely say, you've got appendicitis.'

Turning to Alison, he asked, 'Can I use your phone, I need to call an ambulance?'

'*My God,*' I thought. '*This must be real pain. Shout it from the rooftops pain. He's called an ambulance!*'

The wait seemed interminable. The doctor had to leave and some twenty minutes later, with the arrival of the paramedics, I was being inexorably coaxed along as an object for priority care and attention.

It was drizzling as I shuffled, one pain-filled footstep at a time out of the front door, supported by a male and female paramedic. The cold air hit me and I immediately felt sick. The ambulance doors gaped wide open with the illuminated interior waiting to receive me, but all I cared for was to stand one foot in the gutter and dribble.

Having got me off my feet and onto a stretcher, I was tucked in with blankets and introduced to gas and air; that great double act that had seen a multitude of mothers through childbirth.

The nightmare train of events that was to follow, now began in earnest as I saw Chris and family waving to me through the mirror glass of the rear windows, while Alison joined me and we set off with the siren piercing the night air.

The last time I had been in an ambulance with sirens blaring was to accompany Belinda to hospital after her heroin overdose.

Alison held my hand as I had held Belinda's all those years before.

I was taken to Southmead, a former workhouse that had evolved into a hospital with pre-fabricated units that sprawled across the site in North Bristol.

No bed was free nor, on a Saturday night, was a surgeon available to deal with the diagnosis. Alison and I just had to wait in the stillness of an empty waiting room lit by stark fluorescent tubes that seemed to drain the blood from people's faces. With no refreshment or pain relief for myself, in case I had to be operated on at a moment's notice, the hours ticked by until, around three, two porters arrived to wheel me into surgery.

With the rubber mask placed over my face, a few deep breaths and I was disappearing down a dark tunnel leaving behind the fading image of a masked anaesthetist with intensely tired eyes.

I knew nothing until I woke next morning in the ward and was eventually visited by the duty doctor.

'You've had a lucky escape,' he told me. 'We just caught your appendix before it completely burst. By all accounts, the smell was horrendous. I don't know what you kept in there, but some infection may have seeped into your system, so we'll have to keep an eye on you.'

As with Alison before me, my wound was bandaged and tubes seemed to be coming out of everywhere, my nose, wrist and penis. I felt wretched, being forbidden food and granted only a thimble of water every few hours. I would have to be monitored until my digestive system kicked back into action.

Alison had stayed on, catching a few hours fitful sleep on a spare trolley. She came to see me after the doctor had finished his rounds.

'Darling, how are you? I was so worried. They said it had been very touch and go.'

'Is that what they said? You mean I could have been *a gonna*?'

'I think that's what they meant.'

She stayed half an hour before leaving to ensure Chris and Celia had something to eat before the drive back to Kent.

Various men occupied the beds within my field of view, some

sitting up with neatly buttoned pyjamas talking with their neighbours, others reading the paper, while some lay motionless under the bedding, their expressions distanced and withdrawn.

I envied them the food trolleys throughout the day, bringing meals and cups of tea so, by the time Alison came to visit me in the evening, she found me despondent and withdrawn.

'I'll ring work for you in the morning, darling. They're going to miss you for a few weeks. I've got your sketch pad and a couple of books for you.'

'Thank you, Ali. You've got the car then?'

'Yes, it was nice to get back behind the wheel again.' Her own tiredness was showing, accentuating the lines that had since emerged through her own suffering and anxiety. She had put on weight since her operation, her face now fuller, but her innate beauty still shone through the new frame that harboured her soul.

As each day passed, I was encouraged by the nurse to take a few tentative steps in order to find my feet again and rebuild my strength. By the end of the first week, with some difficulty, I was eventually able to walk down the length of the corridor.

I had started reading Brian Keenan's account of his captivity in Lebanon with journalist, John McCarthy. One passage described how they were incarcerated at one time in a tiny cell together with insufficient space to either stand or stretch to their full length.

The sense of claustrophobia came over me in nauseating waves as I equated their experience a little with my own entrapment in the six foot by two foot six bed.

This had now become my world in which solitary days passed in endless cycles of medication, sleep and a yearning to be free. So much had this become the compass of my existence that I even became agitated by anyone who might sit on and ruffle my carefully smoothed covers.

By the end of the first week, my digestive system was clearly not going to work of its own accord and I was wheeled back into surgery for a more radical incursion into my inner workings. A cut was made from pelvis to tummy button in order to completely remove my intestines, clean them and stuff them back

The original surgeon had mysteriously forgotten to put a drain in my wound and a build up of infection had occurred. Streptococcus

Milleri, a particularly deadly infection, had already claimed the lives of two patents since I had arrived.

I had wondered what all the crying out in the night had been and my curiosity was answered by a junior doctor who had come to ask a few questions about my condition. Two men, one younger than myself had succumbed to the infection and he was curious as to how I had managed to pull through. Despite the pain, I had never considered leaving and clearly it was not to be my time.

I had now added a further scar to my collection, conflicting a little with the snake tattoo, inscribed on my stomach by Helsdon with his cut throat razor. Whilst, by now a little faded, it was still evident and its presence had always been necessary to explain to all who saw it, from Belinda to Kamala and Alison with all others in between.

On my return to the ward, I was drained of energy and despondent at having to start all over again; learning to walk and preparing to eat some real food other than the liquid nourishment being dripped into me through tubes.

Meanwhile, someone in their wisdom had decided to put me on regular morphine injections. Whether because there was a strong chance I might die and it would help me on my way, I shall never know, but it certainly helped with the pain and much more.

Not since my days on LSD in the sixties had I experienced anything remotely akin to an out of body experience, but now I was regularly hovering above my bedridden self, cleansed of pain and scars in a state of prolonged euphoria. I knew it would have been all too easy to cut the cord and float off into oblivion, but I kept returning to hours of sleep and a demi world of trolleys, nurses and cries of distress.

Very slowly, I began to heal, celebrating the day a young nurse wheeled me to the bathroom for a hot bath. I had no inhibitions about my nakedness or the state of my body, despite catching myself in the mirror as a much depleted version of what I had previously known. This shadow before me was more akin to a survivor from a death camp. But, I could only accept what was before me and be glad to be helped like a young child into the steaming water to soak away the trauma of the previous two weeks.

Alison visited nearly every day, punctuated by friends from work, dropping in with *Get Well* cards, books and fruit and telling me how much I was being missed.

It was only early November, but I knew it would be months before I could return.

By mid November, I was taking in solids and walking with the aid of a stick. It was time to go home. Having Alison beside me was like being blessed by an angel. She would insist on me resting regularly, she cooked me food and helped with the medication I had to keep taking.

I returned to work in February the following year; perhaps sooner than I should have, but I was restless in more ways than one.

Since my return from India so many years earlier, I had been thinking back to one of the questions I had asked the Dalai Lama, relating to the use of machines and technology to free us up for spiritual matters. In the early years, I had maintained my efforts at meditation, together with a more creative expression of what I had learned about tanka painting.

But slowly, as life with Alison and the distractions of work, friends and repetitious evenings soaking up what was on offer on television, it all started to be forgotten. The memories of what I understood to be my place in the universe remained memories and I was doing little to reinforce my knowing.

Life had become the drudge I had always feared, full of mostly meaningless activities that merely filled time and provided excuses for the fears that dominated our lives. Fear of lack was the principal calling, preying on worries about money, paying the mortgage and even unemployment.

We had got into the cycle of things to ease the distress, new furniture, clothes, a computer. All things that brought their five minutes of pleasure only to be usurped by the desire for something else. What had happened with being content and having gratitude for being alive in God's universe?

Something had to change for both of us. Our work so dominated our time that something radical was needed to bring us back together. For a while, we resolved to go out together, come what may, every Thursday evening, whether to the cinema, theatre, a meal. This worked well for a few weeks until the *come what mays* crept in - a meeting, a late shift, student work to be marked by next morning. All these diluted our resolve and we were soon back to where we had begun.

Alison was staying out more often after work and I began to wonder if she was having an affair. We still occasionally made love, but the passion had left. Was it from getting older, years of familiarity or something more sinister?

I didn't want to confront Alison in case I was being unduly suspicious, but doubts caused me to wonder about my own future and whether we could sustain something from the wreckage.

This continued for the next two years, our distance increasing with each passing week.

At college, a new lecturer caught my attention and I found myself seeking her company during breaks or savouring a furtive conversation in the corridor. She was about ten years younger than me, still single, but possessing many of the qualities that had first attracted me to Alison on that hot night in Bombay.

In contrast, she had long chestnut hair, energy, exuberance and she even made me laugh; a rare occurrence these days at home.

One afternoon, in the latter stages of the summer term, she invited me to dinner in her flat. Anticipating that Alison would more than likely be out again, I accepted, knowing I was breaking a trust, but excited by the possibilities.

Our conversation was ceaseless; a great outpouring of common interests, which took us through dinner to coffee on the sofa, where inhibition had left the room.

At first, the careless brush of hands, reaching for the coffee pot, but then I found myself being taken back twenty years when nothing mattered and I was free to do what I wished. She had nothing to lose, whereas I had what now amounted to nineteen years of marriage, which could all be thrown away in a moment of madness.

But that moment was upon me as she stretched across to hold my hand, drawing me closer to her as she lay back invitingly across the sofa.

The thrill of the new, seeing for the first time those objects of the imagination, was presenting itself without any conditions.

We saw each other during the summer, for days out, picnics, cooking for each other in her flat and making love.

We even planned a stay in a Devon bed and breakfast, where we led a carefree few days, walking along the cliff tops, sheltering from the summer rain and spending hours in bed together. I was supposedly having time to myself for some sketching but, in truth, it was an idyllic rediscovery of a carefree existence and something of the self I once knew before it became buried in daily routine. But, I knew it to be unrealistic, a fantasy that would ultimately take me full circle to where I was with Alison.

I suspected she wanted children and she even asked me one day if I would give her a baby.

At that point, I knew it had to be over and I ended it soon after returning for the autumn term. She was distraught and angry, causing me to fear she might inform Alison.

Soon after, I sat with Alison and spilled my heart.

'Darling, there's something I have to tell you.'

'I know,' she replied emphatically.

'What do you know?'

'I've known almost from the beginning. You didn't think you could keep that a secret, Adam. Seriously?'

'How did you find out?'

'You mostly, but I've had my spies. You and her were seen in Weston and, quite by chance, Jean Bishop and her husband, down the road, went to Devon for their holidays. You were in plain sight.'

'It's over now. I couldn't live with myself, knowing I was betraying you. But, then, I thought you were having an affair. You were spending so many evenings out. I could only conclude one thing…'

'You were right… I met a doctor.'

Those words seared through me like a hot knife. I looked at her in disbelief, feeling desolate and angry with myself for not giving her more attention.

'After all we have done together,' I said. 'All we have gone though, loving and supporting each other. How has it come to this? Do you love him? More to the point, does he love you? Oh, Alison, I'm so sorry. Can't we still make a go of it. Isn't this what so many couples go through after twenty years? Let's not become another statistic.'

'He's married,' she blurted out, 'with three children.'

'Is the sex better or is it the novelty of the new? That's what it was for me, but I had to learn the hard way, realising that, beyond the sex, it's the you underneath that matters. It is you, Alison, that I love, for so many reasons. Your kindness, patience, the way you giggle in your sleep, your eyes…'

'Yes, it was something new,' she interrupted. 'It was how it had been for us. Why did we lose that?'

'It's not lost, just misplaced. We can find it again. I do love you, Ali. Please believe me. Do you still love me?'

She stared at me with incomprehension, tears now rolling down her cheeks, as if somehow I had brought all this into being.

I took her in my arms and kissed the top of her head, knowing deep down that this was the same Alison who had seduced me so long before.

She looked up at me, her cheeks now stained with rivulets of drying tears.

'Yes, I still love you. I know I've neglected you and spent too much time indulging myself.'

'Then, so have I with my work and I know I've neglected you, for which I'm so sorry.'

I made a resolution, there and then to pull back on my work, conscious still that I was in a vicious cycle of upgrading my knowledge as each new version of software showed itself. What had once been something I had found exciting and challenging, I was now beginning to curse, finding it overwhelming and tedious.

We saw the new century in with friends, watching the excruciating performance of Tony Blair, the Prime Minister, tentatively holding hands with the Queen in a rendition of *Auld Lang Syne* from the Millennium Dome in Greenwich.

Only a few years earlier, he had been eulogising Princess Diana, following her death, and many of us had been pointing the finger at the Royals.

At the beginning of this millennium year, I was to be fifty in a couple more months and Alison fifty-one in May.

This all seemed quite incomprehensible as we wondered where all the years had gone and, on New Year's Eve, I had pondered all the things I would be doing for the last time in the twentieth century - shaving, going to the toilet, having a bath, making love, eating spaghetti, putting a CD on the player. The list went on…

The passing of the twentieth century was one of deep sadness for us both as we had both had our trials, but it had been the time of our youth, when lifetime lessons were learned and we had absorbed so many things that would eventually become comforting nostalgia, from sweet shops to adventures in the woods replete with a bottle of Tizer to the Lone Ranger, popular culture, psychedelic drugs and India. Had I resolved to stay with Kamala, would we have reached this age with the same breadth of experience and common memories?

But ahead lay the promise of a new century, Mayan prophesies of a Golden Age and the end to war.

The following year, those dreams were once again shattered, as the event that would change everyone's lives forever became the reason for endless and complete war in the Middle East and the prelude to the financial crash of 2008.

The Twin Towers, as they came to be known, on the eleventh of September, 2001, was the pre-meditated destruction of the World Trade Centre in New York, although we'd all been fed the official narrative that two planes, hijacked by Middle Eastern terrorists, had flown into the towers. Nearly three thousand people died on that day and, as Alison and I watched the television news, we were horrified to see people plunging to their deaths from the blazing buildings.

It all seemed convincing at the time until people started to point out the way the buildings collapsed, supported by the copy book controlled demolition of Building Seven, into which no plane had crashed.

It was the first great crime of the century, but much more evil was to follow.

As the next few years unfolded, it seemed a madness had overtaken the World. War and the pointless killing and displacement of innocent people appeared nightly on the television with those suffering the most appearing to be women and children, who flooded into refugee camps and undertook suicidal journeys across seas and mountains to find a safe life in mainland Europe.

The world was on the move in unprecedented numbers.

CHAPTER
Twenty-seven

ALISON AND I had learned to look after each other better, often laughing at our mutual foolishness and mistrust at the time of our affairs.

I had taken early retirement and, with the passing of my parents, had inherited a small nest egg. We had often talked of moving abroad, as so many do, and had paved the way by buying a van and converting it into a camper.

It was the best thing we could have done, giving us freedom to roam virtually anywhere we wanted. Several holidays were spent in France, dipping into Spain and Portugal one year.

It was about the time of our fortieth wedding anniversary that our world was suddenly turned upside.

Alison had been called in for her second annual breast screening and had been waiting over two weeks for the results.

I was at home working on a painting at the time, when I heard the letterbox clatter and something falling to the mat. It was Alison's letter, which I propped up in the kitchen for when she got home.

By the time she had arrived, I'd cooked dinner, as I now frequently did, and poured us each a glass of red. We were talking about our days, when I suddenly remembered.

'Oh, I almost forgot. A letter came today. I think it must be your results.'

Like a student nervously opening her exam results, Alison slowly ran her finger along the inset of the envelope and tore it open. She stood quietly leaning against the worktop as she digested the contents, turning the pages in case she had missed something.

'They want me to go in again. Something has shown up on the mammogram and they want to do more tests.'

'Darling, I'm sure it'll be all right. It's probably a mistake. Can you feel anything?'

'I felt before and after the screening, but didn't find anything.'

'There you are then.'

I had tried to make light of it, but knew that Alison was worried sick. She hardly slept that night and for most of the following week until I took her for her appointment on a sunny July morning.

A doctor came to see us before Alison was called in.

'What we are going to do today is another mammogram and a biopsy to test some of your tissue. We'll know some more from the mammogram before you go home today, but we'll have to wait another week for the biopsy results. Are you ready?'

She looked at me forlorn and lost to the world. I hugged and kissed her, squeezing her delicate hand until the doctor coughed a little and asked again.

'Are you ready, Mrs Busk?

My grip loosened and I felt her hand fall away as she sniffed back her tears.

One last smile, a wave and she disappeared across the waiting room through a couple of swing doors.

By lunch time, she was back with me.

'They've found a shadow on the mammogram, which they think could be a lump.'

'What about the biopsy? Did it hurt you, Darling?

'I'm sore and don't really want to talk at the moment. Is that okay?' the tears starting to fill her eyes once again.

'Sure. Do you want to go home now or would you like some lunch?'

'Home. I just want to be quiet.'

She remained silent in the car and went straight to bed on our return. When I went to see her in the early evening to see if she wanted anything to eat, she was asleep and the tea I'd made was untouched and cold on the bedside table.

I curled up beside her and put my arm around her waist.

'We'll get through this, whatever happens,' I whispered.

A week later, she was called in again and got the news.

'I'm sorry to say, it's cancer,' the doctor told her. 'We need to get you in as soon as possible to remove the lump. Hopefully, we can save your breast as we've caught it quite early. You'll have a local anaesthetic and then you'll go on a low dose chemotherapy course to make sure we've got it. Take this leaflet. It will explain and put your mind at ease.'

An appointment was made for a few days later, but Alison was reluctant to go.

'Ali, we've got to go, darling. We'll be late.'

'I can't do it,' she sobbed. I'm already half a woman, now they want to cut up my breast.'

'They said it's only a small incision to remove the lump and a bit of surrounding tissue. You then need rest and the course of chemo to prevent it returning.

'What if I lose my hair? I can't lose my hair. Walking round like a Buddhist nun.'

The thought of her losing her beautiful golden, now slightly greying locks, horrified me too, but I could see no alternative.

We ate well, always fresh ingredients and junk like a pizza only very rarely. We'd tried acupuncture and homeopathy for her hysterectomy, only for her to end up having the surgery. Cancer was the scourge of our age and I certainly knew no other remedy.

It was several hours before I was allowed to see her. As when she had last come out of surgery, she was pale and struggling to walk. She'd been told to wear a good supportive bra to help with her recuperation, but still had a surgical drain to deal with excess fluid, which she would have to empty several times a day until it could be removed in a week's time.

'I've got to start chemo in three or four weeks time, depending on how well this heals. I'm dreading it.'

The following days had me attending to Alison's every need, when she wasn't sleeping. I would help her empty the fluid drain and change her bandages, whilst feeding her home made soups and healthy salads.

The three weeks passed quickly and it was time for the first dose of chemo.

I look back now and so deeply regret that we agreed to it.

Predictably, on the day, Alison was terrified of what lay ahead of her. She had dwelt on the issue, having nursed women who had undergone the therapy and witnessed at first hand the stress and side effects they had suffered.

Like a lamb to the slaughter, she was led into the treatment room, only to return to me further depleted, as if another layer of her beauty and self-confidence had been stripped off her, reaching ever closer to the fragile shell that lay beneath.

Within a week, Alison often complained of dizziness and would have to rush to the toilet to be sick. Then, one day, I heard her crying in the bathroom.

'What is it, Ali, can I help?' I asked, opening the door to find her in front of the mirror with strands of hair lying in the sink.

I put my arms around her waist and kissed her neck, but it only prompted more tears.

'I'm sorry, Adam, I couldn't have been a better wife. I'm so sorry. This isn't what I wanted. Perhaps you would be better with someone else.'

'Don't be ridiculous. You are my wife and I love you. You know I do.'

Alison's hair continued to fall and time came for her to return to the doctor for another check up.

I waited in the corridor outside the treatment room, expecting Alison to come out quickly. Forty minutes, an hour, passed with the silence eventually being broken by a loud, painful scream. I knew there could only be one person behind it.

A nurse came out and I caught her attention.

'Is everything all right with Mrs Busk?' I asked, hoping she would put my mind at rest.

'I'm afraid we've had some more bad news. Perhaps you would like to come in and listen to the doctor.'

Alison was sitting on a trolley, buttoning up her blouse her mascara streaking down her cheeks.

'Ah, Mr Busk,' the doctor said. 'I think it would be a good idea if you sat with your wife, while I tell you what has happened.'

I helped Alison off the trolley and into one of the chairs by the doctor's desk, holding her hand, while she dabbed her eyes with my handkerchief.

He sat down opposite us, his half-moon glasses perched on the tip of his nose as he perused some notes before him. Clearing his throat, he looked up.

'I'm sorry to say that we have found another lump in Mrs Busk's breast and we suspect there is a growth in the other. The chemo doesn't appear to have been working as we had anticipated and it's looking like we may have to do something more radical.'

I squeezed Alison's hand as I had been doing so often of late, but she just stared blankly ahead of her.

'What do you mean, more radical?' I asked.

'He means he wants to take my fucking breast off!' Alison exclaimed.

The doctor visibly reeled at Alison's choice of words, but I could not blame her.

'Is there nothing else you can do?'

We can continue with the chemotherapy in the short term and offer some radiation, but my concern is that it might well be proliferating faster than we can treat it. We have to contain the spread, particularly to the lymph nodes, which can take it to other pats of the body.'

The enhanced treatment was therefore set to start the following week.

I had been offered a small free-lance illustration job and had to go into the city to meet the client, anticipating I might be gone for most of the morning.

The meeting went well and I returned to the house with a spring in my step as I had promised to take Alison out to lunch, by way of some sort of normal distraction from what she was going through.

On entering, I shouted out, 'Ali, I'm back. Are you ready?'

There was no reply with the house being unusually quiet.

I called again, whilst sticking my head round the doorway of each room. She was not in the garden either, so I returned to the hallway, running upstairs two at a time and into the bedroom, thinking she might be having a rest before going out.

I was relieved to find her stretched out on the bed. At first glance, I took what I saw at face value, before I realised she was in her wedding dress and what remained of her lovely hair was crowned by a ring of late summer flowers from the garden.

'Alison! Alison!'

There was no reply. I thrust myself onto the bed and put my ear to her chest, hoping to hear a heartbeat, but she was still and lifeless, her lips blue, hands cold, no pulse and her body unnaturally stiff.

'Alison! Alison! Can you hear me?' I cried, but there was no response. I was no medic, but nevertheless tried frantically to resuscitate her with mouth to mouth and chest compressions, whilst knowing enough to be certain that she had gone.

Then I noticed the bedside table where an empty container of Fentanyl tablets lay on top of an envelope addressed to me.

Seeing my name prompted me to think this was probably the last word she had written. What then would have been her last thoughts?

Opening the envelope, I pulled out the single sheet of paper and unfolded it.

My darling Adam,

If this all works out, these will be my last words to you.

We've had a wonderful life together and you've brought me much joy and happiness.

I am only too sorry that I could not have given you children. It is my deepest regret, which I have lived with through all our years together.

From our time in Bombay, all those years ago, I felt you were someone special and thought about you most days after you left me in that hotel room to start your long journey home.

How ecstatic I was to see you going down the escalator at Warren Street station. At that moment, seeing you again, I knew it was no coincidence, but a divine intervention I could not ignore.

But that was then and now I feel so dark. I cannot go on with this pain and the prospect of more of my body being savaged by a surgeon's knife.

You are strong and I know you will manage to carry on. Find someone new.

Break it gently to Chris.

I know this is not the end and that we will meet again on the other side.

Until then, take care my love.
Your ever loving,
Alison x

P.S: Don't forget India! x

I lay with her until darkness had filled the room then called 999.

Although I told them I was certain she was dead, I heard the siren nevertheless as it rounded into our street and drew to a halt outside the house.

On opening the door, I had thought it just the ambulance that had arrived, but they were accompanied by two uniformed police; a man and a woman.

The paramedics went through the standard procedure of checking Alison's pulse, heart and eyes, only to confirm what I already knew.

'When did you find her?' one of them asked.

'Just before lunch,' I answered truthfully.

'Why didn't you call us then?'

'I knew she was gone and wanted to spend these last hours with her.'

'You should have called us as soon as you found her,' the policeman said.

'Is it a crime to want to spend a little more time with someone you have lived with for forty years?'

He looked shamefaced. 'I'm sorry sir, but this is potentially a crime scene and there is always a risk of disease when a body is left.'

I showed them the empty Fentanyl container.

'She was given these for the pain with her breast cancer.'

'I'm so sorry, sir,' one of the paramedics said. 'These are causing so many deaths these days. Did you say you tried to resuscitate her?

'Yes.'

'Mouth to mouth?'

I nodded.

How are you feeling? Do you have any tightness around your chest?'

'A little.'

'You may have taken in traces of the Fentanyl through her saliva. It's very potent.'

Turning to his colleague, 'George, can you get some Naloxone from the ambulance.'

'Would she have suffered?' I asked.

'I don't know how many she would have had left in the tub, but they act very quickly, causing something we call wooden chest syndrome.'

I looked puzzled.

'Simply put, sir. The abdominal muscles and diaphragm become rigid, causing respiratory failure.'

The police were looking around the room all the while.

'Did she leave a note, sir?' the policewoman asked.

'She did, but it's rather private.'

'I'm sorry, but it is evidence.'

'I'd rather you didn't have it.'

'I have to insist, sir.'

'Can't you take a photo on your phone, perhaps with me holding it?'

'I can do that, if you prefer.'

'Thank you. I appreciate that. This is the last thing she gave me and it's very precious.'

George returned from the ambulance.

'I'm going to give you an injection as a precaution against you having ingested some of the Fentanyl,' the senior paramedic said. 'It works very quickly and should reverse any ill effects you may be feeling.'

'That's as much as we can do now,' the policewoman said. 'We'll arrange for your wife to be collected and taken for a coroner's report.'

I had to sit down on the bed, it was becoming all too much for me. This intrusion into our lives. 'You can take her body, but you can't take my wife,' I said, trying to differentiate the two. 'What happens now? What am I supposed to do?'

'Once the death certificate has been issued,' the police woman began, 'you will need to register the death, notify the authorities to cancel her pension, driving licence, etc. They'll tell you how you can easily do that in one go when you register the death. Then make arrangements for the funeral.'

'I'm sorry,' I said, holding back a sudden urge to cry as I once more saw Alison's still, lifeless body on the bed, 'this is all too much for me.'

'Just take your time, sir. We know this can't be easy for you. Someone from the Coroner's office will be arriving shortly to take the body to the mortuary. We'll stay with you until then. Is there anyone you can stay the night with? It would be best for you not to sleep in here until the room has been thoroughly cleansed. There could be highly contagious body fluids left after she has gone. We can arrange for a company to do it.'

'No, I can manage. I'll stay here.'

The undertaker and his assistant arrived, bringing in a sheet and body bag in which they silently and meticulously started to wrap my darling wife.

'Please stop! I shouted. 'I must kiss her one more time.'

They made way for me to gently bend down for the last time to brush against her beautiful full lips that I had kissed so many times before. Gone was the pulse that had once given her the essential vitality that set her apart from others. She was so still and unyielding.

'Goodbye, my love.'

The men continued with their melancholy task until I heard the zip being pulled to enclose Alison in her plastic tomb. The tears rose once more.

'We can arrange for someone from social services to come and talk with you, if you would like,' the policeman said. 'They can often help you to reorientate yourself after a loss.'

'Thank you. I think I'd like that. When would that be?'

'It should be in the next couple of days. You'll receive a phone call to fix a time.'

Alison was lifted off the bed and the two men gingerly and respectfully carried her down the stairs and out of the front door.

The others followed and, suddenly, as I closed the door behind them, I was alone, bereft and hungry. The best I could muster was a boiled egg, toast and a cup of tea, sitting down at our table to consider what next as I entered my twilight years deprived of

Alison.

I remembered the post script at the end of Alison's note and, from a drawer in the sitting room, I retrieved some papers we had put there.

For some months, Alison and myself had been watching videos by Satyaji, an Indian spiritual teacher, who lived in Northern Spain. We had both been to a couple of meetings he'd held in London and been blown away by what he had to say about our true being.

His teachings had reinforced much of what I had come to understand before I had even been to India and had prompted me into ruminating the outcomes of my several LSD trips. The man had built a big following and was to hold a six week satsang the following spring in Rishikesh on the upper reaches of the River Ganges.

Both of us had decided to go before all these issues had blown up in our faces and I was now holding our visas and plane tickets. Alison's photo stared out at me from her visa, rendering me into a snivelling mess once again. But, I knew she would want me to go and I resolved to make that return to India, despite my many reservations made so many years before, when I was about to leave the turmoil, dirt and noise that, in many respects, had taught me so much.

I ignored the paramedic's advice and slept in our bed that night, lying in the silence and near darkness, trying to feel her presence still with me. At times, I thought I could hear her calling my name and even smell her favourite perfume.

I could not succumb to sleep and, as I lay alone, I remembered that night of the full moon inside the Taj Mahal, when Alison and I had been in the presence of the twin sarcophagi of Shah Jahan and his greatest love, Mumtaz. I had imagined him reaching out in the darkness to touch the fingertips of his dead wife and now I so wanted to touch Alison, my dead wife, but could only imagine her ethereal presence.

I was sure she was still with me, and that gave me some comfort, as my tears welled once more and I drifted into the chasms of deep sleep that, for a few hours, served to remove the pain that overwhelmed me.

I was woken by the phone at about ten. It was the social worker asking if she could come and see me later in the morning.

She was a jovial lady in her early fifties, who put me at my ease as soon as she arrived.

I made her a coffee, while she asked a few questions. How was I feeling? Had I slept? Had I contacted relatives and friends yet?

'Yes, I slept a little,' I answered, 'but, I don't really know how I'm feeling right now. I'm vacillating between deep, deep sadness and an overwhelming guilt.

We lived with Alison's depression for years, much of the time sweeping it under the carpet, but there were many days of tears with Alison taking to bed to forget.

I just hadn't read all the signs. Now it was too late. *Could I have saved her? Had she just waited for an opportunity to be alone, whether it was yesterday or another day, carrying out what must have been a long held plan of which I knew nothing?* These thoughts and uncertainties just poured out of me.

'These are perfectly, natural reactions,' she replied. 'So many people I talk with feel they could have done more to prevent what was probably inevitable. But, you mustn't blame yourself. From what I understand, she had been through a lot of pain and suffering over the years, mixed with her own guilt and anxiety. This latest encounter with cancer was more than she could deal with.

You would have loved and supported her, but she was feeling depleted; an empty vessel of little worth. The most important thing to her was her femininity, her womanhood and this had been violated.'

The woman stayed with me for over an hour, doing her best to assuage my grief, ultimately leaving me more able to put the whole thing in perspective. But, I still ached with what I had lost.

The death certificate was eventually released and I was able to work through the list of things I had to do. Friends were supportive, until the funeral was over.

I couldn't bear the thought of one of those dreadful "conveyor belt" funerals where an unknown official reads a prepared text knowing nothing of the person they are reading about. I wanted Alison to have better than that.

It was late September and the leaves beginning to fall when our friends and Alison's remaining family gathered at a woodland burial ground just outside Bristol. Alison's father had died a couple of years earlier and her mother, now in a nursing home, was too frail to travel. We were having the last throes of an Indian Summer, before autumn set in. Alison was brought in a beautifully made wicker coffin and laid on a roughly hewn stone plinth in the old barn, surrounded by bunches of late summer flowers. Together we remembered her life with stories, music and a little laughter. A plot had been prepared amongst the trees where we all tearfully bade our farewells as she was slowly lowered into the waiting earth.

A few invitations to dinners and parties followed, but I was no company for the gatherings of couples and the invites soon began to tail off.

As the weeks passed, I would regularly drive out to the woodland plot and talk with Alison for hours, telling her the latest news, while desperately trying to maintain that slender ethereal thread that I believed still connected us.

I had become conscious of my isolation in the home we had built together over the years. I would sit of an evening, being aware of so much accumulated clutter that was fundamentally serving no purpose.

Everywhere I walked or in the cupboards and drawers, I would find Alison's possessions; her many clothes triggering memories of places and events in which she had radiated, laughed or even cried. There were all her little personal things, her make-up, jewellery, her phone. What could I possibly do with them all?

I had no daughters or granddaughters to pass them on to, only Chris' daughter, who was perhaps now old enough to value some of them. At one point, I thought of selling the whole house and finding something smaller, but I just could not let go of what had been our nest for so long.

Instead, I had a few car boot sales to get rid of what was truly superfluous, much of it being my own accumulated junk, and contented myself with cleaning and tidying what remained.

Christmas was a lonely affair. I was invited to Chris and his family, our relationship having improved over time with him having become a little less obnoxious. They were all pleased to receive small tokens that reminded them of Alison and duly reciprocated, sharing their Christmas dinner and giving me a few presents; especially a black and white photo of Alison as an eight year old in wellingtons and raincoat pushing her dolls and teddy in her little pram.

Set in a silver frame, this took pride of place on my mantlepiece. She was a little chubby then, but her intense gaze was little different to that which I later came to love.

Twenty-eight

A S THE FESTIVE SEASON rolled into the cold January of 2019, I prepared myself for my return to India. Whilst nervous at undertaking the journey on my own and still lamenting and perhaps a little angry that it should have been the two of us, I was excited nevertheless at the prospect of what the adventure might bring.

Anticipating that I would be away for at least six weeks and quite possibly longer, I locked the house up and caught the train to London. Unlike my first trip when I took a heavy and unwieldy rucksack with me, this time, I confined my possessions to a small case with wheels, reserving the option to buy some Indian clothes when I was settled.

While I watched the English landscape of skeletal winter trees and flooded fields flash past, I reflected on the multitude of events that had occurred since being dropped in Piccadilly Circus, tired and dirty some forty-nine years earlier, wondering what life had in store for me and how I was going to maintain a spiritual dimension to my life. Returning to the sub-continent had always remained just a collection of thoughts and something I never thought would happen, until now.

From Paddington to Earls Court and a quick transfer to the Piccadilly line and I was soon speeding out to Heathrow.

With several hours to pass until my flight at quarter to nine in the evening, I made myself comfortable, nibbling at the food I had brought with me, reading and catching a little sleep.

My experience of flying over the years had been limited to

a couple of European flights with Alison and certainly never boarding a plane of the size in which I was about to spend just over eight hours. This huge capsule, complete with first class passenger beds, was well beyond my comprehension and I was only too pleased that it had sufficient open space to thwart something of my claustrophobia.

Alison and I had booked economy but, with meals thrown in and sufficient legroom, I wasn't complaining. I had managed to get a refund on Alison's ticket and found myself sitting next to an Indian Phd student returning for his father's funeral.

With losses in common, we had plenty to talk about, reminiscing how significant events had played their parts in our lives. Our conversation brought us both to laughter and tears at times as we each recollected one little detail or other that so forcibly emphasised that our loved ones were truly gone.

Occasionally, I made the mistake of calling him, Alison, as I turned in my seat, half expecting to see her there.

By six in the morning, I was watching dawn break over the Afghan landscape, something I had seen many times before from the midst of other travellers and gun toting Afghans, but now a serene, multi-coloured patchwork of snow-capped mountain ranges, meandering river valleys and the vast desert expanses in between.

As we crossed Pakistani territory, the mighty Indus river sparkled in the golden morning sunlight, reminding me of the immensity of this vast continent.

Soon, we were beginning our descent to Delhi; its network of roads and buildings, barely visible through a thick smog of pollution, that were already sending shivers of apprehension through me,

Unlike my last arrival across the land border from Pakistan with hundreds of grubby black market rupees stuffed in my underpants, this time, I was surveyed by eagle eyed customs officials, video cameras and computers, examining my passport and visa barcodes, before giving me the nod to pass through.

I now contemplated another eight hour journey to reach Rishikesh.

I had booked a third class seat on the mid afternoon train as far as Haridwar, from where I anticipated taking the bus for the remaining few miles, but first, I had to get to New Delhi railway station.

The sparkling international airport that was Indira Gandhi, equipped with state of the art electronic paraphernalia and ATM machines, provided the gateway to the new Metro, shaming London's old and dirty system that had once led the world.

As the train emerged into open space, the route gave glimpses of the India I had once known. The comfort, cleanliness and modernity of the train carriage glided along the tracks, oblivious to what lay beyond the tempered glass windows.

Outside, dilapidated buildings provided a backdrop to lines of antiquated flat carts, bearing a few pieces of fruit, a pile of broken biscuits, car parts and old clothes for sale. Coloured saris belied the poverty of the many women sitting here and there in anticipation of a transaction. Green and yellow motorised tuk-tuks wove their way like demented insects through the ever moving web of battered cars, taxis, bicycles and delivery lorries.

Occasionally, an expanse of open ground would emerge between the buildings, seemingly stretching for miles with abundant trees and vegetation.

In small clearings, people had gathered fragments of corrugated iron sheets, plastic and fabric to fashion a dwelling within which they could carve out some semblance of a life.

Stepping out from the modern Metro terminal, the bright sunlight only serving to accentuate the decay that lay before me.

The main road, running between myself and the railway station, was dominated by another endless swirl of tuk-tuks, rendering the safe crossing to the station nigh on impossible.

The India seen from the Metro train now engulfed me, faces pervading my space from all directions. 'Taxi?' 'Tuk-tuk?' 'Hotel?' came the optimistic cries, while vendors displayed their pitiful wares on the cracked and dirty pavements. Cigarette lighters lay spaced out on a coloured cloth, small bundles of beedis, tied together with pink cotton, rested in a carefully crafted pile and neat lines of suitcase wheels waited for the inevitable mishap.

Venturing into the relentless stream of traffic, horns blared in a frenzied cacophony, my presence causing a momentary halt and a parting of the ways as the traffic miraculously flowed around me until I had reached the other side.

Unlike the Metro I had just left, the station had clearly seen better days, part of it having been first opened in 1926 and then partially modernised only in recent years, but its pink monolithic structure was nevertheless dirty and crumbling. The steps to the entrance were mostly bedecked with Indian travellers and those too destitute to travel. Huddled groups of women and children sat staring vacantly ahead of them as if all hope had slipped away long before.

The many porters in their red uniforms touted for work, while some caught their breath from a recent exertion.

Inside the main hall, chaos reigned. A ticket office at one end and an enquiry booth at the other, each besieged by earnest travellers, heads pressed against glass panels that hadn't seen soap and water for what looked like decades. A tariff of prices in red lettering, probably well out of date, was partially worn by the ceaseless rubbing of dirty hands.

I needed to eat before starting the journey and a food stall just off the main concourse displaying stacked boxes of crisps, biscuits and plastic water bottles with a selection of vegetable and egg curries in clear plastic containers.

Ignoring all the usual warnings about street food, I ordered a vegetable curry with a serving of white rice, which was duly placed in a microwave. It seemed to take an age to heat through and, when I eventually sat down and peeled back the plastic seal, the food was tepid. A request for another blast only resulted in a minor improvement, such was the age of the microwave that struggled to emanate any heat. The result was a thirty rupee meal that was not only tepid, but lacked any culinary virtue. Seeing a man with bedroll and begging cup wandering the station, I gave it to him, for which he was more than grateful.

Behind the station building, lay the multitude of railway tracks and platforms that made this station the busiest in India, with trains from all parts of the country constantly arriving and departing. An iron bridge crossed the lines with steps down to each platform, mine being number eleven.

The long platform was the stage for an ongoing play. Whilst

passengers waited with suitcases and bundles, the variety acts of vendors and beggars were playing their parts. A legless man on a trolley, propelled himself along with a sandal in one hand and a tin cup in the other.

An assured and striking man with long grey beard, wrapped in yellow robes and swinging a cane inlaid with ivory, approached, shaking my hand and touching my head as if endowing me with a blessing. Pleasant as he was, his performance only served to achieve one thing. I duly rewarded him with a couple of rupees.

A bookstall sold papers and dog-eared books, a water seller dispensed water from a container on his back, while another hawked packets of biscuits and crisps. Seeing these people emphatically told me that, despite a glossy new airport and Metro, little seemed to have fundamentally changed in fifty years for the ordinary man on the street.

A clamour arose amongst those immediately close by as an entourage arrived and Satyaji emerged from within. It was time to board the waiting train and he was entering the same carriage in which I had booked my seat. Whilst he sat with his small following one end, my seat was at the other. It seemed the most natural thing in the world to be sitting in a railway carriage with an apparently fully enlightened being.

The journey was said to be about four hours long, but seemed interminable, firstly passing through the myriad of buildings that are Delhi and out into open countryside and the many small towns beyond.

Always, there were people, the impression that had first struck me so many years before, but how must the population have grown since?

Crude corrugated iron dwellings occupied spaces in the lee of modern motorway passovers and tucked in alongside brick walls running parallel to the railway. Elsewhere, a hotchpotch of roughly constructed bare brick buildings, of differing heights and states of repair, stretched back beyond the line, many with flat roofs from where washing fluttered and children flew colourful kites in the late afternoon breeze.

A cat's cradle of telephone and electricity cables straddled the spaces between and, even in small towns, clearly defined internet masts protruded high above the rooftops.

Rubbish carpeted the ground with seemingly little community impetus to remove it. Yet, the industry of souls abounded everywhere as they made do with what they had, recycling almost anything and everything, except for the detritus they walked upon. A car workshop retained a collection of battered doors hanging from a beam, in case any could be used at some time to bring another car back from the dead.

Fields had been ploughed and planted with small trees that would one day become an orchard. Boys of all ages played cricket on rough, pot-holed ground, while some men worked on a piece of machinery in order to complete an earth moving job.

Outside one village, a piece of ground had been fenced off, grass planted and a pleasant park with seats had been created.

All the while, the sun was sinking toward the horizon, becoming a more intense nectarine orb with each passing minute.

As darkness swallowed the landscape, inside the carriage official railway vendors, dressed in Indian Railways sweatshirts, walked from one end of the train to the other for the entire journey with cries of, 'Soup, tomato soup!' 'Chai!' 'Crisps!'

Satyaji passed down the passageway between the seats at one point. Putting my hands together in a *namaste*, I caught his eye and he seemingly recognised me, perhaps from a London satsang.

'Oh, my, what a surprise,' he said before clasping my hands and passing on down the carriage.

Finally, drawing into Haridwar, Satyaji and his entourage disembarked at one end to be met by an Indian welcoming party, while I left by the other exit, slipping away to the wide station forecourt and the assault on the senses of insistent taxi and tuk-tuk drivers.

Not being twenty anymore, I did not want to be scouring the streets after dark trying to find an hotel, so I had booked one online before I arrived.

Sifting through the various tuk-tuk personalities, I hit upon a polite and enthusiastic one, who knew exactly where I wanted to go. Lifting my bag onto the seat, he turned the ignition key and the motor sparked into life amid a swirl of toxic blue smoke, setting off with one flat tyre, my spine being jolted every time we crossed over a bump or pothole.

A recommendation in the Lonely Planet took me to the nearby Big Ben restaurant for rice, dal and vegetable curry. I was still not used to doing things on my own after so long with Alison and I was now finding eating alone particularly hard. Nevertheless, it was a satisfactory ending to a long day that culminated in the pleasure of a real, but lonely bed.

An electric tuk-tuk took me to the bus station next morning, where I struggled to make sense of the signage that was no longer in Hindi and English; one outcome of nearly seventy-two years of independence from Britain.

Buses came and went from all directions, some stopping to pick up passengers, others trying to move forward with horns blaring. I had already missed three buses to Rishikesh, as the local people had rushed each one before I had time to collect my thoughts and my bag. A kind man with a smattering of English directed me to one I could board, lifting my case aloft as I passed down the gangway to a seat at the back, where I ensconced myself with my case on my lap.

The journey was a visual feast of much that I had already seen and more. Unfinished, damp buildings covered in black mould. were common sights. New hotels flashed a promise of luxury from the midst of adjacent chaos and rubbish. An unfinished motorway lay forgotten as the jungle and the monkeys slowly reclaimed their territory with a sprawl of vegetation twisting itself round the abandoned concrete pillars.

Elsewhere, temples and statues of deities remained magnets for the devout, while an iron suspension bridge across the Ganges displayed a huge metallic *Om* at each end.

A short corridor of trees and I was entering the outskirts of Rishikesh, passing more workshops, stalls and offices. Billboards advertised various public schools for the aspirational and wealthy, emphasising how important education was for the rising middle class.

The bus drew in to the plot of open ground used for arrival and departures, which still lay some distance from where I would be staying. An obliging tuk-tuk driver loaded my things and set out into the busy street. Ahead, I could now clearly see the rise and fall of the foothills that contained the town and from where the mighty Ganges sprang and flowed through to divide the town into two halves.

Apart from hazardous ferries that daily challenged the fierce river currents, there were two fragile suspension bridges which linked both sides. The downstream, Ram Jhula and, at the top of the old town, the Lakshman Jhula.

My hotel was immediately adjacent to the Ram Jhula with an unimpeded view across the intense jade coloured waters to the temples and low level buildings that fronted a backdrop of tree covered hills. Across it all, hung a veil of smog, arising from the cars, scooters and ubiquitous tuk-tuks, whose pollution hovered within the river valley.

A stroll along the northern bank, took me along the wide ghats that step down to the water's edge, where sadhus of all ages and physical constitution wandered, holding out their hands for alms or carrying out rituals on rocky promontories jutting out into the fast moving waters. One blind man looked as if he had been rooted to the same spot atop a crumbling wall for years, a crude and torn awning protecting him from the sun and rain as he repeated his devotional cry of, "Jai Ram."

Young children, mainly girls, circled around, whenever I stopped to survey the view, asking a few rupees for their little offerings to the gods. With a few shells, some marigolds and a candle placed in an empty aluminium food container, they would offer these little *boats* to the river, watching them float away downstream as they offered a prayer.

The walk back, as the sun was setting, presented me with a gathering of young musicians and devotees from a nearby ashram. Assembled down by the river's edge, they performed the nightly Ganga Aarti, a torch-lit Vedic performance of rhythmic chanting, tablas, harmonium and cymbals in homage to the sacred river.

Alison would have loved all I was now soaking in and I only wished her ubiquitous self was with me savouring all that this place had to offer. Indeed, it was the yearning for her presence that kept me awake for most of the night, my thoughts weaving between a host of memories, only broken by the barking dogs and high pitched scooter horns.

With two days yet until the Satyaji satsangs began, I took the opportunity to take in some other experiences.

To gain another spiritual perspective prior to the main event, I'd seen a poster outside a small ashram, where a Hindu woman, who had lived in Europe and America, would be holding a meeting.

Her philosophy was not so far detached from that of Satyaji, but she differed in her emphasis on celebrating the body. She saw little virtue in detachment, although she agreed that the soul is undiscriminating, having no preference for right and wrong, big or small, yes or no.

She talked of the *inner guru* within us all to whom we can ask our questions.

'We are of this world,' she said, and should embrace it, remembering that life is but a short span and we should make the most of our opportunities, whilst developing the will to love.'

Nearby, in a small building set back from a shady courtyard that opened onto the southern river walk, I noticed the sign for an Ayurvedic centre offering a variety of treatments.

After all the stresses of the last months and weeks, I arranged for a half hour consultation with a young Ayurvedic doctor.

She was petite with beautiful long shiny black hair, dark soulful eyes and impeccable English. She put me at my ease immediately and, having taken my pulse, explained the nature of Ayurvedic healing, centring around balance through diet, herbal treatments and breathing.

I could see she was still quite young and I was curious as to the nature of the training.

'How long have you been practising?'

She laughed a little. 'Well, the training is very intensive, taking nearly three years, which I completed when I was twenty-three and I'm now only twenty-seven.

But, yourself. How is your health generally?' she asked.

'I'm not too bad,' I replied a little melancholically, 'although I could do with a bit more exercise. I've been under a lot of stress recently as my wife died before Christmas and I'm missing her.' A lump rose in my throat and my eyes watered a little.

'I'm sorry to hear that.'

'I often wonder if she would still be alive had she had some alternative treatment. She was severely depressed after being diagnosed with breast cancer and eventually killed herself. I wonder if Ayurvedic medicine would have made any difference?'

'Cancer is an acute condition and I cannot say that it can be cured, but Ayurvedic treatments will help the person to relax and sleep better, removing much of the stress through meditation, yoga and a good diet.'

'I just wish she had held on a bit longer and had the opportunity of meeting you.'

'Thank you, but I would not have been able to offer any promises. But, for you, I am going to recommend you have a massage, oil treatment and a steam bath. These will ease a lot of your tensions.'

An appointment was made for the following afternoon when I was met in the courtyard by Ranya, a pretty young woman, her long hair tied back in a pony tail. She was dressed in a green kurta and trousers, her slightly pock-marked cheeks offset by a red tilak, bright eyes, dark lashes and a slightly turned up nose with a gold ring in one nostril. Her smile radiated through a full set of gleaming white teeth, confirming the *joyful* meaning of her name.

I was led into what had originally been one large room, now subdivided into four smaller spaces with floor to ceiling curtains. A massage couch lay to the left and, beyond, one entered the steam room. It was all a bit crude and makeshift, but had been brightened by religious wall hangings and large coloured photos of the mountains, while an appropriate mood was created with wafting incense and ambient Indian music.

I thought Ranya would be treating me, but I was introduced to her aunt, a thin Indian lady in black trousers and paisley top whose dark rings around her eyes made her look more like eighty than the fifty she really was.

She instructed me to strip off and put on a pair of paper, recyclable underpants before lying on the couch and being covered by an itchy orange blanket.

My masseuse may have looked old, but she knew her job.

Firstly, warm sesame oil was slowly dripped onto my forehead, sending me into deep relaxation and momentary sleep. I could feel the presence of someone else nearby, but was unsure until gentle fingers ran the oil across my forehead and I opened my eyes briefly to see it was Ranya.

The massage that followed was deep and far-reaching, with Auntie's capable hands, pulling, pushing and kneading virtually every part of my body, at times painfully, as the deeply embedded knots were eased out of me.

With this complete, I was guided by Ranya to the crudely fabricated steam enclosure made from wood effect chipboard and lined with aluminium sheets. Sitting on a small stool, the two halves of the top with semicircular cuts were brought down to encase my head. The steam built up over time, opening my pores and leaving the oil from the massage as a greasy film all over my body. A cold shower and I was ready to go, making sure I had booked another session before I left.

Twenty-nine

I WAS UP EARLY, walking to the tuk-tuk stand for a ride to Satyaji's first day at the ashram. The venue was well known to all the drivers, who were ferrying a non-stop stream of devotees through winding, narrow streets, where sacred cows slowly meandered and pigs scavenged along weathered walls where empty slogans and the smiling faces of crooked politicians peered out from layers of torn and indecipherable posters. Local people were opening their shops and stalls - tailors, hairdressers, chai sellers, *loundary* services and bicycle rentals.

A long queue was forming in the street outside the ashram where, in the early morning chill, the gathering devotees dressed in an eclectic mix of jeans, Indian cotton trousers and shirts, with many wrapped in ubiquitous coloured shawls and patterned scarves.

By eight o' clock, we were filing into a large un-shaded courtyard for security checks, before funnelling into one of twelve lines separated by ropes.

The lines quickly filled as the sun rose over the surrounding buildings, beating down on rapidly overheating bodies. A large grey monkey leapt across a wall to oversee the proceedings, looking around and across the crowd as if he knew perfectly well what was going on.

A man living in one of the adjacent flats, came out to clean his teeth, still in his pyjamas and vest, taking some moments to watch the assembly below his balcony. A curious grey squirrel climbed a vertical brick wall, before scuttling into a crevice formed by a missing brick. Screeching Bollywood music emanated from a grille in the wall, while one of the sangha women appeared like a sniper on a rooftop wielding a camera. I imagined the vulnerability of everyone had it not been a camera.

Having waited for the better part of an hour, one of the sangha members passed along the front of each queue, enabling the first in each line to pick a small wooden token with a number on it.

The chosen number denoted in which order the queue would enter the sating hall. On this occasion, out of twelve queues, we were the eleventh.

From the wider courtyard, we passed into a smaller space, shaded by banyan trees and decorated with a scattering of large river boulders. Members of the sangha lined our route, smiling and clasping their hands together in greeting.

Apart from questions to Satyaji, this was a silent retreat, with instructions being passed on by hand held laminated A4 notices; *Silence. Please move closer together. Please switch off your phone,* etc.

At the entrance, we left our shoes in racks before entering the hall and finding a seat, either on the floor or a chair. I opted for a chair, where I could clearly see the stage at the far end, but also the huge television monitor that would give me a closer view of the teacher. Against a backdrop of a mauve cloth with a dominant golden Om, an armchair had been placed for Satyaji with small tables on either side for photos of his mentors and his water. Two large palm fronds framed the central space and a patterned carpet lay on the floor.

At ten o' clock, the corpulent Satyaji entered the hall, being greeted by many of his followers, before climbing the steps to the stage and taking his seat, stroking his long grey beard as he surveyed his audience.

Following his welcome to Rishikesh, he was taking questions from members of the audience, who stood before one of several microphones placed around the hall.

Two hours later, musicians and singers assembled on the stage to bring the meeting to an end and I was stepping out into the crowded street, silenced by the experience.

The sun was hot for February as I walked back along the river bank, stopping to wash my feet and sprinkle my head with the chilly sacred water fresh from the snow melt much further upstream.

Small groups of people and couples who had attended the satsang laughed and discussed the event, whilst I peered out across the tumbling water, trying to find solace in my solitude.

The next day, thunder and rain accompanied me on my tuk-tuk ride, arriving at the bedraggled queue, doing its best with umbrellas and makeshift raincoats to keep dry.

A few wizened men looked out on us with bemusement from the sanctuary of a small temple opening onto the street. A man in rain soaked trousers and jumper was selling thin paper waterproofs at fifty rupees each; so precious was each sale to him that keeping one for himself had not crossed his mind.

A school boy in smart uniform helped his father to open his small shop, selling bottled water, sweets, shampoo, dustpans and what looked like a thousand other items.

There was no lottery on this morning, instead we were all directed as quickly as possible into the ashram hall.

A young Brahmin asked the first question.

'I see a thousand other lifetimes before me, before I can be free, he said. 'What am I to do?'

Satyaji thought for a few moments, before a huge smile crossed his face. 'You can start by putting those thousand lifetimes behind you. What you are looking for is with you now.' He went on to elaborate as, all the while, the young man looked at Satyaji incredulously, not really believing that a lifetime of Hindu indoctrination could possibly be false.

No sooner had Satyaji finished and the Brahmin sat down, than a young Tibetan woman pushed her way to the microphone, ignoring the protocol of the day, to spew out an impassioned speech about the oppressed Tibetans.

She mourned how long it had been going on and tearfully enquired how much longer would it continue?

She spoke for a good ten to fifteen minutes, so enmeshed in what she had to say that there was little space for Satyaji to intervene.

From the Chinese invasion, the humiliation, torture and murder of monks and nuns to the Dalai Lama's exile, she recounted much that I already knew, but clearly raising gasps of surprise from many in the audience.

She was answered by a short parable that illustrated quite clearly how all things happen for a reason and we mustn't always respond so hastily, instead giving any situation time for us to better see the purpose.

I wondered how much time was needed in this case as it was now nearly seventy years since the Chinese army crossed into Tibet, turning the screw ever tighter over the succeeding years.

By the third day, I was brought to tears, such was the love and wisdom exuded in the words of the teacher, that I felt a barrier in my understanding had been transcended as I became the passive observer of my egoic self, watching the futility of much of what I was. As I had previously experienced with LSD and my morphine induced state in hospital, I felt distant from the world about me yet, at the same time, an overwhelming sense of love and Oneness with everything.

On the other hand, a Dutch girl spoke of her disappointment with what she perceived to be her realisation. She had expected trumpets and flashing lights to announce her arrival in a state of awareness. In fact, she was so disappointed, that she was ready to go home. The teacher pondered for a few moments and then enquired whether she had seen any space rockets. Laughter rippled through the audience before giving way to a more serious tone.

'Are you afraid of losing yourself and your life in Holland?' he asked. 'You don't have to go anywhere and you don't have to lose anything, as you are already here now. You don't have to lose anything, unless you want to.'

She was overcome with tears and laughter, owning up to how misguided she had been.

As an ensemble of musicians filled the stage at the end, I noticed people slipping out of the hall to gather outside in readiness to receive a *blessing* from the teacher. I found this both rude and selfish and certainly not behaviour that warranted any sort of special favours.

Food vendors had gathered outside the ashram, the general din broken by the strong and direct cry of 'Coconut, coconut.' A middle aged man in shorts, cotton vest and flip-flops was making holes in the tops of coconuts with a machete and selling them with straws to drink the milk.

I took my now usual walk back along the waterfront seeing, for the first time, garlanded bodies being brought on stretchers to the water's edge, as I had once seen in Benares.

Pyres had been built from whatever wood could be bought or gathered by the families and the process of sending the dead to their destinies had begun.

I had been in India barely a week, yet its lifeblood had surged once more through my veins; exciting, angering, despairing, uplifting me with the ever present flow of people and the visual diversity my few days had already offered me.

I was also getting used to the food, stopping each day for a thali, a traditional Southern Indian meal comprising rice and several accompanying dishes in small bowls all served on a large tray. Not only was it cheap, but also nutritious and filling.

The afternoon following my third satsang, I set out to explore a little more of the town,deciding to take a tuk-tuk up to Lakshman Jula, despite the thunder and heavy rain.

My walk to the taxi rank, where I went every morning, was through almost monsoon conditions, with the narrow streets awash with water and storm drains gurgling up to the surface with all manner of normally concealed and muddy matter, now cascading down to the river. At times, it was necessary to shelter under the awnings of gaudy souvenir shops along the route.

The tuk-tuk wended its way up the twisting road to the upper town, the rain flaps firmly down on both sides, leaving only the tiny back plastic window to provide a view of the journey.

At the top, expensive, western style hotels perched on crags overlooking the tumbling, wild water far below. Vendors sheltered beneath the awnings of their pitiful stalls as the rain washed dislodged earth and gravel across and down the road. Elsewhere, various trekking and rafting companies advertised the experiences to be had on and around the river.

While the main road continued on into the mountains, I was turning down into the town on foot, where I found a hotchpotch of ashrams, temples, guest houses, open air restaurants with steaming aluminium cooking pots, travel shops, healing centres, barbers and endless emporia selling clothes and handicrafts.

A man sat behind the counter of a clean and carefully arranged jewellery shop as a young cow stood on the threshold sheltering from the rain. As I further descended the road, I was constantly confronted with meandering cows, wet and hungry dogs, sadhus and thin, mournful women, crouched in doorways, sheltering their babies.

There came a sharp bend, a steep incline and then a narrowing until the path opened out to the Lakshman Jhula bridge. Far below, the turbulent jade green waters, now iridescent against the stormy sky, squeezed through the narrow gorge.

On one side, the *wedding cake* Trayambakeshwar Temple rose high above the bank in ever diminishing tiers, painted in the ubiquitous orange that shares a third of the Indian national flag.

Swaying perceptibly, the bridge groaned under the interminable flow of pedestrians, whose passion for selfies, frequently blocked the passage of scooters and laden handcarts, weaving from side to side along the narrow breadth. High pitched horns sounded to warn those few beggars with missing or twisted limbs, who had crouched down by the side of the pathway in pursuit of alms.

Casting my eyes downstream, the river widened, now tumbling more calmly between the two banks of waterfront houses, cafés and temples. Here, clumps of trees broke the geometry and flights of steps led to small beaches, where worshippers immersed themselves and tourists took rain-swept boat rides along the river.

Reaching the other side, I found myself in the midst of a Hindu ceremony revolving around the oversized effigy of Lord Krishna, sat cross-legged on a lotus. A large crowd had gathered chanting with candles and displaying hand-held signs. With the rumpus they were making, I wasn't entirely sure whether it was a religious or political gathering.

I was immediately drawn to the road that passed behind the temple, from where bells and chanting were emanating with the onset of sunset.

Passing the many fruit stalls and lines of four-wheel drives returning from having transported clients upstream for white-water rafting experiences, I would occasionally see a familiar face from satsang; one of the girls organising the event or someone

I'd seen in the morning queue. There would be a friendly smile and passing acknowledgement but, beyond that, I would continue alone, all the while becoming increasingly consigned to my solitary state. Everywhere I went, I would hope to see someone I could talk with and perhaps develop a friendship.

Set back from the road and facing the river, lay the Shiva Café, made from wood and rattan, it bore something of a colonial jungle atmosphere. A small garden of banana trees and exotic shrubs led to a covered entrance and a steep staircase to the upper floor, where I was obliged to be barefoot. Here, low tables and long, flat cushions lined the outside walls and pull-down rattan blinds protected the interior from the sun and rain.

There was to be a drop-in music jam later that evening but, in the meantime, an electronic Pink Floyd fusion was playing over the speakers. I was the only customer, sitting alone with a chai, but thinking it might be worth returning later for the music and the possibility of meeting someone.

Darkness had fallen by the time I was ready to leave, passing the temple once more as the bells and chanting had reached a furious tempo and all the roadside shops were lit up by the sparkle of electric light bulbs.

As I walked parallel to the river, the evening congestion could be felt as jeeps, cows and scooters struggled to find space to pass each other on the narrow road that ran between the shops, resorting to much reversing and horn tooting to find a way through.

The shops, set beneath crumbling two to three story buildings, often with balconies and decorative latticed plaster work, were initially Indian run travel shops, jewellers, musical instrument and clothes emporia, where men chatted over a glass of chai and read the newspaper.

But, as I walked further, I found myself within a Little Tibet community of handicrafts and food stalls. All these years later, there were few of the antique artefacts that many escaping refugees had brought with them over the mountains to sell in India.

Instead, the shops were stocked with replicas of prayer wheels, dorjé thunder-sticks, hats and newly made bags, handcrafted wood and metal work and colourful Tibetan clothes.

Tucked away on one side of the street, an open air stall sold

Tibetan momos, the steamed dumplings I had often eaten in McLeod Ganj, but now enhanced with chilli sauce. Ordering eight for fifty rupees, I sat at one of the trestle tables facing the street.

A young American hippy and his friend, still in their early twenties, struck up a conversation as they'd recognised me from satsang.

'Is this your first time in India?' one of them asked.

'No, I came when I was about your age, nearly fifty years ago. In those days, most of us who made the journey travelled overland, hitching and taking whatever transport was available - trains, buses, rickshaws.'

You mean you travelled overland?' he continued, incredulously. 'No plane?'

'No. In those days, you could do things like that. We were much freer.'

As I spoke and downed another momo, my attention was suddenly drawn to the street.

A Tibetan woman about my age, in blue chuba and striped apron, was just passing. I couldn't see her face properly, but something in her gait struck me as familiar.

Casting all formality to the wind, I left my seat and ran out ahead of her, standing directly in her path. As she came closer, she stopped, looking curiously at this grey bearded, somewhat weatherworn Englishman and a spark of recognition registered within both of us.

'Kamala?'

Shock and a little fear were her first reactions as she stopped in her tracks and slowly absorbed what stood before her. Gradually as she dug back through the years, her alarm was replaced by a faint smile irrefutably triggering her acknowledgment.

'Is it you, Adam?'

I immediately broke into tears. 'It's been so long. I'm so sorry about what happened.'

My memory flashed back to that last prolonged kiss and embrace in McLeod Ganj, just before boarding the bus that would take me away from her for all those years.

She hesitated for a few moments as if contemplating the consequences of our reconciliation, then, as before, ignoring all protocol and the witness of passers by, fell into my arms, her hands squeezing me behind my back. People flowed around us as if we were an ancient rock embedded in the stream.

Clasping her warm hands, I stepped back to look more closely. Like me, the years had taken their toll, but kindly. Her hair, although now almost grey, was still long and plaited with beads, her eyes sparkled as they had always done and her lines were those worthy additions earned through life and experience. She still had a good figure, although perhaps a little more full, and was just as partial to coral and turquoise jewellery.

'Is this really you, Adam? It must be fifty years,' her incredulity and a little discomfort apparent in her voice

'I know you must feel perhaps angry at me, but I need to explain what happened. It's been a very long time and a very long story. I've often dreamt of this moment, but never thought it would come.'

Her initial reserve mutated into a beautiful smile as she embraced me once more with our lips joining for a lingering kiss, casting away the years and ascertaining without any doubt that we were together again.

But, I'm confused,' I said, 'what are you doing in Rishikesh? Do you live here now?'

'No. I'm staying with my daughter. She has a shop here.' Taking my hand firmly, in hers, 'Come, I must introduce you.'

'You have a daughter, how lovely. Did you eventually marry then? That nice Tibetan boy, you spoke about? Of course you did, I can see your apron.'

Her lips were sealed as she took my hand and led me further down the street, eventually turning into a brightly lit shop full of Tibetan goods.

A slim middle aged woman was kneeling on the floor with her back to us as she attached price tags to some items spread before her.

'Pema,' Karmala called as we entered, 'I want you to meet someone.'

The woman stood and turned, enabling me to see her face quite clearly under the electric light. She was almost as tall as myself, unusual for a Tibetan, and I was momentarily frozen in my tracks, such was the effect of her presence.

'Pema, this is your father.'

Both of us were dumbstruck, as I looked deep into her eyes and saw, despite her Tibetan features, there was something intrinsically of me that cast no doubt that she was of my seed. She very much had my eyes with an uncanny synthesis of Kamala's and my features that sent me spinning from one to the other.

'My daughter, but how?'

'Don't you remember that last night in the cottage, as the rain came down from the mountains, you loved me,' Kamala said.

'Yes, I felt completely one with you.'

'And so you were. Pema is the proof of our love.'

'Pema, seemed a little embarrassed to hear her mother talking as she had, but was encouraged enough to step forward and survey me as she pulled me into a heartfelt embrace.'

'My daughter. How I have longed for you over these years. So many years, yet, I did not know.'

As we pulled back from each other, not only was I streaming tears, but so too was Pema. With both of us incredulous at the sight of our long lost blood kin, we hugged intensely once more.

'Why didn't you tell me, Kamala? I wrote to you and when you replied you mentioned nothing of Pema'

'I was afraid to. I did not know whether you had found the English girl you had left behind. I just couldn't and then I lost contact.'

'So you brought Pema up by yourself?

'With the help of my mother. She loved her as her own.'

'How were you treated in the village?'

'It was hard at first as Tibetans are not used to a child being born to someone who is not married.'

'Did they have you back at the school?'

'They were so kind and forgiving. Everyone loved Pema, she was such a beautiful child and always laughing. Her name means, *lotus*.

She would play with the other children and was very popular so, very soon, most people forgot about the circumstances. When she was old enough, she was accepted in the school and so was I. Eventually, with so many more children coming to McLeod Ganj, the school was put in a new and bigger building and my job was secure.'

'Did you marry?'

'I met a nice young Tibetan man,' she giggled in the coy manner I had remembered, 'His name was Tsering. He had arrived in the village when Pema was three. Like my father, he was an artist and had learned his skills in Dalhousie. When my father died…'

'I'm sorry, Kamala. I really liked your father. He was such a very good artist.'

'Thank you, Adam. When he died, they needed more artists here in McLeod Ganj and Tsering arrived on the bus one day with a bag and his brushes.

He was very good to me and understanding. He loved Pema, but I made it clear that I didn't want any more children. He still wanted to marry me.'

'You talk in the past tense.'

'Yes, he died suddenly five years ago. It was a great shock to Pema and I. We were told it was a blood clot, perhaps from sitting still for so many hours painting. He was so dedicated to his work and was eventually as good as my father. He received commissions from all over the world.'

'I'm so sorry to hear that, Kamala. You were lucky to have found him.'

'I was, but you know where my real love was?' she replied, looking plaintively into my eyes. 'It was always you and I was heartbroken when you left. Of course, I understood the reasons, but I have often asked myself if we could have made it work.'

'Kamala, we've all got so much to talk about. Where is your husband, Pema?'

'He's a teacher at the same school as our children. They'll all be home soon,' Pema replied.

'I have grandchildren too?' I exclaimed.

'Yes, you have two. A boy and a girl. The boy is twelve and the girl ten.'

'This is turning into the most wonderful day in my life.' I said. 'I cannot believe how blessed I am.'

'I'm going to take Adam to the house,' Kamala said to Pema, 'why don't you shut early and join us?'

I'll do that. I just want to finish labelling these things for tomorrow.'

Pema and I caught glances again, smiling and waving as Kamala and I stepped out into the busy street.

'How long are you staying in Rishikesh, Adam,' Kamala asked as she took my hand again, squeezing it a little to reassure herself it was really me.

'I'm here for the satsangs with Satyaji and I've got another five weeks before my plane leaves for England.'

'Then we've got plenty of time.'

'For what.'

'To get to know each other again, of course.'

I took a deep breath, imbibing the cocktail of Indian aromas and the life enhancing air that now surrounded my newly found Kamala.

Thirty

I T WAS A LONG WALK along the unmade river path to Pema's house, giving us plenty of time to talk alone. As we walked, cows and their calves loomed out of the darkness, as did the occasional hungry dog or goat.

'Tell me, Adam, how has your life been for you?'

I started to tell her how I had tried to find Belinda and of the tragedy that had befallen her and her family. How I had qualified as a teacher and then of my meeting and marriage with Alison.'

'You met her in India?'

'I did, but thought nothing more of it until I met her again in London and she came to visit me in where I lived in Bristol.'

'And you thought nothing of me?' Kamala enquired, almost admonishingly.

'Of course I did. You were in my thoughts for so much of the time I was married, but you have to remember that we had our agreement.

The years ran from one to the other with so many challenges and worries. When Alison was told she could not have children, I thought that was the end for us as I so much wanted a child. But, somehow, we muddled through it all, finding things to distract us and bring some kind of solace.

It never occurred to me that you might have had my child. I thought I had been careful. Had I known, I would have come to you.

Alison then heard that she had breast cancer and one thing led to another, until ultimately it became far too much for her to cope.

I came home one day and found her dead on the bed.'

'Oh, Adam. I'm so sorry,' Kamala said with what I perceived to be genuine concern and compassion. She stopped walking and wrapped her arms around my middle, nestling her head into my chest, as she had once done as a young woman.

'Prior to her death, we had planned this trip to India together to hear Satyaji talk. She left a note in which she urged me to come, despite what had happened.

Travelling alone changed the whole perspective of the trip and, although I was coming to Rishikesh, I was also planning to make the trip to McLeod Ganj to see if I could find you. I'd always had dreams of one day turning a corner and seeing you once again. It looks like karma brought our meeting forward to today and I thank all the gods for that.'

She reached up and kissed me. 'It is as if those years have fallen away and we can now go forward,' she said.

'Of course, this is all very sudden and I've barely had time to think in the last hour. But clarity is sweeping over me and I'm beginning to understand what I must do.

If you'll have me, after all this time, I would like to come and live with you, but things are now much more difficult with visas. I still have a house in England, but I'm sure you would want to be near Pema and your grandchildren.'

'Do you remember Mr Hamilton, the English painter in Dharmkot and the little cottage we spent our night together?'

'How could I ever forget?'

'When he died, he left me the cottage. You know it's not much, but it's a start. As a Tibetan, I could not own Indian property and had very few rights other than as a refugee. But, Pema automatically became an Indian citizen at birth and I passed it on to her to own as long as she let me live there for the rest of my life.

Recently, I applied for and got Indian citizenship myself. Perhaps, if we married, you would be able to stay without any problems as well.'

'Kamala, there's nothing I would want more. I could sell my house in England, we'd have enough money and I'd be able to help Pema and the grandchildren. So, is that decided?'

'Only if you promise with all your heart never to leave me again.'

'I promise with all my heart.'

Once more, her eyes filled with tears, but those of joy. Our ageing shells meant nothing for we were still young within.

'I love you, Kamala and we have our family. *Our* family.'

A dim street light illuminated the path through the trees and an overgrown garden that led to the house where Pema lived. The door was open when we arrived and I could hear children's voices from within. My heart fluttered at the thought of seeing my grandchildren for the first time.

'Tashi Delek, Hello,' Kamala called.

A Tibetan man came to the door and acknowledged Kamala, while glancing at me with curiosity.

'Sangye,' Kamala said, 'I want you to meet Adam. We have known each other for a very long time.'

The man peered as if he ought to know me, but remained baffled.

'I know Pema has told you about an Englishman I met nearly fifty years ago in McLeod Ganj. Well, he has come back to me.'

I sensed that, perhaps, Sangye was a little angry at this revelation, knowing that Pema had been born without a father by her side.

Nevertheless, he beckoned us into the house. 'Come, come, sit,' he said as he directed us toward a sofa and a couple of rattan chairs.

Like so many homes, it was single story with a main living room and two others that served as bedrooms.

The kitchen was very basic with most of the preparation of food being done on the floor and cooked over a small kerosene stove. The bathroom, a cold, functional space, comprised a toilet, washbasin and shower.

Throughout, there were few aesthetic embellishments with mainly cement wall and floor finishes and the only nod to any comfort and personalisation being family photos, a tanka, a picture of the Dalai Lama and hooks to hang clothes and other personal belongings.

'Would you like chai?' Kamala asked as she showed herself into the kitchen and brought out a thermos flask and cups.

I felt a little embarrassed at this first encounter with my potential son-in-law.

While I started to explain my reason for being in Rishikesh and being reunited with Kamala, I heard shy giggling from behind the door. Two faces peered around the door frame and darted back out of site on catching my eye.

'Come on you two,' Kamala said, 'come and meet your grandfather.'

A silence prevailed across the room as the power of these last few words sank in to the realisations of Sangye and the two children that their lives had changed irreversibly in that moment.

Kamala sat beside me, already well practised in her role as grandmother and held the two children on either side of her.

'This is Lipu,' she said, turning toward the boy. 'How old are you, Lipu?'

He hesitated and looked at his feet, then his father, who nodded for him to continue. 'I'm twelve,' he eventually replied.

'And tell your grandfather how old you are, Lasya,' turning to the girl.

She stood to attention and looked me straight in the eye. 'I'm Lasya and I'm ten years old.'

'Well done, well done,' Kamala said as she clapped her hands together, her eyes lighting up with her smile.

At this moment, the main door opened and in walked Pema.

I stood and gave her another hug. 'My daughter. I still can't believe it's possible.'

She smiled and kissed me on the cheek.

'Sangye,' she started, 'you do understand what has happened?'

'Your mother was beginning to explain it all to me.'

The poor man, dressed in conventional shirt and trousers, but clearly of Tibetan stock was keen to understand the true nature of the Englishman now sitting in his house and suddenly the patriarch of the family.

Pema went over to him and put her arm around his shoulders.

'You know that Tsering was not my real father, although I loved him dearly.'

He nodded silently.

'My mother met Adam when they were both very young in McLeod Ganj. He had come overland from England and lived for a few months in the village. During that time, they fell in love, but both realised, with their lives ahead of them, it would be almost impossible for Adam to make a living and support my mother. She would have hated leaving her family to travel all the way to England. It was a dilemma that both of them wrestled with until they both agreed to separate in the hope that one day they might reunite. Before Adam left, my mother conceived me.'

'So, why didn't Adam come back sooner?'

'For the simple reason, he did not know that I was with child,' Kamala intervened. 'We wrote to each other for a while, but I did not have the courage to tell him.

Adam has since lived for forty years with an English wife, who could not give him children and she has now died.

Please sit down everyone as Adam and I have something very important to tell you.'

There was a shuffling as Pema with the two children and Sangye by her side found places on the sofa, while Kamala and I stood. Kamala looked up at me in anticipation, as if I should be starting.

'I can't tell you how wonderful it is for me, after all these years, to have not only found Kamala, just a few hours ago, but also to have found my family, Pema, Kipu Lasya and Sangye. Kamala and I have not had much time to talk and I have only a short time before I have to go back to England.'

There was a groan of disappointment from the children.

'But, it will only be for a short time, while I sort out my affairs. Kamala and I agreed that we want to live together and we are finally going to get married.'

The two children looked at each other excitedly with big grins over their faces as they bumped their bottoms on the sofa and clapped their hands together.

'Where will that be?' Pema asked.

'We've not discussed it yet,' Kamala replied, 'but probably in McLeod Ganj or Dharmcot. First we have to get permission and Adam has to see how long he can stay in India.'

'You're an Indian citizen now, mother,' Pema said, so marrying you should enable Adam to stay.'

'We really hope so,' I said.

With all the excitement, we had quite forgotten the time. We had not eaten and the children had school in the morning.

'Let me take you all out. There is a restaurant by the river called the Buddha Café, where I am told they do very good food.'

'I know it,' Pema said. 'Thank you f..father,' she struggled to say for the first time.

We were lucky to find a table for six of us, as most of those eating had been to satsang that day and the place was buzzing with conversation amid a flurry of waiters carrying dishes of food and the soothing tones of Indian music. It was unusual for a Tibetan family to be in such a place and eyes followed us through the restaurant until we were all seated.

The restaurant lay up steps from the main street near to where I had *found* Kamala earlier in the day. This ramshackle space, constructed from bamboo and rattan, directly overlooked the Ganges with a clear view up to the Lakshman Jhula bridge. The evening air was damp and cold and the rattan flaps had been unfurled to retain some heat, while soft coloured lanterns provided a warm glow over the tables and alcoves.

I didn't think the family had ever been out to dinner and their was plenty to attract their interest. The fabulous choice of food on the menu, the melange of people from all over the world gathered in one place with what appeared to be the common language of English.

I had been impressed how my new family all spoke good English; Pema and Sangye needing it for their work and the children having learned so much already in school. Kamala had spoken good English even fifty years earlier and had since had plenty of time to improve. What level my Tibetan might have been, had I stayed, I would never know.

We had plenty to talk about throughout the meal, principally our wedding, something I had dreaded when first suggested so many years before, but now an event I desperately wanted to come about.

Pema was overjoyed at her mother's happiness and the reality that now her real family was going to be complete. The two of us would look at each other occasionally, perceiving some feature or characteristic that had been ordained by my DNA.

'Adam, I think we must go to Dharamsala as soon as we can,' Kamala said, 'and start the arrangements, but first I want to take you somewhere I think you'll like.'

'Where are you thinking?' I asked, intrigued by her secretiveness.
'I'll meet you tomorrow morning.'

'I normally go to satsang in the morning, but I suppose that doesn't really matter now.'

Light rain peppered our walk back to the house, our laughter only disturbed by the sight of cows huddled in shop fronts, while sadhus and others with nowhere else to go, curled up with damp blankets in whatever partially dry alcove they could find.

As we walked along the dimly lit road, it seemed quite normal for an orange clad sadhu to appear from the shadows, forming his hands in a namaste, or to see a street vendor asleep on his cart.

At the house, I kissed and hugged the family as they went in, leaving Kamala and myself outside for a while longer to talk.

'Kamala.' I started, 'You once said that we are eternal and one with each other and the universe. After today, I am convinced that is true. Why else would our paths cross again after so long?'

'The time is now right for us to be together, here in India,' she replied. 'I understand now that we would have been driven apart had we married before and lived in England or here.'

I took her in my arms and lowered my head to take those lips that had melted my heart before. Little had changed between us. I had previously wanted to give myself to her completely, now there were no questions, no doubts. This was to be our destiny.

'Where do you want to meet tomorrow?'

'Meet me outside the Siva temple, just along from Ram Jhula. Will ten be okay?'

I slept little that night, going over in my mind the events of the day, not really quite believing what had happened. A mantra was being chanted repetitively in a nearby temple and what peace remained beyond the scooter horns on the bridge, was suddenly broken by the arrival below the hotel of a crowd of protesters waving the Indian flag, and shouting, 'Death to Pakistan.'

The young man on night duty at the desk, told me that a Pakistani suicide bomber had killed forty-three Indian soldiers in Kashmir. Now, the protesters were burning an effigy of Imran Khan, the Pakistani Prime Minister, to a background of chanting and banging drums, which went on well into the early hours until the fire had died down and the crowd eventually drifted off.

Kamala did not keep me waiting as I stood in the busy street outside the gates to the temple where a magnificent, effigy of the Lord Shiva in lotus position, rose up from the holy river's edge, it's white marble radiating in the morning sunlight.

I kissed and embraced her as if there had been no bridge of years between us. We were already familiar with each other and needed little re-acquaintance.

'I'm excited,' I said, 'I have no idea where you're taking me. Have you had some breakfast?'

'I had some with the children before they left for school with Sangye.'

'Do you mind if we stop for chai and pourris.' I replied as I drew her into a small café between the glitzy jewellery, clothes and souvenir shops.

'It was lovely to be with you all, last night, and we've not yet been reunited for twenty-four hours.'

She smiled and reached her hand across the table to mine, our ageing flesh now more obvious beneath the lights. But, it mattered little to me and I thought not for Kamala either as we were now so grateful to be in each other's company again.

'Come on, let's go,' she said, as I threw back the last of my chai.

The path led south beyond the Shiva temple until the shops had fizzled out and a few ramshackle chai-khanas remained. Turning up from the river, the bank was lined with a thick covering of trees extending back into what was an almost impenetrable forest.

A small ticket office lay on a rise before us and it was on seeing the information leaflets that I realised where Kamala had brought me.

The Maharishi Mahesh Yogi's ashram had become world famous in early 1968, when the Beatles and a number of their contemporary musician friends and wives had come to stay for a few weeks to study Transcendental Meditation. For Kamala and I, it was almost fifty-one years to the day since those famous residents had woken the world to meditation and all things Indian.

The ashram itself went back many years before, as evidenced by the many domed meditation cells and huge multi-terraced stone structures which once housed monks and devotees.

The Maharishi had taken out a fifteen year lease on the huge site belonging to the Forestry Commission and built bungalows, kitchens and a meeting hall to support his teachings. The site even had its own post office.

Now, as Kamala and I wandered amongst the buildings, we could see what a sad state of neglect it was in as the forest had slowly reclaimed its space, weaving roots and branches through windows and doorways.

Nevertheless, I was excited to see the bungalow where the Beatles themselves had stayed; a double fronted building with a broad verandah, containing numerous rooms, each with its own bathroom.

'Do you know the songs the Beatles wrote here?' I asked Kamala, 'Most of them ended up on the White Album, as it came to be known.'

'I can remember people playing the Beatles in McLeod Ganj. *While My Guitar Gently Weeps*, was my favourite.'

'Yes, mine too, but there were so many others.'

'You used to sing so many of those songs to yourself, when I would come to see you.'

'I think it must have been bit of a racket…'

'Racket?'

'An unpleasant noise. My singing voice has never been that good.'

'I used to like hearing you.'

Looking through into the empty rooms with broken windows and dismembered doors, it was hard to imagine the light and laughter that must have emanated in those heady, hopeful times.

One of the bathrooms, retained its patterned floor tiles and a piece of time worn fabric clung in the breeze to the rotting window frame. Down one side, a solid enamel bath, encrusted in dirt and dust provided echoes of what might have been.

Had this been John Lennon's bath in which he had laid in hot bubbly water composing *Sexy Sadie*. Could McCartney have been in his next door humming the melody of *Blackbird* or George, up to his neck in *Savoy Truffle*?

Ultimately, those echoes were hollow and best left to the jungle, compensated only by the many super realistic wall paintings that local artists had created on empty walls, depicting the Beatles in Sgt Pepper mode with the Maharishi, whilst elsewhere stunning representations of various gurus and mandalas exploded off the walls, some now rain soaked beneath broken roofs.

From the deserted Maharishi's bungalow, where his inner circle of pop favourites would gather on the roof to hear further teachings, the view through the nearby trees opened out to the river and the city while, in the other direction, I could imagine the snow peaks of the Himalayas concealed just behind the highest foothills.

Although much of what we saw was alien to Kamala's experience, we wandered the grounds for a good two to three hours until encroaching darkness forced us to leave. She had learned that the Beatles had meant much to me and I was grateful for her having thought of bringing me.

'I still find it hard to comprehend,' I told her, 'that this place that had once been the focal point of the world's press and TV, where so much spiritual and creative energy had been centred, was now abandoned to the jungle. Ultimately, it will be forgotten altogether when the last of us, who lived through those times and were inspired by the music and the message, have died. All memories will be apocryphal.'

As we approached the river again, a herd of cows was wandering back from the rough patches of grass that had served as their pasture for the day and, closer to the shore, the flames of a funeral pyre were crackling and leaping up over a linen shroud.

Strolling back into town, Kamala stopped at a chai-khana.

'Chai?' she called as we sat outside at a small trestle table, beneath hurricane lamps suspended from the awning.

The chai wallah in grubby white kameez and scarf around his neck brought the steaming chai with a plate of local sweets.

'We must make arrangements to go to Dharamsala,' Kamala said, as I bit into one of the crumbling sweets. 'I came down on the bus, but it is a long journey and you would understand why I don't manage to come that often at my age.'

'Can we get a taxi?'

'Yes, it's more expensive, but much quicker - about nine and a half hours.'

Let's book one then. I expect you want to see more of the family before we leave, as do I.'

She nodded and smiled, the lines in the corners of her mouth and eyes, fanning out across her still firm, soft skin.

'You've been invited to eat with the family this evening, so we better get going.'

Always, with the coming of darkness, the town took on a whole new identity. Lights emblazoned from every crevice or so it seemed, spreading out in multicoloured ripples across the river's surface, further enhanced by the Ram Jhula's reflected golden cables, shimmering in the dark waters below.

The giant Shiva, earlier bathed in bright sunlight, now took on a shiny luminosity from the surrounding lights, its outlines clearly defined against the pitch night sky.

Steaming food was piled high in the restaurants, the spicy aromatic smells teasing the tastebuds as we passed. Street vendors, undeterred by the darkness, made the best of the intermittent street lights to continue selling their trinkets, fruit and vegetables,

Customers laid back in leatherette chairs for an evening shave. A sign offered, *Swidish Massage*, while others invited us to *Indian Cooking Classes*, a *Beauty Parlour,* a *Toilat* and *Colon Hydrotherapy Centre - The way is from backside.*

The family welcomed me with smiles and open arms, when Kamala and I arrived at the house. The smell of spicy food was wafting through from the kitchen as I was invited to sit down and Pema brought me water.

'Have you had a good day?' Pema asked. 'Mother told me she was taking you somewhere special.'

'We've been to the Beatles' ashram. Quite an amazing place, but sad to see all those memories now lost in time and the encroaching jungle. What music did you listen to when you were growing up?'

'Mother had a little radio. She would tune into All India Radio, which sometimes played Western Pop. I would hear the Beatles, Rolling Stones, Elton John, Abba and then there were many Indian groups who created their own style of pop. Over the years, the visitors to McLeod Ganj would bring tape recorders and CDs, so there was always music in the cafés and places where travellers were staying.

But then, I have also been brought up with our own traditional Tibetan music and Indian Bollywood. It's been quite a mix as you can imagine.'

Pema and Kamala brought a low table into the centre of the room, filling it with a succession of dishes from the kitchen. Rice, various curried vegetables, dhal, pickles and chapatis.

'You cook Indian food as well as Tibetan?' I exclaimed with joy on seeing this spread before us.

'Yes, I try all kinds of food. I've got an international cookery book and sometimes I'll even make spaghetti bolognese.'

'Really!' I said with surprise. 'I'll look forward to that, it's my favourite.'

'Pema is a very good cook,' Kamala said, praising her daughter.

'Not really,' she giggled in the way her mother would to show her embarrassment.

'I think she's just being modest.' I added. 'I hope soon I'll be able to help you all find a more suitable house with a modern kitchen.'

The family went quiet as if struck dumb at the possibility of living somewhere more appropriate to their needs.

'I've told Kamala already. We're going up to Dharamsala in the next few days to arrange the marriage. I will then have to go back to England, where I want to sell my house. I should then have enough money to help you find somewhere you really like and your mother and I will have enough to perhaps buy something else near McLeod Ganj and to see out our days. I suppose you've all made your lives here in Rishikesh.'

'I have my job at the school,' Sangye said, 'and we have the shop. The children will eventually grow up and leave home. Have you thought of living nearer to Rishikesh?'

'No, we haven't. Have we?' I said, turning to Kamala for her thoughts.

'We would have to think very seriously about moving somewhere else. I always feel McLeod Ganj and the area around is my home,' Kamala said, quite emphatically.

'And, for me, it is very special too,' I interjected, 'as it is where I met Kamala and had some of the happiest days of my life. If we have bigger houses, it will be easier for all of us to visit and stay for longer.'

The meal went well with the children staying up way past their bedtimes, quietly listening as the grown ups talked of our combined futures and my new life in India.

'How does it feel to be half English?' I asked Pema at one point.

'It's something I have thought about over the years,' she replied.

'Firstly, wondering what my father was like, as mother had no photographs of you, I would try to imagine you and what your life might be like so far way in England.

Every year, as I got older, I hoped that one day I could go there and perhaps find you and see my parents together.'

These last words overwhelmed me with regret for what might have been, causing those tears to well up once again.

'I'm so sorry. I cannot say it enough,' I said, 'but everything is for a reason. Hard as that may be to understand. Circumstances have determined all of our lives. If God had not wanted us to all meet now, it would not have happened. We are all blessed.'

Kamala put her arm around my shoulder to console me as I indicated for Pema to continue.

'I would look at photo books about England and saw how different it was to here, with its pretty villages, rivers, countryside, towns, castles and cities, particularly London. I've learnt a lot about English history too. From the Romans to the Normans and all the Kings and Queens.

Living in India and especially in McLeod Ganj, I was very aware of the British occupation of India over two hundred years. Everywhere I looked, as I was growing up, I would see places like Mr Nazeri's wooden store with all its English advertising signs from the 1930s. The bungalows that the British built all around where we lived and the Saint John in the Wilderness church that could have been taken from any English village.

I've been to Delhi and seen the Imperial Government buildings and have always been amazed at how the little island, that is Great Britain, could rule such a huge country such as India with so few of their own, instead employing thousands of Indians as civil servants and soldiers to keep everything going. Even now, over seventy years since Indian independence, that British influence remains strong.'

I was impressed by my daughter's knowledge and was grateful

that Kamala had been there to encourage her.

'She always did well at school,' Kamala said. 'You always had your nose in a book, didn't you?

Pema nodded and smiled.

'We were all so proud,' Kamala continued, 'when she got a place at the University of Chandigarh.'

'I didn't know you'd been to university, you clever girl. What did you study?'

'Why? English, of course. It was a fantastic three years for me and that's where I met Sangye. He stayed on and did his Masters, but three years was enough for me as I wanted to get back home and start using what I had learnt.'

'What did you want to do, Pema?'

'Write.'

'Novels?'

'One day, I will write a novel or two or three but, for now, I content myself with getting short stories published in newspapers and magazines, which bring in some extra money. That said, I do have ideas for that first novel.'

'The shop must take a lot of your time.'

'It does. One day, I will sell the business or put in a manager. It does provide quite a good living while the children are growing up, so I have to put my greater ambitions on hold for now.'

CHAPTER
Thirty-one

THE NEXT DAY was a Sunday, not much different to any other day in Rishikesh, but I had asked Kamala to join me for the morning's satsang, meeting her at the tuk-tuk stand for a windswept ride to the ashram. Although she had been brought up a Tibetan Buddhist, she was willing to hear other ideas, obviously encouraged by what I had already told her about Satyaji, the teacher.

Our queue was fourth in the lottery, meaning we could have sat on the floor closer to the stage, but our bones deterred us. Instead we chose the front row of the bank of chairs half way back in the hall, from where we could see Satyaji live as well as seeing him greatly enlarged on the big television screen above us.

I could see a few other Tibetans amongst the audience which made me more comfortable about having asked Kamala.

I had been toying with asking a question regarding my LSD experience, just over fifty years earlier, which I had carried with me for the greater part of my life and was foundational in my understanding and, indeed, *knowing* that all existence is One. In that *trip*, I had lost all sense of self and was only aware of pure light, love and truth.

It was only when my ego had partially reclaimed me that I sought to recover that awareness, only to see it rapidly fading away.

It was this that had originally prompted me to make the journey to India in search of a permanent solution, only to be told by Satyaji that I was already that light, love and truth. Everything else was a manifestation of mind.

I had wanted to know whether what I had experienced on LSD was akin to the state of simply being, but the question remained unasked as I could readily anticipate the answer.

Kamala sat quietly throughout the three hours, which ended with a tender and evocative performance by the sangha's pianist and girl singer, leading us to a sombre, silent exit out to the street and the rude awakening from the coconut seller's piercing cries.

With monkeys and goats gallivanting around us, hopeful for a bite to eat, we sat by the river with a view across to the remnants of the Maharishi's bungalow, just visible amongst the trees.

'What did you make of that, Kamala?' I asked.

'I understand the concept of One from Buddhism. It is clear that everything is One, but what I am struggling with a little is the idea of the passive self and the mind. `Trying to separate the two is difficult.'

'If you try to see your true self as not Kamala trapped in that body, but as an entity that merely *is*, which always has been and always will be, it's not so hard. We know that our bodies are finite and will pass, but our true selves always will always *be*, extending to all parts of the Universe.

We are all consciousness and our minds manifest the details that trick us into thinking things are real. The Buddha spoke of losing the ego. Well, this is the same thing. Key to understanding this is the realisation that *all* we ever have is *this* moment. There is no tangible past and the future hasn't happened.

Satyaji often tells the story of the two dormice, One is constantly busy building her nest and feeding her children, never seemingly stopping from her work. Meanwhile, the other dormouse just sits quietly and watches, not becoming involved in the fraught lifestyle of the other, just *being*.'

We ambled along the river bank, hand in hand, eventually stopping at the taxi rank to see about our trip up to Dharamsala.

'We are not having taxi for another two days,' the manager told us, 'but certainly you can be making reservation. We are having special price of five thousand and six hundred rupees. You want?'

I did a quick calculation and realised that the one way trip was around fifty six pounds. I was also aware of the state of the roads, just from my bus journey from Haridwar.

'What sort of car are you using. Is it comfortable for a nine and a half hour journey?

'I can assure you most kindly sahib, that it is the most very comfortable car.'

'So when do you leave here?'

'It will most certainly be this Tuesday morning at seven o' clock.'

Kamala and I looked at each other. 'What do you think, my darling?'

'Let's take it,' she confirmed emphatically.

I paid a deposit, made sure I had a receipt and promised that both of us would be at the taxi stand for seven on Tuesday morning.

We dropped in to see Pema, where she was busy with customers, only having time for a quick hug and a smile before being drawn outside to the chaos of the street and the momo stall, near where I had first spotted Kamala.

'You must have some of these, Kamala, they're fantastic,' I said, as I joined the queue for a plate. We sat on one of the benches and shared the steaming goodies, participating in conversation with several of the young people also eating, as if all differences in years were non existent.

A French girl, lean and cropped dark hair, wrapped in a burgundy shawl, was keen to tell us of the state of things in her country.

'Ze dictator, Macron, 'as become more and more oppressive. E is a Rothschild puppet, oo cares leettle for ze people. Everyvere you go in France, e is making money from us viz speeding fines and taxes on everyzing from fuel to pensions. Zank God, ve 'ave ze gilets jaunes to fight ze bastard banker.

'What are the gilets jaunes?' I asked.

'Ze yellow jackets are people of all ages and classes, oo vant to see an end to tax cuts for ze rich and more help for ze poor. Ve vant a government of social justice.

Macron must go and ve vant to see most of ze old institutions collapse. Ze establishment is old and corrupt. Everyzing. Ze government, police, education, ealth, media. Ze ole system is zere to control ze people and make money. Zey always forget zat zey are public servants, oo are answerable to ze people.

Zen, zere is ze European Union. Ve must see an end to zis corrupt institution, vich is trying to create a New World Order for business and the rich. Ve people have had enough. Ve vant to create a new and loving vorld.'

'That is something that so many of us want to see,' I replied. For some, that goes right back to the 1960s with *Peace and Love*, which somehow got swallowed by *Greed is Good*. But, we are finally entering the Age of Aquarius, which is predicted to see the end to the old order. What is happening in France is just the beginning and we can only wish you success. If the change is going to start anywhere, it will probably be in France.'

'I zank you,' the girl concluded, grateful for the opportunity to off-load her grievances with someone else.

'Have you walked up the river to the waterfalls?' Kamala then asked me.

'No, is it far?'

'We have time this afternoon. We can get away from all these people and find some peace.'

'That's what I've been looking for for years and hope I'm going to find much more of with you.'

'We will, Adam.'

We followed the winding road past the Trayambakeshwar Temple, the *colonial* chai khana and up through the trees with the jade green waters of the Ganges tumbling wildly on its downstream course beside us. Save for the occasional passing motorbike, we were the only ones walking, finding ourselves truly on our own for the first time since our reunion.

At the iron road bridge, the only means for heavy goods to pass from one side of the river to the next, we replenished our water at one of the chai stalls, before turning off the road and onto a steep path that led up through a *Garden of Eden* of diverse trees, exotic shrubs and thick vegetation.

Kamala's fitness and agility, earned through years of walking mountain paths, soon showed me up as the path took us high into the trees, passing families of grey monkeys, who stood their ground as we passed, merely staring at our presence.

A little further, I spotted some piles of animal poo that seemed to be too big for cows.

'Elephants,' Kamala said confidently.

As the path became more twisting and overgrown, it was soon

a stream in its own right with water steadily coursing down from open ground, where it babbled gently over the rocks in mini waterfalls. A few more turns and we were upon the main waterfall that Kamala had promised, cascading down through a narrow crevice in the rock face into a deep pool carved by decades of tumbling rocks and water.

The air was hot, but the water cool as we sat on a rock and dangled our feet for some short-lived relief.

'You brought Pema up well, Kamala,' I ventured. 'She's bright and clever in all sorts of ways. Running that shop, raising the children, cooking and I was so surprised when I heard she'd been to university. Yet, it must have been so hard for you. When did your mother die?'

'I remember, it was a few days after Pema's tenth birthday. She had never got over my father's death and had been ill for a year or so with dementia. Her memory had become increasingly more vague until we couldn't leave her by herself, let alone with Pema. We had to find room for her in the cottage in Dharmcot until she eventually died. Pema was particularly upset as she'd been very close and loved her so much.'

'I'll be sorry not to see your parents again.'

'My mother had a soft spot for you as she knew how much you cared for me. She was sad when we decided to go our separate ways, but was happy to know that you were Pema's father.'

I wrapped my arm around her, drawing her closer as I kissed her on the head. Just a few feet away, a large male grey monkey was sitting on his haunches watching us. We turned and stared at him, myself making faces, until he made a lunge towards Kamala's bag. Not wishing to risk touching him and possibly being bitten, we both shouted and screamed; sufficient to stop him in his tracks. Beating a slow departure, he was content to merely watch until we were lost out of sight down the path.

Kamala wanted to spend her last day helping Pema in the shop and I had already made an appointment for another massage.

By half past ten, I was lying on the couch, stripped to a pair of paper underpants, waiting for my treatment. Using Marma, an ancient Ayurvedic massage technique, Ranya gently applied warm oil to my body and proceeded to work on a number of pressure points, while pressing and pulling my limbs. I had been suffering from intense pain around my heal and arch for which Ranya had brought in a male assistant to work on my feet. The treatment was at times sublime and others intense and excruciatingly painful as they both hit points where toxins and crystals had built up over time.

Such was the state of my body, Ranya even asked Auntie to assist, applying her deep, long stroke massage technique. The encroachment of hands and hot breath to access the various points of my body resulted in either having Auntie's breasts in my face or the young man's balls, as they leant forward to do their work.

Ranya completed the massage with tissue covering my eyes as she dripped warm sesame oil on my forehead before gently stroking her fingers across, creating a sublime absence of self, from which she had to waken me for the steam box and a glass of chai.

I hadn't realised how much stress I had been under with Alison's illness and death, and was grateful for the opportunity to make some inroads into dissipating it. Now that I had found Kamala, I wanted to be able to give my best to her and this could not be done with the physical and emotional pain I had recently been experiencing.

I spent the last evening at Pema's house, enjoying more of her delicious food, before distributing some token gifts to the family. The occasion was as any other family gathering might be with good conversation and laughing children, who were overjoyed at the handmade wooden toys I had found in the town.

By seven next morning, Kamala and I had both had a warming breakfast of porridge and fruit at the Madras Café as we arrived at the taxi stand with our bags ready for our long journey north to the hills.

'I am most very sorry,' the manager said, 'but my driver has not yet arrived, but I can be most certain he is on his way. Would you be liking chai?'

With no choice but to wait, we accepted his offer and took seats in the office.

By quarter to eight, our driver, a thin man in his thirties with neatly combed and parted hair, was standing before us with a big grin on his face.

'I am so very sorry that I am late. Can I be taking your bags?'

We watched him take our things out to the car, a Tata saloon, which looked roadworthy enough and was certainly both clean and comfortable inside.

By eight o' clock, we were on our way, passing out through the southern limits of Rishikesh with its private schools, builders' merchants, electrical shops, luxury hotels and newly built temples, emulating traditional architecture with stone, white marble and painted tiers. Squeezed in between all these were the plethora of workshops, cafés and advertising hoardings, informing and enticing.

Just before the Song River, which would eventually converge with the Ganges, we turned off north, following the river valley to Dehradun.

Kamala looked serene, dressed in one of her best chupas, a coral and silver filigree necklace and her hair beautifully braided on her head, threaded with her favourite turquoise beads.

What thoughts were passing through her as she stared inscrutably out of the window, I could not guess.

I took her hand and smiled. 'Are you happy?'

'Of course. How could I not be?'

Despite the so called *luxury* car, we were not immune from the potholes, which seemed to be more frequent as the journey unwound. The suspension absorbed much of the impact, but we were still jolted from time to time.

Very soon, we were dropping to the Plains, the patchwork of square geometric fields that stretched beyond the horizon and the dual carriageway that would take us into Chandigarh.

As we approached the city, Kamala called out to the driver.

'Can you take us to the MCM DAV College for Women, please.'

I wondered where she was asking for us to be taken until I realised that it was to see Pema's exclusive women's college.

The building was unspectacular, looking not unlike an English secondary modern, built in the 1970s, but more than compensated for by the spacious garden setting and the onward view to the snow covered mountains. Kamala was so very proud of Pema's achievement and clearly cared little for the aesthetics.

Our stop in Chandigarh was an opportunity for some lunch and for me to see if I could make any sense of what I saw compared with my first visit. Of course, I could not. So much had been added since then, that I was totally disorientated. What images I had carried with me for fifty years had clearly been filtered by time and stood little chance when encountering the current reality.

Setting off for the last stage of the journey, I made my confession to Kamala.

'Kamala, there is something I have to tell you.

'Over all these years, I have dreamt of one day meeting you again, but I have always had a reluctance to revisit Dharamsala and McLeod Ganj.'

'Why is that, Adam?'

'It probably sounds silly, but I've had a life-long aversion to going back to things; whether it's been a school reunion, seeing old work colleagues or going to a place with fond memories. McLeod Ganj falls into the last category.

You know how happy we were during my time there. Life was so much simpler then and we expected far less. We walked everywhere, collected water from the well, showered under the rainwater falling from the roof and were totally immersed in nature and relative silence. Of course, we were young and perhaps a little too innocent and optimistic about the future, but somehow things worked.

Since those days, I have read about the way the village has become this huge tourist hub. Not a place that passing travellers, like myself, could casually stop in for a few weeks or months, but now overwhelmed with fast food restaurants, car parks, hotels, meditation and trekking centres. Even Nazeri Cottage, where I had my room for four months, has been demolished and a meditation centre built in its place.

I have looked at photos of Dharmcot too and see so many more houses and other buildings. To be honest, it frightens me. Has the magic gone, only to be replaced with a relentless money-making machine, in the same way Rishikesh has been commercialised?'

Kamala took my hand and snuggled into me.

'Yes, it has changed and not always for the best. There is more work for the Tibetans, but most of the businesses are owned by Indians and, as the village has grown, so more people have come in and this has often led to fights between Tibetans and others. There are young people, who have lost their spiritual way and seem to be only attracted by cheap imitation brand names from China; whether they be clothes, watches, jewellery or phones.'

'It looks little different to so many places in the West, where young people have little direction and are sustained by trashy television programmes, computer games, Facebook and the latest *must have* fads,' I added.

'My house in Dharmcot is still quite unchanged, but the valley is different.'

You have grown with it all over the years, so it has been a gradual change, but I think I'm going to get quite a shock.'

We sat in silence for much of the remaining journey, lost in our thoughts and the passing scenery.

Beyond Chandigarh, we had started to climb again and I even thought I recognised something of the landscape. The monsoon had been about to burst as I had first made my way by bus up the increasingly winding road that cut its way through the trees.

On this day, the sky was relatively clear and the snow capped mountains sparkled in the winter sunshine but, as before, monkeys still emerged from the jungle, chasing our car as far as their legs would take them.

Kangra was another place I thought I was familiar with, only to be disappointed by my lack of recognition. What images I still retained in my memory were impossible to identify from amongst the profusion of new buildings that had sprung up.

I was convinced of the newly rebuilt Siva temple, destroyed in the 1905 earthquake that had devastated so much of the area, even as far as Dharamsala.

I could see it in my mind's eye, topped off by a golden onion and orange flags fluttering on poles. It had lain just off the steep hill from where the bus had dropped me and I had spent the night in the waiting room, bombarded by the booming and flashing of the first monsoon storm.

Today, there had only been time for tea in a relatively unspoilt chai stall, before we were setting off on the final leg to Dharamsala.

My heart fluttered between dread and the vague possibility that I might not be so disappointed, until the road had finally nudged my memory into recognising something familiar.

After Rishikesh, the green vegetation and tumbling rivers made less impact than they had first done, following my days in the mid-summer Afghan desert and the dryness of the Punjab Plains, but the familiarity was nevertheless comforting.

Half an hour of hairpin bends and heartstopping moments followed as a descending bus or lorry forced us to the gravel edge and the ever present drop to the distant valley bottom. And then, we were driving into Lower Dharamsala, as I had always called it.

The long street was essentially an ex-colonial and now Indian entity, populated with banks, post office, government buildings and the expected mix of restaurants, hotels and miscellaneous shops. But it wasn't just these places, as they had always been, there was a darker more overtly commercial aspect that alerted my worst fears. Money changers, fast food shops and glittering merchandise were all the more noticeable beneath the dazzling bulbs and neon signs.

I didn't want to alarm Kamala as I reluctantly took in what appeared before me.

Gone was the gentle bustle I had once known, now replaced by a relentless surge of Indians, Tibetans and foreign tourists, weaving between cars, bikes, jeeps and lorries, emitting their pollution and filling the air with a persistent blast of horns.

'Dharamsala.' the taxi driver announced as he pulled to a halt.

'No, it is Upper Dharamsala, McLeod Ganj we want.'

'I have very clear instructions, sahib, that the final destination is Dharamsala.'

'As we were an hour late in leaving this morning and it is already dark, we would be grateful for you to take us to McLeod Ganj.' I replied.

Seeing he was on a sticky wicket, he reluctantly restarted the engine and rolled on up the main street, emerging out onto the winding main road to McLeod Ganj.

I had taken this short journey many times by bus, the last time being my departure from Kamala. I had even walked it on one of the many paths that led through the woods as I made my weekly visit to Lower Dharamsala for shopping and my treat in one of the Indian curry restaurants.

Nearing the top, the lights of Forsyth Ganj shone upon us briefly and then on into more darkness, briefly glimpsing the Englsh church amongst the trees, before emerging to the lights of a vast car park and finally drawing to a halt where I had bade Kamala farewell outside the Nazeri General Store.

Once the heart of the colonial village, it was now a shadow of its former self, its roof subsiding between the three dormers; the business, like it's lopsided enamel sign, hanging on grimly in the face of the modern onslaught after almost one hundred and sixty years.

Our driver helped us with our bags before we thanked him and watched the car disappear down the road and back into the darkness.

Kamala and I stood in the midst of the maelstrom of noise and people and I shivered in the cold night air.

A quick glance confirmed that little had remained as it was. The wide vista that had been the avenue leading down the main street, previously punctuated by the stupa and the raised dias on which stood the prayer wheels, was obliterated by a new building boasting the *Pastry Den*, *Tattoos*, *McLlo*, multi cuisine restaurant and beer bar. Then there was the *Xcite Rooftop Restaurant and Lounge, Where Party Never Stops.* In quick succession, my eyes took in, *Pizza Hut*, *Lhasa Bar*, *Coca-Cola*, *Tandoori Zayaka,* the *Hot Spot Family Restaurant*, offering, Breakfast, Lunch and Dinner and the *Asian Shopping Hub.*

All this before we had taken a step. Still, I said nothing to Kamala.

'Are you all right to walk to Dharmcot. It's about twenty minutes?' Kamala asked, perhaps anticipating that I may not be up to it.

'I used to take this path most days to and from Nazeri Cottage. Why wouldn't I be up to it, apart from being fifty years older?' I laughed.

I could just perceive the night sky through the glare of neon signs and street lights and could see the moon was full and bright.

'Look we have the moon to guide us.' I exclaimed, trying to find something positive out of the *hell* that now surrounded us.

Collecting our bags, we started the climb up past a few shops, until it opened out, as I had remembered, into a wide compacted gravel track with tall fir and cedars flanking our route. True to expectations, the moon was bright enough and the sky sufficiently clear to light our way, with the path taking on a blue monotone hue, partially obliterated by the clouds of warm air given out by our breath.

'It was somewhere along here,' I suddenly exclaimed, 'I was running down to the village to catch a bus, when I saw you, stopping just long enough to give you a kiss.'

'Ah Adam, I remember that well. I believe I just laughed as I watched you running on down, still clutching your broken sandal. We have some good memories.'

As the path levelled out a little, we approached what had once been my home for four months. A wall and high iron gates marked the entrance to what was now a meditation centre, the entrance embellished with a square arch topped with a Tibetan style pagoda roof, all decorated with oversized aspects of tanka painting.

Save for what I could just make out in the moonlight of the terraced garden, all else had been obliterated. Gone was the broad verandah, the corrugated iron roof under which I had sat up all night through monsoon storms, the laughter of the many travellers who passed through and the sitar music that had wafted between the rooms and on out to the woods and mountains beyond.

Here, I had studied Tibetan tanka painting, struggling into the early hours over a particularly difficult aspect of a drawing or meticulously painting fine lines with a single hair on my brush. I had taught English to two monks who looked after the children in the refugee school and it was in my room that Kamala had first sat for a drawing and I had lightly brushed her forehead with my lips.

Now, all that remained were ghosts and fading memories, superseded by a new generation of seekers, who were not even born when all this had been happening.

The path wound past the centre and on through the woods, where I had taken my bucket to the well every morning for my daily supply of water.

'Let me carry your bag, Kamala. You're not so young either,' I said, as I slung her Tibetan carpet bag over my shoulder.

Emerging from the woods, we had arrived at the spot where I

had remembered the well to be, instead finding a couple of tea and food stalls and a three storey hotel. Beyond, I could pick out houses and other buildings dotted along and up the hillside.

'Just a little further, Adam,' Kamala said, as she guided me on and along the road through the meadows that had once led to the English painter's house and the cottage that Kamala had now inherited.

As we turned off the path, it all came back to me, seeing Kamala washing clothes outside her cottage and me trying to attract her attention after she had secretly retreated to this place.

She had an old fashioned key with a long shaft at the ready, sliding it firmly into the lock and swinging the door open. Light suddenly filled the little hallway.

'You have electricity!' I exclaimed.

'I should think so after fifty years,' Kamala replied.

'She turned the light on in the sitting room, where a fire had once burned and I had taken off my wet clothes to dry after being caught in a downpour on the mountain path down from Triund, now a popular trekking destination.

The once dingy walls had since been painted a creamy colour and were enhanced by pictures of family, the mountains and a couple of her father's much prized original tankas.

'Would you like to light a fire and I'll get something to eat,' Kamala said in a way that was both familiar and comforting.

While she disappeared next door, I rekindled that moment when I had first lit her fire and Kamala had gone to find a blanket for me to wrap myself in.

The fire was soon ablaze with the cedar and oak logs she had gathered and I joined her in the kitchen.

'My. How things have changed,' I said. 'You now have a kitchen!'

She turned to me, proudly showing off her cooker, fridge and sink with hot and cold running water.

'How long have you had this?'

Pema helped me a little and I had some savings, so I now have a bathroom as well.'

'Wow, 'Kamala, I'm so happy for you….and *our* bedroom?'

'She looked at her feet a little coyly and giggled as she would have done as a young woman. Her innate shyness had clearly not diminished over the years.

'Come, I show you the bedroom.'

She turned down the electric hob and led me through the sitting room, where the fire was blazing and throwing out some well needed heat.

The bedroom walls had also been painted and new rugs scattered on the floor, but the furniture remained much as it had been so many years before, including the double bed with its carved wooden headboard.

Kamala sat on the edge of the bed and drew me to sit beside her.

'Well, here we are again. With everything that has passed through our lives, the world has turned and brought us full circle,' I said. 'Can you really believe it?'

She put her finger to my mouth and reached up towards me. The years fell away as I put my arm around her and let her slowly fall back onto the bed as I would a young woman.

'I love you Kamala', I said, brushing a strand of loose hair away from her face and slowly kissing her on those waiting lips, lingering long as I savoured her taste and aroma.

There was truly something very karmic for us in the two chance encounters, fifty years apart, which have led to a love affair that has survived so much.

Kamala had made a noodle dish and, as we sat by the fire eating, a feeling of deep sadness swept over me.

'Are you all right Adam. You're suddenly very quiet.'

No, it's just that… I was thinking about how I've often longed for this moment and yet had to go through so much sadness before I could touch it.'

'You mean with your wife?'

'Yes, but also the sadness of having let you go. Yet, I am here now and so happy, here in your house, but sad about having seen so much change outside.

Arriving in McLeod Ganj was not the joy I had imagined, instead the discovery of a living hell. I just don't know if I'm going to be able to live with that, it is so horrendous. For you it has been a gradual change, perhaps like the frog being slowly boiled in water and not realising he is being cooked. I have been thrown straight into the boiling water and it's choking my soul. I was hoping for tranquility with you but, with all these people and changes, I'm not so sure we'll have it.'

'Dharmcot is different. We don't have to go to McLeod Ganj too often. There are small shops here, where we can buy our essential food and it's really only the trekkers who come up here, most of them looking for tranquillity too. I think you'll grow to love it.'

'I know you're right, Kamala. It's just that I've always held this dream of how things were, not appreciating how things do and must change. Look at us.'

She laughed.

'It's been a long day for us. We need to sleep. Maybe, tomorrow, we can go to the Registry Office in Dharamsala and arrange for our marriage,' she said.

'There's nothing I'd like more. I'm not sure what we will need, but I brought lots of paperwork with me.'

'You sound as if you knew this was going to happen.'

'I didn't know, but I hoped. More than anything, I hoped. I just had to find you and finally seal our love.'

Our lips met again for the umpteenth time that day.

In the bedroom, we prepared for bed with me unpacking the few clothes I had brought on the trip. Rummaging through one of the pockets, I felt something soft and familiar.

'Look what I brought with me,' I said, as I pulled out the white silk khata that Kamala had placed over my neck as we were parting fifty years earlier.

'You've still got it?'

'Of course. How could I not. I've treasured it all these years,' I said as I placed it over her neck and pulled her towards me for another kiss. 'It is the tie that will hold us together forever more. We have an expression in English when a couple are going to marry. They are said to be *tying the knot.*'

And so, with the lights turned out and the moonlight filtering across the room, we lay together as we had last done when our love had made our child.

CHAPTER

Thirty-two

W E WERE UP AT DAWN to catch the early bus down to
Lower Dharamsala, walking back along the path we
had taken the previous evening.

Daylight and the bright winter sunshine cast a better light
on all I had seen the night before. The night had been cold and
a light dusting of snow covered the valley stretching back to the
mountains that soared above us. Despite the new hotels and
eateries, the magic was still there and I thanked God and Kamala
for keeping my faith.

Boarding the bus, I noticed that what a much newer vehicle had
gained in comfort, it had not lost in its restrictions on capacity, as
we squeezed into our seats only to be firmly wedged by standing
passengers before the journey could begin. What had formerly
been a thirty minute ride from McLeod Ganj was now nearer
forty-five due to the badly parked cars along the roadside and the
seemingly incessant flow of private cars and taxis congesting the
road.

Despite the traffic, the Marriage Bureau in Lower Dharamsala
was easily found and we didn't have to wait long before we were
ushered into the office.

Sitting side by side opposite a somewhat plump bespectacled
Indian woman in sari, we were asked some background questions.
She was astounded to hear that we had first met fifty years earlier
and were only now registering to be married.

'This is indeed a most unusual story,' she said, as if she was
intending to put it on public record for the world to know. 'You are

telling me that it is only in the past week that you have rediscovered each other?'

'Indeed, that is true,' I said, 'and we can't get married quickly enough.'

'You realise that we will all have to wait thirty days from the publishing of the wedding announcement, before we can be having the ceremony,' she said.

'That's fine. My visa expires on ninth of April. Does the ceremony take place here?'

'It looks like you will have plenty of time to prepare for the wedding and you will be able to have the wedding here. I am the registrar, so will be able to conduct the ceremony for you.'

'We will be living in Dharmcot and I will be bringing income into India. Will I be able to live here permanently thereafter?'

'That will not be a problem as you are not dependent on the State and you will simply have to change your tourist visa to an X2 visa.'

'So when my current visa expires, I will need to go back to England to sort out my affairs. Do I then apply for another tourist visa for my return and convert that to an X2?'

'That's right.'

It took a few more minutes for us to present passports, my birth certificate and the other necessary paperwork, together with the ubiquitous passport photos. I had brought everything I thought would be important, including Alison's death certificate and our marriage certificate. Kamala was in a similar position, also requiring her husband's death certificate.

Having been born in Tibet, Kamala had no bona-fide birth certificate and was dependent on a document issued by the Tibetan Government in exile and certified by her parents. The confirmation of her May 1949 birth had been acceptable for her first marriage and we imagined it would suffice for the second. The date of sixth of May, 1949 had also been entered in her passport.

'So, if there are no objections, you can arrange the marriage for a month's time,' the registrar said.

'Which will be easiest for Pema, Sangye and the children?' I asked Kamala. 'They will need a day to get here and we'll have to put them up in an hotel.'

'Pema can close the shop any time she wants and I don't think the school will object to Sangye going to a wedding.'

Thanking the registrar, we stepped out into the turmoil of the cacophonous street again, glad to see the bus ready to leave for McLeod Ganj.

Daylight brought some remission to the village, but not much, as Kamala and I had a brief walk around the already crowded streets. My initial perception had been vindicated as the centre of the main street had been built upon with shops and a new temple with the prayer wheels having been moved to an enclosure at the side of the street, appearing to be not as accessible as the originals.

Elsewhere, more hotels, cafés and bars seemed to have sprung up in every available space. What had once been a tranquil walk along to the Dalai Lama's palace, where prayer flags fluttered and an encounter with a passing monk would be met with a *Namaste* or *Tashi Delek*, was now clogged with cars and even an unsightly multi-storey car park, clinging precariously to the edge of the hillside.

The village no longer deserved the designation of village as it had grown like a defiant cancer in all directions, dominated by yet more tourist orientated businesses; most selling fast food or superfluous junk.

Mercifully, Dharmcot had been spared the motor car, with vehicles only being able to access the outer limit and no further. All roads within the village were far too narrow, enabling it, despite its growth, to remain a tranquil retreat from the madness of horns, pollution and impatient drivers, too lazy to walk and with very little interest in the spiritual dimension of the area.

Whereas I had always been conscious of the joy on the Tibetans' faces, evident in their ear to ear smiles and sparkling eyes, many now had a sadness and disenchantment about them. It was heartbreaking.

I was glad to return to Dharmcot and the sanctuary of Kamala's cottage, where we talked of the days ahead.

'How many people do you want to invite?' I asked Kamala. 'I have no one on my side, so it's up to you.'

'There's the family, of course. Then I have friends, who still live in the village. People I worked with at school, even one or two of my ex students.

I will make a list as we will have to arrange for somewhere for us all to go afterwards to eat.'

'Then you will want a new chuba,' I added, 'and I will need clothes. You will have to help me.'

The days passed pleasantly enough, avoiding McLeod Ganj as much as possible and, when we weren't arranging things for the wedding, taking walks through Dharmcot and out into the countryside beyond, where views across the Himalayan landscape took the breath away.

From time to time, we would drop in at one of the little cafés for a drink or a bite to eat, sitting at a window or terrace opening onto the vista beyond.

It remained cold well into March, but we were well stocked with firewood and had each other to keep ourselves warm.

The thirty day wait soon passed and we had arranged the wedding for the weekend of twenty-third and twenty-fourth of March, enabling guests to set aside the Friday for travelling.

With my visa due to expire on ninth of April, I was able to reschedule my original flight that would have conflicted with the wedding and gave myself another couple of weeks with Kamala.

With neither of us having parents to initiate significant aspects of a traditional Tibetan wedding, we decided to keep things simple. By rights, we should not have been living together, instead, treading cautiously in the homes of each other's parents, taking gifts and generally encouraging each side to enthuse about the other.

For us, our die had been cast and it was merely a question of friends and relatives dressing for the occasion and supporting the festivities. Most of the guests were on Kamala's side, although one of Kamala's male friends, Gesar, was *lent* to me for the day as my best man.

On the morning of the wedding, we opened the boxes that had been delivered containing our respective outfits and Chodren, one of Kamala's old students, now in her fifties, came to help prepare her hair and put on her clothes.

I was relegated to a corner of the sitting room to make sense of what had arrived in my box, with the help of my best man.

An hour later, I was nervously pacing up and down outside the cottage, dressed in my new Tibetan boots, baggy trousers, fur hat and a gold braid, knee length chuba wrapped around me, my hands concealed beneath the fashionable long sleeves.

With less than two hours before the midday ceremony, Kamala eventually appeared at the door.

'Darling, is it you? How beautiful you are,' was all I could say.

Chodren stood proudly beside Kamala as she displayed the treasures that now adorned her.

A silk ultramarine ankle length chuba enveloped Kamala, the sleeves and collar fringed with gold braid and white lotus flower motifs decorating the material. A thick cummerbund style belt decorated with stylised cloud motifs and large precious stones in substantial silver mounts.

A length of material comprising rainbow patterns had been cut into three staggered panels and sewn together to create a striking new apron.

Kamala's face had been subtly made-up by Chodren to emphasise her almond eyes and full lips. Her braided hair hung loose, lavishly decorated with large pieces of coral and turquoise.

She was the *Queen of the Mountains* and soon to be my wife.

'Are you ready?' I asked, as Kamala audibly took a deep breath, exhaled and smiled.

'Yes.'

We had arranged for a blessing from one of the monks at the meditation centre, where once my colonial cottage had been. Local people had turned out along the path to clap us on our way as we disappeared into the woods.

Before an altar dominated by a golden Buddha dressed in the regalia of the Yellow Hat, Gelug sect of Tibetan Buddhism, we sat before the priest with white silk khatas draped over our heads and shoulders.

Sadly, for me, the ceremony was in Tibetan and, of course, I didn't understand a word, but I was kindly given a translation from which I gleaned the salient points.

We were encouraged to make our spiritual paths the centre of our lives together, helping each other on the path to enlightenment, whilst ensuring that, as we grew older, we would aspire to transform the trials of life into a path of love, compassion, joy and equanimity.

By deepening our love for each other, so we would aspire to share the feelings of affection, consideration and care for others, thus opening our hearts to radiate love to all beings.

Other points covered negative emotions such as anger and pride; feelings that we too would have to wrestle with from time to time.

Two white taxis, adorned with prayer flags strung across the top of the windscreens, had been ordered to take us separately to the Registry Office, with myself arriving first with Gesar, followed soon after by Kamala and Chodren.

Waiting outside were Pema, Sangye and the children, all beautifully dressed. Pema radiated her beauty in a red and gold chuba, adorned with coral and turquoise necklaces and matching rings on her fingers. She beamed with joy as she watched her parents approach the entrance.

I smiled back at her and felt the love connection between us.

Before we entered, Chodren and Gelug had another duty to perform, an extraction from a traditional Tibetan wedding. In order to confirm ongoing happiness and health, each of them presented us with a decorated arrow head, Chodren slipping hers into the back of Kamala's chuba and Gelug indicating for me to tuck mine into my belt.

Inside, the rest of the guests were waiting as the family took their seats and Kamala and I were accompanied to the front by Chodren and Gelug, where the registrar was waiting. She too had realised what an auspicious day this was for us and had dressed in a green and gold silk sari to celebrate our union.

The civil ceremony was not that different to what might have been expected in England, with the recitation of the vows of love and allegiance and an exchange of the rings that Chodren and Gelug had been looking after for us.

As the registrar pronounced us man and wife, a joyous murmur fluttered through the congregation, signalling approval for us to kiss. Lifting the khata from Kamala's face, I saw the vulnerable young girl I had left behind so long ago, her eyes watery with tears, her lips full and longing for the touch that would finally make amends for all that had gone before.

I eventually flew back to England and sorted through an accumulation of seventy years worth of possessions, wondering what I would need and what might be appropriate to pass down to Pema and the children.

The majority was sent to car boots, junk shops and charity, whilst I retained those essentials that I would want for my life going forward; art materials, a few treasured books and mementos from Alison and my family. So many books had accumulated; many I had promised myself I would one day read, but that day had never come and, meanwhile, years of dust had gathered in the bookcases. Travellers always brought books through, there was a good library in Dharamsala and, if I should really want something in particular, I could order it.

What remained easily filled a container, which I arranged to be sent to Dharmcot, hoping that the arrival of my things in the small cottage would not horrify Kamala. I knew in time, we would need to find a new house to live in, which would easily absorb what I was sending.

Whist I was sorting, an agent put the house up for sale, fully furnished and, within a week, I had a cash buyer offering the full asking price, such was the madness of the English housing market. From the proceeds, there would be sufficient to help Pema and her family, for Kamala and I to buy anew and to keep us in comfort for the rest of our lives.

Within a month, I was back with Kamala, having caught the train from Delhi to Pathancot and then a two and a half hour taxi ride to Dharmcot.

We did find a new house away from the damp of the woods and overlooking the village and mountains. It was large enough for the family to visit and stay in comfort. Nothing could have been better.

And so our lives found a level from one day to another, one of simple pleasures, supported by a few modern amenities and even the internet.

Through the latter, I was able to keep an eye on the coming storm that would soon engulf the world in lies and tyranny.

From the beginning, I knew that Covid was just a fabricated

name for a variant of flu, linked to maximum media coverage in order to create a climate of fear. This fear would be the perfect excuse for the purveyors of genocide to launch a supposed antidote that would, in time, kill millions by way of blood clots, strokes, heart attacks and depleted immune systems, leaving little evidence that the contents of the "vaccine" were the cause.

When the mobile vaccine units arrived in the village, I felt confident enough in our Human Rights, the principles of the Nuremberg Code and the ability to debunk any Covid lies they may choose to throw at us.

One morning, two policemen with batons drawn and a young nurse arrived at the door, each suitably masked and covered in plastic sheeting as if we were undergoing an attack of Ebola and the Bubonic Plague combined.

'We are here to be giving the Covid vaccine,' one of them said in his authoritative manner.

'Thank you. But we are not having any vaccine until it has completed its trials and been proven to be safe.'

'I can assure you that it is perfectly safe,' the policeman replied.

'How do you know this? Are you a scientist?' I asked.

He was lost for words.

'You have to be having your vaccine,' he insisted.

'You should know that the trials won't be completed until May 2023 and that, under the Nuremberg Code of 1947, a person cannot be coerced into receiving an experimental procedure without informed consent. If coercion takes place, the perpetrators can be arrested and tried for Crimes Against Humanity. Usually, the penalty is a long prison sentence or death. Are you prepared to take that risk? Are you also prepared to sign a document whereby you take full responsibility for any injury that might occur as a consequence of the vaccine?'

They were all dumfounded at my replies, choosing not to pursue their mission any further on realising that International Law destroyed their ability to impose this experimental treatment without consequences for themselves. A momentary glance at each other and they were packing their things and leaving, knowing they had been defeated. We didn't hear from them again.

Of course, we kept under the radar as much as possible when

out, wearing masks beneath our noses and not lingering anywhere for too long. But, we had made our stand with the media nonsense.

Despite our unease about the sort of regime that the powers might be trying to impose on the world, I knew it was a global plan and therefore had no regrets about coming to live in India, where space, fresh air and tranquility dominated.

Now, I am at the end of my story and still often ask the question; *'And what of Belinda?'*

I have not seen her since I waved farewell from the back of the bus leaving her village near Cambridge.

What happened to her remains a mystery.

Yet, she remains perhaps the greatest catalyst in my life.

She was the first girl I slept with; exciting and dangerous.

Knowing her led me into a dark underworld of drug dealers and corruption, from which I still have the physical scars.

She connected me to Caroline, her long time school friend, living in a commune in Notting Hill. With her, I had set out on a search along the ley lines and sacred sites of England to find Belinda who had disappeared from hospital, following a drug overdose.

With Caroline, I was awoken to the myths and legends of Glastonbury and the mystical underbelly of ancient Albion. I had shared an LSD trip that had opened my eyes to the infinite and the oneness of all entities; an insight that had ultimately prompted me to make the overland journey to India. But, Caroline, too, fell victim to the forces of evil that swam amongst us and was murdered on a cold spring evening in London.

For a short spell, I was reunited with Belinda, who had found her true self and had emerged as a loving, intelligent mentor for the idyllic time I shared in her cottage, until I realised that I was overwhelmingly compelled to go to India.

She had given me her blessing as I set out on the mad overland journey of some five thousand miles to a place that was only as real as the apocryphal stories of spiritual salvation, mountain and jungle retreats and British derring-do.

Had I not gone, I would not have found Kamala nor Alison,

I just hope Belinda, after all her tragedy, finally found some happiness and peace in her life.

Nowadays, I am content to sit on the verandah and watch Kamala picking flowers for the house, occasionally looking up to smile, wave and reassure me that all is well.

Write a Review

If you enjoyed **The Ethereal Circle,**
I would greatly value your review.
Please return to Amazon/The Ethereal Circle in Books
and scroll down to Write a Customer Review.
Thank You

Read the prequels to the trilogy
(Available in Paperback and Kindle versions on Amazon)

A Hand in God's Till
(The first in this trilogy)

A story of Love, Tragedy and Hope

A vivid portrayal of
sexual and spiritual awakening,
ignited by 1967's "Summer of Love".

Kamala
(The sequel to *A Hand in God's Till*)

Set on the fabled overland trail to India

Kamala will take you through the pain, fear, hope and magnificent
exhilaration of this epic journey

Connect with Me

My Website: http://www.nicholascooper-author.co.uk

Nicholas Cooper

BORN IN WINDSOR, England in
1950, Nicholas Cooper grew up
just outside London, glad to have lived
through the transformational period of
the 1960s that still echoes through our
lives today.

Photo: Angie McKenzie. 2019

He was educated in Somerset at
Queen's College, Taunton, before going
on to art college in Guildford, Surrey.

In 1970, he was one of the few who
successfully travelled overland to India,
spending the best part of a year travelling the country and living
with Tibetan refugees in Dharamsala.

On his return to England, he studied to be a teacher, going on
to work for some years in Illustration and Graphic Design, before
being appointed a college lecturer in Graphic Design at Weston
College, Somerset.

In 2007, he moved to Spain with his partner, the painter, Angie
McKenzie, restoring three Andalucian village houses to habitable
"works of art".

Nicholas started his first novel, *A Hand in God's Till*, whilst still
in Spain, finishing it after returning to live in Ramsgate, Kent.

Kamala was the sequel.

Following five years in Portugal, Nicholas has now returned to
live, write and paint in England, where *The Ethereal Circle* was
completed.

Printed in Great Britain
by Amazon